Pawns
in an
Ancient
Game

Pawns
in an
Ancient
Game

GREGORY C.
RANDALL

WH
WINSDOR HILL
PUBLISHING

ALSO BY GREGORY C. RANDALL

The Cherry Pickers

The Max Adler WWII Thrillers
This Face of Evil
Pawns in an Ancient Game

The Sharon O'Mara Chronicles
Land Swap For Death
Containers For Death
Toulouse For Death
12th Man For Death
Diamonds For Death
Limerick For Death

The Tony Alfano Thrillers
Chicago Swing
Chicago Jazz
Chicago Fix
Chicago Boogie Woogie

The Alex Polonia Thrillers
Venice Black
Saigon Red
St. Petersburg White

The Gypsy King Sci-Fi Adventures
Sector 73

Nonfiction
America's Original GI Town, Park Forest, Illinois

Published by Windsor Hill Publishing, Walnut Creek, California
www.gregorycrandall.info

ISBN-13: 978-1-7365013-3-7 (ebook – Kindle Edition)
ISBN-13: 978-1-7365013-4-4 (paperback)

Cover design by Gregory C. Randall

This novel is dedicated to my two sisters, Anna Marie Randall and Janet Mary Randall Kernan. Two beautiful examples of strong and brilliant women.

Rising on his white horse, the first horseman of the
Apocalypse, Pestilence,
drew back his bow and took aim.

1

The Ardennes
December 1944

By the fall of 1944, the Allied armies had driven the greatest military might of the past thousand years, the German army, backward more than two hundred and fifty miles from the Normandy coast to the German border. Now, three months after liberating Paris, most American soldiers were confident that the war would be over by Christmas. With the Nazis back on their heels, it seemed as if nothing could stop the Allies from racing through the Low Countries, fording the Rhine River in force, and crashing into the heart of Germany. Even considering colossal failures, such as Montgomery's Market Garden ill-advised advance, the Allies' recent victories created a sense of hubris and invincibility. However, the greatest asset the Allies had fighting the Nazis wasn't the tanks and the infantry; it was intelligence and spycraft. The American Office of Strategic Services (OSS for short) was charged with uncovering and then employing that intelligence against the enemy and its positions. In early December, they believed they had the Germans figured out; they were to learn how disastrously wrong they could be.

For the Americans, the OSS and Army Military Intelligence were the lead military agencies that employed foreign-born nationals and Jews—many fluent in German and French—to personally interrogate and gather intelligence from captured prisoners. The enemy knew this and under interrogation would often pass on false intelligence. Yet as Christmas approached that winter of 1944, the opposing armies appeared to have settled into nervous and stalled apprehension, each side believing in a decidedly different version of how to celebrate the holiday.

* * *

The icy December rain had soaked through the lightweight fabric of OSS Captain Max Adler's summer fatigue jacket. He hadn't been warm or dry for a week, and the weather reports for the Ardennes Forest in Belgium predicted no signs of relief. Why he hadn't brought or scrounged a winter coat was beyond him now. *I grew up in Chicago, damn it; I know better.* Now, stuck six feet deep in the freezing mud in the bottom of a foxhole, he prayed just to survive the next twenty-four hours. The cold and the explosions overhead reminded him he was still alive.

After almost a year in Rome and the memory of warm summer days, Max caught up with his OSS intelligence group in eastern France that winter of 1944. The advancing Allied front had pushed forward more than two hundred miles across France to within miles of the German border. The afternoon of December 15 found two unlikely Jews—Berlin-born and Chicago-raised Captain Max (Max to everyone except his mother) Adler and Vienna-born and Bronx-raised Sergeant Jules Faber—at the field GHQ of the 1st Battalion of the 23rd Infantry Division. Their assignment was to aggressively interrogate German officers captured during raids east of Hunningen, Belgium, a small crossroads village three miles west of the German border and in the middle of the Ardennes Forest. So far, they had bupkis.

The winter air left a frozen haze of prickly hoar frost on everything. Twice the day before, they'd gotten lost in the thick fog. Faber not so humorously called the impenetrable soup "pea shit."

The Rhine River was the logistical and natural border to Germany's heartland. Adler and Faber were assigned to this region to find out what the devil was going on. They were there to follow up on persistent and unconfirmed rumors of a German buildup along the Rhine, thirty-five miles to the east; a buildup that many said was impossible. What the two intelligence men quickly learned was that the average German prisoner they captured in the forest represented the dregs, the young and raw draftees culled from Germany's dwindling manpower—most probably sent there as cannon fodder. They knew nothing; some didn't even know they were in Belgium; their officers were green and inexperienced. The intelligence was worthless. Max also believed HQ was not interested in contradictory intelligence such as he found. The immediate German problem, he discovered, was the lack of trained and experienced troops in this part of the front. He wondered, at this stage of the war, why would the Germans not defend their border with their best soldiers? After two hours of browbeating, cajoling, and even physically threatening two German officers, they'd learned nothing. Every hour, Max was certain something was brewing in the forests to the east. What it was, he didn't know. He had learned to leave predictions to the experts. What he needed wasn't more prisoners but a crystal ball.

Now, on this hellish morning of December 16, he sat in a hole in the ground with five other soldiers under a thin and questionable roof of logs and prayed to an absent God for the shelling to stop. During the past three hours, the Germans had fired thousands of rounds from their 88 mm howitzers into the one-mile square of pine and fir where the 1st Battalion was bivouacked. The shells were timed to intentionally explode in the overhead canopy—tree bursts they were called. To the men in the foxholes, it didn't make any difference whether you were shredded by a chunk of hot shrapnel or skewered by three feet of pine tree—you were just as dead. Splinters bombarded everyone. Right now, all Max wanted to do was to take a piss.

He now understood why the latest interrogations had proved worthless. The last two German officers just shook their heads when Max demanded answers. There was no failure of communication; his flawless Berlin German cut away any confusion faked by the two officers. Right now, as he hunkered against the muddy wall of the hole trying to make his six-foot-four-inch body as small as possible, he understood the smirk the German lieutenant made as he was herded away with the other prisoners. Max was positive the son of a bitch knew that unholy hell would be unleashed the next morning.

The surprise German advance caught everyone with their pants down; now they were being screwed up the ass.

"Captain, I need prisoners to interrogate; I need to understand what is happening," Max said to the officer sitting crossed-legged opposite him. The ground shook from the next round of shelling.

"Wait an hour. You won't have to find them—they will be standing on our fucking roof," the captain answered. "I'm not sending my men out—but you, go help yourself." He pointed in all directions.

"This is more than a probe. This is a wedge; they are coming right through here."

"Well, fuck me, now I know why you are in intelligence, Adler. The obvious doesn't escape you." The ground shuddered. "You're right, but my men are still not going nowhere. Until this lets up, we don't move."

The shelling suddenly and mercifully stopped. The soldiers in the hole continued to feel the massive trunks and branches crashing to the ground through their butts stuck to the frozen mud.

"Two options, Adler," the infantry captain said, holding up two fingers. "One, the Germans ran out of shells, which I seriously doubt, or two, they are about to crash into these woods with everything they have. I'd prefer option one, but I think we are going to get option two shoved down our throats. If your jeep is still in one piece, I strongly suggest that you and your sergeant get the hell out of here—right now. My men want to stay alive, not go collecting prisoners or covering your ass. So, I really insist that you get the fuck out of here."

"Sergeant Faber, you ready to roll?" Max said into the gloom.

"Yes, sir."

"Then what are you waiting for?"

The two men scrambled out of the pit. The scene surrounding them was a tortured mass of ripped and shredded tree trunks and branches. The stench of burned wood filled the air. Through the blasted trees, an annoying drizzle of rain mixed with sleet fell. In the eerie late-morning fog, dark forms began to emerge from trenches and foxholes hewn out of the frozen ground. The sickening moan of a man, then others, carried through the quiet forest. Then the yells began for a medic; they came from every direction.

Adler and Faber found their jeep under a two-foot-high pile of broken pine limbs. Three feet away, a forty-foot-long chunk of tree trunk lay parallel to the vehicle. Five feet to the right and it would have cleaved the jeep in two.

"Lucky," Sergeant Faber said.

"I don't believe in luck, Sergeant—but this comes damn close."

To the east, they heard the unmistakable engine roars of approaching German armor.

"Tiger tanks, sir. We need to move," Faber yelled as they

vaulted into the jeep.

"Then go," Max said and braced his muddy body against the dashboard of the vehicle.

The sergeant pushed the jeep hard and fast through the debris. Twice they had to wrench away thick limbs strewn across the road.

"We're in the middle of an advance," Max said. "That's why that smug German lieutenant was silent—he knew something was up. That fucker knew."

Faber swung the jeep out onto the main road and accelerated. Thousands of black tree trunks raced by on both sides. Adler checked his watch—thirteen hundred hours, maybe four hours of daylight left. The gray ceiling was low, maybe a thousand feet—no air cover to save anyone's ass this afternoon.

"Shit," Faber yelled and yanked the steering wheel hard right onto a narrow lane that led to open fields beyond. "Did you see that? A Tiger tank—the son of a bitch came out of the fog like hell's own fucking ghost; he's completely blocking the road." Immediately behind them, the forest lit up from a round fired by the tank; the tree trunks between them gave some limited protection.

"We need to get out of these woods," Max yelled. "Dammit, something was up. I should have seen this coming. The Germans were done—finished."

"It seems, Captain, that the Wehrmacht did not get the fucking memo," the sergeant answered.

Faber jerked the jeep onto another narrow road. The visibility was less than one hundred yards; in some places, less than a hundred feet. The fog protected them from probing German eyes hidden in the forest; however, this same fog also hid what might be sitting in the middle of the road just ten seconds ahead.

"Ambleve is four miles," Faber said. "With luck, we will be there in twenty minutes."

"There you go with the luck thing," Max answered. "Right now, twenty minutes is an eternity. Pull off onto the next road. Go right; I hear something."

Faber slowed the jeep to a crawl and then stopped.

Max stood on the passenger's seat and slowly surveyed the forest that surrounded them; they could feel the vibrations through their boots before they could hear the engines.

"Heavy vehicles, tanks, and half-tracks," Max said. "That way and there." He pointed to the direction they'd just come. "We have ten minutes. Can you make Ambleve in ten?"

"Yes, sir, as long as this fog holds."

The road exited the forest and curved downward clinging to the side of a low hill—one of the hundreds of hills that had funneled armies through the Ardennes for more than two thousand years. The Romans, Charlemagne, and the worst battles of World War I had been fought here, and now another battle was beginning—a bookend to the Germans' westward advance against the French four years earlier. It did not turn out well for the French then, and the Allies would have their hands full now.

Faber crashed through the tiny village of Mirfeld and followed the sign that pointed to Ambleve. Chaos reigned; soldiers were throwing everything they could into jeeps. They raced through the madness and out into the open country. A quarter mile beyond the village, two jeeps and a Sherman tank blocked the road. A dozen nervous GIs stood behind the vehicles; every carbine and Thompson submachine gun was pointed at them. The sergeant stood in the road; he waved his arm up and down, signaling them to stop.

"Where the hell are you two going in such a hurry, Captain?" the sergeant asked, an MP armband wrapped around his upper arm.

"Sergeant, the whole damn German army is less than five miles behind us and will bust through those trees in less than an hour. I suggest that you get the hell out of here or you will be celebrating Christmas in a POW camp. Those artillery concussions are not our guns."

"Right—password," the soldier demanded. He looked past the jeep to the east and the source of the muffled thunder.

"Password? I don't know the goddamn password! We've been in Hunningen the last two days—that is until the Germans overran it this morning. I don't know the password."

"Where you from, Captain? I catch an accent," the sergeant said.

"I'm from Chicago, but not been home for three years. Dammit, Sergeant, get your men the hell out of here. The whole fucking German army is coming."

"Corporal, the captain here says he's from Chicago. Who's the manager of the Cubs?"

"You have got to be kidding me," Max said. "I've not been back in years."

The corporal raised his rifle; the others did as well. The machine gun manned on the tank swiveled directly at them.

"Cubs, manager," the sergeant demanded. "Shit, you even look like a Kraut. We were told that there might be fake Americans wandering around the countryside, screwing up things, switching signs, and causing shit. Maybe you're one of them."

"Hartnett. Gabby Hartnett," Max said. "Least he was when I was there in 1939."

The sergeant looked at the Faber. "Wrong. I think we have some spies. Maybe we should just shoot them and save all the hassle of dragging them back to headquarters."

"It's Charlie Grimm," Faber said. "Least it was him the last time I listened to a ballgame in September. It was on Armed Forces Radio. I was somewhere just east of Paris. I think it was Grimm managing then."

"Yeah, Charlie Grimm. Still couldn't get them a winning season," the sergeant said.

When the sergeant said "winning," all hell broke loose. The lane that Adler and Faber had just driven along exploded as howitzer rounds danced down the road toward the checkpoint. Not waiting, Faber pulled Max back into the jeep and gunned the engine. Five seconds later, they were flying down the hill toward the village of Ambleve. Behind them, hellfire hit the ridgeline and the checkpoint.

Overhead, the shrieking of a plane forced Max to look up into the gray sky. Just above the treetops, the unmistakable shape of Germany's most frightening new aircraft, a Messerschmitt Me 262, appeared. He saw the staccato flashes of its nose-mounted guns as it bore down on them. The ground on both sides of the jeep was ripped by the fusillade. Sounding like a banshee from hell, it screamed past and over the ridgeline and disappeared. Then it returned and dropped a single bomb from its undercarriage.

In an instant, everything was upside down, the explosion numbing. Max tumbled high into the air as their jeep flipped nose over ass down the hillside. He saw Faber fly over him. The concussion knocked him senseless.

Max blinked and dirt fell into his eyes. He couldn't hear anything other than a thick buzz that started somewhere deep in the back of his head or his soul—he wasn't sure which. He pushed himself up and saw Faber lying in a twisted pile, twenty feet away. To his surprise, their jeep, like some arcane cat, had landed on its wheels looking nonplussed about its aerobatic efforts. Faber moved.

He crawled to the sergeant's side and checked him over. Other than his left arm unnaturally bent, he looked whole. His eyes were wide open, and he was conscious.

"Are we dead?" Faber asked.

"Not yet. Can you stand?" Max said.

Max slipped his arm under Faber and slowly pulled him to his feet. Faber gritted his teeth, the pain obvious from his busted arm.

"Let's see if this thing works," Max said, and tried the ignition. After three attempts and an adjustment to the choke, the indestructible chunk of American steel started. Tufts of sod and clods of frozen dirt covered the vehicle. Max reached over the window frame and scraped what he could off the shattered windshield.

"Brace yourself. This is not going to be easy," he said to Faber.

"What the hell was that?" Faber yelled.

"Hitler's newest toy," Max shouted back as he pointed upward. "Our people called it a jet airplane or something like that. Jesus, never seen something so fast."

The airplane twice roared over them, ignoring Adler and Faber both times. Then it disappeared. To the east, as their hearing slowly returned, they could hear the distant concussions of the advancing German artillery.

They drove straight on through the American-occupied village of Ambleve; hundreds of GIs were frantically loading their gear into trucks and jeeps. No one tried to stop them. Outside of the village, they turned right and drove on to Malmedy.

They did not stop in Malmedy either, and the insanity and chaos in the village square mirrored Ambleve. They drove directly to their division headquarters north of Malmedy and ten miles outside the bulge that was beginning to form in the Allied lines by the German push west.

* * *

Three weeks later, the temperature sat at ten degrees above zero. Max, wrapped in two blankets, had still not found a warm coat. And after weeks of bleak, bone-numbing cold, he was getting seriously tired of winter.

Directly in front of him sat two snow-covered German

trucks. All the tires were flat, and their engine compartments were black from fire. The trucks sat where they stopped because they'd ran out of gasoline. The snow-covered humps scattered around the trucks were the winter shrouds of dead SS soldiers. Max stood at the back of the first truck trying to read the panels of wooden crates stacked inside. It was German script; he'd been called in to translate. There was something strange about the crates that alerted the squad that had intercepted the trucks the day before.

"You know what it says on the crates, Captain?" the lieutenant asked.

"Give me a boost," Max answered. Two men from the squad cupped their hands together and helped Max into the back of the truck. Holding the blankets together with his left hand, he clicked on his flashlight and squeezed his way down the aisle and disappeared into the back. The squad watched.

After five minutes, the lieutenant yelled, "You okay, Captain? Everything all right?"

Max materialized between the crates and stood at the edge of the truck's bed. "No, Lieutenant, it definitely is not all right. Have your men move back at least a hundred paces, and make sure to keep the wind at your back."

Max jumped to the road and quickly followed the soldiers.

"What the hell is it?" one of the soldiers asked.

"Don't know exactly, but I'd say it is poison gas. They are still in their shell casings—look to fit 88 mm artillery."

"Thought that shit was illegal under the Geneva Convention."

"It is, but so is massacring prisoners of war. The Nazis work under their own laws. Lieutenant, do not let anyone near these trucks. If they explode, you will be dead. Shit, I don't know how they can be neutralized. Hell, I don't even know what kind of gas it is. But, for God's sake, and yours, do not let these trucks get back into German hands."

2

Kent County, England
Early May 1945

Four months later, Max stood in the greenhouse of the Norcross estate looking at the bright green landscape of an early May day. The lawn, the trees, even a few azaleas promised a season that, like for the world, would be new and fresh. Two cigarettes lay crushed in the ashtray on the ornate cast iron table beside him. Next to it, a telegram sat open. He shivered.

A hand softly placed itself on his arm. "Are you all right?"

"I'm fine." He sighed. "This winter's been hard. We've left too many friends in France and Belgium." He turned to his confidante and lover, Sophie Norcross, and gently kissed her on the lips. "Far too many."

"It will be over soon," Sophie said. "We've pushed deep into Germany; they can't last much longer. Hitler's dead, the Germans in Italy have surrendered, meetings are being held in Germany, only days left."

"And each day paid with more dead."

"Come away from the window. Dinner is early tonight. I have to be back in London tomorrow morning."

Max picked up the telegram. "They've sent for me too. We'll go back to London together."

"I thought they gave you a week."

"Two days is a week in the army."

"For us, two days seems like a lifetime. We are fortunate to even have these."

For Max, the winter had been a war against both the Germans and his own army. After the German advance had been repelled in the Ardennes, Max and Sophie had spent only a handful of days together—one night in Paris and then he was sent back to the front. One early March day, in a German village where captured German officers were being held, she passed through heading north. Orders from MI6—return to London, ASAP. His own assignment was simple: find out what he could about the poison gas found in the trucks. Hers was to ensure that there was a British presence at the interrogations. While the two allies fought this war against the Germans, there was a concern by both partners (and probably rightly so) that some information was not being shared between them. While the goal was the same, each intelligence service—Max's American OSS and her British MI6—had different agendas. Both allies knew that the postwar world would be different. Their agendas reflected the changing politics of their governments.

Max and Sophie had spent the past two years fighting their own war in Italy and France against the Germans. Rome and Paris were now free and had been for more than six months. And while their parts had been small, they had been vital. There would be no medals, no honors, and no parades for them. They lived and fought in the shadows.

"This is for you," she said and handed Max a small box. "I know yours was damaged in Belgium. It keeps good time."

Max opened the box and removed a watch. The white numbers and hands were in stark contrast to the black face. The strap looked new. He turned it over. The inscription read,

"To Max, we will always have Rome."

She kissed him on the cheek. "When you look at this, I want you to think of me. I am very selfish."

He returned her kiss. "Thank you."

Max took her arm and they walked through the house that had been the Norcross estate for longer than the United States had existed. Portraits of Norcross ancestors lined the walls of the hallways. Many wore the uniforms of British officers, men who had served and died in the Americas, India, and South Africa. Each a reminder of a family dedicated to the ideals of the British Empire.

Max Adler's family home in Chicago had portraits as well. Portraits and photographs of relatives lost to the monstrous appetite of a culture and country that had become the scourge of the twentieth century. Photos of family members who were now ghosts and walked among the uncountable dead, lost to the charnel pits of a sick ideology. His parents were some of the fortunate few to escape, fleeing their home in Berlin and settling in Chicago a decade before Hitler's rapacious engine of hate and war began turning its gears. If the Jews didn't have enough guilt in their collective soul, surviving this war only heaped the souls of these dead on their shoulders.

"Are they keeping you in London?" Max asked as Sophie passed him a tumbler of bourbon.

"I don't know, but I don't think so. The rumor is Vienna, or worse, Moscow—God, I hope not, but Uncle Joe is rattling his cage. And my Russian stinks. His unstoppable westward advances are convincing some that he will be even more intolerable after this is over. We need friends inside, so if that's where I'm needed, I'll go. I don't know after that. You? Are you going after that Arab, al-Husseini?"

"I wish," Max answered. "Right now, probably back to the front. I regret having done my job so well. They seem to think that since I discovered that truck full of poison gas, I'm the expert. They want me to find out if there is any left, something that might stop our final assault on Berlin. The Nazis are desperate—why they didn't use that truckload of artillery shells is still being argued. They only thing they agree on is the growing German incompetence. Maybe it was fear of reprisals. But what do I know? And the Arabs, North Africa, the Levant—that's a part of the war we missed. Thank God."

The cook found some canned meat, a few potatoes, and carrots from the cellar, and Lord Edward James Norcross dug out from his secret collection a bottle of Burgundy. A dusty bottle of Madera sat on the sideboard for dessert.

"A toast," Lord Norcross said as he stood.

Max stood next to Sophie, their glasses in their hands.

"Actually, a number of toasts," Norcross said. "First to my darling Donna Marie who has stood by this old soldier and put up with his surly moments and absences. Soon I will be here to spend the rest of our days together. To Donna."

Glasses clinked.

"To my daughter who fights for England as sturdily as any in the army—every time she leaves, my proud heart breaks just a little more. I ache to have you remain here with us. To Sophie Elena."

He turned to Max. "And to you, son, for somehow taming this whirling dervish. You sir, are welcome anytime."

Max smiled and bowed. The Madera survived until almost midnight, then it, too, was lost to the evening. Lord and Lady Norcross disappeared up the stairs and the staff began to close the house for the night. Max and Sophie sat in the library, Max sipping the last of the Kentucky bourbon he'd brought with him two days earlier.

"Outside of my own parents, I do not know a finer couple. I adore your mother and respect your father immensely."

"I think they like you, for a Yank."

"A Yiddish Yank, I'll have you know. It has a nice ring

about it."

"Yes, and at times, a serious pain in the ass as well. There are days when I'm not sure why I've stuck with you these past few years."

"There are times when I wonder about that myself. Our future, as it seems, is in the hands of others, yet here we are—survivors."

"I wish you wouldn't say things like that. It's bad luck to talk about the future."

"All we have is the future, whether it's a day or a week or the rest of our lives."

"It's still bad luck."

"We will make our own luck."

"I thought you didn't believe in luck," Sophie answered.

A cough came from the back of the library. "Sorry, Miss Norcross, but you have an early train."

"Thank you, Charles." Sophie looked at Max and smiled.

"To the early morning and our future," Max said and finished his whiskey.

London
May 1945

His meeting at OSS headquarters in London had been with his old friend Colonel Zebadiah Jones. Jones was, like himself, a survivor. It is always good to have a friend who is a survivor. Maybe Jones's luck would rub off on him, he thought. But then again, Max didn't believe in luck.

Jones began the meeting with a simple, yet gut-wrenching, statement.

"With the hostilities effectively over here in Europe, as of October 1, we will be shut down as a viable military unit," Jones said. "The Office of Strategic Services itself will cease to exist; it's been ordered by President Truman. There are rumors that General Donovan is cooking something else up, but right now I don't have a clue as to what it will be."

"What the hell are they thinking?" Max asked. "You know the Russians are doing everything they can to screw this peace up. Someone has to watch them, and it sure can't be the FBI or military intelligence."

"I know that, and you know that. Hell, the whole intelligence division—as well as British MI5 and MI6—know it.

However, I'm also certain that our British brothers are thrilled they won't have to bother with us anymore. So, officially, in a few months, we are shutting the doors."

"And unofficially?"

"I am supposed to keep a boot in the door here in Europe," Jones said. "There are too many bad guys still causing mischief and mayhem. Even though Skorzeny's homicidal Werewolves never appeared, there's still a chance that something might pop. Our trackers say that dozens—maybe even hundreds—of senior Nazis have slipped through the net we've thrown over Germany. Many of them worked in special divisions dealing with chemical warfare, the concentration camps, and, most critically, their missile program. Donovan wants them found and dragged back to face justice."

"And if they don't want to return to the fatherland or our welcoming arms?" Max asked, knowing well the answer to his question.

"He doesn't want them in the welcoming arms of anyone else. Do I make myself clear, Adler?"

"Absolutely clear, Major."

"Good. Captain, your next assignment is on the table. I'm not sure where this will lead, but the dossier concerns one of these high-ranking fugitives, and your orders, as vague as they are, are inside. The man, Johann von Dietz, is an SS colonel, a very senior officer in the chemical and biological warfare division. The word is that he was also the brains behind it—a scientist with an SS on his collar. I can't tell you how to run this operation; you do well on your own. But if this goes sideways or the OSS does disappear, you will have to make decisions on the fly. Do you have a problem with that?"

"No, sir. None. And where is this SS major?"

"We believe he's in Cairo."

"Really? You are sending me, a Berlin-born Jew, into the middle of the most populous Muslim and Arab city in the whole Middle East?"

"Captain Adler, you are the one who made the connection to Dietz through one of their senior Muslim leaders, Amin al-Husseini. Dietz was involved in the production of that load of shells you found. Our intelligence says that this Nazi may be working for al-Husseini or one of his lieutenants. Rumor is that this lieutenant is a radical French-Algerian hiding in North Africa somewhere; MI6 knows about him. Find Dietz and stop both of them."

"Do you want me to arrest them or just shoot them?"

"I'll leave that to you. However, in Dietz's case, I'm going to guess that he's the one who will be making that decision for you."

* * *

A month earlier, in an Allied prisoner of war camp south of Berlin, Max looked at his watch, then thoughtfully ran his finger over the broken crystal—it still worked but he wasn't sure for how long. The interrogation center was an old, half-broken-down stable; it still smelled of livestock. He looked out the small window to the rows of tents and makeshift shelters that filled the shallow valley between the hills. The POW camp was encircled with multiple rows of barbed wire.

"Who's next, Sergeant?"

"Strange guy. I think he's an Arab or at least from the Levant—there's an arrogance about him," Faber said, looking at the sheet of paper in his hand.

"Why us? Can't we just send him on?" Adler said, looking at the dossiers stacked on his desk. "Colonel Jones wants us to get through the next dozen SS officers and squeeze them. What's this guy's story?"

"Paperwork says he was rolled up with a convoy that was trying to escape south out of Berlin; they were stopped by a roadblock. Everyone peacefully gave up. The few that spoke

English declared their undying hatred for Hitler and love for baseball and Betty Grable."

"Don't they all? Must be in the new *Nazi How to Surrender* manual. This guy?"

"SS uniform, Balkan Handschar unit, Bosnian Muslim. Papers have him from Homs in the French Mandate area of Syria, though. He stood out from the others; in fact, the report from the officer that arrested him was that the Germans would have nothing to do with him. They called him '*Feiger Hund.*'"

"Cowardly dog? Typical for the Germans—if you are not one of them, you are shit, or worse. Does he speak German?"

"Yes, and quite fluently," Faber said. "The file says that he is SS Leutnant Habin Hassan, a Syrian national. He claims he was the number one bodyguard for Amin al-Husseini while the Mufti was a guest of the Führer here in Germany."

"Amin al-Husseini?"

"Actually, Mohammed Amin al-Husseini. The man is the current leader of the North African and Middle Eastern Is-lamic forces—mostly Arab—aligned to fight the British and prevent the Zionists taking over Palestine. He is all over our re-ports as aiding Hitler and the Nazis. He was behind the recruit-ment of Bosnian and Albanian Muslims for Islamic Waffen-SS divisions. He also broadcast incendiary tirades against the Al-lies and the Jews, sort of an Islamic Lord Haw-Haw. There are rumors he was also instrumental in forming execution squads to liquidate Jews found in North Africa in the wake of Rom-mel's advances. All unconfirmed, but it would fit. Twenty years ago, the British, in a shrewd move, made him Grand Mufti of Jerusalem to maintain some semblance of peace between their force and the local Palestine Arabs—a lot of good that did. Al-Husseini is one seriously bad Arab, sir."

"Hassan, he is a soldier?" Max asked.

"Yes," Faber answered. "But there's more, I think. He is a zealot, a true believer."

"A Nazi?"

"No, a fanatic true believer in Islam and the unification of the Arab nations and the expulsion of the French and British."

"And after the British leave Palestine . . . ?"

"The Arabs will likely turn Palestine into something like Buchenwald. They have not covered their intentions with euphemisms—they want the Jews out of the Middle East or dead. And they sure as hell don't want the surviving European Jews flooding into Palestine."

"Neither do the British and French."

"Altogether nice guys. Ready?

"Bring him in, Sergeant."

Sergeant Faber returned, followed by two American soldiers who held a prisoner between them. The man was tall and angular, dark complexion, almost black eyes, a full mustache, and a week's stubble of black beard. His SS uniform was reasonably clean, and there were no restraints on his arms or legs. His facial expression, when he saw Max and Faber, gave away some of the apparent confidence he'd had before he walked into the room.

Max pointed to a steel chair behind the table. "*Sitzen,*" he said in German.

Hassan looked at Adler, smiled, and asked in German, "Are you American?"

"He's sharp, Sergeant," Max said to Faber, also in German. He watched for a change in the man as he sat. Hassan tried to remain stoic. Adler opened the file and studied it. He let the man stew. After few minutes, he looked up.

"Where is he?" Max demanded.

"Who?" Hassan said.

"Your boss, Amin al-Husseini."

"I am but a humble servant of the great leader. Why would he tell me his plans?" Hassan placed his hands together and fingered a string of beads with the fingers of his left.

"Syrian?" Max asked, opening a thick file.

"I prefer Palestinian. Only your friends the British and French call me Syrian. But you will have to ask them what the boundaries of my country are this week." He rolled some of the ninety-nine beads through his fingers; his lips silently moved.

"Your arm patch says you are with the 13th Waffen Mountain Division. According to my reports, that is a Muslim division that fought for the Germans in the Balkans."

"Your reports may be wrong," Hassan suggested.

"They aren't. It also says that most of these same Muslim soldiers left and escaped to Bosnia after the Bulgarians and the Russians overran them. It seems it is also a division of cowards as well. My guess is that uniform, and you, have never even seen combat."

"Your point? We all serve where we are needed."

"So, you were stationed here in Germany," Max said. "You had a nice commission with a Muslim army fifteen hundred miles away, didn't fight, and when the opportunity presented itself, you fled with your boss al-Husseini, like a dog with your tail between your legs."

"Like a beaten dog, a *feiger hund*," Sergeant Faber added.

"We left by different means. Where the supreme leader was going, he did not tell me. I was going home to my family in Homs."

"We will determine when, if ever, you are going home," Max said. "The *SS* on your collar makes you a war criminal. We execute war criminals."

"What, no American fair play?"

Ignoring the remark, Max tapped the folder. "It says nothing here about your education. Your German is excellent. Where did you go to school?"

"The American school in Beirut—my father was a diplomat during the French Mandate. We had privileges; my French and English are also perfect. Then I studied in Leipzig, compliments of the Germans. They were as interested in we Arabs as we were in Adolf Hitler. You do know he is a great leader."

"There are rumors that he is also a very dead great leader," Faber said. "Shot himself . . . in the head."

"He will be missed."

Max looked at the man; he would like nothing more than to punch the son of a bitch in the mouth. He took a deep breath. "Maybe we should turn you over to the British."

"We are great friends of the British," Hassan said. "They, like the French, have done so much for us."

"Bullshit. You hate them as much as you hate the Jews."

Hassan, for the first time during the interview, smiled. "We hate no one, Captain. We just wish to be left alone."

"Joining Hitler's Nazi army, fighting in the Balkans, advising the Germans about Islamic, French, and British intentions. We call that spying."

"Captain, that's what friends do. We help each other against our common enemies."

"Where is al-Husseini?"

"As I said, he did not tell this poor servant where he was going. But I wish him Allah's blessing and reward." Hassan looked at Faber. "Is that soldier a Jew?"

"We are both Jews."

Habin Hassan continued to finger his beads as he stared at the men.

"You have never met a Jew, have you?" Max asked.

"Not a live one."

For two more days, they continued their interrogation of Hassan. On the afternoon of the second day of questioning, Sophie Norcross joined them. Between the three interrogators, Hassan's questioning continued almost nonstop—the man was groggy from lack of sleep. Word had come down through channels that both countries, the Americans and the British, wanted al-Husseini. However, each country wanted the leader of the Middle Eastern Islamic forces for different reasons. The British wanted him to see if he could be useful in Palestine managing the Arab Palestinians and helping with the Zionist issue. The Americans' desire was unclear, but if the British wanted him, they, too, wanted him.

Hassan offered little except the party line. "We will drive the British and French out of all Arab lands—our leader will see to that. With Allah's guidance and laws, we will be great again. And the leader has promised us that we will free our lands of the Jews."

"Hitler made the same promise," Faber said. "That promise, and others like it, destroyed his country and him. He is no more, and we will find his accomplices. There is no place they can hide."

"The world is very large, and Amin al-Husseini has great faith in his people," Hassan said. "And with help from our German friends, we will succeed."

"What help? What German friends?" Sophie demanded, catching the small piece of Hassan's boast.

Being questioned by a woman made Hassan visibly uncomfortable. When she asked a question, he turned his head, trying to ignore her. She pressed on.

"Look at me, you son of a bitch. I asked, what help?" Sophie said. "Who were the Nazis that you had contact with in Berlin?"

"I would have thought you would have arrested and shot them all by now—that's what winners of wars do. Or so I'm told."

"I can make prison more comfortable, if you help us," she said.

"I am comfortable now. Besides, why would I help infidels or Jews?" He turned to Max. "In time your governments will become bored with us and will leave us alone. All you want from our countries is the oil. After that is gone, you will leave. The only thing we have more of than oil is sand—and you are welcome to all of that you can take. I have said too much; I am very tired."

"You said something about your friends, your German friends?" Max echoed. "Who?"

"They have already left; it makes no difference." Hassan's grin was more than Max could bear.

"Look, you son of a bitch, what the hell are you talking about?"

Hassan slowly ran his beads through his fingers, his head down, and his eyes on the table.

"The Führer has provided my leader with the means, the expertise, and the men to achieve our goal of a unified caliphate. It is all in motion; nothing can stop it. Not even you." Hassan looked up. "Jew."

4

Off the Egyptian Coast
September 1945

Just great, a thoroughly soaked Max thought, as he held tight to the hemp rope secured to the bow of the rubber assault boat. To the east, the lights of Alexandria lit the underside of the thin marine layer spread above the Egyptian city. The moon, high above the mist and the ancient port city, was in its waning crescent stage. Ahead, the black desert disappeared at the edge of a flat and glassy Mediterranean Sea. Max hunched his knees as the boat rode over a long swell. After the cold and fog of winter and spring in northern Europe, the breadth of the sky above the arid desert staggered him. Smelling of oil and creosote, the warm breeze blew off the scorched land; it gently passed over him and the two sailors in the boat. The muffled motor pushed them toward the dark beach. The glow of his new watch read an hour to sunrise.

The dark beach was now less than a mile ahead. Behind him, an American destroyer waited for the return of the assault boat and its two-man crew. Max had logged more than a thousand miles in the last two weeks: Berlin, Frankfort, Munich, a plane over the Alps to Rome, a train to Naples, the destroyer, and now a less-than-pleasurable boat ride to the beaches of Egypt. His journey solely based on Jones's information that SS-Obersturmbannführer Johann von Dietz was now in Cairo. Dietz's dossier listed him as a graduate of Technische Universität München, a chemical engineer, biologist, and the presumed inventor of a potent nerve gas; he was also wanted by the Office of Strategic Services and British MI6. On the formal list of Nazi war criminals the Allies wanted, Dietz could be found on page three or four. He was the quintessential Nazi and mass murderer. Not high up like Goebbels or Göring, but certainly a criminal of some interest. The intelligence said Dietz was looking for a new employer, one that would allow him the freedom to weaponize his creations. That hint came from a strange source, one not expected in the mopping up that followed the advance of the Allies into northern Germany and the western suburbs of Berlin. Toward the end of the war, countless numbers of prisoners were interred in massive POW camps across Germany. After the Ardennes, Adler's people in the OSS wanted intelligence, anything that would have aided the soldiers pushing the front deeper into Germany. Now that Germany had surrendered, the prisoners were just a bothersome mob that might, at any moment, bust through the barbed wire and turn on their captors. The OSS was looking for criminals, German war criminals. By Allied order, every captured member of the Nazi Schutzstaffel (SS) was to be arrested as a war criminal and kept separated from the other prisoners of war. The OSS knew that viable intelligence would come only from Wehrmacht or SS officers. By the end of the war, the regular German foot soldier knew only three things: how to follow orders and fight, how to surrender, and how to die. They did all three exceptionally well.

The rubber boat rose high and then fell into a slide on the slick side of a long swell. Max's stomach rolled over. With his wet handkerchief, he tried to rub the salt spray out of his tired eyes.

The chance encounter with Habin Hassan was now just a statistical memory. After the interrogation, he was transferred into the POW system and would, most probably, be released. There was nothing in the Arab's file to suggest otherwise. Max was certain this would happen with the millions of other German POWs. Maybe a few thousand zealots and true believers, mostly SS officers, would stand trial for their crimes. He believed that many of those released officers were criminals. Some probably worth a moment of time at the executioner's gallows, but there was no practical way to expect justice on such a massive scale. He was also certain thousands of German officers and soldiers had escaped Europe and were now in hiding in remote locations around the world.

"Two minutes, sir. Almost there," the ensign said over the noise from the motor.

He saw nothing ahead; Max never thought to question the remark from the crewman. Over the years, he had grown to respect the expertise of the soldiers and sailors he met. A single light flashed on the black horizon, three flashes, a pause, and then two more. The second sailor raised his light and returned the same signal to the beach. The boat rose with a swell, and the sailor washed the floodlight's beam over the shoreline. Max gripped the line tighter. The sailor secured the light and lifted a Thompson submachine gun and charged the weapon. The bow of the assault boat slid up the sandy beach; the ensign cut the motor. Max picked up the light and played it across the sand until it stopped on three men. Like Max, they were all dressed in Bedouin robes and headgear.

"Pleasant trip, Yank?" a voice asked. It carried a decidedly English accent.

"Colonel Michael Rushton," Max said, stepping onto the damp sand. "It is good to see you. Captain Max Adler, OSS."

Rushton grabbed Max's hand and gave it a good shake. "I

suggest that we allow your mates to head back to their ship—in these lands it is very hard to tell friend from foe—and I swear that Arabs can see in the dark."

The ensign handed Max three large canvas bags, and he passed them on to one of the men with Rushton.

"Thank you, men," Max said to the two sailors. "Good luck."

"And to you, too, sir," they replied.

The sailor handed his weapon to the ensign, leaped from the boat, and began to push it back into the Mediterranean Sea. When afloat, he jumped back in. As the first wave lifted the boat, the ensign started the motor. Max and Rushton watched the boat disappear—only the motor's buzzing gave away its location, and then even that was gone.

One of the men took Max's rucksack; the other swung the remaining bags on his shoulders. They followed Rushton and Adler as they climbed up the beach and through the grass-covered sand dunes. Displayed in the gloom of Rushton's flashlight, Max was shocked by the appearance of a massive stone column directly in front of them. He washed his own flashlight over the column and then over the others standing behind it. Intricate stonewalls appeared along their path; the sand gave way to interlocked paving stones. All were broken and showed signs of great age and ruin.

"This way," Rushton said, pointing with his light.

The group turned into a narrow passageway walled in on three sides. Overhead, a canvas awning was strung between the columns. Max had smelled the coffee before he saw the small fire set against one of the walls of the enclosure.

"I prefer tea, but we are always here to help our allies," Rushton said. "Mohammed, pour the American a cup of coffee."

The man sat Max's rucksack on the ground near the fire and filled a tin cup from a small coffeepot. Max took the cup and breathed in the rich Arabian coffee.

"Where are we?" Max asked.

"Someplace relatively safe," Rushton answered. "These are the ruins of a Roman villa from the second or third century. Don't know exactly who—my guess is history has forgotten as well. The coasts of Libya and Egypt are littered with old Roman and Greek cities, villas, and amphitheaters. When I was chasing the Germans across North Africa with His Majesty's Eighth Army, I saw far too many to remember. We fought Rommel across this desert for more than two years. Many of my mates are buried and now lost in these sands."

"And these two?" Adler asked, looking at the two men sitting on the ground, their faces barely illuminated by the fire.

"Mohammed and Ahmed? I trust them with my life. Both are Bedouin, local tribesmen. They have been with me for three years. They speak some English, enough to get by. I speak Arabic—that's why our bosses assigned me to you."

"I'm pretty good at handling myself," Max said.

"Yes, I'm sure you are. But here, Captain Adler, you would be dead in a week, or if found by some of the less savory relatives of these gentlemen, dead in a day. They use long, curved, and very sharp knives here—not pleasant, I assure you. This country is as lawless as your cowboy old west, especially for infidels such as you."

"And you?"

"They trust me, as far as it goes. We owe each other a blood debt. They trust me because I sponsored their oldest boys to a school in England. Smart lads—they are the future of this part of the world. This region is lousy with oil, and we need oil. That's the future, and these men know it. I was told that you will be working under an alias?" Rushton asked, lighting his pipe.

"Yes, Dwight Loomis. I was an army lieutenant in Tunis before I was unceremoniously thrown out of the army. Seems that I'm also wanted for some nasty things in Benghazi, as well."

"I know about the story of Benghazi and the money; I hope the other was for something important."

"Yes, it seems that Mr. Loomis was fooling around with a major's wife. The major is looking for Mr. Loomis—personal reasons. The wife is also looking—for personal reasons as well." Max lit a cigarette. "The world is changing, Colonel Rushton. I hope your friends in this part of the world understand how much."

5

Cairo, Zamalek District
September 1945

Nazi fugitive, SS-Obersturmbannführer Johann von Dietz stood on the balcony of his apartment in the swanky and popular Cairo neighborhood of Zamalek, smoking a cigarette and looking down on the Nile River. He wore an open collar white shirt and gray slacks. He was a thin man of less than average height; his cheeks were a bit sunken and his gray eyes were surrounded by yellow due to the touch of jaundice he'd acquired during the past few months of travel. His hairline had now receded to a point where he considered shaving his head. The nuisance of the remaining fringe annoyed him, but vanity forced him to keep it. His face was almost a perfect oval, and if it were not for his protruding ears, he might even be considered handsome in a Teutonic sort of way. In the vernacular of a movie actor, he looked like a mad scientist. He favored wire-rim glasses; they sat on the bed stand near the ornate glass lamp.

"Come back to bed, Johann. There is nothing out there to see," the woman said from the bedroom. "I am lonely."

From the balcony, Dietz looked back into the apartment,

then back out across the nighttime rooftops of Egypt and Africa's oldest city. The fan lazily spinning overhead helped to dissipate the heat from the day. The haze from all the diesel trucks and cooking fires left an acrid taste in his mouth. A taste that, for some reason, was comforting, almost inviting—it tasted of orientalism. His friends—many newly escaped from Germany and the north—thought that Egypt was a slum, a way station on their route to escape the retribution of the Allies. All hoped to eventually reach Argentina and South America. Dietz found Cairo intriguing and mysterious; the same as he found it eight years earlier the first time he lived here; before the war, before the ruin of his country. Then he'd spent time in its markets and narrow kasbahs. That year, before the war, he spent as a German spy sending reports back to Berlin. His time also helped acquire friends and contacts. Now, just seven years later, the world—his world and Germany's—had radically and irrevocably changed. He held the rank of an important German officer of the Third Reich, but for all realistic intents, now he was an unemployed chemical engineer. Al-Husseini provided well; Dietz just needed to overcome the novel concept of being self-employed, his own man, self-directed.

"I will return shortly, Jasmine," Dietz replied. "Be patient. I will finish my cigarette—and then we shall see."

For the past two years, SS-Colonel von Dietz had watched helplessly as Germany collapsed. His first deployment, the Afrika Korps-chemical division, had been reduced to almost nothing before its defeat in May 1943. He and a small group of officers and men made their escape north to Sicily, while Rommel fled to Germany. After reaching Italy, he continued north and was reassigned to the chemical weapons division. He believed he'd been neutered, both his African experience and his education in chemistry unused. In mid-1944, when the Allies invaded France, he knew the war would end soon. It was obvious to everyone, except the Führer—that Germany was doomed. Hitler's Third Reich would not last for a glorious thousand years; it was remarkable that it lasted thirteen. Dietz was pragmatic. The Allies would decimate his country and take their vengeance; Germany was not someplace that he wanted to stay. Those that had escaped, many of his fellow SS officers and comrades, were now hiding in Cairo, Damascus, and Baghdad. Like him, they, too, needed a purpose. For some, it was the hope to try and foolishly resurrect the Reich and continue with the Führer's intentions of a world free of Jews and communists. For others it was the chance to disappear and hide from the world's need for righteous retribution and its pound of flesh. However, for a few, it was a chance to make money and live well. Germany was now lost to the Allied powers and the Russians. The future for many of these escaped Germans, like him, would be with those who also hated the Allies and the Jews: the Arabs and Islam.

The skills Dietz and many of his comrades carried were far beyond those of the Arabs. These Nazi expatriates sought employment, and the Arabs provided both the opportunity as well as the money. They also provided new identification papers, shelter, and security. During one of his last trips to Berlin, Dietz made it a point to meet with Mohammed Amin al-Husseini at the man's residence outside of Berlin. Much was discussed, but particular attention was made to Dietz's skill as an engineer and scientist and his understanding of chemicals and their application in war. Dietz provided al-Husseini a list of materials he would need if he were to somehow make it to Cairo. All al-Husseini said, as he handed the list to his aide Habin Hassan, was that Allah would provide. It was also arranged, at that meeting, that as soon as they could be accumulated, two shiploads of arms and munitions would be secretly shipped from Greece and hidden in Alexandria, Egypt. The Nazis were retreating northward, and these weapons and materials would not be left for the Greeks or the British. Al-Husseini was well informed about what was happening in the Levant and the Arab lands of North Africa. Long into that evening, Dietz and a small group of influential Nazis listened to the Arab leader talk of his goal of a unified Arab nation, his caliphate. With him as its leader, this new nation then would take its rightful place in the world. With political and religious power gained by the oil extracted from the Arab countries of Libya, Saudi Arabia, and Iraq, this new nation would control the West's economies and their futures. By doing this, al-Husseini prophesized, they would also control their own destiny.

Dietz crushed the spent cigarette against the tile floor of the apartment's balcony and lit another.

"Please, come to bed," Jasmine pleaded. "You need your sleep; it has been two days since you slept. Please, my love, come back to bed."

She was wrong; it had been almost four days. He was exhausted, but his mind continued to churn. The tour of the warehouse the day before went well. A mile off the Desert Road, halfway between Cairo and Alexandria, more than a thousand crates and canisters filled the nondescript corrugated building. Skull and crossbones signs were posted so that the illiterate locals would understand that trespassing was prohibited and potentially fatal. If that didn't convince them, the four permanent guards loyal to al-Husseini and the Muslim Brotherhood would. He fully understood that thievery came second nature to the locals, so every opportunity to make sure they understood the dangers would be made. There was no reason to make enemies of the local population by shooting them; Dietz hoped they would not test the security.

He had also acquired the use of a forgotten British colonial gymnasium lost in a part of the old city of Cairo. With its large open exercise rooms and spacious, well-tiled, and adequately plumbed and ventilated locker rooms, it would be ideal for his chemical factory. The building was a block off Shari Ibn

El-Amri in the ancient quarter of Shubra; access was relatively easy. No one would give it a thought, and the traffic going in and out would be lost in this heavily congested part of Cairo. A sizable garage was attached that could accommodate automobiles and even large trucks. The fact that it said "British Officers Club and Gymnasium" on a plaque near the front door only added to the subterfuge. It also would deter the locals.

The knock on the apartment door was sharp, two taps, a pause, and then two more. Dietz walked back through the living room, stopped by the door to the bedroom, and put his finger to his lips. Jasmine nodded, and Dietz closed the door. He then took the Luger from the table, pulled back the hammer, went to the door, and looked through the small peephole. He smiled and slid back the heavy lock, then opened the door and took a step back as he gently released the hammer and slipped the pistol into his waistband.

The man at the door, dressed in a crisp and neat linen suit, snapped to attention and gave the Nazi salute. He said nothing.

"Come in, Hans," Dietz said. The man, his white Panama hat in his hand, strolled into the room. His bearing was military and athletic. The man was clean-shaven, his hair was dark brown and dropped across his forehead, and his eyes were also brown. What was even more remarkable was his very deep tan. His skin, for a man not more than thirty, was leathery. This color could only be gained by years in the desert, tough years, brutal years.

"Thank you for coming, Hans," Dietz said. "I know it is late." He looked at his watch. "Or early. I'm sorry, but I have lost track of time."

"That is quite all right. It has been a long night for me as well. We were able to welcome three more of our fellow officers early yesterday morning. They landed at the airfield. There were no problems."

"Excellent. They are resting?"

"Yes. The flight from Bulgaria was difficult but free from harassment," Hans said. "They arrived in a Junkers 352. The plane has been secured and camouflaged near the other aircraft; it will be helpful later. We do not want the Egyptians to be aware of its presence. You know how these Arabs are. The pilot was Luftwaffe—his name is Bitner. He has agreed to remain with the plane."

"Excellent," Dietz said. "Cigarette? Schnapps?"

"A schnapps would be welcome, Colonel."

"Here in Cairo, Hans, we will go by our given names. An inadvertent reference to rank or our homeland might be misconstrued."

"Yes, Herr von Dietz, I understand." Hans took the glass of schnapps from Dietz and saluted his superior. "Prost!"

"Prost."

SS-Hauptsturmführer Hans Gottlieb had been a member of the Hitler Youth, the Nazi Party, and a Nazi officer since the spring of 1937 when he became of age and available from the university he attended. Now, at twenty-eight, Gottlieb knew nothing of a Germany that was not under the control of Adolf Hitler. He was a devoted true believer and a loyal officer and friend to Major von Dietz. He had not fully embraced the reality of the collapse of his country, but then again, many of those Germans he had assisted in "immigrating" into Egypt had not accepted this change in the world order either. The Allies wanted to arrest these senior SS and Wehrmacht officers and charge them with being war criminals. If caught, some were bound for the executioner's rope; others for long prison sentences. However, here in Cairo, they were secretly housed in a swank hotel in the Al Qasr Ayni district. This hotel, one block away from the British embassy, was literally under the noses of the British and their residency of the country. These Germans waited, often in great comfort, for the right moment to join the growing Egyptian nationalist movement and seize the country from the British-supported King Farouk. Their expertise would be invaluable to Dietz and the future of his operations.

"This idiot, King Farouk, is certainly making our stay here easier," Gottlieb said as he crossed the room to the open door to the balcony. "Even with this British occupation, his sympathies for the Reich are well known. I'm surprised that he has lasted this long."

"He was pushed into declaring war against us by the British; it was inevitable," Dietz added. "This young king is not long for his throne. He is just a temporary inconvenience. My greater concern is how to remain hidden from the British agents that crawl these streets and fill the rooms of the Shepheards and the Continental hotels. Now that the British have their victory in Europe, they are going to lose the entire eastern Mediterranean, and it will be due to their failure to defeat the Zionists in Palestine. These Zionists, with their American money, are not to be trifled with. My friend, I am confident that with our Arab comrades, we will help the British on their merry way back to England."

"And then we can dispose of the real enemy," Gottlieb added. "The Zionists and Jews in Palestine."

"Yes, these are the enemies we must prepare for," Dietz said. "We have much to finish. Our work, started in Germany, is not done."

West of Alexandra, Egypt
September 1945

The sun was a finger's width above the sand dunes that stretched across the eastern and southern horizon and hid the Roman villa from the highway. It promised a fiery day.

"We can't stay here," Rushton said. "When the Germans were pushed back, they left spies everywhere. In a land as poor and corrupt as this, a smile is suspect, and an American spy could be worth a camel."

"I believe I am worth more than a camel," Max answered.

"You may be right—two camels and a goat."

The two Bedouin laughed and gathered up the rucksacks and other gear that had been stacked against the walls of the ruined villa.

"We should reach Alexandria by midday," Rushton said. "We will stop and reorganize there. While cooler, it is too dangerous to travel at night. It will take us two days to reach Cairo. Why didn't they just fly you into Cairo?"

"MI6 said that you were the best. This was where you were. Besides, it will allow me to become acclimated."

"Acclimated? For the next two days, you will be sitting on hell's doorstep. You could have prepared in London by sitting in an oven at the Ritz."

Rushton had two British Willys jeeps hidden amongst the ruins. They were encamped just north of the main coast road from Marsa Matruh to Alexandria. Camouflage netting covered both vehicles, more to keep local prying eyes away than to hide from the occasional Allied airplane that flew along the coastline. When Mohammed stripped away the netting, a tripod-mounted .50 caliber machine gun was directly behind the driver and front passenger seats. As the jeeps were loaded, Mohammed pointed out the locations of the Thompson submachine guns strapped to the backs of the front seats, Berettas in holsters, and ammunition.

"He is very proud of those pistols," Rushton said. "They were a part of a crate he liberated when the Italians surrendered. He only has eight left—two are in each vehicle, and he wears two under his robe. He smiles a lot, but he has personally killed more than thirty Germans and Italians. He and his brother, Ahmed, are experienced fighters. Ahmed carries the other two pistols. I owe them my life, and they owe me theirs. In this part of the world, there is no greater responsibility than to protect the man that has saved your life. Since you are my friend, they will defend you as if you were me."

"Comforting," Max answered.

"Enjoy it. There are very few other comforts in this part of the world."

By late morning, the temperature was well above a hundred degrees. Max was in the rear jeep, behind Rushton and Mohammed. Ahmed drove steadily and surprisingly well, but they had to follow in the wake of Rushton. The highway could only be described as perdition's own museum for destroyed war machines. Mile after mile, burned-out hulks of tanks, half-tracks, and automobiles littered the road. In a few places, crosses and markers were stuck into the burnt landscape. Camped in among these debris fields were Bedouin tribesmen. In two places Max saw signs, in German, pointing to cemeteries. Another pointed to an Australian cemetery. Max suspected that somewhere in the territory were British graveyards. Now that the war was over, these victors would face different dispositions than the Germans. Germany was in no position to deal with its war dead. Before they mounted the jeeps, the colonel stripped out of his Bedouin robes and was now dressed in his desert uniform; the others, including Max, were still dressed in Arab clothing. Two hours later, as they approached El Alamein, they met their first British roadblock. By then Max was covered in what felt like an inch of Egyptian grit and sand. It was obvious that Rushton was known to these British troops. As they pulled to a stop, the British soldier snapped to attention and saluted. Rushton offered his papers, and after a cursory look, the soldier handed them back. Rushton talked for a moment, then the guards waved them on. As they passed the soldiers, Max wondered what the guards thought as they studied him.

Ahmed closely followed his brother. The day dragged as the heat enveloped the two jeeps; they passed dozens of trucks and other vehicles heading westward. Max nodded off more than once, only to be jerked awake by Ahmed making a defensive move as he dealt with the traffic. They stopped twice; Rushton took a good look at Max to be sure that he was okay.

"Water, drink lots of water," he told Max. "Two more hours—you'll be fine."

This road near El Alamein had cost the lives of thousands of German, Italian, and British Empire soldiers during two murderous years of fighting that swept back and forth across this narrow region from Tunisia, to Libya, to western Egypt. To the north lay the Mediterranean Sea; to the south, a wide stretch of desert called the Qattara Depression, so severe no army could navigate it. A few miles past El Alamein, they abruptly left the highway and headed north on a narrow dirt road. They turned again and followed another road, even steeper and narrower, that wound down the side of a deep wadi that drained to the Mediterranean. In places, the road had recently washed away, leaving a track that only the jeeps could carefully maneuver. The road then abruptly ended; they turned onto a flat section of the wadi filled with lush flowering trees and palms; the verdant valley was not more than a quarter-mile square. Date palms lined the road, small pastures held sheep and goats, and on a low bluff, a cluster of whitewashed buildings looked out toward the sapphire sea.

Ahmed followed his brother toward the structures and parked under the shade of a grove of thick palm trees that intermingled with the buildings.

Rushton dismounted and shook the dust from his uniform; the others did the same from their robes.

"Captain Adler, my home away from home," Rushton said, waving his arms about. Before he finished, a boy, not more than fifteen, walked out from between two of the buildings carrying a silver tray with four tall glasses. "Iced tea, Captain?"

"You have got to be kidding me," Max said, taking a glass and then a long drink.

"We Brits try to drag civilization along with us wherever we go. This is Yousef Abd al-Qadir; he is the son of my cook and the nephew of Mohammed. He is a very bright young man; I have come to rely on him."

Rushton said something in Arabic to the men. They quickly began to remove the equipment and carry it toward another building in the compound.

"Ahmed will take your bags. Yousef will take you to your room—there's a shower, and he will take your robes and try to clean them. We don't want them to look too spanking new, do we? My office is in the opposite direction. Rest. We will have whiskeys at seven and dinner at eight."

Max followed Yousef through a narrow gap in the buildings and into a lush courtyard. A small fountain centered the garden; colorful trees and plants filled the rest of the small man-made Eden. The temperature lowered by twenty degrees and the chirping and songs of flitting birds filled the air. "Your room is here, sir," Yousef said and pushed open the heavy wood door. The room was cool and dark; the floor was red tile with remarkable glazed inlays inserted every few feet. The one window looked out into the garden. "The bathroom is there, towels and soap on the shelves, and the water is safe to drink. I will take your *thobe* and *kibber* and clean them. There is a carafe of water as well as dates and pistachios on the dresser. A bottle of whiskey is there; if you need anything else, just pull the cord by the door. A bell will ring."

Max looked around the room and was surprised at how comfortable it felt and how strange. Two hours ago, he felt like a chicken roasting in an oven, and now like a decadent Westerner at a fine seaside resort.

"Thank you, Yousef, this is more than adequate. Please tell Colonel Rushton I will see him at seven o'clock."

"Very good. I will come and collect you. He is serving dinner on the terrace tonight—very special." Yousef, his arms full of Adler's dusty robes, left.

Max lit a cigarette and poured a small measure of liquor. He studied himself in the dusty mirror mounted on the door to the bathroom and tried to brush the desert out of his beard. Now he wore khaki cotton shorts and fatigues favored by the British North African armies, as well as heavy boots and leggings. Strapped to his waist was his Colt 1911 .45 semiautomatic pistol, the same one he had used in Rome and France. After leaving Chicago three years earlier and joining the army, his six-foot-four-inch frame had matured into a muscular and fit thirty-year-old captain in the United States Army. His assignment, since being essentially drafted four years earlier into the OSS, was to spy.

Max Isaiah Adler was a long way from his home on the near North Side of Chicago, and even farther from when he was born in Berlin, Germany, in 1915. He now understood—after seeing the horrors of the concentration camps—what it would have been to be a Jew in Nazi Germany or occupied Europe. His months in Rome also changed him—he had seen the ultimate in good and evil.

He also understood what it was like to be a Jew in the confusion of Arabic countries and tribes that extended west for thousands of miles across North Africa to Palestine and the Levant and eastward across Saudi Arabia and into Iraq. It wasn't until one crossed into the Muslim world of Persian Iran far to the east that your Arab tribe, your blood family, meant more than any country. For more than five thousand years, this region along the Mediterranean Sea that straddled the Nile River had been the cultural center of the Eastern Hemisphere. It was also home to three of the world's largest, and most interdependent, religions: Judaism, Christianity, and Islam. Over the past millennium, two of these religions fought each other, seeking dominance. Many millions died forging what was called Western civilization, and many more in search of a Middle Eastern caliphate. The Crusades, a thousand years earlier, were never far from the thoughts of the modern Muslims of the Middle East and most especially political and religious radicals like al-Husseini. The Jews were often viciously caught in the vice between these two religions as one or the other fought for dominance.

Max finished his shower. His blue eyes sparkled in the mirror as he pushed the thick blond hair away from his forehead. His looks favored the German ideal, his temperament favored an avenging archangel, and his soul was that of an artist. The war had both aged him and matured him. He was no longer the flippant, spoiled egoist of his youth. Seeing what one human would do to another over ideology cured him of his overblown self-worth. His life now revolved around finding those that would plunge the world again into darkness and stop them.

Max managed a restless nap and then dressed for dinner in somewhat less dusty clothes than what he arrived in. When summoned, he followed Yousef through the garden to the main house. A pipe stuck professorially in his jaw, Rushton stood at the edge of the north-facing terrace, looking out into the Mediterranean Sea. A table had been set with bottles of whiskeys, gins, and other assorted liquors and fixings. A tray of sliced fruits and dates sat off to one side.

Colonel Rushton handed Max a glass. "I understand you favor bourbon; this was given to me by Eisenhower himself when he stayed here for a night. Good chap that man. I see him being your president one day. Excellent leader of men and an even better tactician. This past war was won with valor and logistics; this next one will be much longer and probably end with no clear winner. Religion, mixed with politics, is such nasty business."

They clinked tumblers.

"Handsome watch, Adler. German?"

"Yes, a gift."

"That should make your entry into German society in Cairo a little easier."

"It was not its intent."

Max looked out over the blue-gray sea; at this time of the day, it was hard to see the thin edge of where the sky and sea met. The sun was setting beyond the high cliffs of the wadi; a crimson color slowly washed across the sky and illuminated the soft margins of the few clouds. Then it was gone, and the night opened the heavens.

"Beautiful, is it not?" Rushton asked.

"Yes, it looks so benign. I expect it is hard to live in this desert."

"This desert will kill if you do not treat it with respect. I have lived here for ten years, all as an agent for his Majesty. I split my time with Cairo, our destination. I have grown to love this desert, but—"

"Ten years? Through all of the war and chaos?"

"Yes. First it was my political job, government agent and all. Now, it's as a military liaison for the future, whatever that might be. Even amongst the Arabs themselves, there is distrust. This distrust, even hatred, is of the old colonial powers that have controlled these lands since the end of World War I. Before that it was the Turks, who are not Arabs, who were greatly hated. There's also great suspicion and competition amongst the tribes themselves. And there is a radical movement growing amongst the ultra-religious. The most powerful is the Muslim Brotherhood located in Cairo. This is the group that al-Husseini is cultivating. And now, the Palestinian Zionists—natives and refugees from Europe, financially supported by Americans—are causing problems. There is a power vacuum developing here and underlying all of it is the intransigence of us British, and the French as well. Captain Adler, just between us, Britain and France are bankrupt. We cannot support these countries and fight this growing religious conflict. The smart Arabs, especially the radicals, know this and will use this knowledge to push us out. And, if they acquire the skills of these escaped Nazis officers, they may just succeed."

Yousef entered the terrace and stood off to one side. When Rushton acknowledged him, he nodded.

"Dinner is served. I believe the kitchen has prepared a small feast for us. Eat well. The next two days will be difficult."

Dinner was a banquet: flatbreads, couscous, a lamb *shakshouka*, and usban sausage. It went well with the Chianti that the men shared. They finished with thick coffee and a sweet bread called *leka'ek*.

"Dinner was wonderful," Max said. "My compliments. I have never had anything like it."

"In this culture, the women stay separate from the men. As such, they are timid when it comes to us Europeans. I will make sure the cook knows your pleasure."

They finished the evening with brandy and cigars. They talked more of the future—one they hoped for though did not expect.

"I understand that you worked with Sophie Norcross in Rome," Rushton said, mentioning the MI6 agent for the first time. "I have known Sophie and her family since she was a child, especially when she was in Rome at her grandparents' villa. Strong willed, I'll give you that—a mind of her own. Are you close?"

"This watch was a gift from her; it's a convenient reminder." Max wasn't sure how much to say.

"Is she in London?" Rushton asked.

"No. I don't know where she is. Right now, for the army, there is peace; for us in the spy game, there is never peace. We go where we are sent."

"So true. I understand that your time in Rome was difficult."

"Yes, at times extremely difficult," Max admitted. "Yet, I would not trade it. We shared a lot over the past three years."

"Volunteered, did you?"

"In a manner of speaking—my language skills were helpful as well as my family's connections."

"You are Jewish, am I correct?" Rushton said matter-of-factly.

"Yes, by blood and heritage. Not sure by practice. The Nazis saw little difference. All they needed was the excuse; for millions of those murdered, blood was enough."

"Be careful here in these countries," Rushton continued. "The Arabs use any excuse to maintain control, and for them, blood is also enough. The Germans and men like Amin al-Husseini, want to continue their war. They will use their own people as proxies in their fight. When you walked into our lights the other night, I thought that a German had landed. That is something that you can use."

"That is our intention. I am to become one of the Nazis that I hate."

Rushton looked at Max and scrunched his brow. "I wish you luck, there are some about who wish us gone. The boy will wake you at four o'clock. We will be on the road by five—as I said, the next two days will be difficult, even for an old desert rat like me."

Max fell into a deep sleep that only changed when he had to take a short walk to the bathroom. He left the lights out; only the faint glow of the stars and the moon from the bathroom's high window aided him. As he stood peeing in the chamber pot, he heard the door to his room being pushed slowly open; he thought of the boy. Was it four o'clock already? His watch glowed 2:25. The sound made by the door, almost imperceptible, was wood being dragged across sand. He stepped back against the bathroom wall and saw a black shape reflected in the mirror; considerably taller than Yousef, it stood in the open door. The man, with one sweep of an arm, drew out a dagger. The curved steel flashed in the dim light as he raised the knife, lunged at the bed where Max had slept, driving the blade into the mattress. Pushing himself away from the wall, Max leaped into the room and slammed his shoulder into the shadow, driving it against the far wall. A muffled cry of shock filled Max's ear as the two slammed into the partition. He continued to drive the man forward, easily lifting the attacker off the ground, while pinning and trapping the thin, yet muscular and wiry man's arms against his own body. He smelled like sour offal. The assailant twisted and tried to free his arms. Max, feeling a sharp pain on his thigh, bashed the head of the man against the wall. The only sound was the sharp ring of the knife when it hit the floor. Continuing to push forward, the two men grunted and cursed, then crashed through the window and tumbled across the paving and out into the garden. Max shifted his right hand to the man's throat and the other to the assailant's right wrist and hand that was desperately reaching for something inside his robes. Max squeezed the attacker's throat like a vice, his fingers crushing the jugular vein. He squeezed with all his power on the man's neck; the man bucked and fought against the stranglehold. As the man slowly faded under Max's unrelenting pressure, the night was shattered by gunshots and screams.

7

A foot shorter than the American, the attacker regrouped and managed to rip away Max's hold on his neck and stagger back a step. The attacker reached into his robe and pulled out something black and began to swing his arm upward toward Max. From behind Max, a shoulder slammed into his side, followed by the report and flash of a pistol. The attacker, his pistol still pointed at Max, staggered backward then collapsed to the floor.

Yelling and shouts came from the other rooms aligned along the courtyard. More pistol shots shattered the night, then all was quiet. Seconds later, lights flickered on around the compound. Max ran into his room and grabbed his Browning. When he returned to the courtyard, he looked at the man on the ground. The lamp, now on, over Max's door, cast a dim light on the man's face. He was obviously dead; a bearded Arab, dark, leathery, with a finger-sized hole above the left eye. Max turned to the man who had slammed his shoulder into him; it was Yousef. The young man held one of Mohammed's Berettas in his right hand; Yousef walked over to the body and spit on the corpse.

"Are you okay?" Max asked.

"It is I who should be asking you," Yousef said. "He was

here to kill you."

Three men ran down the walkway to Max's room—they were Rushton, Mohammed, and Ahmed.

"Good, you're alive," Rushton said, then looked at the man on the floor. "This fool—did you shoot him?"

"No, it was Yousef. He saved my life."

Rushton rolled the man over and pulled away his *kaffiyeh*.

"Arab, not from round here," Rushton said. "Damn." Rushton saw the blood on Max's leg. "Is it deep?"

"A nick. I'll wrap it later. You know him?"

"No, most likely Algerian," Mohammed said. "Bounty hunter, I suspect. There's another one outside the colonel's room."

From the end of the corridor, two more men appeared; another man was held between them. The prisoner was dressed like the dead man—black robe and black *kaffiyeh*. One of the men holding the prisoner spoke to Rushton in Arabic, then he pushed the prisoner to his knees. Mohammed asked the kneeling man something, also in Arabic. The man spit on his feet. Mohammed grabbed the man's headscarf and yanked it off. He then grabbed the man's long black hair, jerked his head back, and in one slash cut the intruder's throat. He held the man while he gurgled and tried to grasp at the wound. Mohammed threw the man on top of the intruder Yousef had shot.

"Jesus, Rushton," Max said. "Did he have to do that? He could have told us who sent him."

"The man would have said nothing, and besides this piece of shit killed one of my guards—that's how they got in. The guard was Mohammed's cousin. There was nothing on earth I could have done that would have stopped him from exacting his revenge."

Two more of Rushton's men appeared, and the bodies were quickly removed.

"Are you going to call the authorities?" Max asked.

Rushton laughed. "Don't be naïve, Captain Adler. We are the authorities. They will bury the bodies in the hills; they are lost to all except Allah. We, however, need to leave now. There will not be another attempt tonight, but I will not tempt fate. We leave in an hour."

The jeeps were assembled in the courtyard, and additional supplies were stacked in the rear cargo areas. Jerricans of water and gasoline were strapped to the sides of the vehicles; the weapons looked cleaned and well oiled.

Colonel Rushton walked through double doors that led to the main living quarters of the compound; he was dressed like a British field commander, even down to the lanyard and Webley revolver in a holster. He sported a Field Marshal Montgomery type of beret.

"Going to show the colors, Adler. Being a colonel has its advantages, and I've never been released from service. How's the leg?"

"Good. Lucky, though."

"Walk with me."

The two men crossed back through the house and to the terrace, the dark Mediterranean spread out before them. To the east, the sky was beginning to lighten, the dim glow of Alexandria on the far eastern horizon. Rushton offered Max a cigar.

"Tell me why you're really here. I was handed less information than I'm usually given, which seems to be typical with you American OSS types. Even your office in Cairo, run by a particularly strange bloke, gives out little information. Now, after last night, I assume that someone thinks that you are worth more dead than alive. How the word got out, I'm not sure—but I'm going to find out."

"If you hadn't—"

"Executed the man? I could no more have stopped Mohammed than I could have stopped the wind. He was honor bound; all the others in my security detail are his relatives. It needed to be done."

"I have no idea who could have said something. No one outside of three or four people knew I was coming."

"We work for large organizations, and since the end of the war, security has become lax. I can see it in the cables and the occasional visitor who drops in. London thinks I run an escort and tourist service. We also know that in both our intelligence operations there are those, for a few pounds or dollars, who would sell their own sisters. I'll send the information to London, let them figure it out. Right now, I want to know why you are here and why I should give a shit about you."

Max inhaled and blew out a cloud of blue smoke; it drifted in the still air.

"Mohammed Amin al-Husseini."

"The son of a bitch is somewhere in France, I'm told," Rushton said. "The man is a Palestinian, Jerusalem-born, lived near Hitler in Berlin for most of the war. Been a thorn in the side of my people in Jerusalem for almost twenty years. He sided with the Nazis; he should have died with them."

"The man and his organization," Max said, "are helping fugitive SS officers and Nazi personnel escape to Arab countries. Some have been seen in Baghdad, Cairo, Alexandria, even Beirut."

"We'll find them. The blighters can't hide forever. Besides, like us, they stand out like goats in the parlor."

"Everything right now focuses on Palestine and Egypt," Max said. "The British, you guys, want to hold on to them. The Zionists and the Jews fleeing Europe and Russia want Palestine for themselves. You are doing everything to prevent the Arabs and the Zionists from throwing you out. And the Palestinian Arabs want the Jews out as well—all very simple. Except it's not. And in Egypt the Muslim Brotherhood, with their intrigues and assassinations, is doing what it can to destabilize an incredibly weak and stupid monarchy. It's just one happy party."

"That's for damn sure; you know your history," Rushton said. "But consider this, too—the Egyptian army is also a serious problem, something left over from the Ottomans. They want the power and Egypt's future; they see the Brotherhood as chaos. So, why are you here? Why the cloak and dagger, and why have I been ordered to help you get to Cairo? You could have just flown in on Pan Am, walked into the Shepheard's Hotel, poured a bourbon, and just asked."

"I'm not sure anyone would have answered your question," Max said. "The reason I'm here is one very nasty Nazi, SS-Obersturmbannführer Johann von Dietz. We believe he is in Cairo. He is in the employ of al-Husseini to further develop strategic chemical weapons, research that he headed up in Wuppertal-Elberfeld, Germany, after he fled North Africa. We found intelligence on the research and initial deployments of an extremely potent and deadly gas. There were reports of his active applications of the gas at one of the German concentration camps. Dietz avoided capture in central Germany by three days. We understand that he escaped through the Balkans, where he was able to board a boat and reach Alexandria. That was two months ago, just before the war ended. He realized he needed to get his murderous ass out of Germany before we found him. It also appears that he took at least four other SS officers with him. We also believe there is an extensive network of escaped SS officers here in Egypt. Some we want captured, some need to be prosecuted, and some we want dead."

"Good luck with that. There are almost twenty million people in Egypt, and the Arab quarters in Cairo are some of the dirtiest and most overpopulated dens of shit in the Middle East. You could lose a battalion in the ancient quarter, and they would never be seen again."

"That's why I intend to have Dietz come to me," Max said.

"How?"

Max handed Rushton a German passport. In the growing light the Englishman saw the Nazi eagle and swastika prominently displayed on the well-worn cover, while inside he saw a portrait of Max Adler in an SS uniform; the rank was colonel. The name listed was Max Adler, a Berlin address, the religion Catholic. Then Max handed him another passport—this one said United States of America. Inside was a photo of Max in an American army officer's uniform, rank lieutenant, the name Dwight Loomis.

After inspecting the documents for a minute, Rushton said, "I have been given the information on this Loomis chap. You sure you want to go forward with this charade?"

"Dwight Loomis was a close friend. He was one of two good friends I lost due to the Nazis and this war. I thought he wouldn't mind my using his name and his history."

"And how is this man going to lure Herr von Dietz?"

"This passport"—Max tapped the red American passport—"tells everyone I'm an American. It can be easily checked to find that I was dishonorably discharged for my political and personal activities and general attitude toward the end of the war. I'm traveling the Middle East trying to find a job with an oil company. Even my family wants no part of me. You have the information on my illegal activities in Benghazi; make sure the word gets out. However, in this other reality"—he held up the Nazi passport—"I am Max Adler, SS officer with an engineering background, who fled Germany—like so many of my comrades—to save my ass, to find a better life, and, hopefully, a well-paying job. I am using the fake cover of being an American in Egypt as a cover for my German and Nazi SS past."

"Where are you actually from?"

"That is top secret, Colonel. That is one thing I can't tell you. Maybe, when this is all over, I will. Until then, you will just have to trust me."

"Is Adler your real name?" Rushton asked.

"Maybe, maybe not. Like where I'm from, you will just have to accept it."

"Trust is hard to find here in the desert. However, it can be earned. Yousef wants to work with you, be your aide and assistant. Your Arabic is not even marginal; he would be helpful. He also said that you obviously need someone to protect you. He told me to remind you that you cannot refuse his wish."

"I can't. I work alone," Max said, protesting.

"That's not what Miss Norcross said. She said she saved your ass a few times in Rome."

"She may be confused; it was her ass a few times as well. So, maybe I could use the support. What about his family?"

"His mother hopes that you will pay him a lot of money," Rushton said.

"Nice family."

Daybreak was still two hours away when the two vehicles pulled out onto the highway. Yousef now sat in the back of Max's jeep. Early traffic was filling the road, an equal amount going east and west. In the relative cool of the morning, battered trucks, prewar cars, and even camels and donkeys along the shoulder mixed together and carried the commerce between Egypt and Libya. Many of the trucks were obviously artifacts from the German army. On some, paint was slathered over the palm tree logo of the German Afrika Korps. Others slashed an X through the faded insignia. In this part of the world, if it was salvageable, it was salvaged.

From Rushton's compound to Cairo was another three hundred kilometers. Two searing hours later, they rolled to a stop at another of the British-controlled checkpoints. After Rushton finished with his greetings and vouched for his passenger, Dwight Loomis showed his passport.

By eleven o'clock that morning, they had traveled six and one-half hours, stopped to eat once, peed, and drank two liters of water, each. Max had no idea of the temperature; his Bedouin robes and *keffiyeh* seemed to keep some of the intense heat out. However, every time he closed his mouth, he felt the grit of the Egyptian desert grind against his teeth. The wind buffeting the open jeep suggested that he was only ten feet from the doors of a blast furnace. At noon, Rushton signaled to Ahmed to pull off the road. A cluster of palm trees filled a small depression a few hundred yards from the highway. Some native tents were spread haphazardly amongst the dunes and the depressions.

Yousef and Ahmed set up their tents along a stretch of the beach. That evening, Max and Rushton walked through a British cemetery where thousands of Rushton's comrades lay. They were the only living souls walking among the dead.

"I knew many of these men, Captain," Rushton said. "Some were fathers, some were husbands, some, to be honest, were assholes, but none of them had to die here in this forsaken land, thousands of miles away from their homes. The same could be said for the Germans. Politicians! Maybe we should construct a cemetery somewhere in this desert where politicians must go to be buried. That might dissuade them from being so . . . political."

"Doubt it. I think it's an incurable disease," Max said. "But don't lose the thought. I like it."

Max slept fitfully under the blanket of stars. The moon, still in its waning crescent, hung low above the desert. The thin surf rolled up the sand, then escaped back into the sea, the repetition finally lulling him into sleep. His last thought was of the Great Pyramid.

Dietz and Gottlieb crossed Gomhurriya Street, climbed the short, broad stairway populated with a beggar or two, walked between the terraces thick with tourists and British officers, and into the lobby of Shepheard's Hotel. Dietz was dressed in a crisp buff linen suit, espadrilles, and a tightly woven Panama hat. His neat paisley bow tie was snug to his white cotton shirt. He slowly removed his sunglasses and placed them in a leather case, snapped it shut, and slipped it into his pocket. Gottlieb was more casual, linen slacks, white shirt with an open collar, no hat.

"What time were they expected, Hans?" Dietz asked Gottlieb.

"Four o'clock, sir. They were tired and wanted to rest from their trip from Alexandria. May I suggest the terrace?"

Dietz removed a silver cigarette case from his jacket pocket and selected a Dunhill cigarette. Gottlieb lit it with a lighter. "Ja, I could use a drink," he said.

* * *

The terrace of Shepheard's Hotel was one of those iconic meeting places found in most exotic settings throughout the world. These places, such as the reclaimed bar at Raffles Hotel in Singapore, the recaptured bar at the Ritz Hotel in Paris, and the now reopened bar at the heavily damaged Adlon Hotel in Berlin, were spots to see and to be seen, as well as to meet, to plan, and plot the overthrow of regimes and countries. How many revolutions had had their start over cocktails in the American Bar at the London Savoy? Only the winners knew. This day, even in the summer heat of Cairo, the terrace was crowded.

Gottlieb saw a table off to the side in the shade. Four men stood, obviously diplomats of some kind, and prepared to leave. As Dietz and Gottlieb approached the table, three men, clearly American, pushed their way through the confusion of tables and said something to one of the men who was leaving. The man nodded. The Americans sat.

"I'll have a few words with those men," Hans said. "That is our table—we saw it first."

"*Nein*, Hans, *nein*. Let them have it. I do not want a scene. I believe they are in the oil business; their dark tans are not ones like the diplomats. In fact, if you look at their hands, these are not men who have walked away from much during their lives. It is not worth the fight. There, another table. Come, Hans."

The Americans paid no attention to the two men. Dietz had called it correctly—all three worked for Texaco, the American oil company. Now that the countries of North Africa were at peace, rumors of oil fields in Egypt and Libya were being explored. In fact, in the late summer of 1945 across the breadth of North Africa, they and hundreds of others were there hunting for oil.

"We live in wondrous and strange times, Hans," Dietz said as he crushed his cigarette in an ashtray. "The failure of our cause, the collapse of the fascist ideal, and the rise of mongrel nations such as the United States have irrevocably changed history. Hope is given to the undeserving and the worthless. We are now on our own, cut free from our homes, our friends—at least those that are still alive—and our country. We, and a few others like us, have no orders and no one to give them to. We are able to offer our expertise where needed—for a handsome fee, of course."

"It feels strange, sir. At times I feel lost, adrift, as if waiting for something," Gottlieb said.

"We have survived because we are smart and lucky. There are those that were smart and are now rotting in prison in Spandau, most probably waiting for a date with the executioner. And there are those that were lucky and found a berth on one of the last U-boats to escape Europe. They will probably spend the rest of their lives hiding from their own shadows. But we smart and lucky few are here, where the war, our war, will continue."

"Are you sure of these men, these Arabs?" Gottlieb asked.

"As sure as I can be of anything in this country," Dietz said. "I have known Mahmoud a long time. He should be here with his eldest son. The boy is a bit of a hothead but dedicated to the future of Egypt. He is a member of the Muslim Brotherhood, a strong political party that has risen from within the Egyptian population, not unlike our own Nazi organization. They want the British out. They are currently protecting King Farouk who is a fool and an irresponsible wastrel; someday he will be assassinated or overthrown. There is money to be made working with the right people, and I believe that these are the right men—at least for now. They are also very close to the Algerian."

Two well-dressed Egyptian men walked onto the terrace and scanned the tables filled with businessmen, smartly dressed European women, small clusters of British officers, and groups that were obviously tourists. Both men wore dark suits, ties, and a maroon *tarboosh* with a black tassel. They recognized Dietz at the same moment the German saw them. As the two Egyptians wove their way through the terrace's wicker tables and chairs, the two Nazis stood. The Egyptians bowed, then raised their fingers from their hearts, to their lips, and upward to their foreheads in the traditional greeting.

"*As-salamu alaykuma, effenis*," the older said.

"*Wa'alaykumu s-salam*," answered Dietz. "Mr. Malouf, my associate Hans Gottlieb."

"My oldest son, Amir," Mahmoud Malouf said, taking his son by the arm. "Welcome to Cairo."

They exchanged handshakes and Dietz offered the men seats.

"Is your family well, my old friend?" Dietz asked in German.

The man answered, "Yes, exceptionally well. Amir's brother was able to leave Germany last year. A blessing, considering what has happened."

A waiter sat a large carafe of water on the table and asked about drinks, then scurried away.

"I hope that the warehouse and other facilities are adequate?" Mahmoud asked. "The building is my cousin's; he appreciated the rent that was paid in advance. He will pay no attention to what we are doing—at least until the next payment is due."

"Tell him thank you for us," Dietz said as he watched three British officers walk through the congested front entry to a large black automobile that pulled up to the curb. He thought their swagger had substantially increased during the past few months. Winning will do that, he thought.

Amir leaned in a little and quietly asked, "Are the weapons also there?"

"My son," Mahmoud whispered, "that is for another conversation, one where it is less public."

"Quite all right, Mahmoud," Dietz answered in a low voice. "Yes, all is being prepared as we discussed. It will take some time, but what you need will be there. I can also add that there may even be more surprises. There was much to either destroy or to find alternative uses for at the end of the war. One never knows what's in a gift box until it is opened."

"I apologize, and thank you," Amir said.

"And you, my friend," Dietz asked. "How is Cairo now that the Allies have won the war?"

"Strangely quiet. The British, as expected, are all puffed up. What is most troubling are the factions throughout the region trying to find their place in this new world. From Tehran to Riyadh to Jerusalem to Morocco, it is, as you say, all up in the air. Also, of course, the biggest threat is the Jews and their Zionist occupation of Palestine. They give the British and the French something to be concerned about."

"The war has bankrupted them," Dietz said. "Trying to keep their empire together will be impossible. The war with Japan is still being fought, and it may go on for many years. They may win, but the cost will destroy them."

"It will be the corrupt Americans that will rule the world," Amir said. "They are a godless country run by the Jews."

"Have you ever been to the United States, Amir?" Dietz asked.

"No."

"Then I would hold your opinion until you have visited it," Dietz said. "I did ten years ago. I lectured at universities in New York, Chicago, and near San Francisco. It is a vast and extremely wealthy country. The worldwide Depression barely made a ripple here in Egypt. There, in America, it was devastating. Yet they fought us and defeated us. Now, after the war, it is a manufacturing behemoth. Never, ever, underestimate the Americans."

They drank their strong coffee and nibbled *ghorayebah* butter cookies. After an hour, the two Egyptians offered their thanks and left.

"I realize, sir, that we need them. But again, I ask, can we trust them?" Gottlieb asked as he watched them enter a taxi in front of the hotel.

"When I was stationed here before the war began, I was an officer assigned to our embassy. I spoke some Arabic, English, and French, a talent that few on the staff had. The result being that I was often asked to attend meetings where I would verify conversations that required interpreters. Hans, it is amazing how often the thrust of a conversation can change or be misinterpreted by the wrong word or even inflection. I like to think I became invaluable. My university training in chemistry was also helpful during discussions with our oil companies and industrialists who wanted entry to this part of the Middle East. That is where I met Mahmoud Malouf. His is an old Egyptian family; in fact, he likes to brag that they can trace their ancestors back to the pharaohs. My guess—his ancestors are buried in tombs all over Lower Egypt; dried up husks just waiting to be stuck in some museum. However, even though he professes to support the Brotherhood, he has one vice that was easily satisfied: money."

The two Germans left Shepheard's and Gottlieb drove them north into the Shubra district and the gymnasium that Dietz had rented. Inside they met with the German team that was reassembling the equipment that Dietz had smuggled out of the Balkans ahead of the advance of the British.

"Did everything arrive?" Dietz asked a short, rotund, bald gentleman holding a clipboard. "There were thirty-three boxes."

The man saluted and nodded his head sharply. "Yes, all the boxes have been accounted for. We were lucky. The voyage was an adventure; I would not like to do it again. Two boats in our convoy were sunk by British aircraft; we took some damage but managed to survive. The British are blockading everything in this part of the Mediterranean. However, they are more afraid of the Jews escaping to Palestine than watching for old freighters such as ours. Luck was with us."

"Excellent, Bruno," Dietz answered. "How long before you are in production? I would like to make a demonstration soon. It would assure our backers that their money is well spent."

"It will take at least a month. We are missing the basic raw materials and chemicals. They were too difficult to carry and too dangerous."

"Leave that to Hans and me. Are the new men here?"

"They will arrive this afternoon," Bruno said. "I will start them on the mounting brackets and stainless-steel tubing. After that, the tables and workbenches will be assembled. It will all be as it was in Sarajevo. Were you able to locate a generator?"

"Yes—it will be here long before you need it. The British commissary in Alexandria, I imagine, wonders how it disappeared."

"Along with the trucks and refrigeration units, as well." Bruno laughed. "These Arabs are very good at liberating things."

"I suggest you remember that," Dietz said. "When word gets out—as it eventually will about this place—you will become a target yourself."

"We are prepared. If necessary, an example might be made."

"Be careful. Do nothing until we have discussed it."

"Yes, sir."

Dietz and Gottlieb spent the next hour reviewing the plans and schematics for the chemical factory they were reassembling. Malouf supplied additional personnel, mostly manual labor used in relocating plumbing in the floor and finishing the rooms with white glazed tiles. The gymnasium's old showers and locker rooms made the conversion to a modern research chemical lab easier than if they had started with an empty building. The service doors off the alley were wide enough to allow the large glass-lined steel tanks to be moved into the squash courts; incredibly, these had survived the trip from Sarajevo undamaged.

"Herr Koch, do you foresee any problems?" Dietz asked the man, still holding his clipboard.

"No, just get me the materials I need. We can then proceed."

"The primary ingredient is being loaded on a ship in Trieste—it is all that was left of the plant in Bavaria. The canisters are labeled 'Fertilizer.' There are sixty-two twenty-liter glass-lined canisters."

"An adequate amount to start. In time we will be able to manufacture our own."

Satisfied that all was well, Dietz and Gottlieb returned to the major's apartment.

9

The Pyramids, Cairo
September 1945

Max and Rushton pulled to a stop at a roadside inn five miles north of the pyramids. It was an elegant survivor of the British colonial days when Cairo's growth pushed west past the Nile River. The three largest pyramids stood ominously, as they had for almost five thousand years, above the clutter of houses and buildings that butted up against the desert. Beyond, to the east, the rough and hazy skyline of Cairo left a dark, brooding stain across the horizon.

"The boys are staying with friends; we will stay here for the night," Rushton said. "Tomorrow you can assume your role as whomever you are playing. Lord knows if I understand it."

They checked in separately. After Max was able to shower off the thick coating of dust, he dressed in clothes fitting the role of an American expatriate looking for work. He bundled up the Bedouin robes and *kaffiyeh* and left them in the corner of the room. Rushton would take the clothes with him when they parted.

The inn was an old home built by a well-to-do landowner in the last century. The physical touches made it look like a

British interpretation of an Arabian architectural nightmare. The central courtyard, with a small pisser for a fountain, reminded Max of Rushton's compound, but that was the full extent of the similarity. This sad place was grimy and in need of renovation. But then again, from the moment they neared Cairo, Max thought everything needed renovation. To his eye, everything looked like it was made old.

The bar faced the cloistered courtyard; Rushton sat on a stool at the far end, nursing a tumbler of clear liquid.

"Gin and quinine," Rushton said. "You just never know around here. Malaria, chum—nasty thing, that."

Max looked at the hawk-nosed bartender wearing a red fez. "The same."

"This all reminds me of the British Empire and its once glorious past," Rushton said, looking around the hotel. "Once resplendent in its reach and power, now barely able to piss in a straight line. I am watching an end to centuries of our power and influence. Max, it seems to all be ending in a whimper."

"I don't know what to say," Max said.

"There's nothing that can be said. It was foretold a hundred and fifty years ago at the battle of Yorktown—your George Washington did that. We've become a tired and exhausted nation. It's your turn into the breach. America's run will be considerable, but only God knows how long, but then it, too, will end. Such is history."

"Yes. History always is written by the winners."

"True, until the revisionists arrive, and slather new lipstick about." Rushton paused. "Yousef, is he upstairs?"

"Yes, setting my things out. Cleaning what he can, badgering the butler on the floor—seems like a good kid."

"He is, and so is his family. He's related to Mohammed through some strange tribal thing—Lord knows, but they understand it. You take care of that boy and make sure he returns to his family. I'm not sure how Mohammed would take it if anything happens to him."

"I understand, but the boy seems to have some skills himself."

"For the last five years, since he was ten," Rushton said, "he has been caught in the never-ending tide of war that washed across this portion of Africa. He survived, and let me tell you, you will never find a better scrounger. Tell him what you want, and he will find it, or a good replacement. Half the parts in the jeeps came from destroyed American equipment. So, take care of him."

"Not sure who will be taking care of whom."

Rushton finished his drink and signaled to the bartender. The man nodded while he finished making Max's drink.

"How many of those did you have before I came down?"

Rushton smiled and took a deep breath. "Not hardly enough."

Two couples walked into the bar and sat near the pisser. They were loud and raucous. They spoke Portuguese.

"Brazilians," Rushton said. "Probably the only people left with money in the Southern Hemisphere."

"There are the Argentines," Max added.

"Corrupt. They will be lucky if they don't implode. There's revolution there. Peron is organizing the opposition—people are mysteriously disappearing—so Argentinian."

The inn they were in was for those that couldn't afford the Mena House. The road from Cairo was lined with these second- and third-tier guest houses and hotels, for the most part clean and reasonably dust free. A visitor would pay extra to make sure that they got a room on the top floor—the evening breeze was better and the chances of stepping on a scorpion in the middle of the night were somewhat less, and the stench from the street was reduced.

After dinner, Max lit a cigar, and Rushton his pipe. They walked the pathway that extended out into a grove of date palms that surrounded the inn. The night still held onto the heat of the day, but without the sun, the stroll was tolerable. Somewhere beyond the palm grove, a radio played an American jazz tune. Jimmy Dorsey's clarinet drifted through the trees.

"Surreal," Max said.

"Egypt is surreal—if you remember one thing, remember that. This guy you're chasing, he's that dangerous?"

"From what we have, yes. The stuff he was working on at the IG Farben chemical plant in Wuppertal-Elberfeld is about as toxic as it can get. When we went through the plant, we found records that they were building another facility near Sarajevo. Johann von Dietz's name was all over everything. We sent in a team to find the plant in Yugoslavia. Tito wanted nothing to do with us. Our guys got out a day before they would have been thrown in prison."

"The plant?" Rushton asked.

"It was empty," Max said. "The whole thing had been packaged up a month before the end of the war. The locals said a number of trucks arrived, were loaded, and then quickly left. The rumor was that it was sent to Dubrovnik. From there, your guess is as good as ours."

"You think it's here, in Cairo?"

"The records at IG Farben say that Dietz was the manager of the Sarajevo facility. The authorizations for the Sarajevo plant were also under his name. If Dietz is here, the plant is here. All this fits with his service records; you got to love the Germans for their bureaucratic efficiency."

"And what is this chemical, something like World War I's mustard gas?" Rushton said.

"Worse, far worse. This stuff will kill you in ten minutes. It's colorless, odorless, and literally rips your lungs apart before you die. It's named after the four German scientists that discovered it. Just before the war, they were looking for a new pesticide. What they ended up doing was inventing SARIN gas. You mentioned mustard gas. This material is almost thirty times more deadly."

"God damn. Why here?"

Max held up his hand and ticked off on his fingers. "Al-Husseini, a brewing Arab revolt, the power vacuum, the Zionists, the British, the French, money. Shit—pick one or pick all of them. The plant is sophisticated and very complicated. One mistake and it will kill everyone in the room, maybe on the whole block. I'm assigned to find and stop Dietz, the facility, and anyone else he's brought in."

"Why not more men? Cairo is a huge city."

"Might incite a panic if we go public. We also want to find out who's connected to this. There's a lot of shit up in the air right now, and that includes the Russians. They want this as much as we do, or so we think. They may have their people here. We hear rumors that they are collecting scientists like it's a sale at Macy's and sending them to their own facilities deep in Russia. They are poaching experts in chemicals, airplane design, even rockets. They are given two options: work with us or die. One day they are here, the next day gone."

The men walked in silence for a while, each wondering what the next few weeks would be like.

"Is Sophie involved?" Rushton asked.

Max stopped and, in the dark, looked at Rushton. "This is an American operation; the British are here for logistical support. MI6 is not involved," Max said.

Rushton relit his pipe. "Her grandfather and mine fought in India and South Africa together. I'll give you that she's a handful, but she's also like a daughter to me. Be careful."

"Yes, but she still has scars, real and imagined. Some won't easily heal. When this all settles down . . ." Max paused. "Look, Rushton, I'd rather not talk about the two of us. Bad luck and all."

"Understood."

Later that night, while Max lay in bed, he looked at the time on his watch. He also wondered why he'd been so evasive about Sophie. *Hell, she's the love of my life—I think about her all the time. I'd do anything for her. If so, why won't I talk about her?*

Two days later, Max said goodbye to Colonel Rushton just outside the entry to the inn. Earlier, Yousef had brought down Max's luggage; it was stacked neatly along the drive at the base of the steps. Yousef now wore the traditional Egyptian *jellabiya*, and the long white cotton garb hung to the top of his sandals. Instead of a *tarboosh*, he wore a cotton turban made from the same material as the *jellabiya*. A taxi idled in the drive. The transformation in Max's appearance startled Rushton. The beard was gone, his hair was now dyed dark brown, short, and close-cropped to the sides. Yousef had proved himself to be an excellent barber. While his face had developed some color during the ride from Libya, Max allowed himself a touch of makeup that he applied to his face (where his beard had been) and arms—a soldier's tan. But, strip away the shirt, and his upper arms, chest, and back were Aryan white.

"Damn, you could have fooled me. You look well weathered and traveled," Rushton said. "Might give you a little cover. Stay safe. I'll see you at the Mena."

After the twenty-minute ride through congested traffic, Max stood outside the taxi and looked at the layered two- and three-story façade of the Mena House Hotel. He ignored Yousef as he unloaded the bags. The steps from the drop-off climbed to a short porch that led to the covered entry; bric-a-brac trim hung from the eaves. It was here, at this same hotel two years earlier, that Roosevelt, Churchill, and Chiang Kai-shek had met to discuss the wars in Europe and the Far East. He wondered about the debates and conversations, especially with Chiang about the Japanese in China. Max remembered where he was in September 1943: Rome, hunting a nuclear physicist, desperately trying to hide Jews, and helping escaped prisoners of war to avoid the Nazi SS.

"A room for Dwight Loomis—it was telegraphed to you three weeks ago," Max said to the clerk at the front desk. "Here is the confirmation." He said Dwight Loomis loud enough to be heard over the soft din of conversation in the lobby. A small bus arrived just after his taxi had dropped them, and a dozen tourists had followed him into the hotel. The talk was of camels and the pyramids.

"Mr. Loomis, welcome," the clerk said. "Your key. The room, on the third floor, has an excellent view of the pyramids. Your luggage?"

"My man is taking them up. I will need an extra key."

Yousef was standing across the lobby near the entry, trying to avoid talking with one of the hotel porters. Max was surprised at how calm and professional he was.

"I am going to the bar," Max said to the clerk.

"Yes, sir, excellent. The bar is that way. Do you wish to have someone take you?"

"No, I'll find it."

He crossed the lobby and gave Yousef the key. They talked briefly, then Max left and headed down a long corridor. He passed the dining room, and through the large glass windows saw the pool—and above the surrounding palm trees, the pyramids. In the bar, he found a table in the corner of the dark, wood-paneled room and ordered bourbon with ice. A group of British officers sat in the opposite corner. One, a colonel, suspiciously eyed him. After five minutes of staring, the colonel stood and walked over to Max's table.

"American whiskey?"

"We call it bourbon; this particular brand is from Tennessee. Do you know where that is, Colonel?"

"Somewhere in the middle part of your United States. Closest I've been is Washington, D.C.—meetings at your Pentagon. Colonel Michael Rushton, 8th Army," he said loud enough to be heard and extended his hand to shake.

Taking the outstretched hand, Max said, "Dwight Loomis, Chicago, Illinois."

"Jolly good, Mr. Loomis. I have to ask, a young man like you, military age and all, why are you here in this backwater?"

Max smiled and sipped his drink. "I've wanted to see the pyramids and the Nile since I was a kid. Tomorrow is the day."

"Traveling alone?"

"Why, yes. Here for a couple of days, then onto Cairo. After that, maybe Jerusalem."

"And why Cairo and Jerusalem?" Rushton asked.

"Colonel, I really am not in the mood for the third degree. Why all the questions? I'm just traveling through. You a cop or something?"

"To where?"

"Again, with a question. Tell me, Colonel, why aren't you in London or Germany rounding up Nazis? It seems that there's probably a lot of them running around all over Europe. And your being here, in this nice bar, with your buddies makes me think you're hiding out from your boss. Are you?"

Rushton smiled, ignored the question, and cleared his throat. "I was just wondering, not many tourists yet. Mostly what we see are diplomats and their families, and of course, businessmen. Americans are usually here for Egyptian cotton and oil. What are you here for, Mr. Loomis?"

"We have this old saying in Chicago," Max said. "Goes back to the time of Al Capone and the gangsters. It goes something like: 'None of your fucking business.' So, if you don't mind, I'd like to finish my drink, stop at the restaurant, order room service, and go to my room and unpack. I'm exhausted, and your questions are boorish and tiring. Good evening, Colonel Rushton." He stared up at Rushton and withdrew a Lucky Strike cigarette from its pack and lit it.

Rushton glared at Max, began to say something, thought about it, then turned away and marched back to the officers. He retrieved his cap and swagger stick and, after saying a few words to his mates, left the bar. The remaining officers stared at Max for another few minutes; then they left.

Max's room had a small balcony that overlooked the pool. Yousef found a radio station playing a mix of Egyptian and classical music. The lights illuminating the pyramids had been turned back on. There on the balcony, attended by Yousef, he ate a dinner of lamb and couscous with a bottle Chianti. The sauce reminded him of an Algerian restaurant in Paris that he and Sophie shared, chunks of tomato and zucchini, onions and chickpeas. Just one night when they both were in Paris, a night where neither slept, neither cried, and neither regretted.

Outside of that night and this lonely meal on the balcony, he couldn't remember another more delicious and histrionic dinner. One came close—a hot Christmas dinner with his OSS buddies in a bombed-out wreck of a building, a week after nearly having his ass blown off by a strafing German jet plane in the Ardennes.

The next morning, Max was up early. Yousef had laid out his clothes; he dressed as a tourist fop, full safari gear, pith helmet, and scarf. Yousef smirked at his appearance; Max felt embarrassed. Someone in Rushton's group would make a few calls, maybe even find the name *Loomis* on a list. The day would be interesting.

The pyramids and the sphinx commanded the view and landscape to the west of the hotel and adjacent residential complex. Connecting the hotel and the pyramids was a causeway that crossed an ancient wadi. As he hiked toward the three most dominant pyramids, the pathway and bridge took him back almost four thousand years. Beneath the causeway, he was shocked to see a golf course winding its way through the flatland below these greatest of Egypt's monuments. Obviously, there had been a Scotsman in one of the marketing groups that managed the hotel: "Come for the ancient Egyptian civilization, the monuments to dead kings and queens, the inscrutable sphinx, and Scotland's contribution to the modern world, golf." Max was sure it made sense to someone.

These wonders of the world had fascinated him since he was a child, and now here they stood, mesmerizing. For the next two hours, he wandered through the complex, read the plaques, even bought one of the booklets. He passed on the camel riding. The reasons for his being in Egypt and Cairo were forgotten—even if only for the few hours of his adventure. As he stood in front of the recently excavated forward portion of the Sphinx, he was jostled by a group of young Egyptian children. All had their hands out, begging for a few coins. The dozen or so other tourists surrounding him tried to ignore their noisy demands.

"Hard to find something like this in America, right, Loomis?" a familiar voice said, keeping up the charade.

"There is nothing like this in America or even Britain, for that matter," Max said, seeing Major Rushton pushing his way through the urchins. "If I remember correctly, when your ancestors were piling stones on top of each other at Stonehenge, these people were building monuments to their gods. Seems to make all our European cultures smaller."

"Irrelevant. They are gone. We are here."

"Brilliant. Spoken like a true imperialist." Max walked slowly away from the crowd and toward a vantage point that took in the whole panorama. Rushton followed.

"Nice show last night, Major. Were your guests impressed?"

"Yes. In fact, one of the officers—Lewis with our local police constabulary—is looking into who you are and where you came from. I assume the story will be good?"

"Should hold, but I'm staying here only a day or two, then into Cairo. Be careful about what you tell Lewis—I want the notoriety, but I don't want my cover blown. Tell him what you need to, but right now only three people know I'm in Cairo, and two of them are standing here. Dwight Loomis may be on some of your lists, but shortly he will disappear. I'd not like to have the British or the Egyptians chasing him for too long."

Max lit a cigar and walked back across the causeway to the hotel, leaving four thousand years of history standing silently behind him.

The Sinai Desert, Egypt

Dietz's secret airport was hidden 120 miles east of Cairo and deep within the Sinai Desert. Its location was specifically picked because of its almost equal distance from Alexandria, Cairo, Jerusalem, and even Amman. All these capitals and cities were less than two hundred miles from the end of the runway—a four-hundred-mile round trip, a critical element of his operation. While he hoped for a closer location to Cairo, the airport's Sinai location was far from normal commercial and even military air routes in this part of the Middle East. The airport had been secretly begun three years earlier by one of the Muslim Brotherhood technical groups using funds provided by the Berlin regime. All this was done under the noses of the British 8th Army, as it chased and was chased by Rommel and his Afrika Korps back and forth across North Africa. Its political cover had been logistical support for a cement factory under development by a division of the Egyptian army, a division that was also under the control of the Muslim Brotherhood and supported financially by Amin al-Husseini. In reality, it was a Nazi airbase providing for the defense of the Suez Canal from attacks from the east. That was its intended use after Rommel had thrown the British out of North Africa and the Middle East. Now Rommel was dead, Hitler was dead, and Germany was defeated and destroyed. The airport survived, and Dietz was not someone to waste an opportunity.

Dietz and Gottlieb left the Cairo apartment before the sun and heat began to climb. Dietz discovered anything could be bought in Egypt for the right price. Their vehicle was a sturdy Horch 901 German staff car. Stripped of all insignia and anything that suggested the Afrika Korps, Dietz had it painted a dusty gray, and a sign on the door panel read, "Sinai Oil and Gas." He enlarged the gasoline tank in the vehicle's undercarriage to carry forty gallons. Racks on the sides allowed for six additional jerricans of fuel. He also replaced the hard military seats with fabric-covered cushion seats. Even the canvas top was replaced with better fabric.

Traveling in the desert poses problems; to make a mistake might get one killed. Most important is the heat; the second is the dust and grit; and last, acquiring fuel. A camel may be able to walk through the desert for almost a week without water. A vehicle will only go as far as its gas tank will allow. For the Germans, the trip would be short, just overnight, but a fuel reserve was critical. It was Dietz's fourth visit to the airport since he'd arrived from Berlin, and it was Gottlieb's second. Their route would take them east from Cairo toward the city of Suez (an important port for the Gulf of Suez as well as a gateway into Egypt, Alexandria, and the Mediterranean Sea), across the canal on a car ferry, and then on to the airport. The opening of the Suez Canal in 1869 only improved the city of Suez's place in the world as a transportation gateway. It was also the primary reason for Rommel's push eastward. If he had captured the canal, he would have been able to control the movement of British ships and weapons to both the Middle and Far Eastern wars. It was an opportunity that he failed to accomplish—twice.

Egyptian authorities inspected their paperwork as they waited for the ferry. Dietz recognized the officer in command as one of the Muslim Brotherhood.

"Is everything in order?" Dietz asked.

The man smiled, looked at the papers again, and handed them back. "Yes, Mr. Strauss, everything is in perfect order."

Gottlieb slowly drove the vehicle onto the ferry and sandwiched it between four camels and a herd of goats. Directly behind him, three fully loaded donkeys were tethered. None seemed phased by the boat trip.

"Do you have family in Germany?" Dietz asked Gottlieb as they stood next to the staff car as they motored across the canal.

"My parents—they live near Düsseldorf. My brother, Rudy, has been missing since Stalingrad; my sister died during an air raid on a factory she worked at."

"I am sorry to hear that."

"We have all lost someone. It was my father who encouraged me to escape Germany. Through friends, I traveled south to Trieste and then by boat to Egypt."

"Your father, was he a party member?"

"Yes, for more than fifteen years now," Gottlieb added. "He was too old to join the army but served Germany by working for the city of Düsseldorf. He was in charge of the sanitation department. That is where I received some of my early training in the use of chemicals, especially chlorine."

"I'm sorry about your brother and sister," Dietz said.

"Thank you. They are two of the reasons I am here. Again, I appreciate the opportunity."

"And there is another reason you are here?"

"Yes, *mein herr*, vengeance."

* * *

The Sinai Desert is relatively small as deserts go; almost fifteen Sinai Peninsulas would fit into the massive Sahara Desert
farther to the west. However, its historical importance to the
three major religions born in this nearly empty region in the
northeast corner of Africa and most western part of Asia is
almost impossible to fathom. It was here the Israelites wandered for forty years after escaping the Pharaoh and Egypt before entering Israel; the Ten Commandments were given here;
the burning bush and other important rituals and traditions of
Christianity, Judaism, and Islam developed in its rugged and
stark mountains. Modern Western cultural and religious traditions were born out of the Bible that evolved within this desert,
and so did mathematics and moral law. This triangular chunk
of desert and mountains, enclosed by the Mediterranean Sea
to the north, the Red Sea to the south, the Gulf of Suez to the
west, and the Gulf of Aqaba to the east, has provided a cultural and military buffer for Egypt for more than five thousand
years. It was also an excellent place, with adequate funds and
proper camouflage, to hide an airport.

* * *

Traveling the rough road to the airstrip took more than three
tortuous hours. Except for the five miles of paved road near
the ferry crossing, the rest was gravel, potholes, collapsed
shoulders, and the occasional Bedouin family clogging the
route with their camels and donkeys. It was noon when Dietz
and Gottlieb crested the rise that overlooked the airport; the
heat rose in shimmering waves, almost obscuring the complex.

"It is well camouflaged," Gottlieb said. "Even from here, it
is impossible to see."

"Yes, they have done well. We will hold here while I send
a message."

Dietz stood and climbed into the back of the truck. A metal box was secured to the interior side panel; opening the door, he removed a set of headphones and clicked a switch. The dial on the front of the radio brightened.

"Strauss to Aqaba, Strauss to Aqaba," he said and listened to the crackling static.

He repeated the call.

He waited and listened. "Be advised, we will be there in ten minutes. Over."

"Yes, I hear you," his headphones barked. "We spotted you thirty minutes ago. Over."

He clicked off the radio. "They had already spotted us. Shall we go?"

Gottlieb maneuvered the truck down the small hill toward an enclosed valley at the bottom of sandy-gray hills that melded with the massive boulders strewn about the valley floor. When they were less than two hundred yards away, the sandy-gray shapes became low metal buildings under camouflage netting. Three men stood in the shade of a small grove of date palms, waiting.

They snapped to attention and saluted as the truck came to a stop, their arms extended.

"Good afternoon, Captain Hofer," Dietz said, moving amongst the men and shaking hands. "I've brought you a few things to make your stay more comfortable—they are in the crate. Have one of the boys move it to your lodging."

"Thank you, Colonel." Hofer pointed to one of the Arabs standing deeper in the shade. Two of the men went to the truck and began to remove large trunks. "Also, bring in the colonel's and lieutenant's bags; put them in their rooms."

"Some food and other necessities," Dietz said. "I also found a few German newspapers, most of them filled with Allied propaganda, but I thought you might like a little information about home. We will stay the night, and we will return to Cairo early tomorrow morning. How is our project?"

"We are ahead of schedule."

"Excellent."

The five Germans walked under the shade of the netting. This portion, held upright under dozens of long poles, was as large as a soccer field. In places it was secured to the ground; in others, raised in peaks. Toward the northerly end of the netting, a section extended out over a Junkers 352. The massive transport plane, patched with squares of bright metal along the fuselage and on the wings, sat with its side door open. Nearby, dozens of open and empty wooden crates sat on the sand, as well as a hundred jerricans. A Fieseler Fi 156 or Storch, as it affectionately was called due to its long, fixed landing gear that reminded someone of a stork, was tied down next to it.

One man, an athletic-looking German, was working with the Arabs servicing the airplane. Wiping his hands on a cloth, he walked to the group, clicked his heels, and saluted.

"Colonel von Dietz, I'd like to introduce you to Captain Bitner. He flew the plane in," Hofer said, hooking his thumb at the Junkers.

"Captain," Dietz said.

They exchanged pleasantries and Gottlieb was also introduced.

"We loaded fuel as we flew," Bitner said. "Luckily, we only had a few hundred miles to go beyond its normal range. We escaped Sarajevo just before the airport was closed."

"Captain, you flew that in?" Gottlieb said.

"Yes, sir. We left in the middle of the night three days ago and arrived here just as the sun was rising the next morning. Uneventful."

"The holes in the fuselage and wings?"

"That was during the portion of the flight from Obertraubling," Bitner said. "We were the last plane out—chased over the Alps into Yugoslavia; thankfully, the fighters gave up. We brought the last of the plane's parts—those were added to the crates from last spring."

"Excellent. And you will fly the jet?" Dietz asked.

"I am yours to command, sir," Bitner said.

"Excellent."

"This way, sir. She is an impressive beast," Captain Hofer said and turned toward a building.

They walked to the metal hangar, also under the netting. Dietz knew the building was thirty-five meters square. Its height was no more than five meters; the Junkers would not have fit inside. The rolling doors of the hangar were open, facing east. The hum of a generator mixed with the soft purring of the wind through the netting. Overhead lighting illuminated the single airplane sitting inside.

"There are no propellers," Gottlieb said, looking at the aircraft. "How the hell does it stay in the air?"

"The two engines are under the wings," Bitner said. "Essentially those blades you see through the front cowling spin at amazing speeds, compressing the air. Then, in a chamber behind these blades, this compressed air is injected with fuel and ignited. The expanded gas is then directed out through a nozzle at the rear of the engine. This push of gas out the back pushes the aircraft forward. Actually, quite simple—simpler than a prop motor."

"For some reason, Bitner, I prefer propellers," Gottlieb said. "I want to see what keeps me in the air."

Bitner smiled. "I understand. Nonetheless, this thrust—this push of exploding fuel—can make this small plane, not bigger than a Messerschmitt, fly three times faster than the Junkers, and almost twice as fast as any enemy fighter. We can, and have, literally flown circles around P-38s and Spitfires. Nothing can catch us. Unfortunately, this is one of the last jets, as they are called, produced at Obertraubling. In its nose are cannons, and it is also equipped with releases on the wings for dropping bombs."

The group walked around the aircraft, admiring its shape and sleek design; the body was painted with a gray-brown mottling on the top of the wings and fuselage; the underside was dusty blue.

"Beautiful," Dietz said. "You have done well. How does she handle?"

"I am excited every time I fly her; I was up early this morning. I kept to the mountains and the desert floor; she excels at everything I try. Our current limitation is fuel and replacement parts. We have some parts for the engine, but we must be careful. Just before the Americans seized the airfields and manufacturing facilities in Germany, I was able to rescue some parts, but not all that we may need. My scroungers are still looking in the Russian areas, but if caught, they are summarily executed. Our best hope is in the Allied areas."

Dietz shook Bitner's hand. "Excellent. The Reich will be proud."

"Our nation will return, I know it," Bitner said, looking Dietz in the eye. "And with the help of these Arabs, we will be able to exact some revenge on the bastards."

"Yes, Captain, we will," Dietz said. "But right now, I am not sure who our best target is. We are working with the Mufti's people. This part of the world is a target-rich environment."

12

Shepheard's Hotel, Cairo

Max's taxi stopped in front of the steps that led to the terrace and the intricately carved wooden front doors of the Shepheard's Hotel. The valet, dressed in an arcane military-style uniform, opened the vehicle's door and stood aside as Max exited. From the front seat passenger side, Yousef exited, went to the trunk, and opened it. Max, ignoring Yousef's labor, proceeded up the steps, past the well-populated terrace, and into the grand lobby of the hotel. An attendant at the doors, in a similar uniform as the valet, pointed to the reception desk. Max thanked him.

Even Max, who over the past five years had been in some of the grandest hotels in Europe, was impressed. Beyond the polished stone columns at the entry, twin ebony nude female figures flanked the entry to the lobby. In an ancient Egyptian style, the walls and arched hallways employed stone in alternating colors of black and white for a dramatic effect. And, spread across the stone floor were thick oriental carpets. At the reception desk, Max introduced himself and slid his passport across the counter—when the receptionist opened it, it read "Dwight Loomis."

"I see you will be with us for a month, Mr. Loomis," the young man said. "Baggage?"

"My man is bringing it." Max looked across the lobby and saw Yousef guarding Max's four bags. "There." He pointed. "And I assume there is room for my valet?"

"We have space available in the dormitory; it can be added to your bill."

"Thank you."

"You are welcome, Mr. Loomis. If there is anything else we can do for you, please use the house phone."

The real Dwight Loomis had been a university friend of Max's in Chicago, six long years ago. Before the war, Max had goaded Dwight and another friend, Dominic Fallace, into attending an American Nazi rally on Chicago's North Side. There had been a brawl and Dominic was severely injured—soon after, he died. Max still carried the guilt of that death with him, and not one day had passed that he didn't think of his friend Dominic. Dwight Loomis, an architect, enlisted the summer after Pearl Harbor. He trained as a Marine infantryman in San Diego, and during the battle for Tarawa, died from a sniper's bullet. The ache in his heart over the loss of his friends never left him. Max, who had fought the Germans in Rome and France, and who found and saved a nuclear physicist in Rome, still mourned his two great friends. Dwight would be proud that he used his name as an alias, even if he were a dishonorably discharged soldier. The goal was the capture of this SS killer.

Max walked to his man and handed him the key. "Take the bags to the room and unpack. Have the valet on the floor brush out the linen suit and press my shirt. Leave the case with me." He looked at the small black case with its black leather handle. "I will bring it up later. Here are a few pounds—find yourself something to eat."

"Yes, sir," Yousef answered. "Anything else?"

"Yes. Ask about any German or Austrian nationals that might have found their way here to Cairo, and be seen in the lobby, on the terrace, or anywhere in the hotel. The staff will talk to you a lot faster than they will talk with me."

"Yes, sir."

"And, Yousef, be very careful."

The boy smiled. "Yes, I will be very careful."

Max walked the length of the lobby to the Long Bar located in one on the corridors that extended out from the lobby. At the bar, he placed the case on the floor and ordered bourbon. He was the only person at the bar.

"I have a dozen kinds—be more specific, effendi," the bartender said. "Kentucky? Tennessee? Which?"

"Tennessee," Max said.

"Excellent choice." The bartender turned away from the white marble countertop and rummaged through a dozen bottles on the shelves behind him. Finally selecting one, he turned to Max and held it up. "Neat or ice?"

"Ice, if you have it."

As Max looked at the clock mounted high over the shelves filled with hundreds of exotic liquor bottles, he heard the ice rattling into a crystal tumbler. The clock read 2:33.

"Just arrive?" the bartender asked, his accent indecipherable. In fact, Max couldn't peg its original source.

"Yes, I was at the Mena House last night. I'll be here for the next month."

"I'm Joe Scialom, a fixture here behind the bar for almost ten years."

"Dwight Loomis, Chicago, United States."

"A pleasure." They shook hands.

Max sipped his drink and looked around. The Long Bar had a tradition of "Male Only." Pity—much too nice to waste on a bunch of drunken men.

"Chicago, Illinois?" Scialom said. "I hear a touch of some-

thing else there in your English. I know eight languages; sometimes, they tell me more about the people than the people
themselves. I hear a soft overtone of German or even Yiddish
in that American accent. Your family is from Germany, maybe?"

"Joe, anything right now is possible in this fucked-up world
we live in. So, for the moment, let's leave it at Chicago. That
okay with you?"

"Yes, Mr. Loomis. That is perfectly okay with me."

Max finished his drink, left a large tip, picked up his case,
and walked back into the lobby. In an alcove of the hallway,
a seated couple secreted themselves trying to ignore the people walking about the hotel. Max couldn't help but noticed the
brunette; her makeup and attire were perfect. It was obvious
they were not married to each other. He took the elevator to
his floor and walked the richly decorated hallway to his room.
Yousef had performed well as an amateur valet. Max's clothes
were carefully put away, his jacket had been brushed out and
pressed, and his shirt neatly hung in the closet. Max lit a cigarette, went to the window, and opened it. The noise from
the street filled the room as quickly as the heat. With the din
came the smells of dung and vehicle exhaust. Two streetcars
squealed by each other as trucks and cars moved chaotically
along Gomhurriya Street. He crushed the cigarette in an ashtray, closed the window, and then closed the thick curtains. In
moments the heat was gone, and except for a few flies buzzing
about, the room was dark and quiet. He lifted the phone receiver and paused, waiting for the operator.

He told the woman the number he wanted and waited.

"Rushton? Loomis here. We need to talk. Name a bar—not
here at my hotel—where we can meet . . . Grand Continental?
Good. Tomorrow morning at eleven. Excellent. See you then."

Max still wasn't sure he wanted the British in on this project. They had little control over anything that happened here in

Cairo, and he was positive there were leaks in London at MI6. With his own service in disarray, he wasn't sure whom to trust. The British believed they controlled Egypt; it was one of those fantasies that they told themselves to continue funding these colonial outposts. The OSS wasn't sure if anyone could control Egypt, ever. Now that the war in Europe was over, maybe it didn't mean anything to anyone anymore. Many in Washington wanted to leave Egypt and the Middle East to those that knew it well, the Bedouin and the flies. However, learning that the Russians were here, he faced new problems. From photos he'd seen in London, he recognized Natalia Petrov as the female half of the amorous couple in the lobby. Whether she was here waiting for him, or just trolling for any new face, was irrelevant. The real issue was that Stalin's people were here in Cairo.

He placed the black leather case on the table and opened it. Inside, nestled in a velvet receiver, sat his Browning M1911. It was scrupulously clean and well oiled. Two boxes of .45 caliber hollow-point bullets, as well as three additional magazines, were snugly secured in their own cavities. Also inside was a dark brown and well-oiled leather shoulder holster tooled with a basket weave pattern. The holster had been a gift from Sophie Norcross. He ran his fingers across the leather and wondered where she was. He ejected the magazine and cleared the round from the chamber. He rechecked the magazine, loaded the ejected bullet, and inserted the magazine back into the pistol. He then began to load bullets into the other empty magazines.

The tap on the door pulled him out of his thoughts.

"Yes?" Max asked before opening the door.

"It is Yousef, effendi," the boy whispered through the door.

"Did you get something to eat?" Max asked after the boy entered the room.

"Yes, it was quite good. In fact. I'm meeting with some of

the staff after work. I am shocked that they are meeting at a bar. My uncle would not be pleased."

"Be careful. These city boys can be tough."

"My sister could beat them up, but I will be careful. Are you going to dinner?"

"Yes. I will eat here in the hotel dining room. After that, I will have a cigar and take a stroll around the park."

"You must be very careful, Mr. Loomis. Do you wish me to go with you?"

"I will be okay, and thank you, Yousef, for remembering my new name," Max said, looking at the pistol on the table.

"Of course, effendi, of course. We all, sometimes, wear different masks. My uncle told me that."

"Your uncle is a very wise man."

"Yes, he is. And he is also very dangerous, Mr. Loomis."

Petrov in Cairo? The last place she had been seen was in Yalta during the conference between Churchill, Roosevelt, and Stalin. That was in February. Now, in late summer of 1945, the war in Europe was over, President Roosevelt was dead, Hitler was dead, Mussolini was dead, Churchill had been tossed from office only a month earlier, and the retributions in Britain had begun. Only Russia's own devil, Stalin, was left to cause havoc and chaos.

During the briefing before he left London, Max noticed Petrov's picture among the dozens of people he might see in Cairo. Her beauty stunned him.

"If you see her, Max, be very careful," Colonel Jones said during their review of possible foreign agents he might see in Cairo. "She is like the soft black kitten that purrs in your ear before she slashes and bites. We are not sure if she is an assassin, a spy, or a witch. I would consider her all three. If she is in Cairo, she is after Nazis. She's a bounty hunter; remember that. If she can't have them, no one can."

Of course, the "postwar" Russians were in Cairo, and had

been in Egypt for years, before and during the war. This game would be played three or four ways. The British, the Russians, the Americans, and the wild card, the Zionists, all were chasing Nazis. What Max wanted to find out was if there was a fifth player at the table, the radical Islamic faction belonging to Amin al-Husseini and the Muslim Brotherhood. He was sure they were—all he needed was proof.

* * *

Husseini, a Jerusalem native, had spent a significant portion of the war as Hitler's guest in a country house outside Berlin. For years, the Nazis had given him a generous allowance to be used for his intrigues and conspiracies. His political and cultural enthusiasm for Germany's National Socialism only increased his hatred for Zionism and anything Jewish in the Levant and Palestine. In the Middle East for more than twenty-five years, he had waged a limited, and yet somewhat successful, religious battle between the followers of his brand of Arab nationalism and the British. The British, in an effort to compromise the leader, made him the Grand Mufti of Jerusalem. A move they now regretted.

Husseini became Hitler's Islamic lapdog. The Mufti formed Muslim military battalions for the Waffen-SS from Bosnian and Eastern European Sunni Muslims. He broadcast radio diatribes against the Jews of Europe and America. He received Hitler's support for his dream of an independent pan-Arab state, a caliphate. He also viciously fought the idea and establishment of an independent Jewish state in Palestine. Now that Hitler was dead, Husseini was on his own to challenge and fight his real enemy, the British. In one bizarre way, they were allies; the British did not want the Jewish state to form either. A Jewish state would create a tactical and political problem and only add to their weakening stranglehold on the Middle East. The enemy of their enemy was their friend—the problem was figuring out which one was which.

Before Max left Germany, he had been told that Husseini was currently a guest of the French in Paris. Max was sure he was invited by the French just to annoy the British and Americans. In time, he also believed, Husseini would return to the Middle East, and most probably first to Egypt and Cairo to meet with his followers and ask those mercenaries and fanatics to join his cause against the West and the Zionists. Max was also certain Johann von Dietz was in Cairo to meet with Husseini. Max's orders were simple: frustrate and stop the Germans from doing whatever they were trying to do.

13

After dinner, Max crossed Gomhurriya Street and strolled to the park almost directly across from Shepheard's. The Ezbekieh Gardens, a park expanse of elegant ponds and gardens, had stood on this site in the center of Cairo for centuries. In its southeast corner stood the Royal Opera House. It was an important part of Cairo and the neighborhoods that immediately surrounded it. The temperature had fallen, and it was now a remarkably comfortable evening for midsummer. Many wandered the grounds in their evening finery, a mix of Arabs, Europeans, and Egyptians.

In more devout Arab cultures, a woman never walks alone outside the house and almost never without her husband or a senior male relative. Cairo was different. Here, Western culture had invaded, and many Egyptian women were beginning to dress like sophisticated European women. The Europeans generally disregarded cultural and Islamic religious strictures, and some were almost rude showing their disrespect. They might wrap a scarf over their hair, but most acted as though they were walking the Champs-Élysées in Paris. Egypt's modern women were adopting this European look, but with a bit more conservatism. Most religious leaders were not happy.

Max saw Natalia Petrov standing alone on the ornate narrow bridge that crossed an inlet of one of the park's ornamental ponds. Her appearance, even by Egyptian postwar standards, was deliberately shocking, even scandalous. Her sheer white dress, with its open back, clung enticingly to her shoulders, and then draped to her slim hips. Its hem stopped fashionably mid-calf. Finishing the look were deep burgundy pumps, and the color of a silk scarf, draped over her shoulders, matched the clutch handbag she held under her left arm. Smoke from her cigarette, held in a black holder, hung about her dark brown hair like a soft aura.

Max straightened his fedora and relit his cigar. *No time like the present.*

He stopped directly behind her and watched as the smoke from his cigar drifted into her halo.

She turned on the heel of the left pump. "I saw you in the lobby at Shepheard's," Pavlov said. "Are you following me?" This was asked, not as a challenge, but more as, "What are you doing the rest of the night?"

"Actually, no," Max answered. "And I'm sorry that I didn't see you. I must be losing my touch. Were you hiding in some dark recess or corner?"

"No, I was there with a friend. Sadly, we are not friends anymore."

"To lose *your* friendship must be a very difficult thing to do. He must have been a very bad boy."

"I can deal with bad boys," she answered with a smile. "No, he was worse. He was a liar and a thief."

"Now I understand. Hell hath no wrath as a spurned woman. My name is Dwight Loomis."

She extended her hand. "Natalia Petrov. American?"

"Guilty. I'm not that good at guessing. Polish?"

For a flash of a second, Max noticed a look of disdain and revulsion but it was quickly gone.

"No, I'm Russian. In fact, what is called in the West now,

a White Russian. We still believe that the czar will return and save our country from that madman Stalin."

"That madman saved your country from the Nazis; he can't be all that bad."

"My family left Odessa as refugees in 1920 and came here to Cairo—actually Heliopolis. Sometimes I think I'm as much Egyptian as Russian—but I am not a Bolshevik. They are all murderers and scum."

"Sorry, Miss Petrov," Max said. "I didn't mean to get you all worked up. May I suggest we start over?"

"It's entirely my fault," Petrov answered. "Yes, let's. Are you staying at Shepheard's?"

"Yes, for the month," Max answered. "Nice place; stayed in better though."

She slipped her hand into her bag, retrieved a fresh cigarette, and mounted it. He lit it for her. "And you do what? You Americans always seem to ask that."

"Yes, strangely we do. I'm looking for a job—oil, exploration, or logistics, any of those things. I'm good with figures and mechanical systems."

"I have been told that Cairo is where you might find a job like that," she said, blowing a cloud of smoke into the air. "Mr. Loomis, all that bores me to death. Always chasing money—how droll and uncivilized."

"Are you always this argumentative, Miss Petrov?"

She paused, nervously took another drag of her cigarette, and quickly blew it away. "I apologize. Yes, I do seem to jump in with both my feet. Maybe that's why I'm so alone."

"That I find hard to believe," Max said. "Greta Garbo said something like that in a movie, a Swedish actress playing a Russian. Miss Petrov, you remind me of that character—a dancer I think she was."

"*Grand Hotel* and she was a ballerina. My feet are too large to dance, though my parents forced me to try."

"Parents are like that, always meddling. And what do you do, other than pose on bridges and look alluring?"

She tapped the cigarette on the railing. "Thank you, Mr. Loomis—these lips of mine do get me into trouble. I am spending a few weeks here visiting family and friends, before leaving for Istanbul. The evening is pleasant, don't you think?"

Max appreciated the change in subject, but the fencing match they were engaged in would garner no points. The thrusts and parries, while interesting, were leading to a draw.

"Yes, but it is getting late. I came in from Benghazi two days ago and stopped at the pyramids. I'm still shaking the desert out of my hair. So, if you don't mind, I'll head back to the hotel. May I escort you?"

"I'm fine here. I am at another hotel, for now," she answered, tossing the cigarette into the pond. "I will see you tomorrow, hopefully?"

"It's possible. I have a few appointments in the morning. A cocktail on the Shepheard's terrace around four o'clock?"

Petrov smiled. "Yes, that would be nice."

Max couldn't help but think the smile was one a black widow might make a moment before she bit the head off her mate and wrapped him in a silk tuxedo.

* * *

Petrov watched the American stroll through the dimly lit park and disappear in the direction of Shepheard's. There were obvious points about the man that didn't exactly fit. He'd spent time outside; the tan was deep, not red as many newly arrived in North Africa. His look and ancestry were German, hard German, war hard. He spoke English, actually American, if there was such a dialect. She'd heard it enough over the last few years interrogating Americans detained during the war. And there was a slight inflection in the vowels, an almost Germanic note. The Americans were fond of their slang and curt edginess. She understood that. They were cocky and innocent; they were also as foolish as they were rich. This American was trying too hard; her impression of Loomis was a man trying to be someone he was not.

Halfway back to the hotel, she met the man who had sat with her in the lobby.

"He says his name is Dwight Loomis," she said. "Is there word about such a man?"

The man grinned. The look seemed to twist his narrow face like he'd sucked a lemon. He brushed away a breadcrumb that had stuck to his thick black mustache. "Yes, I have heard of this man—the news came in just yesterday. He crossed the border a few days ago from Libya. The British tried to intercept him, but he escaped. My sources think the man might be either American or possibly German. I can only attest to the story I've been told. But if the British want him, who knows, there might be something."

"Yes, it is very curious. Besides, he is good looking," she said wistfully. "What can be wrong with that, Dimitri?"

"I am not the one to ask, Major. If this man is one of the fugitive Nazis, I will find out. Then what you do with the son of a bitch is not my concern."

"Patience, my friend. Your family will be avenged."

* * *

Max took the steps up to the hotel entry two at a time, turned right, and found a seat on the terrace. The evening noise on the boulevard had lessened from the chaos of the afternoon. Yet, even at this hour, the terrace was full of lodgers and their guests.

He ordered a Campari and soda and waited. He had Yousef leave a new note for Rushton at his hotel and to meet him that evening. He was certain little on the telephones was not overheard by someone. The meeting tomorrow would be watched;

tonight, though, maybe not.

Rushton was on time, this time dressed in a linen suit and open shirt. As he sat, he pointed to the drink in front of Max and put two fingers up. The waiter nodded and headed toward the bar.

"Strange city, Cairo," Max said.

"Intrigues, spies, whores, religious fanatics, flies, and sand—what's not to like?" Rushton said. "As I said, I've been here for ten years, and only been home once. Now you are here, all cloak and dagger business. Will this damn war never end?"

"Ending this war is not my concern; stopping the next one is." Max slipped his hand into his suit jacket and retrieved a photo. "This is Dietz." He placed the photo on the table. "The nasty SS officer I told you about."

"And what am I to do?"

"Keep your eyes and ears peeled for any mention of the man or his comrades. As I told you, the poison gas he is involved with is extremely deadly."

"Bad stuff. Lost my father to that stuff in the Marne. May I keep this?" Rushton said.

"Yes. Also, the Russians are here," Max offered.

"Yes, they have been here most of the war. Anyone in particular?"

"Natalia Petrov."

"Foul bitch, that one. We think she's responsible for the death of three of my local agents. Her muscle, as you Yanks call it, is a bastard named Dimitri Smilitov. A Chechen who likes to use a knife."

The crowd on the terrace had thinned, and the sound of a piano drifted through the open windows, a nostalgic Gershwin piece that Max couldn't remember the name of.

"Is this bloody war ever going to be over?" Rushton repeated as he lit his pipe.

"I'm the wrong one to ask. Like you, I've been fighting these assholes since 1939. Mine have been both a private and public war, initially with one man. Now, it's a war between the West and the East. And we, Colonel Rushton, are soldiers in that fight."

"My boy," Rushton said, tapping the back of Max's hand, "whoever—and for Christ's sake don't tell me—they are, to them we are just pawns in an ancient game. A game that has been played for thousands of years and will still be played long after our bones are dust."

14

Cairo, Egypt
October 1945

Max and Yousef left the hotel early the next morning; they walked along Boulevard Muhammad Ali. Their goal was the ancient Citadel, the dramatic and massive mosque and castle that overlooked Cairo; it was the historic heart of old Cairo. Cairo was new to both of them.

"I want to be back by three; I have a date," Max said.

"With the Russian woman?" Yousef asked.

"You are very perceptive, Yousef."

"We will be back in time; I will make sure of it. My uncle has told me much about this castle. It is very important to the history of Egypt; it has been here a very long time."

The two outsiders, a clandestine Jew and a Bedouin Arab, walked around the Citadel's walls that encircled the Muhammad Ali mosque, museums, and historic cultural buildings. Later, while Yousef prayed in the mosque, Max wandered through the grounds of the massive complex. A following of children, beggars, began as he inspected the collection of buildings. He handed out a few coins until they were gone. When he passed through the narrow passageway that was the original entry to the castle, he tried to envisage the carnage of the Mameluke slaughter where five hundred notables were murdered in this narrow corridor; it unnerved him to imagine the political will required to wreak such havoc—all to ensure complete political control. He recalled that Peter the Great, the Russian czar, accomplished the same thing by exterminating the bothersome Streltsy. On a much more horrific scale, so had the dictators Hitler and Stalin.

"There are ghosts everywhere, effendi," Yousef said when he returned to his boss.

"Yes, I can sense them too," Max said. "They prowl the dark halls and corridors; I've felt a chilled breath when I walk into a room as if someone has passed. The dead populate this hill and cry for vengeance. Are you done?"

"Yes, effendi, I'm done, thank you. I prefer the desert to these haunted rooms. Would you care for tea? I saw a shop as we climbed."

"Tea and crumpets—what's not to like?"

The two sat in the shade of the colorful awnings that extended out over the wide sidewalk that fronted the narrow street. The tea was rich and thick; the biscuits were hard and inedible.

"This Russian, do you trust her?" Yousef asked.

"No," Max answered.

"Then why?"

"It is important that I have her confidence."

"Why?"

"You are beginning to sound like a child, Yousef. There are dangerous people involved in this, people who will kill for politics and pleasure. My job is to stop them. This woman may be one of the keys."

"I admire the British, but they are not Arab or Egyptian. I think that someday they will go home, and we will be left with our troubles and our past glories, like that haunted Citadel above us. When I looked at the pyramids, I was amazed that people so long ago could build such things. This city, it confuses me. I cannot wait to get back to my uncle."

"You are young," Max said. "I think you will grow old wondering about these things, and you will become wiser and understand them better."

"Maybe."

They took a trolley down from the castle to the park across from the Shepheard's. Yousef returned to the room. They arrived just before three.

Max looked over the gathered crowd on the terrace. The faces had changed, but the mix was the same. Sitting alone to the rear, in the shade of a large umbrella, sat Natalia Petrov. She wore a wide-brimmed orange straw hat and chocolate brown dress. Her gloves, even in the afternoon heat, matched the color of her hat. She also wore sunglasses; their black glass completely hid her eyes. He was not surprised; he had pegged her as a fashion horse. He amended the thought to a fashion thoroughbred.

"May I?" he asked as he pulled back one of the chairs at her table.

She waved the cigarette, in its gold holder, like it was a magician's wand. "Please. I wondered if you remembered."

"To forget would have been a sin," he replied.

"You Americans—so cute." She signaled the waiter.

"Boodles and tonic," he ordered.

"It is said that Churchill drank Boodles."

"I know for a fact it was Johnnie Walker scotch. Yet, look where it got him," Max added. "Thrown out on his own ample ass by his own people. Citizens can be so shortsighted and unforgiving."

"Such a pity, but then again elections and the opinions of the people mean so little in the grand scheme of things. I was a child when the czar and his family were killed. I remember people celebrating. Me, I was sad that the beautiful Anastasia, only a little older than I, could die. She would be forty-four now. I wonder how things would have been."

"Not much different. That German madman would have rolled through your country like a hailstorm over a wheat field, no matter who was governing. Stalin probably saved Russia—either die for him or die for a dead king."

"For an American, you are smart. I sense the heart of a poet. We Russians admire poets."

"Yes, but most of your poets are droll, extremely sad, and mystical. I like our optimists, like Robert Frost."

"There is nothing better than a fire, in the dead of winter, reading Pushkin."

"I rest my case—young, fiery, political, romantic, debt-ridden, and dead in a duel before he was forty. Yes, he was the quintessential Russian."

Petrov raised her Pernod and smiled. "And educated. I did not expect that from a disgraced American trying to find a job in Egypt."

It was Max's turn to smile. "I see there must be some interest on your part. If not, why waste your time researching a guy like me? It also means that you have resources, something I am very short of. What do you know about Texaco, British Petroleum, even Royal Dutch Shell? Do you know if they are hiring?"

"You men and your need for salvation through work. Me, I enjoy the minutes and hours. Later tonight, I'm having a delightful dinner with an Albanian prince, or that's what he said he is, on his houseboat. Tomorrow, some shopping at Cicurel's and Chemla's, tea with friends. Never a dull moment. I am not one of those droll Russians you mentioned. No, not me. I'm as modern as they come."

The terrace was now completely full. People stood in the shadows of the hotel lobby waiting for a table to open. They were there so they, too, could see and be seen. Spotting Yousef standing next to one of the hotel's ornate iron columns, Max finished his gin and tonic, pushed out his wicker chair, and stood. "Madame, if you would excuse me, my boy seems to want me for something. I've certainly enjoyed the conversation. Literature and politics—all in one sitting. So Russian."

"I enjoyed this as well," Pavlov said. "Leave a note for me at the desk if you wish to discuss Dostoevsky or Turgenev. You, Amerikanskiy, intrigue me."

Max left a British ten-pound note on the table, bowed slightly, and left, following Yousef into the hotel.

When the change was returned, Petrov took the money, neatly folded it, and placed it in her handbag. She also stiffed the waiter.

The next morning, Max took coffee in his room; small cakes were set to the side of the tray. They tasted of almonds and lemons. Yousef laid out his suit, shirt, and tie. After a bath, he dressed.

"Thank you, Yousef. You are becoming a very good valet. You were late. I asked for you, and you were not in the dormitory."

"I was playing the job of a spy," the Bedouin said with a smile. "I have much to tell you."

Max lit a cigarette and carried his cup to the chair near the window; the early sounds of the city of Cairo waking up pushed their way through the gap in the double windows.

"First, my uncle would be proud—I was a good nephew last night, even though some of the servants and valets did get drunk and acted, for Muslims, most incorrectly."

"I will make sure that Mohammed finds out about your good behavior. Colonel Rushton will also be pleased."

"Thank you, effendi," Yousef said. "But the real news is that there are at least two gentlemen who visit this hotel regularly. The permanent man on the front steps, who opens car doors and greets guests at the bottom of the stairs, thinks they are Nazis. He tells everyone that he sees everything and everyone in Cairo, and I also believe he cannot keep from bragging either. He has been at the top of the steps for the last seven years. Before the war, he says, one of the men would visit the hotel, stay a few days, then leave. Then, for many years, he did not stay at the hotel—then, just two months ago, he returned. In fact, he was here two days ago meeting with important Egyptians, men who he cannot—or won't—mention their names. My guess—they are with the Muslim Brotherhood. Dangerous people."

"Fascinating. You are very good at being a spy, Yousef."

"Thank you. They think me a kid, so they just brag. But I listen good."

"'I listen well,'" Max said, correcting Yousef. "Did they hear a name for the man?"

"No, but one of the waiters on the terrace called him *al-fuyran alwajh*. From their description, he comes close to matching the photograph."

"Alfuyran alwajh?"

"It means 'rat face' in English, or something close to it. He generally stops at the terrace before noon, stays for a simple lunch, then leaves. Sometimes another man, a big tough-looking man, is with him. My new friend from the stairs says that he is the driver and speaks German. He drops rat face off then leaves to park the vehicle. Sometimes he returns, sometimes he doesn't. Rat face then sometimes meets with others—most are Arabs or Egyptians."

Max sipped his coffee and thought for a while, then sat at the desk and wrote a long letter, folded it, and placed it in an envelope. On the front, he wrote "M.R." He then wrote an address on a slip of paper and handed them to Yousef.

"Please take this letter to Colonel Rushton—same place as last time. Tell the man at the door—he will be in uniform—it is critical that Colonel Rushton receive this letter immediately. Wait for an acknowledgment from the colonel. Then return here; look for me on the terrace."

Yousef slipped the letter under his new *tarboosh*, smiled at Max, bowed, and left.

Three hours later, Max, hidden in the shade just off the terrace, sipped a cup of black coffee. Dozens of the men and women arrived, shook hands, kissed, bowed, saluted, and in many other ways greeted each other. Some sat for a few minutes then left; others drank their coffee or tea and watched. Some, like Max, were obviously waiting for someone. The soft tap on his shoulder startled him. It was Yousef.

"The colonel says all is well."

"Excellent. Take the rest of the day off. I'll be back to the hotel late."

"Yes, effendi. Be very careful."

"You are becoming like my mother," Max said.

"Yes, effendi," Yousef replied.

A lanky Arab stood at the top of the steps. His white *jellabiya*, unlike most of the men walking the street, was crisp and clean. Max guessed it was provided by the hotel. He also guessed the man was Yousef's talkative informant. For the past hour, the man helped guests and visitors out of taxis, carriages, cars, and even a Rolls-Royce. He directed them up the steps, he carried bags, he even shooed away the vagrants who stayed too long near the entry. Max was impressed with the man's dedication to his job, especially as the temperature rose. When a dark red Mercedes-Benz sedan pulled to the curb, the man was quick to the rear passenger door and bowed slightly as Johann von Dietz exited. Dietz passed a coin to the man, then leaned over the front passenger's window and spoke to the driver. Dietz then turned and climbed the steps to the hotel. At the landing, he scanned the crowd. Someone waved at him; he then weaved his way through the tables. He quietly snapped his heels at the table, bowed slightly, and then sat. The man at the table was an Arab, dark, with a crisply trimmed beard. Most of his face was hidden behind the folds of his *kaffiyeh*.

Max waited. Ten minutes later, the Arab stood, shook Dietz's hand, then left through the hotel. From his table, Max watched the Arab walk briskly through the lobby, where four men—bodyguards, he assumed—joined him. He disappeared down one of the interior corridors.

Max turned back to Dietz as another man joined him—the driver of the Mercedes, he assumed. He carried himself as military, German military. Max had interrogated hundreds of these men; they were different from your usual Wehrmacht grunt soldier. Max recognized the face from photos: Hans Gottlieb.

Well, no time like the present. He stood, left an English pound note on the table, and maneuvered himself through the tables toward Dietz. Halfway there, the driver stood and headed toward the steps. Max, easily four inches taller than the man, intentionally crossed the terrace to intercept him. When they passed, Max turned his shoulder into the man, knocking him into a table of four professionally attired English women. Tea and biscuits flew into the air.

"*Dummkopf!*" Gottlieb yelled at Max.

"Sorry. I am so sorry. Are you okay?" Max asked as he looked Gottlieb directly in the eye. "Ladies, are you all right? I am such a lout, and you, sir, I am most sorry. Are you okay? I didn't mean to injure you. Did I?"

Gottlieb looked at Max, and then the ladies. Then pushed his way past them. A waiter quickly approached the table.

"Let me buy your lunch. My mistake, sorry. I'm so clumsy," Max said to the women. "Waiter, put this on my room tab—Loomis, Dwight Loomis. Is that okay, ladies?"

The four women, obviously due to their business attire, were probably connected to the British ligation. Stunned, they could only nod their appreciation.

"Waiter, remember, Dwight Loomis."

"Yes, *effendi*, I understand," the waiter said as he began to pick up the bits of biscuits and crockery on the floor.

"Excellent," Max said as he watched Gottlieb walk down the sidewalk that fronted the hotel. He assumed he was going to get the car.

Max looked to where Dietz sat, three tables away. The German stared at him as he lit a cigarette. Max was pleased. The lure had been cast in front of the fish. Max continued on, intent on just passing by Dietz, hoping the lure might get a nibble. It did.

"Excuse me, sir," Dietz said in deeply accented English. "Did you say your name was Dwight Loomis?"

"Why, yes. Do I know you?"

"I don't think so, but we may have a mutual friend. He has talked about you often."

"Not sure how to answer that. I've only been here a few days. Don't have many friends here or, for that matter, anywhere. So, what is this, a scam? A shakedown or something?"

"Please sit. Let's see if we can clear this up. It's not often that my friend Hans gets knocked about, even if on purpose."

"On purpose? Why would I do that?" Max said as he took a seat across from Dietz. "He doesn't look so tough."

"He is very tough, as you say. And does not take to being assaulted."

"Don't know anyone who does. You seem to know my name. What's yours?"

"My name is unimportant, but yours, Mr. Dwight Loomis, is not. I was told someone with that name had crossed the border from Libya a few days ago, and the British are looking for him. Now, I ask myself, why would the British be looking for an American—I assume you are an American?"

Max nodded.

"Excellent. So, Dwight Loomis, why are the British interested in you?"

"Seems I skipped out on a hotel bill in Benghazi and the bastards reported me."

"I find it hard to believe that the British would muster a small armed force to chase down a deadbeat such as you," Dietz said.

"The British can be so serious at times and are notorious for not being able to take a joke."

"Joke?"

"Other than the hotel bill, it seems that a few thousand British pounds may have come up missing from the officer's mess in Benghazi. Now, I had nothing to do with that either, I assure you. But they think otherwise—that might be another reason."

Dietz smiled at the man. "Yes, they might not like that. Now, how can you wander about here in Cairo using the name Dwight Loomis and not be arrested?"

"Are you with the local police or something? Why should I tell you?"

"Just interested," Dietz said, crushing his cigarette in the ashtray.

"Well, Mr. Unimportant, it is now officially none of your business too. I have an appointment, and if I don't leave now, I'll be late. So, if you don't mind?"

"Where is your appointment? I can drop you. Hans knows the city quite well, and I am leaving."

Max studied Dietz. "Well, I'm not sure. As I said, you could be a cop—or something worse."

"I assure you, Mr. Loomis, I am definitely not a cop. So, where are you going?"

"The American embassy."

"It is on the way. Come. Hans is out front. I can have you there much faster than a taxi."

"You sure you're not a cop? You're not just taking me for a ride, are you?"

"Mr. Loomis, if I were a cop we would not be sitting here. I can assure you of that. And taking you for a ride? I don't understand."

Max looked down to the street and the red Mercedes idling at the curb, the convertible top closed. Hans stood next to the door.

"Sure, why not. Thanks. Still, won't you give me your name?"

"For now, just call me Johann."

"Well, that's a step in the right direction. Sure, Johann, why not."

Max followed Dietz down the steps, past Yousef's Arab informant, to the car. The surprised look on Gottlieb's face made Max smile. "We meet again," Max said as he waited for Dietz to climb into the rear seat.

"He's okay, Hans. We have an understanding," Dietz said.

"*Jawohl, Mein Herr,*" Hans said.

Max slid into the rear seat next to Dietz. Hans closed the door and walked around the front of the automobile. After he had entered, he put the car in gear and slowly pulled away from the curb. On cue, Max felt something hard jam into his left rib cage. Looking down, he saw the pistol's sight and cocked hammer of a Luger.

"Now, Mr. Dwight Loomis, who the hell are you really?" Dietz demanded, jamming the pistol even harder into Max's side.

"Be very careful, Major Johann von Dietz. You leave a mark on this suit, and I will make you pay to clean it."

"You know who I am?"

"Yes, as well as your able captain there, Hans Gottlieb. Both of you are well known to us."

Behind them the squealing of tires and the blaring of car horns drowned out their conversation. Out the rear window a black sedan could be seen weaving its way through the traffic.

Max yelled, "Hold on!"

The speeding car crashed into the left rear fender of the Mercedes, throwing the two men in the rear seat hard against the interior paneling. Gottlieb quickly recovered and accelerated. Then another hard, rear-end collision almost forced the Mercedes onto the sidewalk. Hans pulled the wheel left.

"Go, go," Dietz shouted as he looked through the rear window. As they increased speed, the black car again slammed against the side of the Mercedes.

"Guns," Max called out.

Dietz saw the three Thompson machine guns at the same time as Max, their barrels sticking out of the windows.

"Faster, Hans," Dietz yelled.

The rapid staccato firing of three tommy guns shattered the air. Max felt the bullets impact the rear trunk of the sedan, then saw the holes materialize in the windshield, and as the black car roared past them, they fired again, hitting the motor. Steam instantly exploded out of the engine compartment; the hood flipped open as smoke billowed out after the explosion of steam. The black sedan roared by and into the street traffic of Cairo. The Mercedes slid to a stop as Hans pulled to the curb. Max slowly sat up right, Dietz was prostrate on the seat, under Max. Hans held the steering wheel tightly.

Max, blood running down one side of his face, leaned back against the upholstery and asked Dietz, "Are you all right, Major? You are not shot?"

"Yes, I'm not injured, just get off me."

Max, extracting the pistol from the footwell, now held Dietz's pistol close to his side.

"Hans, are you hit?" Dietz asked.

"Nein, mir geht es gut, ich bin nicht verletzt."

Dietz seemed stunned by Max's concern, since he asked him in German with a Berlin Accent.

16

Dietz removed a small medical kit from the bullet-ridden trunk of the vehicle and applied a compress to the bleeding scratch on Max's forehead. A mixed crowd of Arabs and Egyptians were beginning to gather along the sidewalk; the three men ignored the attention.

"It is not serious—you were lucky," Dietz said. "Why the hell did you do such a stupid thing? You could have been killed; you don't know me."

"Your safety is paramount," Max answered, still in German. He slipped the pistol into his suit coat; drops of blood now covered the front of his shirt. He also dropped the small pocketknife into the same pocket—the knife he had used during the chaos of the attack to make the small cut on his forehead.

The compress stemmed the light flow of blood. Dietz, seeing the nature of the wound, said, "It is stopped. I have a small plaster; would you like me to cover the cut?"

"No, not necessary. It's minor," Max said, taking the compress and holding it against his forehead. He turned to Hans who had finished looking into the engine.

"Damaged, but I believe it can be fixed," Gottlieb said. He glared at Max. "Were they after you?"

"Me?" Max said, switching to English. "No, not me. No one knows I'm here in Cairo, no one. I would suggest that they might have been after the major and you, Herr Gottlieb. Not very good, were they? Simple target, middle of the day, three machine guns—such amateurs. I caught a glimpse, they looked Egyptian."

"We should be dead," Dietz said in German. "Thank you for protecting me. Your German is from Berlin. Am I correct?"

Max ignored the question. "We cannot stay here; the police will arrive any moment. We must leave. Can Hans take care of the car?"

Dietz said something to Hans. He was going to protest, but Dietz waved him off. "I will go with this man; I will meet you later at the apartment."

Max and Dietz pushed their way through the crowd of on-lookers, leaving a very upset Hans to talk to the police. Sirens could be heard and were getting louder.

"Quickly, Major. May I suggest the rear entry to the Grand Continental? I need to clean up and I can also use a drink."

The men hurriedly made their way along the two blocks to Cairo's second-most famous hotel. Max spent a few minutes in the restroom trying to wash away some of the blood on his face and shirt. The bleeding had stopped, and he dabbed it gently until there was no sign of blood. He wanted to see if Dietz would wait for him, as well as have him consider what had just happened. When he came out, he was pleased to see that the Nazi's curiosity more than made up for his caution.

"I owe you a drink," Dietz said.

"And I accept. But for right now, I'll buy."

They found seats in the rear of the bar. Max went to the

counter, leaned over to the bartender, and placed a twenty-pound note on the counter. "We have been here all afternoon, my good man. Do you understand? There will be another if you are asked."

The man straightened his white jacket and then slipped the note into his pocket. "Yes, effendi. I understand. Drinks?"

"Two schnapps."

"I will bring them to you."

"Thank you."

Max took the seat next to Dietz, smiled, and in German said, "Now, Major, why would those men want you dead?"

"I have no idea," Dietz offered.

"A man of your professional reputation in this flea-ridden city? Obviously, someone wants you dead. The British? The Americans? Hell, even the Arabs?"

"You ask too many questions. However, I have one for you. Who the fuck are you?"

Max extracted a pack of cigarettes, they were Lucky Strikes, and offered Dietz one; he took it. "I think you may have dropped this." He removed the Luger from his pocket and passed it under the table to Dietz. "It is an excellent weapon; I would be disappointed to lose it."

"Thank you. It was a gift. Now to my question."

"I am like you, a German who is looking for a job. Now that we have lost, some of *us* must continue with the fight however we are able. I managed to find my way here through Italy and Sicily and then on a very leaky boat to Benghazi. My papers and my language skills have served me well; English is my second language. I lived for a time in Chicago before returning to Berlin in 1939. There, I worked for Colonel Otto Skorzeny and his people up to when it all began to collapse. Unfortunately, Colonel Skorzeny now languishes in an American prison. I am the only one left alive. He suggested that if I could make it to Cairo, I should try and find you. As I said, I'm just a simple lieutenant looking for a job."

"From what I see, you are hardly a simple lieutenant. Do you have a name?"

"Max Adler, SS-Hauptsturmführer. Retired." He smiled at the irony.

Dietz took the glass of schnapps and offered a toast. "Prost, and to the future, Herr Adler."

"Prost."

"I can promise you little. I will make a few calls, and then we will see. I am a very cautious man. When was the last time you were in Berlin?"

"April—all was chaos. The Russians were pushing from the east, the Americans from the west. We were able to escape at night in a Junkers held together with wire; we barely made it over the Alps. Herr Dietz, I wouldn't wish that on anyone. We refueled at one of the last airports our people held north of Milan. Our goal was Egypt. Somewhere over Sicily, we were shot down; the crash-landing on a beach killed my comrades. I alone escaped. That is where my English skills helped. I was able to find an American officer's uniform that fit."

Dietz's eyebrows rose.

"The man was alone; they won't find his body. I then headed to the coast, where I stole a boat. Libya is too damn hot; I can tell you that."

Dietz laughed. "You will get used to it."

"Only if you are an Arab. It was there, in Benghazi, that I took a few days of rest at the British officers' club."

"And the name Dwight Loomis?"

"The name of the unfortunate American officer. Surprisingly he was from Gary, Indiana. Do you know it?"

"I have never been to the United States," Dietz lied.

"Well, it made my cover better. I knew the city from my time in Chicago. Luck sometimes smiles, even on a shit soldier like me. I was also able to pick up some spending money."

"That was stupid. I assume that is the reason they are looking for you?"

It was Max's turn to smile. "They won't miss it."

"I need to make a call. Do you mind Herr Adler?"

Max raised both his hands. "Do I have a choice?"

Dietz was gone for ten minutes. When he returned, Max was sure the hook had been set.

The bartender set two additional schnapps on the table. Max passed him another twenty. A few minutes later, two Egyptian policemen walked into the bar and directly to the bartender who was cleaning glasses. They talked for a few minutes; the bartender shook his head no a few times. The policemen looked around the bar and then back to the bartender. They then pointed to Max and Dietz; the bartender said something then shook his head again. Disappointed, they left.

For the next twenty minutes, the two men talked about the war and the stupid mistakes that had been made. They both agreed that if they could fight the war again based on hindsight, the outcome would have been very different. Gottlieb came to the door of the bar and waited.

"My driver is here," Dietz said. "Can I still take you to your meeting?"

"No, I've just had the meeting I wanted. I will return to my hotel. This has been fortuitous, Major. I hope that we can talk soon."

"Here is a phone number—call me tomorrow. I will see what I can do." Dietz passed him a paper.

"Thank you, Herr Dietz. I appreciate the opportunity."

"That remains to be seen. Good day, Herr Adler."

Max returned to his hotel. Yousef was waiting in the room.

"Are you all right, effendi?" Yousef asked as he poured two fingers of bourbon for his master. "Your forehead. What happened?"

"A scratch. I did it myself. But everything went well, very

well. Thank you for getting the message to the British. The operation was executed precisely, and no one was hurt."

"I watched from the hotel; I was sure they killed you. I prayed to Allah that you were spared."

"I was praying as well," Max said, as he pointed to the bottle. Yousef refilled the glass. "One mistake and we all would have been dead."

"The colonel laughed when he read the note. Since I can't read English, I assume that they were instructions and they were carried out as requested."

"Perfectly. Any drive-by shooting you can walk away from is a good shooting."

Yousef didn't understand the subtlety of American humor.

"Please have this shirt cleaned and my suit pressed. I will need it later. After I change, I'm going out."

"Yes, effendi."

Max returned to the Grand Continental and took a table in the restaurant. Colonel Rushton walked into the room twenty minutes later. He watched Rushton scan the room, then walk to his table. Rushton was dressed in the same linen suit he wore the day before. To anyone he looked like a British civilian, a businessman.

"I see you are in one piece; my men were not sure. I was working on a response to the home office if I had to explain your demise. The hard part was explaining my role in your death."

"Thanks. I owe them all a pint. Dietz is very confused and will spend most of the day trying to confirm my story; some of your people in the government may get a call. My guess is he's going to have a lot more questions the next time we meet."

"We are ready, and then what will happen?" Rushton asked.

"I will call him tomorrow—here is his number. Your people may be able to trace the number to an address. I assume it will lead nowhere, but at least it's a start."

"And then?"

"I hope he will offer me a job. Then, maybe, I will find out what Nazi Germany's most notorious chemical warfare expert has in mind for the Middle East."

Cairo
October 1945

For seven frustrating days, Max waited for a return phone call from Dietz. As Dietz had requested, he dutifully returned the call the next day. Rushton's people chased the phone number down. It was to an answering service buried in the narrow streets of the Bulaq district. When they approached the manager at the address to get additional information, they were stonewalled. It seems there was not enough *baksheesh* for the man to change his mind and give up Dietz. Rushton guessed that the man had other clients who also respected his discretion. To give up one would ruin his reputation. They tried everything; when they returned the next day, the phone operation had picked up and moved. No one in the building knew where. Max was concerned that his cover was blown.

Cairo is a dangerous city to be lost in. It is interwoven with narrow streets where a car or truck cannot pass and grand European-style boulevards and parkways crisscross the various districts. The noise is omnipresent—the calls to prayer from a thousand minarets, the braying of camels and donkeys, the pounding of hooves and metal wheels against the stone streets, the vendors yelling, even the tooting of the trucks and taxis added to the urban chorus. Max was becoming mesmerized by this city. Within a week, it began to seep into his dust-plagued pores. It had that same allure as Rome; crowded with bright and historic detail, yet full of the laments and echoes of a million dead voices demanding their wretched stories be heard. A week after placing the unanswered call to Dietz, the front desk handed him a letter. It smelled of jasmine.

> *Dear Mr. Loomis:*
> *You are cordially invited to a small formal reception to be held on the yacht the* Nile Princess *on this Saturday night. This is to celebrate the arrival of the new Russian ambassador to Egypt. The yacht will leave the pier below the Bulaq Bridge across from the Gezira Palace at 7:00 p.m. Your name will be on the list. Wear something nice.*
> *Sincerely,*
> *Natalia Petrov*

More puzzled than surprised, Max cautiously wandered about Shepheard's hoping that he might accidentally run into the Russian spy. No such luck. The next morning luck took a turn, a strange and coincidental one. As he was having breakfast, Yousef handed him an envelope; the outside was addressed to "Herr Loomis." The script was decidedly Germanic, the notecard also written in German.

> *Please meet me at the Gezira Palace Hotel, tomorrow morning at 9:30 a.m. Be in the lobby. I will find you.*

Everything about the note said Dietz. Yet, no signature or return address.

"I asked the front desk who dropped the note," Yousef said. "They answered that it was a messenger, a kid actually. It was left at the desk early this morning, before prayers."

Max smiled at the smart and resourceful boy. That afternoon, Max and Yousef walked the length of Foud El-Awwal Avenue to the Bulaq Bridge. The bridge's crisscrossing ironwork supports reminded Max of bridges that crossed the Chicago River. From mid-span, they could see both the *Nile Princess* moored at its pier for Petrov's Saturday evening outing, as well as the Gezira Palace Hotel. Its ornate ironwork façade gleamed in the morning sun.

When Yousef asked why they were here, Max replied that, as spies, it was always a good idea to case the joint.

"What is this 'case the joint'?" Yousef asked as he watched the triangular-shaped sails of the feluccas push their way upstream against the current.

"Learning the lay of the land, understanding the different ways in and out. You never know when the front door is the last place you want to head. It's good to know where the back doors and escape routes are."

"I understand," Yousef answered. "Yes, we will case the joint."

They looked down on the upper decks of the *Nile Princess*—her name was emblazoned in neon along the long upper cabin. There were two decks with wide promenades above the main deck.

They crossed the bridge and went into the Gezira Palace Hotel. After an hour admiring the marble floors, the interior gilt, and the layout, they went into the gardens. Facing the river, numerous doors exited out under the arched portico, each arch filled with a shop or boutique. At the rear of the hotel, a well-tended ornamental garden, a swimming pool, and a dining terrace extended southward toward the quintessentially exclusive British Gezira Sporting Club.

Crossing the street to the river, they stopped at a vendor's stand and shared a casual lunch. Yousef described each newspaper-wrapped portion; for Max it was as exotic as everything in Cairo.

"My mother makes this," Yousef said. "Hers is much better, not so much grease."

"She will be glad to hear that. What did you think of the hotel?"

"Very, very nice. Not as beautiful as the Shepheard's, but nice just the same. Effendi, if you are to meet this man here, have him come to the front of the hotel. It is more public."

"Thank you. I agree."

"Where would you like me to be?"

Max put his arm on the boy's shoulder. "I'm going alone. You will stay at our hotel. I will be back by noon—do not worry."

"It is my job to worry. I should be here, with you. If there is a problem with the language . . ."

"We will not be speaking Arabic; we will talk in German. Therefore, you must wait. I will be fine."

"Will the British officer be there?"

"No, just me," Max said.

"I do not like this, not at all," Yousef objected.

Max paced back and forth along the pathway that paralleled the Nile's riverbank and smoked a cigarette while Yousef did his midday prayers. The yacht for the ambassador's event was secured to the bank with thick hemp lines. Would the boat stay moored, or would he be trapped on a party boat with dozens of Egyptian bureaucrats, British politicians, Russian Bolsheviks, and other itinerant spies aimlessly cruising the Nile River? Natalia Petrov would obviously be there; he knew her public protestations about Stalin were a part of her cover. As far as he knew, she believed Stalin was a god. So, was this a date, an interview, or a chance to ferret out something else from him? He would give her every opportunity to find out.

The meeting with Dietz was another matter entirely. He had heard from Rushton, and there had been inquiries about

Dwight Loomis. All innocently made through government agencies—Dietz learned nothing new from those. If Dietz had contacts in Germany, it was a different story. While setting up Max's legend, Major Jones had done some digging and found at least six Max Adlers in the Wehrmacht and SS ranks. Two had survived the war, or at least so far as the records showed. Both were soldiers, not officers. Jones and his people developed a plausible story for Adler: Berlin-born down to the neighborhood and street, his history with the Nazi Youth, the date of his joining the Nazi Party, Leibniz Universität Hannover, engineering major, never married. He had been assigned to Skorzeny's 502d SS Jager Battalion, and during the final days of the war, he was with the SS-Jagdverband Mitte when it was part of the Ardennes offensive. The paperwork was perfect and so was the legend. If he were questioned, he knew the Battle of the Bulge as well as how the elite SS operated. He was confident that Johann von Dietz would have difficulty breaking his cover. Max hoped he wouldn't try.

The Sinai Desert
October 1945

The Me 262 flew ferociously low over the desert, the exhaust from its twin jet engines kicking up a mile-long dust storm in its turbulent wake. The jet banked high and tight inside the natural bowl created by the ragged range of mountains that enclosed the airfield. Seconds later, it was taxiing to the fuel truck parked near the camouflaged hangar. Dietz was impressed.

"If we had a thousand of these machines and another year, the war would have ended differently," Dietz said to Hans. "There was nothing in the air that would have stopped us."

"Yes, I agree. Unfortunately, we didn't," Gottlieb said. "However, we can make an impact now. Do you think it wise to allow the pilot to continue to fly it? Things break and parts are impossible to find."

"I will talk with him. How is the development of the mixture?"

"For the moment, we are proceeding slowly," Gottlieb said. "Until the proper combination is developed, it is difficult to determine the exact timing for the mixing and dispersal. We are also concerned that aerosol spraying may rapidly decay the chemicals, destroying their effect. I suggest that at the proper time we try a test—a live test."

Dietz watched the plane slow to a stop. Two men threw wheel chocks under the front gear and tires under the wings. The cockpit canopy opened and Bitner waved.

"An excellent idea," Dietz said. "I suggest somewhere remote yet easily verified after the test. We need to quantify the results. Find me possible targets."

"Yes, sir."

"What a magnificent piece of machinery," Bitner said when he reached the men. "She responds like a lover to the lightest touch."

"I am concerned about replacement parts," Dietz said, lighting a cigarette.

"I am as well. I will leave her in the hangar until we are ready to test the weapons. While I would love to fly her every day, I will be patient."

"Thank you, Bitner. My thoughts exactly. There is also less chance of accidentally being seen. The delivery systems—how are they coming?"

"A few more adjustments," Bitner said. "When will I have a facsimile to test? We can do the testing on the ground."

"Three weeks, at least. The manufacturing is proceeding. Hans and I are returning to Cairo in an hour. Is there anything you need here?"

"A case of beer, a carton of cigarettes, and a gorgeous blonde with big tits," he said with a laugh and cupping his hands out from his chest.

"I will see what I can do," Gottlieb said. "The hardest will be a decent beer."

"Yes, Mein Herr. I would like the blonde first."

"Wouldn't we all."

Dietz and Gottlieb returned to the Cairo manufacturing

facility late that evening. Much of the plant had been reassembled, and Dietz was pleased with the progress. The pipes and tubing had been reconnected in a complex configuration that led from the large glass-lined tanks to two larger tanks. In another room, modern metal working machinery sat waiting for the raw materials so that precisely shaped bombs and dispersal systems could be manufactured.

"The compressors, Otto?" Dietz asked the man standing in the room with a clipboard.

Otto Vort was the engineer responsible for the reassembly.

"They perform exceptionally well; we are keeping the chemicals at the warehouse until they are needed," Vort said.

"Excellent. I will let you know when you are to proceed."

"Major, a strange message was sent to the phone service," Vort said, handing Dietz a note.

Dietz read the note from Max Adler inquiring about employment.

"Hans, what do you think about this SS officer?"

"I think we need to be very careful. He could be who he says he is, or he could be an American spy," Gottlieb answered.

"I agree, though I tend to think he is one of us. If he is, we can use him. Contact our friend in Cologne and have him look for Herr Adler's records. Have him pass on what he can, but be careful. If this Adler is an American agent, I'll give you the honor of eliminating him."

"Yes, Mein Herr, at your command."

Dietz handed a note to Vort who had delivered Max's message. "Get this to the service and have them respond to the man's call; this letter will do."

They finished the tour of the facility. The damaged Mercedes was parked in the garage of the facility; next to it was the Horch staff car.

"The engine was unharmed—just the hoses and a nick to the fuel line. It was easily repaired. The police were not interested after they saw me. Seems they only cared for Egyptians that might have been in the area. Anything to do with Europeans was not their concern."

"As expected," Dietz said. "Did the British show up?"

"*Nein.* They couldn't be bothered, I guess," Gottlieb said.

"Or they knew all about it, maybe were involved. We will test this man and find out what he knows, and then we will see if we need him."

* * *

Abdul al-Khaldi sat on the carpeted floor and leaned against the huge pillows placed against the wall. Through the dark rain-streaked window, he could make out the silhouette of the Sacré-Cœur basilica on the hilltop of Montmartre. Across from him sat Amin al-Husseini, the Grand Mufti of Jerusalem. A tray filled with cakes and an ornate copper teapot filled the space between them. They were alone in the small Parisian apartment.

"It is good to see you again, my son," al-Husseini said. "It has been too long."

"Yes, my leader, too long. However, you have spent too much time with these infidels. It is time for you to return to Jerusalem and your people. These Europeans are worse than dogs. Your people need you."

"Yes, but the Nazis served us well. We received weapons, and even now there are escaped German officers helping us in Baghdad, Damascus, Jerusalem, and Cairo. We will do what is necessary to prevent the Zionists from seizing Palestine. I have heard that many of our Bosnian men in the Handschar SS divisions are escaping the communists and finding their way to Syria and our friends in Palestine."

"Yes, that is happening," al-Khaldi said. "Some are accompanied by their German officers—they will be helpful as the French and British leave."

"Allah willing," Husseini answered.

"Yes, the Germans were helpful, until they lost." Al-Khaldi twisted uncomfortably against the pillows. "We are, as always, alone. I have fought the French in Algeria for fifteen years, and my father before that. I will continue to fight them until we have our country back. I am uneasy with these so-called accommodations the French have given you. They could easily turn you over to the Americans or the British."

"The British will want me to broker peace in Jerusalem. I will only go to throw out the Zionists. Allah will provide."

"There are those that want you dead, my leader."

"If Allah wills it, I will be a martyr," al-Husseini said. "But I see a hard future ahead for us. In time, your homeland will be free of the French and the Transjordan free from the French and British. It will then be up to us to remove the Zionists from Palestine and Jerusalem."

Abdul al-Khaldi was thirty-five years old and had been raised in one of the encircling slums of Algiers. His formal education stopped when he was twelve. He'd memorized the Koran like a good Muslim, fought the French gendarmes while in a street gang, and eventually married a woman who bore him three sons. During the push of the Allies into Algeria and the collapse of the North African German forces in May of 1943, his apartment was bombed, and his family killed. He joined the radical Islamists in Algeria and during the next two years became an assassin and able leader of a small faction that pledged their loyalty to Amin al-Husseini. He escaped to France soon after France was liberated and disappeared into the Arab quarters that were beginning to develop around Paris. When word was received that al-Husseini was in Paris, he let the man's followers know that his heart, mind, and knife were at the Mufti's command.

"If Allah wills it, my leader," al-Khaldi offered, "your ca-liphate will extend from the Atlantic Ocean to the Persian Gulf.

The nations will fear you, and you will again sit in Jerusalem."

"Thank you, I dream this as well. However, my son, I have called you here to assist me in an important matter. I have initiated a number of actions in both Egypt and Palestine that will both challenge and put great fear into the British. I prepared a group in Egypt while I was in Germany. They are in Cairo and beginning to put into action everything I have planned. However, my friend, I do not trust them. That is why I am asking you to go to Cairo to be my eyes and ears, and if necessary, my sword."

"Your request is my command, my leader."

"Excellent. In four days, there is a freighter leaving Marseilles going to Cairo. On board is a cargo of farm implements and crop seed. These are to be guarded by you and two trusted members of your group. There will be no problem leaving the port, and our people in Alexandria will ensure a successful arrival. I want you to memorize these orders and take full control of the operation in Cairo." Husseini passed an envelope to al-Khaldi. "The German, Major Johann von Dietz, will understand. If he objects, tell him that he and his fellow officers will be well taken care of."

The Algerian looked at the pages and the photograph of Dietz sitting with al-Husseini. Even though he could not read the German that was written, he would proceed as directed. "Yes, my leader, I understand."

Cairo, Egypt
October 1945

Max, in the guise of Max Adler, crossed Fuad El-Awwal Avenue and retraced his steps from the previous
day. The morning was fresh and surprisingly pleasant,
especially after the heat of the past week. When he reached the
Bulaq Bridge, he stopped and watched the dense traffic heading toward the upscale Zamalek district and the British Gezira
Sporting Club with its polo grounds and exclusive facilities for
British officers. Zamalek, an island in the Nile River, was to
Cairo what the Northside was to Chicago—there, money and
power lived. Beyond the island and the El Bahr El Ama canal
lay farmlands waiting for Cairo's eventual westward growth.
The river itself was filled with a hundred feluccas, with their
slender and tall triangular sails, heading upriver against the current. They would swing the sail low as they passed under the
bridge in a measured dance not changed for a thousand years.

Max, retracing his steps, crossed the river down to the
Gezira Palace Hotel. Stopping under the shade of a tree, he
checked the Browning snug under his linen suit coat.

A dozen scenarios worked in his head, all on how Dietz

would respond. He would give him a job or not. He would dangle an opportunity to see how he would react. He would pass him on to Hans and let his captain figure out what to do with him. Or, would he embrace him as a fellow SS officer and welcome him into whatever the operation was. Or he would shoot him. Max was certain that any offer would require time to ensure his loyalty. After that—he hadn't a clue.

Smoking a cigarette, Max looked like a dozen other tourists and businessmen that milled about the hotel after their breakfast. Some were obviously waiting for someone; they checked their watches frequently. Others scurried through, heading back to their rooms. Almost every chair was occupied, and most of the guests held an open newspaper. He saw papers from Cairo, London, and Paris. The news from home was welcome, no matter how old.

Max spotted Dietz and Gottlieb before they saw him. The strategically placed potted palm tree he'd hidden behind gave him a chance to watch the Germans. They looked furtively around the lobby, obviously looking for him, but at the same time looking for possible British agents and police. When they were a dozen steps away, Max popped up in front of them.

"Herr von Dietz, a pleasure to see you again," Max said in German. "And you, too, Herr Gottlieb. I've been looking forward to this."

Both men were startled by Max's sudden entrance, and stiffened, expecting an ambush.

"Herr Adler, it is good to meet you again," Dietz said. Recovering, he extended his hand. "Very good indeed. There is a corner table in the bar that I've reserved. It is quiet and less public. Is that acceptable?"

"Yes, Mein Herr, very acceptable," Max added with a touch of enthusiasm in his voice.

"Good."

The table overlooked the gardens, where people strolled

the grounds. Wheelbarrows filled with plants and debris sat on the lawns near the gardeners. Even in a world upside down, the flowers needed planting and watering.

"Coffee?" Dietz asked as he signaled to the waiter.

"Please," Max answered. "I've grown fond of this strong Arabian coffee. Makes our German coffee seem anemic."

"When we could get coffee," Gottlieb added with a snort.

Max smiled. *Good, he is more than a watchdog.* "I went for almost three months without coffee during the last battle of the Ardennes. It was more valuable than gold."

"And you were where during this battle?" Dietz asked as he ladled sugar into his coffee.

The steam and aroma rose; Max blew across the cup. "I was with Colonel Skorzeny's 150th SS Panzer Brigade. We were part of the force that was parachuted behind enemy lines to cause havoc and confusion. Along with the cover provided by the miserable weather and the blitzkrieg by our forces, we were able to accomplish our mission. Unfortunately, supply lines and lack of fuel became the real enemies. I avoided capture along with five others in my squad until the end of January. We were overrun but managed to regroup west of Berlin, just ahead of the advancing Americans. I have told you the rest regarding our escape."

"*Your* escape. You were the only survivor," Gottlieb corrected.

"I assume that you have resources and have checked me out? Ask Colonel Skorzeny; he's in some prison camp, I suppose. I have not heard if he was killed or executed. Find a commander from the 150th; ask them. I was one of the few Germans who could speak American English, knew idiomatic phrasing. Shit, I even know about baseball."

"Baseball?" Gottlieb asked.

"Hans, you do not have enough time or imagination for me to explain baseball to you, but I assure you every American soldier does. It helped me once when my team was confronted by a roadblock. You know the Cubs?"

"Cubs? Young bears?" Hans said.

"You see, Herr Dietz. That is what I mean. It was cold, wet, dangerous, and deadly work. I heard reports that the Americans did not take kindly to our impersonations. More than a dozen of our men were executed for wearing American uniforms. It was all a mess from the beginning. I lost friends, comrades I'd fought with during the last three years from Russia to the Ardennes. It was a measure of how much we had lost. Nonetheless, that was last winter; today you gentlemen can't tell me that you are here because of duty and honor. At some point in every war, the survivors must do what they can to survive. I am here to continue the fight. If you don't want me, fine. There are others that want my skills; I understand they are looking for officers in Damascus and Baghdad. I hear the pay is excellent."

"They are cesspools of arrogance and stupidity," Gottlieb said.

"So, I'll try elsewhere. Yes, Baghdad; even Tehran. I've got nothing but time."

"Herr Adler, what do you bring me? Yes, we have done some research, and I am aware of Operation Greif. I was tangentially connected to it. My services were not requested, but we were prepared. Your description fits with what I have learned. I never met Colonel Skorzeny. But his reputation is legend."

"I believe he is at least four legends; he would vouch for me," Max said, praying that they couldn't find the SS Nazi colonel and ask him who the hell SS-Captain Max Adler was. Being a spy requires a lot of bullshit. "My skills? My English is perfect, an excellent resource with the British controlling Egypt. I also speak Italian and French. I was born in Berlin and intimately know the city, or what's left of it. I know radio communications and some mechanical engineering. I am an excellent shot with both a sidearm and a rifle—the skills of a professional soldier."

"Can you fly an airplane?" Dietz asked.

"No, but I have spent hours sitting next to the pilot of our Junker before it crash-landed, so landing is not my specialty," Max said with a smile. "I am familiar with most of our field weaponry. I'm also very good at avoiding capture."

"What do you know about chemical weapons?"

"Almost nothing, thank God. They scare the shit out of me. There's enough out there in a battle to kill you without worrying about the air you breathe, and the stuff could blow back on you. Why?"

"Just asking."

"That's not what you are doing, is it? Chemical weapons, mustard gas, phosgene?" Max said.

"It is unimportant," Dietz said. "Are you willing to follow orders?"

"Whose?"

"Mine and those I order you to follow."

"Of course, Herr Dietz. As I've said, I'm a soldier, a German soldier. I am at your command."

"Excellent. Herr Gottlieb will pick you up at your hotel tomorrow morning. There are things he will show you. Be prepared for a long day."

"I'll cancel my date to the opera."

20

That afternoon, after returning from his appointment with Dietz, Max sent Yousef to a clothier recommended by the hotel. He was to rent a white double-breasted dinner jacket, pants, shirts, shoes, and tie. He had responded to Natalia Petrov's invitation through the hotel but had not received a confirmation. When Yousef returned, he was pleased to see labels from important Saville Row shops sewn into the jacket and shirts. He'd requested two shirts just in case he'd ruined one before the event. He intended to give the outfit a try and see if there were women out there that might like to share a drink. In addition, Major Rushton had asked him out to dinner with his wife at the Gezira Sporting Club for Sunday, the day after the *Nile Princess*. He was certain that his new employer, Herr Dietz, would not be at one of North Africa's most exclusive British dinner joints.

Gottlieb was waiting at the curb the next morning with the red Mercedes. The bullet holes were still quite evident, but the windshield had been replaced. Max was curious as to how they could find a replacement for the shattered windshield so quickly.

"Good job on the windscreen," Max said.

"There is a very excellent repair shop here in Cairo," Gottlieb said. "Herr Dietz does business with them; they are most accommodating."

"I expect so. And where are we off to?"

"You will see."

They passed over the Bulaq Bridge, through the Zamalek neighborhood, and across the canal flanking its western side. They continued west until they turned north; the signs at the intersection read "Alexandria." For the next two hours, they passed some of the most verdant fields of corn, vegetables, and date palms that Max had ever seen. The Nile Delta, almost as famous as its pyramids, was more than what Max had imagined. If Cairo was the heart, the countless villages they passed in the delta were the soul of Egypt. These fields had been tilled before the time of Moses and the Jews in Egypt—the same Jewish tribes that played a critical, if not problematic, role in the history of Western civilization during the past three thousand years. Jews that, even now, were dying as they tried to wade the beaches of Palestine in suicidal efforts to return to their ancient homeland and reach the new Israel. Max's private thoughts, if Gottlieb could have read them, would have ensured Gottlieb putting a bullet in his head.

The road paralleled the railroad tracks from the port of Alexandria to Cairo. Reaching the heart of the delta, they turned into a warehouse complex south of a village of mud buildings and straw roofs. Rail spurs turned off and disappeared amongst the dozens of one-story brick buildings. Gottlieb stopped the vehicle at a double gate in a chain-link fence topped with barbed wire. Three sizeable corrugated metal buildings stood behind the fence. Gottlieb talked with the armed guard at the gate and handed the man a bag. He smiled in return and then opened the gate. They stopped at a building—a skull and crossbones had been stenciled on the side.

"It's to keep curious eyes from becoming curious fingers," Gottlieb said. "There are things inside that will kill you if poorly handled."

"Great," Max said.

A single guard stood in the humid shade near the roll-up door to the structure. A smaller man-door stood to the right. Hans removed a key from his pocket and unlocked the steel door.

"God, it's hot," Max said, as he surveyed the dozens of crates and large pieces of strange equipment neatly placed around the room. He noticed two massive steel cylindrical tanks with iron supports centrally placed in the room.

"A drawback," Hans said. "But the major assures me that it does not affect the equipment or the chemicals."

"Chemicals? There are chemicals in those tanks?"

"Agricultural chemicals, pesticides. Quite effective, I'm told—but I'm not a farmer. Over the next few days, we are going to move these crates and tanks to our operation in Cairo—that will be your job." Hans turned to a man that followed them through the door.

"This is Mahmoud. He is handling the logistics. He speaks English; he was trained by the British and in some circles has their confidence. He is also a member of the Muslim Brotherhood. His allegiance is to Hassan al-Banna and, through him, Amin al-Husseini, our sponsor."

"Mohammed Amin al-Husseini?" Max said. "He's involved? It is good to have friends in high places."

"You know of al-Husseini?" Gottlieb said, surprised.

"Absolutely. I listened to his broadcasts and revelations about the Jews in both Europe and Palestine. We are working with him?"

Gottlieb didn't answer Max's question.

"Mahmoud and I have things to discuss," Hans said. "Look

around, get a feel for the number of crates and how we will move them. We will transfer them next week; our Cairo operation will not need these until then."

Max watched the two men leave, then meandered through the complex looking at the crates and the tanks. Outside of addresses stenciled on the boxes that said "Sarajevo," there was nothing that said what was inside. In the farthest corner, crates were stacked six high. Max smiled. They looked perilously unstable. He looked around and leaned his shoulder against the boxes—they rocked twice then toppled. The topmost crates hit the concrete floor and partially split open. The noise echoed through the building. Gottlieb and Mahmoud ran through the brightly lit doorway.

"I'm all right, just fine. Knocked over some boxes, sorry," Max yelled as he quickly looked inside the cracked wooden boxes.

Even in the dim light, he could see dozens of German MP-40 submachine guns still greased and in their original paper packaging.

"What the hell happened, Adler? Where the hell are you?" Hans yelled.

"In the far corner, under the skylight," Max yelled back.

Hans and Mahmoud reached him in seconds. Gottlieb saw the broken box, looked at Max, and removed his Luger from its holster.

"Hell, Hans, I was just looking through this area and backed into this stack of crates. You should have told your men not to stack them so high. This was an accident just waiting to happen. Look around; there are piles of these everywhere. Nothing should be higher than four crates. We cannot afford another accident. Everything is fine. No need for the pistol."

Hans returned his pistol to its holster.

"That MP-40 is a magnificent weapon. Saved my ass a few times, I'll tell you that," Max said. "These look brand new. Excellent. They will come in handy. Mahmoud, do you have a hammer? Won't take but a minute or two to put these crates back together—not a good idea to leave it open."

Gottlieb, confused by Max's remarks, looked at Mahmoud, and asked in Arabic, "Hammer?"

Later, after Max had rebuilt the damaged boxes, they walked through the other buildings. They also contained crates, but no cylindrical steel tanks.

On the ride back to Cairo, Max asked, "I assume there are more weapons in the other crates?"

"That is not your concern," Gottlieb answered.

"The hell it isn't. If I'm moving them, I need to make sure they are secured and hidden from the prying eyes of the local police, as well as the British. I didn't come all this way to be arrested for smuggling. I've had experience hiding and disguising things, so I need the manifests and crate numbers so they can be hidden from curious eyes. I can bullshit my way through all this if I'm stopped, but only if I know that the boxes with the weapons are safe."

They drove on for another hour before Gottlieb said something. "I will get you the list. They are twenty crates of weapons out of the one hundred and thirty. Three contain ammunition. They are for the Brotherhood. Keep them separate; Herr Dietz wants to hand them over, personally. The date has not been set. The Egyptians are waiting for al-Banna to return. He is currently out of the country."

"Not a lot of trust going on here, is there?"

"We are comfortable with the arrangements; not your worry."

"Hans, of course it's my worry. I'll be leading the small convoy loaded with these crates; it's me the British will hang if I'm caught. When the time is right, I'll make it work."

"Mahmoud will be helpful."

"I'll take your word on that. Me, I don't trust any of them.

It's a solid bet that the Egyptians care little for our work against the British; they have other agendas and goals. They would as likely cut our throats as to offer us coffee. I want to make sure their goals don't conflict with ours."

21

Gottlieb dropped Max at the curb opposite the Opera House, two blocks from the Shepheard's Hotel. Max had convinced him that it would be better if they weren't seen together.

"We do not need your help until Monday; take the week-end off," Gottlieb said as Max exited.

"Where do I meet you?" Max asked.

"There will be a note left at your hotel. Be prepared for a few days away from Cairo."

"And where will we be going?"

"You will know when we get there."

When the Mercedes made the turn and disappeared, Max hailed a taxi.

"Do you speak English?" he asked the driver.

The man nodded.

"Good. Turn right at the next corner—you will see a red Mercedes. I want you to follow him."

The driver looked at Max and hesitated. When Max showed him a five-pound English note, he floored the accelerator. They caught the Mercedes at the next intersection and waited three cars back as the traffic policeman finished waving through cross traffic. When he signaled for them to proceed, they followed.

"Keep the cars between us," Max said.

"Effendi, the car—it is red. We cannot lose it," the driver said.

"Be careful. If we are spotted, I will throw the note out the window."

"Yes, effendi."

They wound their way through the Bulaq district then back across the Bulaq Bridge into the Zamalek district. Gottlieb turned north and paralleled the Nile River. Dozens of swank apartment buildings faced the river, their ornate balconies and terraces sitting in the shade of the late afternoon sun. Max saw the rooftops of hundreds of houseboats that lined the Nile's bank. Beyond the houseboats, the ubiquitous sharp-pointed sails pushed feluccas upstream. The neighborhood reminded him of the swankier arrondissements of Paris. Even the architecture, with its ornate iron balconies, looked like the *ruelles* of the Left Bank.

The Mercedes slowed and turned into the front parking area of a reasonably new twenty-story apartment building.

"Pull over here and wait," Max said to the driver as he watched Gottlieb stop.

The attendant at the entrance bowed to Gottlieb. Gottlieb said something and the attendant nodded, then stood next to the car. The German went inside.

"We wait?"

"We wait. But in five minutes, I want you to drive around the block, okay?"

"You are the boss, effendi."

The attendant left and went inside. He returned with a small bucket, and cloths draped over his arm. The man lightly

wiped down the vehicle, removing the dust. For one moment
he stood back, looked at the bullet holes, and shook his head.

"We can take a lap, driver."

"I don't understand," he answered.

"Around the block."

"Yes, effendi."

When they returned to their vantage spot at the curb, Dietz
and Gottlieb stood next to the now shiny Mercedes. Its canvas
roof was now up. Dietz was dressed in evening clothes; Gottlieb was still dressed the way he had been during the day.

Max made a mental note that Gottlieb probably didn't live
here with Dietz. They talked for a moment with the attendant;
the man smiled and nodded, then quickly waved his fingertips
to his chest, lips, and forehead.

"Nice job being a doorman," the driver said. "Don't have
to deal with all this bloody traffic. Maybe I could do a job like
that."

Max smiled at the remark—people are the same everywhere. "When they leave, we will follow."

"Yes, effendi."

The Mercedes wove its way through the streets of Zamalek and eventually over the same bridge they had crossed an
hour earlier. Gottlieb turned and followed the river past the
Cathedral of All Saints and the Egyptian Museum. There they
turned onto Antikhana Street and down the fashionable boulevard, past the famous coffee shop and bistro, Groppi's. Ahead
lay the Abdeen Palace.

In his preparation for his insertion into Egypt, Max had
been given a cram course of the most recent history of Egypt
and the American version of the involvement of the British
in its Egyptian affairs during the past seventy-five years. The
most recent meddling occurred a little more than three years
earlier when the British ambassador, Sir Miles Lampson, forc-
ibly tried to have King Farouk I abdicate for a government

more amenable to the British. This led to the British surrounding Abdeen Palace and forcing the king to form a new government, one not supported by the people. This forced cooperation had subsequently increased the opposition by the people to the monarchy and the ruling Wafd Party. It also turned the Egyptian military against the British.

The Mercedes stopped at the elegant iron gates and guardhouses of the Abdeen Palace; they stopped up the street at the curb. As the Mercedes idled, three more limousines queued behind. Two guards walked to the side of the vehicle. One of the guards leaned in to hear something, then extended his hand, received some papers, spent a moment looking at the documents, handed them back, and then saluted. The salute was similar to the Nazi salute. The soldier took a formal step back and turned to the guard inside the gates. Two men then pushed the gates open. Gottlieb drove the car into the courtyard. The next vehicle pulled up to the guards.

"I don't think we can go in there, effendi," the driver said.

"That's all right—I've seen enough. To the Shepheard's Hotel."

When the driver heard the destination, Max saw him brighten for two reasons. It meant that Max was probably wealthy and would pay him; and the other—he would pick up a similar wealthy fare.

Max mulled over Dietz's entry into the palace. Even before the British forced the new government on Egypt, King Farouk I had been an admirer of the Nazis and Adolf Hitler. There had been instances where he would go out of his way to embarrass or otherwise needle the British by showing preferences to Germany. Only when the Germans were obviously defeated did he throw in with the Allies. Max was certain that whatever Johann von Dietz was involved in, some in the palace knew what it was, and most probably had the support of the king.

* * *

Max scanned the evening crowd on the terrace. Only one face appeared that he knew, Rushton's. Catching his eye, Max then nodded his head toward the hotel's interior. At the Long Bar, Scialom poured him a bourbon on the rocks. He lit a cigar and wandered over to the darkest corner of the room. As per policy, only men were allowed in the Long Bar, and even though there had been an attempt by a woman or two to crash the policy, the bar had held fast as a male bastion. Rushton squinted, trying to see into the dark recesses. Spotting Max, he grabbed the drink that Scialom offered, and sat across from the American.

"I'm in," Max said. "They trust me a little but not a lot. You can tell your people that I'll let them know what's happening when I know. Right now, it's the most dangerous time—one slip and it's my throat."

"Nasty business, this. I'll pass it on," Rushton said. "Do you know where they are? What they are up to?"

"Not a clue. I spent the day with Gottlieb driving around the Nile Delta looking at warehouses. They are trying to find someplace to store equipment here in Cairo; I'll try and find out what. Damn humid and hot, I'll tell you that. I need a shower and a decent meal. You available for dinner?"

"Can't. Dinner out tonight—wife's friends. God-awful boring, I'm sure," Rushton said. "Well, here's to the spy game." He smiled and lifted his glass.

Max saluted. "Yes, to the spy game."

Late that evening, Yousef was relieved when he opened the door to Max's room and found his boss standing there. He quickly looked for bandages, scrapes, and even bullet holes.

"I'm fine, no problems," Max said.

"I was crazy all day," Yousef said and quickly looked around the room. He removed Max's jacket from the chair and began to shake out the dust. Seeing the pistol in its holster hung on the chair, he asked, "Does it need cleaning? Did you fire the weapon?"

"No, leave it. And I didn't fire it. Quit worrying, Yousef; I'm just fine. I'm going to take a shower."

"Did you have something to eat? Should I get you something for dinner?" Yousef asked.

The quick lunch that Max and Gottlieb had at the warehouse was a memory. He felt his stomach react positively to the word *dinner*. "Yes. Can you find me something downstairs in the kitchen? Something with meat—a hamburger or a sandwich."

"Hamburger?"

"Just ask. Also some wine or something alcoholic."

As Max stood in the shower, the Mercedes passing through the gates of the palace kept replaying in his head. What would Dietz be doing in the palace of the young King Farouk? What was the event? What were his connections? It was obvious that the Egyptian government was involved with these Nazis in some form or another. To be allowed to just waltz into the royal palace required more than an invitation. There had to be some history to this. While the Egyptian charade was to play nice with the British, it was more obvious than that. Like the pyramids, the Egyptians would be here long after the British were thrown out. The same thing had happened to the Romans and, fifteen hundred years later, Napoleon and the French, then the Ottoman Turks, and soon the British. Max decided—beyond his job dealing with Dietz—that he needed to find out what the Germans were doing to help the expulsion of the world's greatest, albeit current, colonial power.

22

The Nile River, Cairo

Yousef said, "Allah be praised, you look like the proper English gentleman, effendi," as he admired Max in his tuxedo. "And to think you smelled like the back end of a camel less than three hours ago."

"Very funny, Yousef," Max said, studying himself in the mirror. "This mother's boy does clean up well, don't you think?"

"Yes, not bad for an infidel, spy."

Max passed on the information about Dietz and the Abdeen Palace to OSS in London in a coded message. In the return package, he'd been told, in great detail, about Churchill's ignominious ouster and the new government in England. How it would change things in Egypt and North Africa was yet to be seen. The war with Japan was drawing to a gory close, but when it would finally end was anyone's guess. Dozens of ships passed weekly through the Suez Canal heading to the Far East filled with men and material. He wondered about Dietz and what his targets were. The canal was certainly in the top five; the others were guesses. Damascus and the French. Jerusalem was a two-for-one—Zionists and British. Cyprus and the British garrisons. Hell, there were even pockets in and around Cairo that could be targeted. But targets for what? Sure, chemicals of some kind, maybe a bomb, maybe the water supply?

When he entered the cab at the bottom of the steps, he told the driver his destination, the *Nile Princess* across from the Gezira Palace Hotel. "And take the Khedive Ismail Bridge."

"But, effendi, that is the long way."

"That's all right; I have time."

He did not want to be early, and this would give him the opportunity to see more of Cairo. They headed south on Shari Abdn to Shari el Tahrir. There they continued west past Tahrir Square and across Khedive Ismail Bridge. Reaching Gezira Island, they turned north and passed the El Zuhriya Gardens, the polo grounds of the Gezira Sporting Club, and eventually reached the Gezira Palace Hotel. The *Nile Princess* was moored to the pier directly across the street from the hotel. The sun was setting, spreading a red blanket across the sky. The white wedding cake of a ship turned to a rose color.

At the top of the gangplank, two uniformed Russian guards stood at attention, while a third reviewed invitations. The well-dressed guests milled about on the sidewalk and garden area along the street waiting their turn. After inspection, the guests proceeded down the ramp in twos.

Max finished his cigarette and retrieved his invitation. As he took his place in the queue, an arm, bare and bejeweled, slipped into his.

"I understand that Tolstoy is back in fashion," Natalia Petrov said.

"Considering Stalin's reading habits, I doubt that," Max answered. "Thank you for the invitation; I'm suitably intrigued. And you look stunning."

"Thank you. I really hate to go to these things alone. It can be awkward."

"I'm sure you never go alone."

"Well, if I ever did, I would be embarrassed."

Max was certain nothing could faze this woman—well, maybe not having a backup magazine for the Tokarev pistol probably strapped to her inner thigh. Other than that, he was sure nothing had ever embarrassed Madame Petrov. Considering the dress she was wearing this evening, he did wonder where the pistol was concealed.

A swing band played on the main deck, and on the upper deck, a trio of Russians played traditional Slavic music. Their dour squeezing of the notes reminded Max of the Russian poets that he and Petrov had discussed.

After a tour of the decks, she said, "I must pay my respects to the ambassador. We do not see the world the same way, but the old fool does represent my country."

"How big of you," Max said. "I'll be hanging around somewhere upstairs near the bar."

The boat lurched as it cast off its lines and swung into the flow of the Nile River; the engines pulsed through the deck of the vessel. As Petrov leaned in to give him a European peck on the cheek, he looked across the deck at the dozens of guests who were engaged in conversation. Max's gaze stopped. In an intriguing red chiffon Abaya with an embroidered and beaded bodice in silver, a woman stood alone. A woman he'd never expected to see in Cairo—never. The woman was staring at him; she was not happy.

"I have people to see," Petrov whispered in his ear. "Be good. I will find you later." She pulled away after she ran her hand slowly up his leg. She then turned toward the stairs and left. Max, glancing back and forth between the two women, felt both discomfiture and fascination at the same time. His biggest question was why, after three months, was Sophie Norcross in Cairo?

Sophie's frown changed to a curt smile. She tilted her head toward the doors and the promenade that wrapped the deck.

He nodded and passed through them. His head spun. Why the hell was she here? Moscow—why wasn't she in Moscow? What did she think he was doing? And, good God, Petrov! How was he going to explain that? He took a spot at the rail and fumbled with a cigarette, trying to light it. A flame magically appeared.

"And why are you fooling around with that Russian tart?" Sophie asked in Italian as she lit his cigarette. "She will eat you alive."

Every nerve in his body tingled a most unexpected but welcome feeling. He was also disgusted with himself; he hadn't thought about her in days.

"She is nothing to me, *mio amore*, nothing," he quipped back.

"Don't push it, Max. I'm as surprised to be here as you are. They didn't tell me anything about you. This is still a shock, albeit a pleasant one, *mia cara*."

Max's mind raced. "We can't talk right now—too many things happening. You don't know me, and I certainly don't know you. The Russian is looking for the same thing I am. I'm close. Where are you staying?"

"At the Semiramis. I have a wonderful room overlooking the Nile."

"Alone?"

"None of your business. You?"

"Shepheard's."

"Always first class; be careful, Max." She smiled. His heart jumped; how he'd missed her. She turned and walked away down the promenade, her red chiffon drifting like a cloud behind her, and disappeared inside. Two Egyptians standing at the railing watched her every move.

Max returned to the room through the same doors, and walked to the bar. Petrov strolled up and took his arm. "Interesting crowd. There's a few White Russians, a few Bolsheviks, the second layer of Egyptian officials, a few diplomats from the various legations and embassies, and of course a few I can't recognize. I was also told there's a striking Frenchwoman breaking hearts on the second deck; she's in a red dress. How gauche and tawdry."

"Maybe I should look her up?" Max said.

"I would begin to lose my favorable opinion of you, Mr. Loomis."

"I'll guess, to lose that, it would be very difficult to regain that opinion."

She ignored the stolen remark. "Some fresh air. Care to join me?"

"Absolutely."

He lit two cigarettes and handed her one. Cairo silently drifted by on the port side as the *Nile Princess* slowly powered upriver. They passed the illuminated All Saints Cathedral and the Egyptian Museum behind it. Beyond and above Cairo and its glitter of lights sat the Citadel, floodlights washing its flanks. The *Nile Princess* slowed as it neared the swing section of the Khedive Ismail Bridge, the same bridge that Max had crossed a few hours earlier. Small boats drifted down the river, while others powered upriver. Another nearby party boat, its decks illuminated, passed downriver through the now open span.

"Thank you," Natalia said. "I usually use my holder."

"I think you can handle it; it's just the two of us," Max said. His eye caught movement near the party boat.

A small speedboat appeared from behind the party boat. It abruptly turned across the wake of the boat and headed directly at the *Nile Princess*. The lights from the bridge temporarily illuminated two figures standing at the controls. The boat did not change course as it accelerated.

"Strange to see a boat traveling that fast at night," Max said, pointing to the speedboat. "With all the debris in the river, they could collide with a log or something and disappear in a flash."

Petrov looked to where Max was pointing. The speedboat was less than two hundred yards away.

"What the hell is he doing?" Max said. The speedboat increased its speed. "God dammit, they are going to ram us," he yelled.

The craft, now less than a hundred yards from the party boat, adjusted its heading and aimed directly at the center of the *Nile Princess*, directly below where Max and Petrov stood.

Max grabbed Petrov's arm and pulled her with him as he turned toward the bow. "Run, now."

The only sound was the loud buzz of the speedboat's motor as it raced toward the hull of the ship. He took one glance down and saw that the forward portion of the speedboat was covered with a tarp. He also watched the two men jump from the boat when it was a hundred feet away. Max continued to pull Petrov to the bow. "Run!"

The explosion knocked them to the deck; they tumbled into each other against the railing. Natalia screamed from the pain of hitting one of the stanchions. Behind them, fire shot up the face of the hull a hundred feet into the air. The *Nile Princess* shuddered and rocked from the impact and explosion. Max helped Natalia to her feet. She winced from the pain in her side; he continued pulling her to the bow. A second explosion rocked the deck followed by the screeching and tearing of the tortured hull of the boat. Then the human screaming and yelling began.

23

The Nile River, Cairo

Max, standing in the bow, saw that the *Nile Princess* had turned toward the nearby shore of Gezira Island. He guessed that the captain was trying to beach the boat before it could split in two and sink. Unfortunately, without power, the momentum of the boat slowed with every yard it traveled through the water. The engines were destroyed; the terrorist attack had been executed well and hit the *Nile Princess* just at the bulkhead where the fuel bunker and engine compartment were. The boat's wooden superstructure furiously burned, forcing people to jump for their lives into the crocodile-infested river. The *Nile Princess* only had four small lifeboats. The two portside—directly above the impact—were now burning.

The two remaining lifeboats, on the starboard side, were slowly being lowered the ten feet to the river. A dozen men tried to climb over the railing to reach them; they tipped and spilled the men into the river, fouling the lines. Both boats became jammed and useless in their davits. The screaming increased as the panicked passengers saw a woman, engulfed in flames, fall from the upper deck into the river. The fire on the port side forced the guests to the starboard side as the *Nile Princess* began to awkwardly list. More people jumped into the river.

Max yelled into Petrov's ear, "We have to jump. Can you swim?"

"Yes, and in much colder water than this. But I can't in this dress."

"Don't tease me," Max said as he stripped off his tuxedo, jacket, and shoes. "Now would be a good time."

In less than ten seconds, Natalia Petrov stood on the sloping deck of the bow in her bra and panties, the elegant dress, slip, and shoes in a jumbled pile.

"Nice, very nice," Max said.

"And this, *Amerikanskaya*, will be all you will ever see," Petrov said with a flourish and a coquettish smile. She then climbed to the railing and somersaulted into the Nile.

The lights from the fire and Cairo shimmered on the surface as he watched her swim to the nearby shore. He started to climb the railing to follow Petrov, then dropped back to the deck. *Sophie. Where the hell is Sophie?* He forced himself through the panicked crowd as others followed Petrov over the railing. Most of these older people wouldn't survive the plunge into the Nile, but they had no choice—the option of burning to death was more terrifying. Women screamed and men yelled, a dozen languages added to the confusion and babel. The river's current was aggressively trying to suck them away from the shore. The captain was doing everything he could to steer the boat using the momentum of the current, but it was a losing battle. With each terrifying minute, they gained a precious foot toward the shore. The fire had now consumed a third of the ship and was burning toward the stern and bow. Max wasn't sure it would stay together. More people pushed past him and dove or fell into the river.

Working his way down the starboard side and through the

mass of tuxedos and luxurious gowns, Max spotted a flash of red. It appeared—then disappeared. He pushed on. The shore was now less than a hundred feet away, the fire exploded through the salon windows of the starboard side, showering the passengers with broken glass. The boat was now effectively cut in two by the blaze. Max, through the flames, watched Sophie climb the railing wrapping the stern, her dress on fire. She held tightly to one of the metal deck supports, took a quick look around, spotted Max, waved, and then jumped into the river. Max spun and ran back to the bow and, without stopping, flung himself into the Nile River.

With practiced speed, Max swam away from the lights of Cairo toward the black riverbank of Gezira Island—it was closer, maybe a hundred feet. Ahead, the river was burning. The fuel from the ruptured tanks was spreading across the water; flames from the ignited fuel rose hellishly twenty feet into the air. When necessary, he dove under the flames and swam as fast as he could. His Olympic training, now ten years old, surprised him as he remained calm. The water surrounding him was a surreal orange hell. When he surfaced, he heard screams and calls for help.

As he swam, a woman, eyes bugged out, face covered in oil, grabbed at him with her nails, which were sharp and long. He had to save her; she wrapped her arms around him and tried to climb his back, forcing him deeper. He broke free and swam to the surface; she reached for him again, her wild fingers around his neck. He had no choice but to slug her, knocking the woman out. He rolled her onto her back, and with his available arm around her, pulled against the current. Lights appeared on the shore, floodlights of some kind. They must be from the British garrison on the island. With each stroke, he pulled them to the riverbank. Fifty feet from the bank, he heard voices, English voices. A length of rope hit him in the face; he frantically reached for the rope's end. Finding it, he grasped it and was quickly pulled to the bank. Strong hands grabbed him under his arms, and he felt the woman being taken from him.

"You okay?" a voice yelled in English.

"Yes, I'm okay. The woman?"

"She's coughing up most of the river, but she'll be fine, mate. What the hell happened?"

"I don't know."

Max climbed up the muddy bank and looked back at the inferno that was the *Nile Princess*. Its decks were empty as it slowly drifted away. Down the river he heard muffled cries from the survivors still in the river; sometimes a voice yelled a name or something that Max couldn't understand. But what he heard most were the screams of those that were found by the crocodiles—they cut him to his soul. Then there was a silence, a silence that held to the riverbank full of people, like the thin fog that was forming in the cool of the evening.

Reaching the top of the riverbank, he saw a dozen small boats helping those that hadn't reached the shore. In the distance, the wailing sound and flashing lights of a fireboat neared the catastrophe. More boats were visible heading toward the fiery pyre. Max saw the faintest shape of a powerboat trying to throw a line around the bow of the *Nile Princess*. Max knew they were trying to move the boat back into the river to keep it from drifting into the dozens of houseboats moored on the shore. It was not going well.

The road above the river was now littered with survivors. The klaxons of the ambulances and trucks from the British rescue force on the island wailed. Headlights and spotlights waved and reflected on the road and into the trees that lined the river. They reminded him of the bombing raids in Rome where the fascists lit up the sky with spotlights looking for bombers; here those lights looked for survivors.

A disheveled man in his fifties grabbed Max by the arm and in broken English asked, "Have you seen my wife? Her name is Maria. We are with the Bulgarian embassy. Have you seen her?"

"No, sir, I haven't. I'm sorry."

"She was with me until we reached the riverbank, then her hand slipped away. I can't find her."

The man stumbled away; looking down toward the river, he yelled "Maria" a dozen times before he, too, disappeared. Others walked the bank looking for friends, comrades, and lovers. Sunrise wouldn't be for another eight hours.

Max climbed back down to the river and helped as many as he could reach higher dry land. Many were on the brink of collapse; some could barely breathe. Others, along with the soldiers, helped pass the survivors, hand-to-hand, up the steep slope. On the road, British medical personnel began to triage the more seriously injured. Many were burned on their face and hands, other had broken fingers and arms when they were tossed to the deck by the lurching boat, while still others suffered from exhaustion and fought to just stay alive. A quarter mile up and down the river, Max looked at the victims, helping where he could, waving to medics when needed. His apprehension grew; he had not found Natalia or Sophie. The apprehension turned into a fear that began in the pit of his stomach and spread.

Standing in the road, Max was caught in the headlights of a vehicle. It slowed and then stopped.

"Jesus Christ, is that you, Max? You okay?" a familiar voice said. "It's Rushton, Colonel Rushton."

Through the bright lights, Max tried to focus his eyes on the man not five feet away. "Rushton?"

"Yes, Rushton. I was having dinner at the club when we heard the explosion. Our men are out here, and I'm temporarily in charge of the rescue and recovery. Is that the *Nile Princess*?"

"Yes, the *Nile Princess*. Michael, Sophie was on the boat. I don't know why but she was on the boat," Max said.

"Sophie Norcross was on the boat?"

"Yes, she jumped. Her dress was on fire. Have you seen her?"

"No, but I'll get my men looking. What happened?"

"The boat was attacked by a speedboat equipped with either a mine or high explosives. My guess it was also filled with gasoline. Two men were on board. They jumped off just before it struck. Too dark to see who they were. The boat was targeted—there's no doubt in my mind. They rammed into the port side, midway, near the engines. In seconds, the whole boat was on fire. People panicked. Some jumped in the river. The others . . . I don't know how many stayed on the boat—they are probably dead." Max looked down the river; the boat still burned but somehow a line had been secured. The line and a small tug kept the *Nile Princess* away from the shore and the houseboats. Great arcs of water could be seen hitting the vessel from the fireboat.

"Why the hell were you on board? Was Dietz there?"

"No. I was invited by Natalia Petrov as her guest. It was a welcoming party for the new Russian ambassador. Hell, I wonder if he made it? The guy was so fat he'd have fed ten crocs."

"Sophie was on the boat?" Rushton repeated.

"I briefly talked to her; she was working. She was stunned to see me. I've got to find her."

"I need to get to my men. Up this road is the club; I've set up a triage station there in the parking lot. Everyone is being taken there. They will take care of you until I get back. Did your Russian make it?"

"I don't know."

"I'll keep an eye out." Max watched Rushton pull away and head farther up the road. Max began to jog toward the club. After a hundred feet, a taxi pulled up next to him.

"Need a ride?" the driver yelled.

"Yes, sir. I absolutely need a ride. I'm going to the club."

The taxi pulled to a stop under the porte-cochere of Gezira Club while a continuous stream of jeeps and trucks came and went. Dozens of people sat on the ground trying to gather their wits about them. Inside, a dozen more, mostly women, tried to fix wet and torn clothes. Many were crying. Some had a dazed look that Max had seen in the faces of soldiers after a battle. The staff tried to help those that they could. Max searched the lobby for Sophie.

A voice with classic British panache was ordering about everyone, staff and victims alike.

"You there," the man said, pointing at Max. He was dressed in the formal dress uniform of a British sergeant. "If you are well enough to walk and don't have anyone inside, I need you outside. There is no room here, and my people tell me there are dozens more on the way. You, sir, out."

"Sergeant, I'm looking for two women. The first was wearing a red dress with silver beading. The other, when she dove off the burning boat, was just wearing her underwear."

The man paused for a moment, then snapped his fingers. "The woman in red, was she French? Did she speak French and have dark brown or black hair?"

"Yes," Max said.

"She's all right. Her dress was burned a little, but she is fine."

"Where is she?"

"She left in a hurry," the sergeant said. "Took a taxi—where she went I haven't a clue. The other woman—in underwear, you say? No one has arrived in that condition—I'd have heard, I assure you. No, only the woman in the red dress."

Max unconsciously patted his wet pants, looking for a cigarette. The pack of Lucky Strikes was in the pocket of his now thoroughly burned formal jacket lying on the deck of the ship. Maybe the rental agency would at least take back the shirt and slacks. He looked down at his stockinged feet—he'd be charged for the shoes as well. A cigarette miraculously appeared from a soldier.

"Thanks. Mine are somewhere in the Nile River."

"Keep the pack, mate, no worries. As I say, any burning boat you can escape from . . ."

". . . is a good escape! Thanks." Max took a long drag.

"I heard you asking the sergeant about the woman in red; hard to miss her, I'll tell you, sir."

"You saw her?"

"Yeah, I'm the bloke that got her the taxi. I asked her where she wanted to go. She said the Semiramis Hotel. Then she was gone."

"Was she okay? Was she hurt?"

"No. Looked good, though, considering what she'd been through."

"Thanks," Max said.

"No worries."

"Can you get me a taxi?"

"I'll give it my best Aussie try."

24

Yousef demanded an answer. "Effendi, were you on that boat?" Max stood in the room in his stockings and poured himself a bourbon—then another.

"Yes," Max finally said. "I was on it and barely escaped. Many people didn't. I need to change; I've got to find someone. They are supposed to be at the Semiramis."

"I'll get the shower started," Yousef said and headed toward the bathroom.

"No time. I must get to the Semiramis Hotel."

"The woman who invited you, that Russian? Is she there?"

"No, someone else—an old friend I saw on the boat."

"A friend, from where?" Yousef asked.

Max started to take off his damp clothes.

"England, but she speaks French. My guess is she's working."

"Working on what?"

"I don't know," Max answered, then unconsciously said, "I didn't know how much I missed her, until tonight." Gathering up his shirt and pants, he handed them to Yousef. "Maybe we can get the rental service to take the shirt and pants. The jacket's going to cost me a few pounds."

Yousef looked at Max's feet.

"And the shoes—they are gone too," Max said as he stumbled around the room in his underwear, mumbling.

Why is she here in Cairo, and what about Moscow? Two minutes more—all I needed were two minutes. The dress, it was on fire . . . they said she made it. Maybe it was someone else I saw? How the hell would they know?

He turned to Yousef. "I'll finish cleaning up. Get my linen suit out. I want a cab in ten minutes."

"At this time of night?" Yousef looked at the clock; it read 3:25.

"I don't give a damn about the time. Go downstairs and get me a taxi, and make them wait. Tell them there'll be a big tip."

After Yousef went downstairs, Max dressed. He slipped the holster, with his Colt, over his shoulder, glad that he'd not worn it to the ship. Then stuffed two packs of cigarettes and matches into the jacket pocket. He took the stairs to the quiet lobby. One man stood at the reception counter, and no one sat in the leather chairs that populated the room. Through the entry doors, he saw Yousef standing next to a taxi talking to the driver through the window. Max stopped at the hotel's entry, retrieved one of the packs of cigarettes, and extracted a cigarette. As the flame touched its tip, something hard jammed into his right kidney and a thick German voice whispered in his ear.

"You will come with us, Herr Adler. If you try to make a scene or attempt to escape, I will kill you right here. Do you understand?"

Max nodded and dropped the cigarette to the tile floor.

"And if you attempt to reach for the pistol under your jacket, I will shoot you. There is an automobile parked behind the taxi at the curb. You will climb inside. Any attempt to escape—"

"I know, I know—you will shoot me. I get it."

A man dressed in a dark suit passed him on the right. Max still felt the pressure of the barrel of the pistol. He followed the man. When they reached the top of the steps at the terrace, Yousef looked up and started to walk toward the trio. Max quickly shook his head, no. Yousef stopped, a puzzled look on his face.

"Tell the boy we don't need a taxi," the man behind him said.

"Boy, no taxi tonight. I have a ride with these gentlemen," Max said in English. He slipped his hand into his pocket and flipped a shilling to Yousef. "Something for your trouble, and tell M.R. I won't be at the meeting."

Yousef caught the coin in midair. "Yes, effendi. Thank you, I understand. No problem." Yousef bowed and touched his chest, lips, and head, and took a couple of steps back.

"Good lad," Max said and turned left, the pressure of the pistol against his ribs pushing him along. The first man walked around the car and climbed into the back seat.

"Get in," the voice said; the pistol dug deeper.

Max did as ordered. Another man sat inside the car, next to the window. As Max sat, a black cloth bag was jerked over his head, and he felt a pinprick to the side of his neck. He tried to reach for his Browning, but the drugs acted too quickly. In seconds, he fell into a black hole.

Stunned by his boss's actions, Yousef watched helplessly as the Fiat pulled away from the curb and accelerated up the almost empty boulevard. His mind raced. M.R.? Those were the initials of the man his boss sent messages to, the English major. Effendi was also going to look for a woman, someone who was on the boat. Should he go to the Semiramis Hotel and find her? What would she look like? He said a red dress. Should he find the British major?

"Hey, kid, you want this taxi or not?" a voice yelled from inside the vehicle.

He made a decision. "The Semiramis Hotel," Yousef said as he climbed inside.

"You got money, kid?" the driver asked.

"Don't worry about that. Allah will provide."

"Allah better have piasters," the driver said as he turned onto Ibrahim Pasha.

Yousef's mind raced. How would he find the woman? Was she a guest? Would anyone know who she was?

"Faster," Yousef said.

"No problem," the driver said and pushed the accelerator.

The massive Italianate Semiramis Hotel overlooked the Nile River near the Khedive Ismail Bridge. Across the boulevard from the hotel stood the barracks for the British Army of Occupation, located in the old palace of Kasr al-Nil. The taxi slowed and stopped in front of the columned front portico.

"Now, will Allah provide?" the driver said, his hand out.

Yousef handed the coin his boss had flipped him. "This is more than enough." He left the taxi and climbed the front steps. Three Egyptian Arabs stood at the top of the steps; two held large push brooms. They looked at the kid and turned their noses up. An Egyptian could tell a Bedouin from a mile away.

"Friends, I need your help," Yousef implored.

One of the men turned to the boy. "What can we do to help a desert rat like you? Go back to your donkey and your mother."

"Please, you know about the fire on the boat, the one earlier tonight?"

"Yes, we could see the flames. They were a hundred feet high over the bridge. Yes, so?"

"Did a woman, a European, come here to the hotel a few

hours after the fire? She was wearing a red dress; she was on the boat."

The three men turned to each other and talked for a moment; Yousef could not hear what they said.

"It's possible, why?" one asked.

Yousef, thinking quickly, said, "A man, my boss, sent me to find the woman. He helped her escape the flames; she said she was staying here. He wants to find her. So, can you help, or will you be an ass? It is important."

"An ass? You impertinent little shit," another said. "Maybe there's a coin or two in it if we help?"

"I make no promises. Well?"

"Yes, a pretty European woman climbed these steps about two hours ago, in a red dress—it was singed along the hem. I've seen her a few times."

"Was she alone?"

"Yes, a taxi dropped her off."

"Do you know her name?"

"No."

Yousef studied the three men. "What is the night manager's name?"

"Monsieur LeBlanc. He does not tolerate street urchins."

"Thank you." Yousef pushed his way through the men and into the lobby of the hotel. "You can't go in there," he heard as he walked into the deserted lobby.

A thin man with gaunt cheeks and a red tarboosh stood behind the reception desk studying papers that were spread across the desk's surface. Yousef had to cough to get the man's attention. He slowly raised his eyes, and through his wire-rimmed glasses, he studied the boy.

"Yes," he said. Then added, "Get out, get out now. I'll have you thrown out on your ear."

"Please, effendi, that is totally out of the question; nonetheless, I need the effendi's help. One of your guests, in a red dress, was on the *Nile Princess*, the unfortunate boat that exploded tonight. I have some of her personal things that were recovered. I need to return them to her."

The man stared a long time at the boy, squinting the whole time. "There were a number of our guests on that vessel—two are still missing. Give me the articles. I'll see that Countess Conti receives them." He held his hand out.

"And let you get the reward for returning them? Not a chance. I carried these all the way from the British Gezira Club, and you make the money for my work? That will not happen."

"And what are these articles?"

"None of your business, Monsieur LeBlanc. They are personal and valuable. So, what room is Countess Conti in?"

Yousef watched the manager, believing he could see the arcane gears in his head grind.

"I will not give you the room number, but I will call her room. She will be very upset to be woken, I'm sure. However, you little shit, what you have better be good."

"Excellent, Monsieur LeBlanc. I will wait near the entry."

"Better yet, stand over by the shoeshine stand where you won't be so conspicuous."

Yousef walked across the lobby in the direction that Monsieur LeBlanc had pointed. He took a position near the last chair and waited. He felt like his head was about to explode. Where was his boss? Who was this woman? Where would he find the colonel?"

A woman in gray slacks, white blouse, and a rose-colored *kaffiyeh* draped over her shoulders crossed the lobby to the manger's desk. Yousef watched as they briefly talked, then the woman turned and headed directly for him. He was stunned by her beauty and grace. If this was the woman from the boat, and she was a friend of the boss, he was more than impressed.

"Are you the boy with something of mine from the boat?" she asked.

He nodded, too stunned to say anything.

"What's your name?" she asked in English.

"Yousef."

"Well, Yousef, what is this thing you say you have?"

"My boss told me he was coming here to find you, but just before he left Shepheard's, he was taken by two men. He told me to find you."

"Your boss? Is he a tall American, blond hair, good looking?"

"Yes, that is Mr. Loomis. He is this much taller than me with hair the color of the desert. I am his valet and servant; we have been together for more than two weeks. We came from Libya. His looks? I guess he's okay, Countess Conti."

"You know my name. I'm impressed."

"I try to pay attention. Were you on the boat?"

"Yes, and your boss and I briefly talked. We knew each other during the war. You said he was taken by two men?"

"Yes, he said he was coming here, to this hotel, to find you. He wanted to make sure you were all right. I waited with a taxi. When he came out of the hotel, two men—they looked German—were with him. I think one had a gun. He told me to find M.R. and tell him to cancel the meeting. What meeting, I don't know. So, I came here to find you."

"Good decision. Do you know who M.R. is?" Sophie asked.

"Yes, it is Colonel Rushton," Yousef answered.

"Colonel Michael Rushton?"

"Yes, Madame. Colonel Michael Rushton. I have known him my whole life."

"So have I, Yousef."

25

Max's wrists were secured to the arms of a wooden chair; his feet were tied to the chair's legs. His head suffered like he'd gone ten rounds with Joe Louis. His dry tongue felt the coarse fabric of the bag tautly pulled over his head; the cord around his neck slightly choked him. He not only felt like shit; he felt stupid as well. He didn't know which was worse. When the bag was jerked off, stupid won.

"Well, Mr. Dwight Loomis or Herr Max Adler, or whoever the hell you are, what's going on?" Johann von Dietz asked.

He stood five feet away, holding a thin cane in his right hand; he impatiently kept striking his left palm. Max was sure that if Dietz struck him, he wouldn't be as gentle.

"Is this how you treat your comrades, Herr Dietz? Kidnap them from their hotel, throw them in the back of a car with a bag over their head, drug them, then tie them to a chair? God, my head hurts. What the hell is going on?"

Looking around, Max realized that he'd been stripped to his slacks; the rope cut into his wrists.

"Where's Hans?"

"He has things to do. It does not take two of us to find out if you are a traitor. I have experience in this, I assure you."

"Traitor? What the hell do you mean?"

"You were on the *Nile Princess*, the party boat that burned tonight. Why were you there?"

"What's it to you? You said I had the weekend off after my field trip with Herr Gottlieb. I'm new in town; it was a chance to enjoy the evening. Mingle some with the locals."

"You needed an invitation to get on board. The Russians are very particular about who they invite to their parties. So, why were you there?"

Max smiled; he saw the confusion on Dietz's face. "A woman—actually she claims she's a Russian princess. We met on the Shepheard's terrace the other day, hit it off, and she sent me an invitation to the party. It was the day before I found you on the same terrace. Her name is Natalia Petrov, pretty in a modern, Russian tart sort of way. During the war, I developed a thing for Russian women. However, I quickly learned they often don't play fair. I wanted to see where it might lead."

"Herr Adler, you were seen entering the boat with her."

"Actually, we met at the pier. We talked for few minutes, and then she left me to go talk with someone—I don't know who. When the *Nile Princess* caught fire, the last I saw of her was when she jumped overboard. How do you know all this?"

"We have friends who watch everything that is happening in Cairo, especially with our enemies. You know she is a spy."

"I thought as much. That's one of the reasons I was with her, to see where it might lead. I expect the communists are trying to persuade some in the government to side with their interests, which I believe do not coincide with our interests. I also think she is trying to recruit or kill our brothers who have managed to evade the Americans and the British and reach Cairo. But that's just a guess."

"Yes, that is true. Why didn't you tell me about this?" Dietz asked.

"Tell you what? It was just a date, nothing more. She's adorable in a sort of murderous pussycat and mouse sort of way. It's a failing on my part. I'm drawn to women like that. She looked like fun."

Dietz put the tip of the cane under Max's chin and pushed slightly.

"No need for that, Herr Dietz. I'm lucky I wasn't killed in the accident. I escaped, and I hope so did Petrov—I'm not sure how many others survived."

"The latest count is thirty are dead; a dozen more are missing. Some that were rescued were badly burned. Two were found mangled by crocodiles."

"Petrov? The ambassador?" Max asked.

"They are among the missing, not that the Bolshevik pigs will be missed. Considering the girth of the ambassador, there are probably some very well-fed crocodiles sunning themselves this morning."

Max took a chance and added, "Just before it struck the ship, I saw two men jump from the motorboat that carried the bomb. I assume that you have an idea as to who is responsible."

Dietz smiled. "I might, and yes, there are some in the government who do not want the communists in Egypt. Did you tell anyone what you saw?"

"No. I swam to shore, managed to find a taxi and get to my hotel."

"And why were you leaving the hotel at four this morning? It was obvious to my people that you were going somewhere."

"Yeah, that's another thing. Why were your people waiting for me? It's beginning to look like you do not trust me."

Dietz dragged the stick across Max's chest and stopped just below his rib cage; he pushed slightly. "I trust no one, Herr Adler, no one. And I trust least those who push themselves on me. Now, where were you going?"

"A woman, a gorgeous French girl I met on the boat. I wanted to find out if she survived. She told me the hotel she was staying in."

"What about your Russian princess?" Dietz asked.

"Who cares about her? Once we were on board, she abandoned me. Said she had things to do. And also said things that were not nice. That was fine with me—free food and booze, what's not to like? While I was standing at the rail, I met a woman—a real knockout—we were separated when the boat exploded. I wanted to find her and see if she was all right. Ask your spy whether there was a swell-looking French gal in a red dress. If they didn't see her, you must fire them—they're blind as the sphinx. And as I was leaving the hotel, your boys interrupted my search. Why was that?"

"What hotel is she staying in?"

"She said the Grand Continental. I told one of the boys in the lobby to hold a taxi. I was headed there."

"She may have lied to you."

"Would not have been the first time a woman lied to me. Such are the foibles of love and war. But I wanted to find out."

"Her name?"

"We didn't get that far, but she's French. When I answered her in French, she lit up. I think she's from Paris. We just started talking when the boat was attacked."

"And it wasn't this Petrov woman you were going to see?"

"No. As I said, the Russian's a piece of work. I hope she made it to shore, but not my problem. She's a spy? Not surprised—she acted all Mata Hari like. So, Herr Dietz, what are you going to do with me?"

"Did the Russian say anything to you? Do you think she knew who you were?"

"No, we did not discuss politics, just poetry and literature—Russian literature. She believes me to be Dwight Loomis, an American expatriate, and someone with a dodgy history wanted by the British in Benghazi. The same history you know. Nothing happened to change that. If she's dead, I'll miss her— more for what might have happened than for what we had."

"Adler, you are an incurable romantic and a fool."

"Yes, that's me, Herr Dietz, a foolish romantic."

Max watched Dietz pick up a stiletto from the table. Dietz slipped it under the ropes and cut them. As Max bent down to untie his own legs, he looked over his shoulder and saw a man in a dark suit, the same man that had jammed the gun into his back.

"Herr Dietz, you said you might know who was involved with the attack?"

Dietz tapped Max on the shoulder. "Captain Adler, you ask too many questions. Corporal Reese." Max heard the man's heels click to attention. "Get the captain's shirt and jacket."

"My pistol," Max said. "It's a souvenir from the war. Something I acquired in the Ardennes; I would like it back."

"Corporal Reese will give it to you when you get to your hotel. It is heavy and uses hard-to-find ammunition. Why do you carry it?"

"A memento of the fickleness of war. An American aimed it at me, pulled the trigger, and it jammed. I took it from him, just before I killed him."

"Luck?"

"I do not believe in luck, Herr Dietz."

Reese dropped Max off at the steps of Shepheard's and handed the pistol to him. The sun was high, and the heat already had pushed some of the Europeans from the terrace. Max walked into the lobby, and before he could make it to the elevator, Yousef nearly tackled him.

"Boss, are you okay? Where have you been?" Yousef inspected almost every inch of Max as they both entered the elevator. "Who were those men? Where did they take you?"

"Not now, Yousef. I need a shower. I also need to get to

the Semiramis Hotel—the woman."

"I have her," Yousef said.

"What do you mean, you have her."

"In your room."

Max burst out of the elevator and ran down the hallway; he pushed the unlocked door open. Sophie stood in the center of the room, smoking a cigarette. Seeing Max, she threw herself into his arms.

"I didn't know what to imagine, where to find you, nothing," she said.

"I was headed to the Semiramis to find you," Max answered.

"That's what your boy said. He found me."

Max turned to Yousef. "Thank you."

"Effendi, when they took you, I didn't know what to do. I went to the Semiramis Hotel and asked questions, and I found the countess."

Max looked at Sophie; she winked and wrinkled her nose.

"From there we went to find the colonel," Sophie said. "Colonel Rushton said that he saw you on Gezira Island at the club."

Max turned to Yousef. Yousef pointed to the couch along the wall behind the door.

Colonel Rushton, smoking a pipe, sat on the richly embroidered couch with its ornate pillows. Max, for the first time, smelled the Turkish tobacco.

"Michael. God, it's good to see you—right now it is good to see anyone."

Rushton tapped the pipe in the large ashtray next to him and set it down. "What the hell went on this morning?" he asked.

Max told them everything that happened after he left Rushton on the road in Gezira, through the abduction and his return. "I'm sorry, Michael, but dinner tonight is out of the question, now. Please tell your wife I'm sorry."

"I will. You think your cover is safe?" Rushton asked.

"I hope so. However, I do not trust Dietz to tell me the truth. He has something big going on, and I need to find out what." He turned to Sophie and kissed her cheek. "But what are you doing here? I thought you were in Moscow or Russia somewhere?"

"I was, for only a few weeks. Then I was sent to find Petrov and see what she's up to here in Cairo. There are reports of money being funneled into the communists here—she is part of it. They also found, in Alexandria, two dead SS officers that had escaped Germany. Both had been executed. Home office speculates that it might have been Petrov or a Cossack that works for her," Sophie said and then looked at Max. "Two more things, MI6 never said a word about you being here. Then again, I don't think the OSS informed them of exactly who you are and why you are here either. The colonel knew, of course, but only what the OSS wanted him to know. Second, I'm also after a French-Algerian assassin who is working for al-Husseini. He is an extremely dangerous man. We believe he is coming here to coordinate with the Muslim Brotherhood and prepare for Husseini's return to Egypt and Palestine—as well as set up operations against the British and the French."

"Interesting. I'm after an SS officer, Johann von Dietz," Max said. "The man escaped from Germany and is involved with chemical weapons; he has connections to Husseini as well. Yesterday, they took me halfway to Alexandria to a warehouse full of German weapons and supplies that look like chemicals. I think I can find the warehouse, but I sure can't tell you how to get there. It is possible they are working together."

Rushton stared at Max; Max caught the look of rebuke.

"Sorry, Michael, for being a bit untruthful. Not sure what I should have told you after I returned. Saying we were looking around was enough for then—now you know the truth." Max could see that Rushton still wasn't pleased but would get over it.

"If Husseini comes back to Egypt, it will be with the help of the Brotherhood," Rushton said, refilling his pipe. "We will try and intercept him, but he's such a political force here that if we arrest him, there will be more trouble than leaving him alone."

"What does this Algerian bring to the Brotherhood?" Max asked.

"A brutal hatred for the French, the British, the Americans, and the Jews," Sophie said. "He is a known assassin, and with his skills, he can organize the rabble that makes up a lot of the Brotherhood and turn them into fighters. If your man Dietz has other Nazis with him, they may be able to build a strong militia. One that can cause trouble for the current government and potentially for the British as well."

Max remembered Dietz's visit to Abdeen Palace. "Suppose there is support within the king's government, suppose that Dietz has the ear of important government officials, and suppose the king is one of those listening?"

Rushton relit his pipe and took a long pull. "Then we may be royally fucked."

26

It was late in the afternoon when Max awoke. After Rushton and Sophie separately left the hotel, Max crashed. Before he fell asleep, he counted on his fingers and thought it had been more than twenty-four hours since he'd last slept. He was sore, and his back ached from the jump into the Nile River. How he got into bed was a mystery.

After a shower, he dressed in his remaining clean suit, secured the pistol under his jacket, and left the bedroom for the main part of his room. The smell of Rushton's Turkish tobacco still hung in the still air. Yousef was on his knees, facing an open window, doing his early evening prayers. When he was finished, he stood.

"Your mother will be very proud of you," Max said.

Yousef smiled. "Are you well? After the countess and the colonel left, you collapsed on the couch; I made sure you got into bed. There are dates and pastries on the table. Would you like some ice water?"

"Thank you, Yousef. However, right now"—Max checked his watch—"I need a bourbon."

"Shall I pour you one?"

"No, I'm going downstairs to the bar. Have my suit cleaned and return what remains of the tuxedo back to the shop. Find out how much I owe them; I will pay for it. You can have the evening to yourself. I will be busy."

"With the countess?"

"You ask too many questions."

"How will I learn, if I do not ask?" Yousef said with a smile.

"You are also too young to ask certain questions."

Yousef slightly bowed. "Yes, effendi."

He took an English newspaper from the front desk and went into the grill, not the Long Bar. Exclusiveness was not what he was looking for; he was hoping to find a spy. He ordered a bourbon on ice.

The front page described the accident on the Nile River and the unfortunate deaths that resulted, but it mentioned nothing about a speedboat or an explosion. The most current report was that twenty-eight bodies had been recovered from the river and the burned ship. Dietz's information was close. The boat had been successfully towed to the eastern riverbank and avoided crashing into the houseboats. It was a complete loss. The captain survived but was badly burned. Four people were still missing; one of those was the Russian ambassador. There was not a published list of the survivors or the dead. At the end of the article, it was reported that the Russians were blaming the Muslim Brotherhood for the explosion. They were demanding a full investigation. After what Dietz had hinted, the Russian accusations were probably more right than wrong.

Max signaled to the bartender for another, and he turned to the society pages of the paper—they reminded him of the tawdry pages of London's *Daily Mail*. However, here it was about the local Brits and the comings and goings of a colonial class seemingly unaffected by the just-concluded war. It was as if they lived on a desert island, but in the case of Cairo, an island entirely surrounded by desert sand. When he looked up, a small burly man dropped into the seat across from him. Swarthy was the first word that came to his mind; the second word was Petrov. He'd last seen this man sitting with Natalia Petrov a week earlier in this same bar. He knew he was not the woman's lover; she would be far more selective. No, this man was muscle and brawn—the bullet to Petrov's pistol.

"Where is she?" Max asked, slowly folding the paper. He extracted a cigarette and lit it. "Did she survive the swim?"

"Yes, Madam Petrov is alive."

"And you are?"

"I am Dimitri Semitov, a friend of Madam Petrov. She asked me to find you; she was concerned about your safety. Personally, I don't give a shit—you Americans are all assholes. But I do what I'm told."

"A man who can follow orders, excellent. However, why are you here? I'm alive; you can tell her that. And my condolences about the Russian ambassador."

"He was a fat pig; it is good that he is gone. He was some party *apparatchik* from Georgia, a friend of Stalin. Why he was sent here I do not know or care. We will have to wait and see who is sent to replace him. I don't expect anything better."

"My, a cynical Russian—who would have thought. So, you are here to . . . what?"

Semitov extracted a fat cigarette from a case and tapped it on the tabletop. He took Max's matches and lit it. "I am here to escort you to Madam Petrov; she would like to see you."

"As you can see, I am too busy. Tell her if she wants to see me, I will be in the park on the bridge tonight at eleven. She knows where."

"I was told to bring you to her, now." Semitov slowly opened his jacket to reveal the butt of a revolver.

"And I told you no." Max, like Semitov, slowly opened his

jacket and revealed his pistol. "Mine's bigger."

Semitov stood and turned toward the door.

"Eleven, and tell her not to be late. And, Semitov, I don't want to see you there, understand?"

The Russian turned back to Max, extended his fist; his stubby thumb stuck out between his thick fingers and he raised it defiantly.

"And fuck you too," Max replied.

Later that evening, Max ordered dinner; he'd grown fond of steak and kidney pie while in England and was pleasantly surprised as to how good the Shepheard's version was. The local beer was not nearly as good.

As he crossed the lobby, Yousef intercepted him.

"Did you get something to eat?" Max asked.

"Yes, effendi—they have a dining room for valets and servants. The food is not bad. It will be on your bill."

"I should pay you more."

"You don't pay me anything," Yousef answered.

"We'll work something out. Did Colonel Rushton say anything to you when he left?"

"Yes, the colonel said he would be at his club, then to the officer's barracks across the road from the Semiramis Hotel. He and the countess would like to see you for breakfast. They said the Semiramis Hotel."

"I need you to tell Colonel Rushton that I can't. I have an appointment with the Germans. He will understand."

"Yes, effendi. What time will you be back tonight?"

"Late, very late. Don't worry."

"I always worry; it is my job."

"I should give you a raise."

"Yes, you should. Good night," Yousef said and quickly walked through the lobby toward the back stairs.

After an excellent late dinner, Max strode down the steps to the street and headed toward the Ezbekieh Gardens.

For a Sunday evening, the garden was crowded with couples walking around the small lake and grounds. Someone was playing the oud, the sound from the string instrument drifting amongst the palm and orange trees. The finger taps on a tabla drum kept the rhythm. Max stopped short of the small bridge that crossed the pond and paused. He then slipped into the shadow of a large date palm. Across the pond, Petrov and Semitov stood in the light of an overhead light fixture; she was smoking a cigarette. Semitov was scanning the crowd, obviously looking for Dwight Loomis. He said something to Petrov, then walked away. She stood alone on the path, looking toward the bridge.

From the opposite side, Max purposefully walked toward the bridge. Petrov spotted him and waved. He waved back.

Approaching each other on the bridge, Max saw a wide bandage wrapping Petrov's left arm. A thin orange silk wrap crossed her shoulder and over the forearm. She took his left arm with her right hand and steered him to the railing, and then kissed him on the lips.

"That was for saving me last night," she said.

"You are the one that jumped into the river in your underwear—an image I will remember fondly my whole life. I hardly call that saving you."

"I should have stayed to help the ambassador—you made me jump."

"That's one way to remember it, but thanks all the same. Your arm?"

"I cut it climbing the bank of the river; my ankle as well. You don't look injured."

"Swam to shore, caught a taxi to the hotel, got drunk. Since I didn't know where you lived, I couldn't find you. Your associate was kind enough to pass on my message; tell him thanks."

"I will."

"You are not too upset about the ambassador, are you? He

was a Bolshevik and a member of Stalin's circle, and you being
. . ."

"A White Russian?"

Max smiled at the admission. "If you say so. Me, I'm just
a kid from Chicago. I know so little of these things. Chicago's
politics have always been tough, but Stalin plays by a whole
different set of rules."

"He says little, demands a lot. That's why I will never go
back. My country is lost. Is that why you are here, Mr. Loomis?
Are you also lost?"

"I think we are now beyond discussions of Tolstoy and
Pushkin, Madam Petrov. My country did not appreciate me,
so I was thrown out. The only things they allowed me to keep
were my passport and name. I need work. That is why I'm
here."

"How can you afford such luxury, if you are so . . . unap-
preciated?"

"My family is well off, and I'm an embarrassment. They
are more comfortable if I'm here than in Chicago—less to explain. So, for the time being, my accounts are covered, but for
how long I'm not sure. That's why I'm interested in working
for an American or British oil company—seems like a big future in energy." Max paused and lit a cigarette. "Enough about
me. You're intriguing. What's your game?"

"Game? I do not play games."

"Sure you do. I ask myself: What's a great-looking dame like
you doing in Cairo? You say you're hiding from the Russians,
yet you attend soirees on yachts. You wear very nice clothes
and go to the best parties. You are not afraid to strip to your
very pretty undergarments in a flash and meet strangers on a
bridge at night. Yes, I do wonder about you, Natalia Petrov."

"My, my, you ask so many questions. Like most Americans
I've met—you all ask too many questions."

"And where have you met these Americans?"

"I have spent time in America. It was before the war. I was traveling with a friend from Leningrad. We were staying in Washington, D.C. He was in state politics."

"Washington, D.C., is not like America, that I can tell you. It will give you the wrong impression of us; the real Americans are in the country, the small towns. They are the ones that fought the war and won it."

"Russia is like that. The workers and the peasants—they are the heart and soul of Russia."

"I understand Stalin came from a small town and working family, not aristocracy. I would not think that you would lean toward the peasants."

"More than twenty million of my people died in the war, all by German hands and guns. A whole generation was lost. There is much to remake."

"And Stalin will do this?"

"There is an old proverb in Russia: 'When the rich make war, it's the poor that die.' Stalin has made sure that the poor died in this war, million upon millions of them."

"So, the cobbler's son, the pauper, is now the rich man."

Before Petrov could answer, three men walked onto the bridge, two from one side, one from the other. Each wore the long white *jellabiya* and a red tarboosh. Two of the men drew long knives from within their sleeves. One yelled, *"Allahu ak-bar,"* and they charged, blades flashed in the lights.

Max instinctively reacted. He withdrew his pistol and aimed at the lead attacker. He put one round in the middle of the man's chest. Max spun in the other direction. The lone assailant took a round from Max in the shoulder and fell over the railing into the pond. The third stumbled over the dead man and then spinning around, raced to the end of the bridge; he didn't make it. From behind Max, a pistol shot almost deafened his right ear. Petrov had fired her small pistol at the flee-ing Egyptian. The man tumbled onto the gravel path at the end of the bridge.

Max looked at the men on the bridge. "We need to get out of here, now," he said to Petrov. "We only have minutes until the police arrive." He grabbed her arm.

She cried from the pain to her injured arm, then pushed it away and stared in bewilderment at Max. "Who the hell are you? Who carries a canon under their jacket?" She looked at the men, then back at Max.

"Now," Max said but then saw Semitov standing at the foot of the bridge. "A lot of good that worthless asshole did." He grabbed her arm again and pulled her down the bridge and into the shadows of Ezbekieh Gardens. Semitov, like a shamed dog, followed.

27

At the edge of the garden, Max hailed a taxi and put Petrov into the back seat. When Semitov tried to get in, Max pushed the small man back and yelled, "*Nyet.* Find your own damn ride."

Semitov began to reach into his jacket. Max raised the pistol he had not returned to his holster and pointed it at Semitov's forehead.

"It's okay, Dimitri, I will be okay," Petrov said from inside. "I will see you in the morning."

Semitov backed away, buttoning his coat as he did. The loathing on his face scrunched up his inflated red cheeks until his two black eyes sat glaring on top of them. Max climbed into the cab and slammed the door.

"Where do you live?" Max demanded. The sounds of police sirens could be heard.

"Who the hell are you?" Petrov demanded again.

"Live? Where the hell do you live?" Max fumbled around in Petrov's handbag until he found the pistol. He dropped the magazine onto the seat and ejected the chambered bullet.

"Damn it, Natalia, where do you live?"

"Garden City, on the Corniche, facing the Nile, near the British embassy."

"Driver, the British embassy on—"

"Effendi, I know where it is. What happened back there?"

"Not your concern," Max said. "Just drive."

Leaving Semitov standing in the street, the taxi circled the Opera House and headed south. In silence, they passed Abdeen Palace and turned west toward the Nile River. The traffic was light. At the British embassy, Max asked, "Where now?"

"The Corniche parallels the river. Turn south in three blocks. Then you can let me out. I never want to see you again."

"We are beyond that. After what just happened, we are forever linked."

The driver slowed as they turned onto the Nile Corniche; to the taxi's right side the moon reflected off the river. On the opposite bank, lights were visible from the structures and houseboats along Gezira Island.

"Here," Petrov said. "Just leave me here, then go away."

The taxi stopped.

"I'm taking you to your apartment," Max said. "Driver, wait."

"You pay before you get out," the driver said. "Pay, now."

Max threw coins on the front seat. "That should cover it." Then, taking Petrov by the arm again, he guided her out of the car and to the sidewalk. As soon as the door slammed, the driver took off.

"Even the taxi drivers don't trust you," Petrov said.

"It's not the first time. Which is yours?"

Petrov stopped and held out her hand. "The Beretta. I want my pistol."

Max handed her the small, well-worn pistol.

"The magazine."

"You have others. I'll keep this one."

"You bastard!"

"A bastard that saved your life," Max spit back.

"How do you know they were after me? It could have been someone from the British trying to get even—it may have been *you* they were going to kill. Or maybe it's for the lies *you* are spreading."

For the first time, it occurred to Max that she might have the glimmer of an idea there. For the moment, he put it to the side. "They were after you—maybe because they didn't finish the job last night."

"Who are you? Who goes on a nice date wearing a pistol? Who does that? Spies do that, secret government agents do that, and goddamn liars do that."

"And someone who doesn't trust anyone they meet does that," he countered. "I have no idea who you are, a Russian, a Cossack, a Georgian Bolshevik, and a liar as well? Maybe Stalin is your fucking father."

She slapped him. He was surprised by its strength; it stung and hurt.

"Another reason to keep the pistol's magazine," he said with a laugh. "And who am I? I am who I said I was. Maybe we'll meet again. Good night, Natalia Petrov, *dasvidanya*." He handed her the Beretta.

She spat on the ground. "*Svin'ya.*"

A rare late-night taxi turned the corner and headed down the street toward them. Max waved. The taxi slowed.

"Madam Petrov, maybe I'll see you sometime on Shepheard's terrace. Please come unarmed." He climbed into the taxi and left Petrov standing at the curb.

As the taxi pulled from the curb, Max turned and watched Petrov out the rear window. He then leaned in and said to the driver, "Turn at the next intersection and stop. Then turn around and slowly pull to the side of the road. I'll tell you where to stop."

"Yes, effendi," the driver answered.

From this new vantage point parked along the Nile, Max watched Petrov pace back and forth along the curb. She did not go into the apartment building. After ten minutes, a sedan slowly drove up the street. When it reached Petrov, it stopped. She immediately got in, and the sedan pulled away and headed toward them. Max slipped down in the shadows and watched as Dimitri Semitov accelerated past them.

"She had another date, effendi?" the driver asked.

"Looks like it. Women can be so fickle."

"Yes, effendi. Where to, effendi?"

"The Semiramis Hotel."

The driver smiled. "Yes, effendi."

* * *

After Petrov climbed into the front seat of the car, she said nothing to Semitov. She stared out the window, watching the lights reflect off the Nile River.

"It did not go as planned," Semitov said.

"No, I was expecting something else from the American when your men attacked. A different reaction, maybe whimpering and fear—pissing in his pants would have been good. I got a soldier's response, a very well-prepared soldier. This American is not who he says he is."

"Who is in this fucking city? Everyone is someone else. I even wonder about my mistress—for all I know, I might be fucking a French spy."

Still looking in the glass of the window, she stared at the back of the head of Semitov. *Such an ass.*

"Your men, what happened?"

"One died, one badly injured. My men want this American; they want him dead."

"In time. However, for now, I need to find out why he is here. All those reports from Benghazi may be just stories to confuse us. He is staying at the Shepheard's Hotel. See what additional information your people can find out about this American, Dwight Loomis."

* * *

Max said into the lobby phone, "Did I wake you? I'm sorry."

"Never be sorry for waking me," Sophie said, sleep obviously in her voice. "What are you doing up so late?"

"I had a date."

"Figures."

"Can I come up?"

"Maybe I have a date."

"Then I will be up even quicker. What's the room number?"

She told him. "But wait ten minutes. A girl needs to freshen up a bit."

"I'll give you five."

When he knocked on her door, it was closer to ten minutes. She grabbed his hand, yanked him into the room, and kissed him hard. He did nothing to stop her.

"I hope we're alone," Max said when he came up for air.

"Obviously." She nibbled his neck.

"No biting." He reluctantly pushed Sophie back and sniffed the air. "You tend to leave marks."

"You do not trust me?" she said.

He sniffed the air. "No Turkish tobacco and no Colonel Rushton. Of course I trust you." He grabbed her and kissed her like a man desperate for life; she returned his advances. After a series of preliminary rounds, they tumbled into bed. Only when an embarrassed, early morning sun poked its head through the slats covering the window did they stop.

"Room service?" Sophie asked. "The coffee is very good."

"That would be great—I missed you," Max answered.

"I could tell, and I missed you. This is the last place I

thought I would ever find you."

After the coffee had arrived, they went to the room's small balcony and, wrapped in hotel robes, looked out over the illuminated morning rooftops. From a dozen minarets, the call to *Salah* echoed through the streets.

"It has been bizarre the last few weeks," Max said. "But I'm close."

"Can you tell me?"

He told her everything and added things he hadn't said the night before when Rushton was in the room. She listened quietly. They had spent almost six months together in Rome fighting the fascists and the Nazis. When the war moved north, past Rome, they returned to London, then to Paris where another adventure saved the Allied High Command. The war pushed then eastward across Europe and Max was assigned to the front in the Ardennes. He survived the Battle of the Bulge, as it was now being called, and returned to OSS headquarters in London. What their relationship was remained hard for either of them to define—the war continually got in the way. Now peace was doing the same thing. If pressed, they would have said they were committed, but to what still needed sorting out. Commitment is a lot different than committed. If they were afraid of anything, it was time and what would happen when time was all theirs and they were no longer under orders. God and country were two strong beliefs to fight for. They had fought for each other for so long, at times they thought it was just them against the world. But to have time for just themselves—to be committed, to take a vow—scared the devil out of both of them.

Max played with the magazine from Petrov's pistol, pushing bullets in and out of the magazine. He stopped and looked at one of the shells. It was odd.

"What do you think?" he said, handing the bullet to Sophie.

She took a few seconds. "It's a blank 9 mm, loud but ineffectual. Whose are they?"

"Madam Petrov's. I took the magazine from her pistol before I returned it to her."

"Worthless. Did she shoot at the attackers?"

"Yes, after I did."

"I'll bet that the attackers were surprised when real bullets showed up to a knife fight."

"Yes. What was her angle though? To save me, impress me?"

Sophie lit Max a cigarette and refreshed his coffee.

"This Natalia Petrov is a Russian spy and a liar," Sophie said matter-of-factly.

"Shocking, isn't it?"

"And the OSS and Director Donovan believe that she's here to poach Germans."

"Yes, just like me. The difference being that she wants them for Stalin, or dead. Me? I want to know what they are doing, then stop them. The problem nagging me is—what does Dietz want? To attack the British; that's why you're here. To attack the Jews in Palestine; not sure what that accomplishes. To be blunt, the Jewish problem is one that neither of our countries really gives a damn about. They just want it to go away. But Dietz's target? I don't know."

"The Algerian doesn't give a damn about the British," Sophie said. "It's the French he's targeting. The British are incidental and would be welcomed collateral damage. For him and al-Husseini, it is the Zionists and the Jews in Palestine and the French mandate, Syria. Al-Khaldi is a real threat. That's why I'm here, to sort it out, and help de Gaulle. Everything MI6 sees is British-centric, but we know in this region of the world is a six-sided box. The British on one side, the French on another, and the Muslim Brotherhood and the Islamic radicals are opposite the Zionists and Palestine. However, the two remaining sides, the top and bottom, are you, the Americans, and your newfound hegemony, and the expanding world of the Soviets. Try and put a bow on that present."

28

Alexandria, Egypt
Mid-October 1945

Abdul al-Khaldi, dressed as a successful European businessman, walked down the gangway of the Greek freighter *Taurus*. Behind him, two longshoremen carried his bags. He breezed through customs, his papers and passport identifying him as a French national and importer from Marseilles, his name Amir Duchamp, French-Algerian. Both the British and Egyptian customs authorities inspected his luggage. Finding nothing suspicious, they waved him through. On the street, outside the long pier where the *Taurus* was tied up, a young Egyptian man stood near a taxi; he held a sign that said in Arabic: "Monsieur Duchamp." Al-Khaldi nodded to the man and pointed to the bags. The Egyptian driver placed the bags in the trunk as al-Khaldi watched. He then opened the taxi's rear door and allowed al-Khaldi to sit.

"Welcome to Egypt, sir," the driver said in French.

"*Merci*," al-Khaldi answered. "How long to our first stop?"

"About an hour and a half, Monsieur. Do you wish to have something to eat?"

"I ate breakfast on the boat this morning. I can wait until

Tanta."

"There is a thermos with cool water as well as some dates and dried apricots."

"Excellent, your name?"

"Ismail, Monsieur."

"Good, please proceed."

They crossed the Nile River at Kafr el-Zayet and proceeded through the lush Nile Delta. There was no conversation between the two until they reached the outskirts of Tanta. When they approached the gates of the warehouse complex, Ismail slowed, then stopped. He nervously waited as the guards talked with his passenger. The senior guard went to the phone in the small guardhouse and called someone. A minute later, Hans Gottlieb left the largest warehouse and crossed the grounds to the gate. He held a photograph in his hand. When he reached the gates, he waved to the men in the taxi to get out. Al-Khaldi looked around the facility and nodded to Gottlieb. Hans looked at the photo, then at al-Khaldi. He smiled and extended his hand; al-Khaldi instead first extended his right arm and hand in a Nazi salute and said *heil* before shaking Gottlieb's hand. Gottlieb smiled.

"Welcome, Monsieur Duchamp. Let's get out of the sun." He turned to the head guard. "Make sure they have enough petrol and find the kid some food. We will be back in an hour."

The guards saluted, said something to the driver, and pointed to a covered area of other parked vehicles. Gottlieb and al-Khaldi walked toward the warehouse.

"Your men are retrieving the boxes, Herr Gottlieb?" al-Khaldi asked.

"Yes. In fact, they called me when they saw you leave the ship. They will bring them here late this afternoon. Your voyage, was it pleasant?"

"As far as it goes. The cook was Greek—I'm very tired of mutton."

"Herr von Dietz has an excellent cook, and only the best lamb is served. I'm sure you will be comfortable."

"Comfort is a luxury. And is, for the time being, something that we cannot afford. Is everything proceeding on schedule?"

"Yes. In fact, we are ahead of schedule," Gottlieb said. "The Cairo facility is in full operation; the first canisters are being manufactured. They will be ready for testing next week. The chemicals will be delivered in two days."

"The weapons?"

"Let me show you," Gottlieb said as they entered the warehouse. For the next hour, the two men opened and inspected crates of rifles, machine guns, grenades, ammunition, and even uniforms. The uniforms were originally for the Balkan Handschar units; they had been stored at the chemical facility near Sarajevo. "We are having insignias produced to give your troops special identification. You will meet the Muslim Brotherhood leadership in two days; they are assembling their militias."

"Excellent. The Mufti is pleased. He has given to me the honor of coordinating the various operations. I will tell Herr von Dietz and the Brotherhood leadership everything the Mufti wishes when we meet. There is much to coordinate, but I see that German efficiency has again shown us how to proceed."

"Thank you. The kid will remain here. I will drive you the rest of the way to Cairo. There is much to talk about, and it is only for our ears."

Late that evening, the Mercedes pulled to a stop in front of Dietz's apartment building. After Gottlieb and al-Khaldi left and disappeared into the building, the doorman parked the car away from the entry and removed al-Khaldi's bags. Placing them on a cart, he wheeled them into the lobby.

* * *

Max asked Sophie, "Was that your guy?"

"Yes, that's him," Sophie said. "Our people in Alexandria said he's traveling under a French passport and the name Amir Duchamp. They must have stopped at the warehouse on the way here. Five containers filled with farm equipment were included on the ship's manifest. They were offloaded a few hours after the boat docked and loaded on trucks; they are being tailed. I should know exactly where they went tomorrow."

In the dark shadow along the street in front of Dietz's apartment building, Max and Sophie sat in an appropriated taxi, sharing a cigarette.

"Seems like old times," Sophie said. "Like that time we waited for Schmidt's birthday to end. I still don't know why you stopped those partisans from killing him."

"I still don't either. Considering what followed, I guess I should have. History is full of stupidity and lost opportunities. That was one of mine. So, you have your boy here—what are you going to do about him?"

"He is part of a much larger action," Sophie said. "We're positive he is connected to the Muslim Brotherhood and al-Husseini. His skills can do a lot of damage, but we also need to know what is going on. This connection to Dietz and the Nazis here in Egypt opens the doors to a lot of nasty stuff, both here and in Palestine and Syria."

They waited an hour, and then Gottlieb walked out of the apartment building to the Mercedes. He turned the car around and headed out onto the street, away from Max and Sophie.

"Are you going to follow him?" Sophie asked?

"No, it's a good bet he's going to his apartment. Let's see what happens here, at least for the next hour."

Forty minutes later, two black Citroens pulled into the driveway. Four men exited from the rear seats. They were dressed in European suits; all wore red tarbooshes. The drivers exited the cars, stood at attention, and waited.

"Two of those guys are Brotherhood," Max said. "I saw

them talking to Dietz on the terrace at Shepheard's last week. I assume that the others are as well. I confirmed their identities from mug shots that Rushton had. One is a professor of history at Cairo University; the other is a director of one of Cairo's largest banks."

"They do not sound like radicals," Sophie answered.

"They aren't. That is the power of the Brotherhood. They cross many boundaries of Egyptian life. There are also factions within the organization that are at odds with the leadership. Some in the OSS guess there are more than a million members of the Brotherhood, a formidable number. A small percentage would make a significant militia, especially with all the unemployment and dissatisfaction with the current government leaders and the British. It's our guess that they have members in the army."

"MI6 thinks the same."

The lights in the apartment lobby brightened; six men left the lobby, Dietz leading the way.

"Grab the camera," Sophie said. As she watched the men, she heard the camera's shutter click a dozen times. "Maybe we can figure out the others."

After shaking hands, four of the men returned to the cars. Dietz stood at the entry with al-Khaldi and watched as the cars left the property. Max and Sophie slipped into the darker recess of their taxi to avoid being seen.

They looked back at the entry. Dietz stood there smoking a cigarette. Al-Khaldi was enthusiastically waving his hands and walking about. Dietz watched, saying nothing until his cigarette was finished. He crushed it on the paving.

"I wonder what that's all about?" Max said.

"I would guess that the meeting went well; everybody seems happy," Sophie said.

"If they're happy, we're in deep shit."

29

The Sinai Desert
October 1945

The high-wing Fieseler Fi 156 flew low and slowly through the mountain passes seventy miles east of the air base. Dietz, with his three airplanes, formed a significant air force for al-Husseini's organization. The Storch, with its two occupants, had been scouring the valleys looking for one thing: Bedouin.

"They are hard to find," Gottlieb said from the seat behind the pilot, Bitner. "We were informed that a small tribe had set up their camp in one of these wadis." He looked at his watch. "Thirty minutes more, then we return."

"Yes, sir," Bitner said and banked the aircraft around a sharp outcrop of the escarpment that held to their left side. A wide valley opened in front of them.

"There, that's it," Gottlieb said. "Circle around the camp; I'll mark the map."

The single-engine plane did a slow turn over the camp. The sheep, gathered on the northern flank of the long tents, began to scatter. Gottlieb saw that the boys in charge of the flock were having a tough time controlling them. He said nothing.

Horses were tied to stakes in the ground and pulled against their leads; a dozen camels sat on the ground but began to climb to their feet. As the aircraft made another pass, a dozen men exited the largest tent and looked up.

"This will do. How soon will you have the airplane ready?" Gottlieb asked.

"It is ready now," Bitner said. "What we need is to have the weather cooperate—no wind. That means early in the morning before the sun begins to stir up the air. We are about eighty miles from the airfield. I can leave and return in less than forty-five minutes, well within the range of the fuel. In fact, I suggest that we only fly with two-thirds of a tank—less weight."

"No, full tanks. I want to see how it performs fully loaded, as it will be in the real action. No surprises. Is that acceptable?"

"Yes. No surprises."

Bitner turned the plane back to the airfield. For the next hour, both men sat with their thoughts.

* * *

The next morning, Gottlieb, back in Cairo, waited for Max Adler a block from Shepheard's. He'd left a message for Adler the night before. The message said simply: "Be at the southern corner of the Ezbekieh Gardens. You will be away for three days—bring a change of clothes."

Gottlieb watched Adler, a leather satchel over his shoulder, cross the street in front of the hotel and walk toward him. Herr Dietz had accepted this German as one of their own. He was not so sure. Everything about him was almost too German, and his history was almost too American as well. He now wished that he could have been with Dietz during the interview with this man after the attack on the *Nile Princess*, but he was too busy recovering the two men who had jumped from the speedboat. The major said Adler had a plausible excuse for being on the boat, and now he would be helping with the operation. Dietz trusted the man; Gottlieb did not.

"Good morning, Hans. Where are we off to?" Max said as he sat in the front passenger's seat.

"We are going back to the warehouse. You are to inventory everything today and begin to deliver the crates to our Cairo facility tomorrow."

"And where is that?"

"I will show you."

Gottlieb drove through the rabbit warren of streets and alleys of the Shubra district until he came to a large roll-up door at one side of a courtyard. He had Max mark the route on a detailed map of the district. The courtyard was just large enough to turn around a medium-sized truck.

"Tap on the door three times," Gottlieb said. "Then pause, then three times more. When the door rolls open, drive inside." Gottlieb got out and knocked on the door.

He then walked away from the Mercedes and up a narrow alley that intersected the courtyard. There was no one in the courtyard. Even the usual mix of street urchins and beggars were missing.

He then walked in behind Adler as he drove the Mercedes into the garage, the door closing behind them.

Gottlieb showed Max where the crates were to be placed when he returned from the Delta warehouse. The Shubra facility was unremarkable. There were a dozen wooden crates stacked on one side of the room—some were open and empty, others still secured. As they stood there, a steel door opened on one wall and a German stepped out dressed in a lab coat. He was trying to light a cigarette. When he saw Gottlieb, he immediately turned around, threw the cigarette to the ground, and closed the door behind him.

"And where does that lead to?" Adler asked.

"To someplace that does not concern you," Gottlieb said. "You will move the crates from the warehouse and leave them here. It will take you two days; you will make two trips each day. The first trip we will include the two large tanks that you saw, then the rest as you see fit. The tanks will go there—use the overhead hoist to move them. After the last trip, you will leave the trucks here in the garage."

They climbed back into the Mercedes; the steel door remained closed and secured.

"You drive," Gottlieb said. "You might as well get used to the route. I've done it too many times."

For the next two hours, they wound their way north through the Cairo traffic and then finally out into Nile Delta. Gottlieb had to correct Max twice as the neared the village of Tanta.

They were waved through the front gate. They parked near the central warehouse building.

"Follow me," Gottlieb said, and quick marched toward a smaller warehouse. He removed keys from his pocket and unlocked the door. The only light inside was from four skylights. Bathed in the light were three trucks, all British Leyland "Hippos." They were painted desert brown and beige. On each of their doors was stenciled, "Sinai Oil and Gas," with the symbol of an ancient Egyptian bird.

"I assume that you requisitioned these from the British?" Adler asked.

"They have many; they won't miss these. They should be more than adequate to carry the crates and the chemical tanks. I have three experienced Egyptian truck drivers who are loyal to our cause and that of the Mufti and the Brotherhood. You will coordinate with them the loading and the unloading. There are adequate personnel here and in Cairo; the tanks are the most critical. They need to be in Cairo by tomorrow night. The rest of the crates will follow."

"Yes, sir," Adler said. The heat became oppressive as they walked deeper into the warehouse.

Gottlieb stopped and turned to face the SS officer. "To be honest, Adler, I do not like you. Nonetheless, you have the favor of the major and I follow his orders. However, one fuck-up or you lose one box or crate, and you will discover that the desert is very large and one can easily get lost."

"I understand; I am a soldier. Like you, I do what I'm told. To be honest, I have not warmed to you either. When this is over maybe we will have time to become friends; there is still much to accomplish. And it is not helping the cause to carry enmity among the troops."

Gottlieb stared at Adler, the response not at all what he expected. "I will see you tomorrow afternoon. Now let's meet your drivers and the men who are working here."

Gottlieb and Adler exited the warehouse, and the man was introduced to a dozen men. Three were the drivers. Only the drivers spoke English and some German.

"German?" Adler asked Gottlieb.

"Yes. They worked for the British during the war, driving trucks to al-Alamein and Tobruk. They also drove for the Germans when they advanced across North Africa the first time. They are the lucky ones. Between here and Benghazi, a lot of their friends are dead and buried along the main highway."

"Yes, I saw the cemeteries."

Gottlieb looked surprised, then remembered. "I forgot that you came here from Benghazi. They are loyal members of the Brotherhood; they know what to do."

* * *

After Gottlieb had left for Cairo, Max spent the rest of the afternoon looking into boxes and crates—the military equipment and ordinance stunned him. There was more than enough to arm a small army.

A cot had been set up in a small office located in the rear of the warehouse; Max thought that it could have doubled as an oven. One of the guards brought him dinner wrapped in paper; he also included a couple of cold bottles of Coca-Cola. Surprisingly, they tasted wonderful.

That evening he stood outside and smoked a cigarette; the moon's crescent hung above the fronds of date palms that filled the fields beyond the fence line. The smell of dung fertilizer and wood smoke hung in the humid air—they were surprisingly comforting. Illuminated by the faint light, the only person he could see at the gate was the guard. The rest of the men and the drivers had gone to their homes or wherever they slept. This whole operation was beginning to stink. He was here, isolated in the Nile Delta, in a warehouse full of some of the nastiest chemicals man could create, with enough weapons to arm a company of soldiers—and no support and no way to call for backup. When Major Zebadiah Jones said it was his operation, he wasn't kidding. Did Dietz believe him? He sure as hell wasn't going to get any support from old Hans, that was obvious. Right now, he had to play this out, get back into Cairo, and find out what Dietz was doing.

He stood in the darkness at the base of the still warm metal wall of the warehouse and sipped the second Coke; the moon left a thin veil of light across the compound. When the light in the guardhouse went out, it surprised him. Maybe they turned if off to help their night vision. He reached into his pocket and found his cigarettes to light another. He looked toward the guardhouse—a shadow passed in front of it and crossed the compound. The shadow disappeared among the vehicles in the parking area, then reappeared and crossed over to the warehouse. Max drifted over to the base of a massive palm and leaned back against the trunk, all but disappearing. The shadow was now methodically working its way along the face of the warehouse; it stopped when it reached the door. Then the shadow slipped into the warehouse.

Dammit—all Max had were his hands. He'd left his pis-

tol under the cot in the sweltering warehouse. Whoever it was
sneaking about was most likely as well trained as the assassins
at Rushton's. He envisioned long curved knives and a garroting
rope. He slipped his way next to the warehouse door, grabbed
the door handle, and waited. Not finding Max asleep on his
cot—whoever came out would be pissed. The beam of a flashlight washed across the ground just inside the door, then the
flashlight appeared, and then an arm. When the hand of the
other arm appeared, a glint of the moon flashed off the blade
of a curved knife. Max slammed the door forcefully against the
frame. In the faint light, both forearms were pinned between
the door and the jam, the flashlight spun through the air, and
the blade of the knife stuck in the ground. He also heard the
surprised scream of the man behind the door.

Max, in one motion, picked up the knife and grabbed the
nearest arm. He jerked the attacker toward him; the door flew
open, and the whimpering man toppled to the ground. With
both arms broken, the man tried to pull a pistol from his belt.
Max kicked him in the side and removed the Luger from its
holster.

"Do not move," Max ordered in German. "If you call out
or even twitch, I will cut your throat. Do you understand?"

"*Jah*," the man blurted. "But why did you do this? I was
sent to give you a message from Cairo."

Max was sure the message was a knife plunged into his
heart or a slit throat. He washed the flashlight over the man; it
was Corporal Reese, Dietz's assistant at his interrogation.

"And that message was what?"

"God, my arms hurt. Why did you do this?"

"The message—what is the message?"

A rifle cracked behind him. Max spun around as the guard
at the gate ran up to the two men; Max washed the approaching man with the flashlight. When Max turned back to Reese,
the man was lying on his back, obviously dying. The flashlight

illuminated a bloody hole in the man's throat. Reese's gurgling ceased when his heart stopped.

The guard said something in Arabic that Max did not understand. When the guard saw that Max was still standing, he realized that he'd shot the wrong man. He turned the rifle toward Max, but Max, seeing the guard's initial reaction, already had the Luger pointing at the man's face.

"German? Do you speak German?" Max demanded.

The guard lowered the rifle. "Yes, I speak some German."

"Why did you shoot this man?"

"He was attacking you."

"He was on the ground."

"Maybe he had a knife or something."

"Who gave you the orders to shoot, who?" Max demanded.

The man stood holding the rifle, unsure what to do. He looked down at the man then back at Max.

"Who told you to shoot me?"

As the man started to say something, three shadows rounded the corner of the warehouse; flashlights washed the ground. Then, spotting Max, they turned all the beams to the faces of the guard and Max.

"Get those damn things out of my face," Max demanded. "Turn those fucking lights off."

The guards did as ordered and began speaking Arabic. The gate guard said something, and the guards swung their rifles up at Max.

"Herr Adler, please lower your pistol," a voice with a French accent said from behind the men. "There is no reason to die here."

30

The Nile Delta
October 1945

Max lowered the pistol he'd retrieved from Reeves; at the same time, he played the flashlight on the face of the man giving orders. Stunned, he did everything he could to stop his arm from automatically rising and shooting the man. It was Abdul al-Khaldi.

"Good, thank you," al-Khaldi said. "We do not need any more unfortunate accidents."

"And you are who?" Max demanded. "You weren't here when Herr Gottlieb introduced me to the team. Who are you?"

"I am a friend of the cause, and an associate of Herr von Dietz and Herr Gottlieb; my name is irrelevant." Al-Khaldi turned to the men who had arrived with him and spoke in Arabic. None of the men surrounding al-Khaldi were among the drivers and warehouse staff that Max had met earlier. Two of the men then picked up the unfortunate Herr Reese and carried him around the corner of the building.

"I was told that Herr Reese was an experienced soldier. I am astonished that he was caught—"

"Caught? What do you mean *caught?*" Max demanded.

"The wrong word, I apologize," al-Khaldi said. "I meant surprised. I sent the corporal to find you and bring you to me for introductions, and this guard accidentally shoots him." Al-Khaldi pointed at the man and said something in Arabic; the man lowered his head. "I will deal with him later." Al-Khaldi's German was rough and awkward on Max's ears. There was also the hint of a French accent.

"You still haven't told me who you are—and, by the way, your German stinks. You look Algerian, with some French thrown in for measure. I worked with your people in France— you still seem to have a problem with the French."

The man smiled and then said, "Fuck the French. I am a liaison for some very important people to the cause. You do not need to know anything more than that. Herr Dietz will tell you when he deems it appropriate."

"I would still like to call you something other than Frenchy."

Al-Khaldi marched his way to Max and lit his face with his flashlight. He had to look up into the blue eyes of the much taller man. "Never call me that again, or I will gut you like a fish and hang your intestines in a tree for the vultures to eat. Do you understand?"

"And testy as well," Max replied.

"You will address me as Monsieur Duchamp."

"Certainly, Monsieur Duchamp. Am I under your orders now? I would have hoped that Herr Gottlieb would have told me himself."

"You will proceed with your tasks as Herr Gottlieb ordered. My men will also assist the loading—it will proceed quicker. I am expecting deliveries from Alexandria early this morning; my men will handle the unloading. I will remain here during your deliveries tomorrow as well."

"Anything else, Monsieur?"

"Go to bed. You have a long day tomorrow."

"It's too hot in there, and tomorrow is already here."

"So it is," al-Khaldi answered and walked back the way he came; his men followed. Only Max and the chastised guard remained. Then the guard turned toward the guardhouse and disappeared into the night.

The next morning, Max pushed away the mosquito net he'd hung over the cot; the building had cooled during the night and was just becoming tolerable. He'd wanted to sleep out under the stars, but he gave up comfort for the simple fact that the small rear office in the warehouse had a lock on the metal door.

There was a knock on the door as he finished washing his face in the small bathroom off to one corner of the office. A shadow moved against the frosted glass.

"Breakfast, effendi; I have breakfast," a voice said in German from beyond. "Coffee."

When Max opened the door, a young boy stood just outside with a tray. Max heard his stomach growl in anticipation.

"Put it on the table. Thank you."

The boy did as he was told, then left. While Max would have preferred a good American breakfast, the thin breads, dried fruit, and almonds did make a dent in his hunger. The coffee was thick and stimulating. He finished dressing, walked through the warehouse and out into the morning air. Ten men were standing just outside, smoking cigarettes.

"Your orders, Herr Adler—where do we start?" one of the drivers asked.

For the next two hours, they loaded the two tanks, one to each of the two trucks; on the third truck they loaded fifty of the smaller crates. Heavy canvas tarps were draped and secured over all the loads.

They left for Cairo midmorning with three trucks and a total of six personnel: Max, one driver, and one passenger led the small caravan. Max's "partner" was a young Egyptian who spoke English and Arabic. Anwar said he was a college student at Alexandria University, was studying political science, and had joined the Muslim Brotherhood after the riots of 1939. After Max asked a few probing questions about the Germans and the war, he came to the sad conclusion that the man had little understanding of the European war and its history. Anwar was focused on Egypt, the hated British, and the need to remove the Jews from his country. He lumped in the king and his family and government with what was wrong with Egypt.

"Did you know the king and his people are really Europeans—in fact, Albanians of all things? All imposed on us by the Ottoman Turks. I spit on their feet," Anwar said.

Max smiled and thought of the Great War's English king and his very close family relations in Germany—and the fact that Kaiser Wilhelm II was a grandchild of Queen Victoria and in 1914 he and his adversary George V were cousins. Seems the political and royal inbreeding in the Middle East were also not that unusual.

"Will you go back to your studies?" Max asked.

"Yes. When we take our country back, I will go back," Anwar said. "Then I will travel—I want to see America. Do you know this country?"

"Yes, I visited it once, before the war."

"What is it like?"

The road took a deep dip, and the two bounced in their seats. Max looked out the side mirror and watched the other trucks as they passed over the same hollow. On both sides of the road, as far as he could see, were fields of lush green plants about four feet high.

"Do you know what these plants are?"

"These are cotton fields—our most important crop. As a child, I worked on my uncle's farm. I spent five years growing the miserable plants. I never want to walk a field of cotton again."

"You sound like you are becoming one of the bourgeois

elite, Anwar."

Anwar laughed. "Possibly. My feet are in the soil of the Nile Delta, my head in the academy in Alexandria, and my heart with the Egyptian people."

"You asked about America. I only saw a little of it. Imagine a city where the buildings are taller than the pyramids—that is New York City. There are lush forests that crawl over the mountains for thousands of kilometers, grasslands that are larger than the Mediterranean Sea, and in the western regions, mountains that are higher than anything in Africa. It is a wild and very spacious land."

"Is that why they defeated you Germans?"

Max turned to the young man and sensed a trap. "We were never defeated. We lost because our people did not have the fortitude and will to fight on. We simply ran out of time. That is why I am here, and that is why you are here, to find more time to correct the errors of the past six years. Is that why you are here, Anwar? Tell me the truth." Max was sure he was ordered to ask probing questions.

"Yes, Herr Adler, that is why I'm here—to help my people."

"How fucking admirable, 'to help my people.' You're a soldier. That is why you are here, that is why I'm here. We do what we are told to do, we follow orders, we fight, and, if necessary, die for the 'people.' Is that what you believe? Are you willing to die for the 'people'?"

Anwar started to answer, then stopped and looked at the fields of cotton. Small tufts of white were beginning to show in amongst the green.

"The picking will start soon," Anwar said.

"Yes. Even during revolutions, the cotton needs picking, grapes need to be harvested, and wheat reaped. That is always the problem with political revolutions—life and the survival of the people get in the way."

Reaching Cairo, the trucks wound their way through the narrow streets of the Shubra. Max had memorized the route, yet when he saw the neighborhood mosque with its blue tile and gold dome, he was relieved. He banged the proper signal on the metal door; the other trucks idled in the courtyard. When the door rose, the three trucks disappeared into the building.

The Shepheard's Hotel
October 1945

After two days and nights of hauling crates from the delta to Cairo, Max returned to Shepheard's Hotel late in the evening, exhausted. The loading and unloading, as well as the travel in the August heat and humidity, took its toll. He slept for a few hours on each end of the trip, then turned back to repeat the reloading. They were stopped just once on the second trip south when a roadblock had been set up on the northern edge of Cairo, but a few hundred piasters eased the concerns of the soldiers. Standing in the late afternoon heat, he had to admire the audacity of the *official* thieves. Max also began to realize there was something to the loose clothing that the men wore; he felt the heat trapped in his European shorts and heavy cotton shirt. And, outside of the fact that the men smelled like sour camels, he eventually began to acclimate to the strong aromas of the Nile Delta and its occupants.

He climbed the stairs to his room, fully expecting to see the concerned face of Yousef holding a tumbler of ice and bourbon. He pushed open the door and, not seeing the boy, became concerned. The room was a mess; two chairs were overturned, as well as a table. The windows were uncharacteristically open, the noise and fetid aromas drifting up from the street below.

"Yousef!" Max yelled.

The sound of something falling over and crashing against the floor came from the bedroom; Max drew out the Browning and held it to his side. He advanced to the door and heard a moan. He took a quick glance in and saw Yousef, using the back of a chair, trying to pull himself upright. It spun out of his bloody grasp and tipped onto its side. Yousef followed and collapsed onto the floor into a pool of blood that extended out from his young body.

Max rushed in, bent down, picked up the boy, and placed him on the bed. He stripped off the bloody *jellabiya* and gasped when he saw the cuts and abrasions on Yousef's skin. The cuts were deep, some to the bones in the boy's arms and legs. Max counted six on the upper torso. Seeing the drying blood on the floor, Max couldn't believe the boy had survived this long.

"Yousef, it's Max. Stay with me, be quiet—I'll get a doctor."

"Don't leave, effendi. It was the Russian," the boy weakly said. "The one who was with the woman."

"Be still; let me make a call."

"No, I have to tell you. He came to the room; he was looking for you." Yousef took a long shuddering breath. "He pushed his way in, tied me up, demanding to know where you were. I said nothing."

"Good lad, stay with me." Max reached the phone and called Rushton.

"Now, Colonel. It's Yousef. Bring a doctor. Hurry."

The boy held Max's hand; he could feel the strength ebbing from the boy.

"Was Semitov alone?"

"Yes, he caught me by surprise. I thought it was you coming to the door." Yousef started to cough. Then blood began to dribble out of the corner of his mouth. His breathing became noticeably shallower. "I would have stopped him; I would have."

"Yes, Yousef, you would have. Shhhh, the doctor is coming."

Yousef, his eyes pleading, looked at Max. He took another long and raspy breath and squeezed Max's hand, trying to hold onto what little life was left in his body. Then the air slowly left him, taking the boy's life with it.

Twenty minutes later, Colonel Rushton burst through the door, another officer with him. Max held Yousef; blood covered his arms and hands. He sat near the door, on the floor of the bedroom, pointing the Browning.

"You okay?" Rushton said as Max slowly lowered the pistol.

"No, I'm not fucking okay. They killed Yousef. What the hell did that accomplish?"

Rushton and the officer walked into the bedroom. A minute later, Rushton handed Max a wet towel to remove the blood from his hands. "Clean yourself up," Rushton said.

The other officer joined them in the main room of the suite after Max had washed his arms.

"This is Colonel Pitt. He's a doctor."

"You are late, Colonel; the boy could have used you four hours ago. Then again, it's all my fault—I should have been here." Max looked up; Sophie walked into the room.

"Yousef?"

"In the bedroom," Rushton said.

Sophie touched Max's cheek as she walked by; a tear ran down her own cheek.

"Where the hell are they, Rushton?" Max demanded. "I want to know what you know about these Russians. They've been in Cairo a long time—you have to know. Where do they live? Where is the hole they crawl out of?"

For the next hour, the three intelligence officers discussed their options. The least controversial was Semitov. They were the judges, jury, and soon-to-be executioners of the Russian, that was a fact. There was no discussion of justice or law. No arrest would be made—the man was dead. Their bigger concern was Petrov's role in this murder, not that they materially cared. They wanted to know what she knew about the Nazis, the Brotherhood, and the involvement of the Russian government in what was now becoming a very serious conflict between the communists and the British. If Russians were now meddling in Egyptian state affairs, Rushton and Sophie needed to know how much and how deep. All Max Adler wanted was to put three bullets in the gut of Dimitri Semitov and watch him slowly die.

* * *

They kept the police and the Egyptian authorities out of the disposition of Yousef's remains. The hotel accepted the British version of what happened—"a sad, but natural death," Colonel Pitt told them as he removed the body. There would be no report, no investigation, no arrest, and no trial. That was decided early on. Max and Rushton would hear of nothing else. Rushton would see that Yousef would be quickly returned to his family according to the customs of his tribe and religion.

Rushton came through and gave Max and Sophie the last known addresses of both Natalia Petrov and Dimitri Semitov. It was an art deco structure built near the Kasr el Aini Hospital on the southern boundary of Garden City. It overlooked the ancient Nile canal that separated Cairo from Roda Island. It was about ten blocks south of where Max had dropped Petrov off the night of the attack on the bridge in Ezbekieh Gardens.

32

The Sinai Desert
October 1945

Captain Bitner said, "I'm uneasy about these chemicals," as he walked around the Messerschmitt inspecting the assembly of copper tubing and aerosol spray heads secured to the jet's underside. "Is this shit going to kill me when I open the valves? You lose me, and you lose the plane—not a good result of a test."

"Captain Bitner, the chemicals will be in two containers," Dietz said, pointing with his stick. "One pressurized container is mounted here and another there. They lead to the single container here. This is where the mixing will occur. The system is sealed until you opened the aerosol nozzles. The pressure from the two original containers will drive the chemicals together in the single tank; from there they will be sprayed out of the eight nozzles, four on each side of the trailing V-shaped assembly. The turbulence created by the aircraft will allow for a greater dispersion. The material is like water—it will drop and settle quickly. It is not like smoke or other unstable gas."

"And this is effective?" Bitner asked.

"Extremely," Dietz continued. "Our comrades at the Wuppertal-Elberfeld facility developed the mixture—it is called SARIN. When the material is applied to the skin, clothing, or is breathed in, death will occur in less than ten minutes. We did not have an opportunity to conduct and test with a plane such as yours. There were tests with slower aircraft, and while successful, the plane and pilot were at risk due to slower speeds."

"As I asked, what are my risks?"

"At your speed, you will leave the material well behind you. It will be a watery mist that will drop quickly," Dietz said. "If a second pass is necessary, the material will have cleared the airspace making it safe. You have already noted the gauges and on-off lever in the cockpit. As long as you hold the lever back, the material will be dispersed. When the stick is released, it will shut off. I estimate that a dispersion time of three to four seconds is all you need over the target. I suggest that you start the sprays as you approach and release the stick after you count to three. About half the material will be discharged. A second flyover should empty the canisters."

"Why two containers?" Bitner asked.

"Only when the two are mixed does it become SARIN. Until then, the two components are relatively harmless—only when mixed do they become active. So, for both our sakes, it is better they remain separated until needed. We have enough supplies to make six of these pressurized containers. We will make more, but for now this is all we have."

"I will take the jet up and see how it performs with this 'equipment' secured to its belly," Bitner said. "At the speeds I will fly, I want to make sure that these tubes don't rip away and damage the airplane. It would be a shame after all the preparation that this becomes a disastrous suicide operation."

"Yes, I understand. Be very careful."

"The operation is tomorrow?"

"Yes, weather permitting. Hans and I will fly ahead of you in the Storch, and radio you the conditions. It will take us about an hour to reach the camp; you should be ready then. The flight time—"

"I estimate it to be about twelve to fifteen minutes. I will make one pass out of the sun from the east, make a circuit around the valley, and then another on the same flight path. I will then return here. Total time should not be thirty minutes."

"We will remain above you, observing. For this operation, I have added a red dye to the solution. It will allow us to observe the cloud as it settles. It is imperative we understand the effects of the turbulence created by the airplane."

The conversation sounded to the casual listener like the men were discussing a simple crop dusting of a field of corn—not an encampment of a Bedouin tribe.

Late that evening, Gottlieb returned to the airfield in one of the British Leyland trucks. Two small crates were wedged in amongst the other boxes and bags labeled fertilizer, seed, and pesticides. The small crates had skull and crossbones symbols stenciled on their sides. Considering the other materials, they did not seem out of place if the truck were stopped and inspected.

"Any difficulties?" Dietz asked.

"None. Even the British were asleep at their posts."

"Good. Take the truck to the hangar. We will remount the canisters. The jet is fueled and ready."

* * *

The next morning, the slightest sliver of the moon stood in the western sky as Gottlieb, with Dietz sitting directly behind him, left the tarmac of the airfield. The Storch rose noisily to eight thousand feet, well above any ridgelines and mountains in this part of the Sinai Desert. Gottlieb banked the plane to a heading of 122 degrees. With this southeastern heading, it would take them about fifty minutes to reach the camp. They would take a slow turn over the valley before taking two low-level passes over the encampment. Dietz's intent was to draw out as many of the tribe as possible from inside the tents before the jet would make its pass.

They spotted the village as the sun broke over the ridge-line to the east; the mountains cast long, sharp shadows over the folded landscape. Dietz radioed Bitner. They made another circular pass over the valley. There were a few Arabs walking around the tents. Gottlieb banked the Storch and dove down the slope of the hill to the west of the dozen black tents clustered on a geologic bench above a wadi that turned and disappeared behind a red and brown escarpment. At the height of not more than fifty feet, the airplane passed over the tops of the tents. Gottlieb brought the plane about in a full circle and made another pass. Two dozen men and boys now stood outside the tents watching the plane roar over their heads. More Bedouin were leaving the other tents. Just as before, the camels began to awkwardly get to their feet; Dietz saw the horses yanking at their ropes. The sheep moved as a confused mass; it was as if a white cloud chaotically drifted across the burnt sand.

Gottlieb climbed, returned to five thousand feet, and slowly followed his earlier circular path around the valley.

Dietz looked east. The sun flared and reflected off the wing of the approaching Me 262. He tapped Gottlieb on the shoulder and pointed. The jet raced toward them at an impossible speed. Gottlieb softly banked the Storch, allowing Dietz the best view at the jet. At more than five times the speed of their plane, it raced across the desert floor. A second before the jet reached the cluster of tents, a red cloud blossomed in its wake. The bloody cloud roiled in great billowing rings as the jet's powerful engines spun the air. In a flash, the jet sped past the Storch, banked again, and did a roll before heading away and directly at the sun.

Mesmerized by the speed and agility of the plane, Dietz

almost forgot the horrid work that they were performing. He watched as the jet made another pass; the first red cloud had settled on everything in the encampment. From their vantage, they could see the sheep racing in all directions, a pink color to their wool. The red cloud again bloomed.

The jet again curved upward to them, waggled its short wings, and then disappeared into a canyon slashed into the mountain. The jet instantly appeared at the top of the canyon and then disappeared, leaving its red stain on the valley floor.

"Take a pass—I want pictures. We need to confirm the dispersion," Dietz said.

Gottlieb lowered the nose, and the Storch slowly descended to the floor of the valley. It took four minutes to reach the cluster of tents. Dietz looked at his watch—fourteen minutes had passed since Bitner's first overflight. At five hundred feet, the airplane made a slow turn over the tents. All the sheep were in grotesques piles; the camels and horses lay contorted and twisted, many still jerking and twisting in agony. Human bodies lay everywhere. The black cloaks were women; the white-clothed bodies were probably men. Smaller forms lay next to the black forms. He clicked photo after photo until the film ran out.

"Lower?" Gottlieb asked?

"Do you wish to die, Hans?"

"No."

"Then no lower."

On their second pass, a man stumbled out of the largest tent in the center of the camp. As Gottlieb brought the plane around, the man raised a rifle and fired once at the cockpit. A hole instantly appeared in the forward windscreen, and the plane lurched to the right as Gottlieb twisted in his seat. He shoved his hand against the wound to his left shoulder. Blood appeared between his fingers. Dietz looked back at the Bedouin. He'd already fallen to the ground.

"How bad, Hans?" Dietz yelled over the roar of the engine.

"Feels like it busted my shoulder. You need to get a compress on it from the medical kit. It is directly behind you."

Dietz found the bag and removed a large gauze bandage and pushed it under Gottlieb's shirt. He then tried to fasten a broad bandage around the man's chest to help apply pressure.

"The bleeding has slowed; can you still fly this plane?"

"I'm trying. I can feel the shock hitting me. Look down. Is there someplace we can land?"

"Land? We cannot land here. The airstrip is only a half hour away—you can make it."

"Would you rather land or crash, Major? Right now, those are the only options. I can set it down, you can patch me up, and I can take an hour or two to recover. Or I can keep flying until I pass out, which is coming very quickly." Gottlieb's head rolled toward the right.

"I see a stretch of river bottom to the left—looks smooth. Can you make it?"

"There's no other option."

Gottlieb slowed the plane and aimed toward the widest part of the wadi. The airplane, known for its amazing ability to land in less than a hundred feet, floated in like a giant bird, dropped down on its fixed gear, and came to a gentle stop.

"Excellent job," Dietz said, pushing on the man's shoulder. Gottlieb, unconscious, slumped on the stick. The airplane lurched forward. Dietz reached over the pilot and flipped off the ignition switch. The aircraft jerked to a stop.

Dietz pushed open the door and climbed to the ground. He then unbuckled Gottlieb and pulled him from the cockpit. Unbuttoning the man's shirt, he removed the gauze and looked at the wound. A hole the size of his little finger, and just above the clavicle, oozed blood. Gottlieb moaned, then opened his eyes.

"You will live, Captain. Just a small puncture. Rest while I redress it."

"We landed?"

"Yes. I'm not sure how. You passed out; we were lucky."

Fifteen minutes later, Gottlieb's upper left arm and shoulder were wrapped in gauze and medical tape. Dietz gave him water.

"We need to get out of here," Dietz said. "It may look like no one lives here, but the Bedouin own these hills. Once the word is out about the camp, our lives will be worthless."

As Gottlieb rested, Dietz walked the area immediately around the plane and down the wadi that had been their runway. He pitched a few larger boulders out of the way as he stepped out of the length of the spit of sand on which they had landed.

Returning to Gottlieb, he said, "Two hundred and fifty feet, then there is a drop of about five feet, and boulders too big to move on each side. Can you do it?"

"I wish I'd had another hundred takeoffs—the few dozen I've made were all on oiled sand or tarmac. This will have to do. Give me another half hour, then we can go."

They had only brought a thermos of coffee and two canteens, no food. It was nearing eight o'clock and the morning heat was already beginning to fill the canyon. If they couldn't leave, the desert and its inhabitants would not show them any mercy.

"We need to turn the plane into the breeze blowing up the wadi," Gottlieb said as he stood. He rocked back and forth.

"I can do it. You rest."

"Just push against the fuselage, just in front of the tail. It will spin on the front landing struts. I'll tell you when to stop."

Dietz took his position and pushed; the tail wheel stuck in the sand. He quickly scooped away the buildup and began to push; Gottlieb joined him by pushing with his back. Once the aircraft started to roll, realigning the plane was easy. Both men breathed heavily.

Dietz looked toward the hills spread out above and beyond them. "Company," he said.

Dust rose from a trail halfway up the side of the mountain. "Are you ready?"

"I'd rather crash and burn then have one of those barbarians find me. Let's hope your count is correct," Gottlieb said as Dietz climbed into the rear seat. Gottlieb took his seat, buckled in, and started the engine. It roared to life, shattering the quiet that had filled the wadi. Pushing the brake as far as he could, he increased the revolutions until the motor roared. He checked to make sure the flaps were correct, then released the brakes. The plane nearly rose off the ground like a great gray-green stork. In seconds they were a hundred feet off the desert floor flying down the narrow wadi and then they exploded out into the open desert.

Cairo, October 1945

Max and Sophie sat in Rushton's car outside the apartment complex of Petrov and Semitov. The colonel had given them the location. The four-story building was modern in design, unlike the others along this section of the Corniche. Even in North Africa, the effects could be found of the modern architectural movement of the 1920s. The building would have fit perfectly along Rue St. Germain in Paris.

"Not very pretty, if you ask me," Max said looking at the stucco and concrete structure. "Not sure they left out any geometric shape, circles, squares, and what is it with those handrails?"

"Just shut up. I don't need the *New York Times'* architectural critic giving design lessons on a stakeout," Sophie answered.

"Well, it affects my sensibilities," Max lamented.

"Just ignore it."

Max lit a cigarette and held it out the open window; Sophie had informed him that she'd quit. *What else had happened when they were apart?* Two hours passed; the lights in the upmost floor went on and off in various windows—obviously, someone was home. They both watched the front stair of the building, hoping that Semitov would appear. Rushton's intelligence said that Semitov's apartment was on the third floor, in the rear. Petrov's was on the top floor with a view of the river. In front, a dark-colored Citroen, possibly the one that had picked up Petrov a few nights earlier, sat against the curb. The lights in the upper flat went out.

"Either she's going to bed or out," Sophie said. They waited.

Two shadows walked down the steps to the sedan. One, obviously a man, went to the passenger's side; the other, a woman, slid into the driver's seat. The car's headlights came on and washed the street ahead of the vehicle; the rear running lights and one brake light tapped bright red, then the car pulled away. The light on the right side was out.

"Should be a little easier to follow if the traffic thickens," Max had said after returning from breaking the glass of the taillight an hour before.

"You are so smart," Sophie said.

"That's why you love me," Max answered. "For my smarts."

She had ignored the comment.

Max accelerated behind the sedan but left his headlights off. When they reached the busy Khedive Ismail Bridge, he allowed another car to slip in between them; he then turned the headlights on.

"Where are they going?" Sophie asked.

"Gezira Island," he answered. "However, I'm fairly certain it's not the British Sporting Club."

"Dietz?"

"That's what I'm thinking. Gottlieb said that the major was away for a few days in the desert—didn't say where. He would return tonight or tomorrow. My guess is that Petrov is going to his apartment to wait for him."

"And how do they know where he lives?"

"They are spies," Max answered sarcastically.

"Cute."

"It's the only place in Zamalek that would interest them. If they turn north, we'll follow."

"I suggest that you let them go north, then we'll follow a few minutes later. The streets are empty; they'd spot us in a second. If it's Dietz they're after, we will meet them there."

It was a good call on Sophie's part. Max pulled to the side of the road near the polo grounds and watched as Petrov turned north. When they followed five minutes later, they passed no other cars until they reached the southern residential streets of the Zamalek district. They drove past Dietz's apartment building; Sophie looked at the cars parked along the curb. She said nothing until they disappeared around the turn of the road that fronted the Nile River.

"The Citroen was parked between two sedans. Go around the block and park on the side street. We'll walk in."

Five minutes later, Max and Sophie stood near a tree deep in the shadows that had a perfect, unobstructed view of the parking court of the apartment.

"We'll wait and see what happens," Max said. "If Dietz is here, they may try to get into the building and nab him. If not, they could try and grab him outside. In fifteen minutes, we'll move the car."

A red Mercedes passed them and pulled into the parking court. Within seconds Petrov's sedan pulled out of the spot between the cars and sped toward the Mercedes. Max and Sophie started running, chasing both cars.

In the overhead lights of the courtyard, Dietz climbed out of the Mercedes and starting walking to the trunk; the Citroen pulled to an abrupt stop directly behind him. Before it completely stopped, Semitov was already out the door, his arm high holding a pistol.

Max and Sophie, running but still hidden in the shadows,

heard Semitov yell, "Hands on the car, now."

Dietz reached inside his jacket for his pistol, but Semitov pistol-whipped him to the ground. Dietz tried to stand.

"Slowly, Major, very slowly," Semitov ordered. "Hands up."

The major did as told, his hands high.

"Are you okay, sir?" a voice from the lobby entry asked, as the doorman walked toward the pair.

Semitov swung the Makarov to the doorman and fired. The round knocked the man to the cobblestones. He turned it back on Dietz. "One move and you're dead."

Semitov, his attention only on Dietz, did not see Max appear in the dim lights cast by the lobby entry. He was just ahead of Sophie. The sedan's horn blew when Petrov saw Max. Semitov looked first at the Citroen and then at the man running toward him. Max had his Browning up aimed at Semitov.

"You son of a bitch," Max yelled in German at Semitov.

Dietz, seeing the opportunity, pulled his own pistol and was preparing to shoot Semitov. The Russian, his pistol still aimed at Dietz, fired a round, just missing the German. Dietz ducked behind the Mercedes. Two bullets hit Semitov in the chest. One fired by Max and the other by Sophie. Semitov—surprise and shock on his face—tumbled dead to the pavement. Leaving her partner sprawled on the cobblestones, Petrov spun the car around; the squealing of the sedan's tires ripped the night as she fled.

"You? Why are you here?" Dietz yelled.

Max walked to the body of Semitov and fired one bullet into the man's skull. "Herr von Dietz, my sources told me that there might be an attempt on your life. We waited for you just in case. We were lucky." Looking down at the dead Russian, Max asked Dietz, "Do you know this man?"

"No, I've never seen him."

"He's a Soviet agent—Dimitri Semitov is his name. Very nasty. He killed a close friend of mine. He deserved worse than he got. I assume that he was here to kidnap you. If they were going to kill you, they would have just shot you."

"They?"

"The driver is a notorious Russian agent, Natalia Petrov. She works with the Russian Main Intelligence Directorate. They collect Germans with talent and expertise in all sorts of scientific endeavors. If you didn't go with them, they would have killed you right here. Very simple—if they can't have you, then no one can."

Dietz looked at Semitov's body. "Like the Americans or the British?"

"Exactly, sir. Yes, especially the Americans."

"We need to go, Max. The police will be here shortly," Sophie said in Italian.

"Yes, my dear," Max answered in Italian. He turned back to Dietz. "We need to get out of here. Leave Semitov and the doorman where they are—that will confuse the police. You and I will head to the Shubra facility; you can return tomorrow. I don't think anyone saw you arrive, at least anyone alive."

"And her? Who is she?" Dietz asked, his Luger still in his hand.

"A very close friend. I will explain it all soon. We need to go, *schnell!*"

Dietz looked at Sophie, then Max. He slipped the pistol into his jacket and walked to the passenger side of the Mercedes and climbed in. Max blew Sophie a kiss and took the driver's seat. As they pulled away from the apartment building, Sophie left the bodies in the courtyard and walked to the car parked in the shadows around the corner.

* * *

Dietz said, "What the hell just went on, Herr Adler? Why were you here? Not that I'm not glad. You saved my life—again."

"I have been following those two. I spotted them as I left

the Shubar facility yesterday. I trailed them to their apartment. I recognized them as Russian agents."

"And how would you know that?" Dietz asked, lighting a cigarette. "Unless, of course, you are more than what you seem or say you are."

"Could you light me one of those?" Max asked. When Dietz handed him a cigarette, Max, his brain doing circles and flips, quickly tried to develop a plausible story.

"You were right when you guessed I was more than just a captain in the Schutzstaffel. Until I was able to escape the advancing Americans, I was working with SS-Brigadeführer Walter Schellenberg and the Reichssicherheitshauptamt, the RSHA. I was one of his investigators and worked with him when he was dealing with the Mufti in Berlin. I helped move the Mufti from Rome to Berlin. For a period, I was Schellenberg's liaison. That is why I'm here. Like you, I realized that if there were a future, it would be here in the Middle East, not South America where many of our comrades have . . . retired."

"They are traitors. The fight is here, not in some peaceful and forgotten part of the world."

"My view exactly, Major. When I saw you on the terrace at Shepheard's, I thought why not, take a chance. Seems to have worked out."

"And the Russians?"

"During my time with the RSHA, I came across their pictures. When I saw them, I knew they were on to us, so we followed them."

"The woman with you?"

"She is a close friend from Paris. She is Italian, a fascist. She worked for the Vichy government in Marseille in their information and translation division and was extremely helpful to the RSHA. She escaped just ahead of de Gaulle's people when they took Marseille. We agreed to meet here in Cairo if we could. She is quite competent."

"And good looking as well."

"A bonus."

Max wasn't sure how much of his concoction Dietz was buying, but it sounded good to him—he was buying it. The Schellenberg connection was easy. He'd spent more than thirty hours interrogating the general after his capture by the British. Max had a lot more if needed. Schellenberg was one of Amin al-Husseini's Nazi associations that, along with Hassan, helped to fill in the gaps of the Mufti's wanderings around occupied Europe. Max still had not figured out why the Americans or the British hadn't just crashed into al-Husseini's Paris apartment, put a gun to his head, and arrested the son of a bitch.

"I met Schellenberg once, at a dinner party in Berlin. Very young—about your age, I think," Dietz said.

"He's a few years older. The last I heard was that the British had captured him, probably squeezing him for everything he has. His connections to the Grand Mufti probably concern the British, especially after everything the man broadcast from Berlin. While I was a liaison with Schellenberg, I never met the Mufti. I understand he has a lot of pull around here."

"Yes, significant influence. I met the Mufti in Berlin; he is the essential component of everything we are doing. He is the primary funding source for this operation. In effect, we are working for the man."

"Strange and very small world, isn't it, Major?"

"That it is, Herr Adler, that it is."

34

Shubar District, Cairo
October 1945

Max stood outside the roll-up door of the Shubar facility. Dietz banged on it with the proper signal and
waited. The small security panel slid open, and a moment later the door swung open as well. A man who Max did
not recognize, stepped forward and saluted. Dietz returned the
gesture. Within seconds, the roll-up opened and Max drove the
Mercedes inside. The space where the three trucks were the
day before now held the Mercedes and an old weather-beaten
Horch staff car. Dietz stood near the door; Gottlieb next to
him. Max noticed that his arm was in a sling.

"Herr Gottlieb, good to see you," Max said as the roll-up
door closed behind him. "Fall down or something?"

Gottlieb glared at Max, then said, "Herr Adler, you always
seem to be in the right place at the right time—that makes me
suspicious."

"Herr Dietz might think it fortuitous," Max answered.

"Stop it, you two. Hans, if it weren't for Max here, I'd be
dead, and you would have to run this operation by yourself,
and you know it's more than a one-man job. The base is wait-

ing for the final canisters; how soon before they are ready?"

"Two days," Gottlieb answered, his eyes still not off Max.

"Has al-Khaldi, arrived in Cairo?"

"No, but I expect him in the morning." Gottlieb turned to Max. "I understand there was an incident at the warehouse?"

"Yes. One of the guards shot Herr Reese; he died," Max said. "I'm not sure what the guard was thinking. For all I know, he believed it was me."

"Reese is dead?" Dietz said, and turned to Gottlieb. "Why didn't you tell me?"

"Yes, the guard believed he was going to attack Adler," Gottlieb said. "He was confused and mistakenly shot him. Al-Khaldi took care of Reese's body. We have been busy; I was going to tell you when the time was right."

"The Algerian was at the warehouse? Why was he there?" Dietz demanded, still staring at Gottlieb and ignoring Max.

"He told me that he wanted to see if everything was in order and prepared. He looked around, inspected the weapons, told me he was pleased with what he saw, even though he was obviously concerned about the security. He will go over all that with you when he arrives."

"You have been very stupid. You should have told me all this as soon as you arrived from the warehouse," Dietz said. "Al-Khaldi knows nothing about what we are doing. He should not have been there." Without saying anything more, Dietz stomped through the back door of the garage and into the facility.

"Are you coming, Max? There is much to discuss," Dietz added before he disappeared.

"Yes, sir, right behind you." Max, surprised, followed Dietz into the facility; Gottlieb brought up the rear.

The white-tiled entry hallway provided access to a dozen doors aligned along its length. Each had a number painted on the glass panel. No other markings or signs were posted. Most of the glass panels were dark.

At the end of the hall, the last door was identified with the number eight. Dietz stopped, unlocked the door, and motioned for Max to enter. He and Gottlieb followed. Inside, a dozen men in white laboratory coats busied themselves over industrial machinery. The sounds of metal being cut and drilled filled the air. Like the hallway, the room's walls were tiled in small white squares from the floor to the ceiling. The men, their faces covered in gauze masks, sat at long steel desks. The hum of the ventilation system provided a background of white noise and static over the sounds of the tools.

"Impressive," Max said as he looked around.

"The building used to be a British gymnasium—now it is our factory. Ironic, don't you think?" Dietz said as he walked around the tables picking up steel canisters and checking notebooks. He talked to a few of the men. "It has been very convenient for our use, and here we are right under the noses of the British."

"Obviously a manufacturing facility," Max answered.

"An astute observation, Herr Adler. Here we build and then assemble the various canisters required to carry the chemicals. Each must withstand enormous pressures, temperature changes, and the buffeting of winds up to seven hundred kilometers per hour."

"Seven hundred kilometers an hour—why?" Max said. "That is an impossible velocity. And chemicals, what chemicals?"

Dietz smiled and said nothing. It was like the Cheshire Cat smiling at the inquisitive Alice.

The three men left the machine lab and proceeded down another corridor; only two doors faced this hallway. The first door read "Officer's Bath"; they went in.

"This was the Turkish bath and shower area—it has excellent ventilation," Dietz said. "This room, just off the gymnasium and the basketball courts, is the heart of the facility."

The two large tanks that Max had delivered dominated the room. Both sat on their own steel carriage with wheels that allowed them to be easily moved. A metal table was placed next to each, while secured to the table were canisters that looked like the ones manufactured in the previous room. Midway along the table, steel tubing extended from the canisters and into a series of valves. The valves rerouted the lines from the tanks.

"Here we take the chemicals from the larger tanks and compress them using a standard air compressor. We need to reach a very specific pressure reading on that dial on each canister."

"The purpose for all this?"

"Max, my boy, I thought all this was obvious, but then again I have been a chemist my whole life. I don't understand the general ignorance of people, even those seemingly as well educated as you. This is a toxic gas facility. In those tanks—the ones you brought a few days ago—are the chemical components that we transported from our facility in Bosnia. If we were exposed to these two chemicals for less than two seconds—I won't bore you with their long scientific names—we would die an excruciatingly and painful death in less than ten minutes. The mixtures are extremely corrosive, so we need to be careful. The final product has a very effective but short life span—that is why the canisters, once used, are then discarded."

The sophistication of the facility surprised Max. In fact, even though he was aware of the poison gas programs in Germany, he was shocked to see that one had been delivered and rebuilt in Cairo. "Is there a name for this concoction?"

"It was named after the German chemists that created it; it is called SARIN. We have found it to be extremely effective. Our tests have exceeded our projections."

"You have tested this?" Max asked.

"Of course—in fact, just the other day. The mortality rate was probably one hundred percent; we did not do a ground inspection. There is almost no residue, there is no odor, and it is colorless. Our test used colored dyes to assess the proper spread and dispersion. Our review of the post-application photographs has shown excellent penetration and coverage."

Max fought down his revulsion and slowly inhaled. "I am impressed, but then again, I would not have expected less. RSHA reports I had read in Germany, before we were forced to flee, hinted at the facility in the Balkans. However, the knowledge of what was operational, and what was not, was controlled. I expect that the Mufti is involved with this as well?"

"The Mufti can afford to be generous after all the money the Reich gave him over the years. Yes, he has provided the funding, the access, and the security, especially here in Egypt. These men are engineering and chemistry students and members of the Muslim Brotherhood. They are applying their theoretical knowledge in more practical ways. Through our connections to the leadership of the Brotherhood, we have integrated our services with members that have the expertise to utilize the conventional weapons you also transported from the warehouse. At the proper time, we will initiate an attack that will be coordinated with their fighters."

"This gas will kill anyone in its path. What about the Muslim forces—won't it kill them as well?"

"Again, integrated coordination and specific targets. Our attack will cause massive disruption and confusion; the British are not prepared for this type of aerial assault. In the chaotic vacuum created by the attacks, the Brotherhood will seize strategic strongholds and services. From these locations, they will expand outward until the whole country is under our control. These are the first steps to free Egypt of the British."

"Aerial assault? What aerial assault?"

"Do not be concerned with that; it is being handled elsewhere," Dietz said.

"And the Egyptian army and the king?"

"We control many significant positions within the army and the king's staff. They, like us, are waiting for a signal to begin."

"And who controls this signal?"

"The man you met at the warehouse," Gottlieb said. "Abdul al-Khaldi. He is close to the Mufti and has important information for the leadership of the Brotherhood. What that information is, we do not know."

"He does not know about most of the details of this operation," Dietz added. "There are some in his circle I do not trust. Nevertheless, Herr Adler, does all this adequately scare the shit out of you?"

"Yes, Herr Dietz, all this *does* scare the shit out of me, but at the same time makes me proud once again to be a German and a member of the Reich."

"Excellent, Max," Dietz said as he put his arm around the SS captain. "We are very concerned about spies! That is where Herr Gottlieb is most experienced. His time spent in the SS as a coordinator with the Gestapo . . . taught him a great deal. So, while I have opened my operation to you, you understand of course that from this moment on you cannot leave this facility. Your assistance is greatly appreciated, but secrecy is paramount. There are only two people I implicitly trust: Herr Gottlieb and myself. Everyone else only knows parts of the plan. In fact, after a certain point, even I don't know the Mufti's and the Brotherhood's overall plans. We are mercenaries, plain and simple. Hans will show you to your room. Don't worry—the operation will commence soon. You can then go back to that delicious-looking Italian tart. Then, after we are successful, we will have a new order in this part of the world. And after our triumph here, the Führer's war against the Jews and the democracies that support the Zionists will continue in Palestine until they are all wiped from the face of the earth."

35

They were running, and the alley was dark; the rain fell hard, making the stones slippery. The screams from the pursuing Nazis filled the narrow space and echoed off the walls: "*Halt, halt, stop, jetzt!*" Bullets ricocheted off the cobblestones, throwing sparks. Sophie reached for Max; he was gone. She spun toward the attacking soldiers and fired. From every soldier she hit, fire erupted and two more soldiers formed in the flames and began advancing. She shot again. More soldiers appeared and more fire. She continued to pull the trigger until there were no more bullets. The alley was now a wall of soldiers and fire.

"Help me," Max screamed. "Help."

The pleading was from under the stones, under her feet; she saw Max's face in the wet glaze of the rain. "Help!" The heat was becoming unbearable; she looked at the flames, then at Max. She fell to her knees and with her hands tried to push away the rain, tried to reach Max. The fire began to engulf her, and she began to shake.

"Sophie, wake up, wake up."

"Max?" she yelled. "Max!" Her eyes fluttered open. Michael Rushton stood over her, gently shaking her shoulder.

"You're okay; it was only a nightmare—that's a good girl."

Sophie slid upright in the large chair in her room; the sun still streamed through the window. She took a deep breath to clear away the mental chaos of the dream.

"How long was I asleep?"

"Not long—a couple of hours. You needed it."

"How about you? You haven't slept in days."

"I'm a soldier. I'm used to it."

"Max? Anything?" Sophie asked.

"No. I haven't heard anything, and no one has reported seeing him at the hotel or anywhere else," Rushton answered.

"It's been two days. If he could, Max would let me know what's happening. Even though Dietz was grateful, I don't trust him."

"I wouldn't trust him or any others in his operation," Rushton said. "They could be anywhere in Cairo."

"They still must be in the city," Sophie said.

"Yes, I agree. Dietz would not allow his facility to be too far away. Control is paramount."

"Max talked about bringing in the materials from the warehouse in the delta. Did your people find it?"

"Yes, got the call an hour ago," Rushton said. "They have it under surveillance. I told them to just watch; maybe we can catch a bigger fish. Right now, all I'm hearing is that there is a weak force guarding the buildings, no more than a half dozen men. No one has entered or left since our people arrived. We might be too late."

"Max is certain it is some type of chemical agent, a nerve gas or something similar. The conventional weapons he saw could support a battalion of men. The chemical components and the weapons are now somewhere in Cairo." Sophie stood and began to pace the room.

"And your target, Abdul al-Khaldi?"

"Max ran into the Algerian at the warehouse. This ties him to Dietz and whatever they are planning. Al-Khaldi arrived alone in Alexandria without any support or aides. He picked them up here. Al-Khaldi now has his own men; Max guessed they were Muslim Brotherhood."

"If it's the Brotherhood, then al-Banna is involved," Rushton said. "He controls the group. I'm sure he has hundreds of fanatics trained by the Egyptian army, all loyal to him and the cause."

"Based on the number of weapons he saw, you are probably right. Who is this al-Banna?"

"Sheikh Hassan al-Banna is an intellectual and Egyptian radical. He formed the Muslim Brotherhood in the late 1920s as a way of combatting our power in Egypt and the region. He published articles and gave speeches challenging British colonialism and the failure of the institutional monarchy. He's been very public about his unhappiness with us in this country. We are well aware of him, but for the most part his objections revolve around social injustice. Hell, it's his own people who exploit the poor, not us. If it weren't for us, this part of the world would fall into complete chaos. Sunni on Shia, Egyptians on Saudis, Muslims on Jews, and everyone on the Christians—we are here to preserve the peace."

Sophie wondered how much of what Major Rushton said he really believed.

"You are probably right. If al-Khaldi needs help, it would have to come from al-Banna. Do you know where al-Banna is?"

"I will find out. My last report was that he was up north near Alexandria; his family is from the area. I will check and see if he's shown himself here in Cairo. We also believed that there is more than a political connection between al-Banna and al-Husseini. They have much in common, especially with the

Nazi Reich. Hitler provided money and ideological assistance to the Brotherhood. Many of the Bosnian soldiers trained by the Nazis for their Muslim SS divisions have escaped to the Levant and here in Egypt. All in all, a very bad pot of soup."

"If we find al-Banna, then al-Khaldi will not be far away."

"And hopefully, Max and Dietz."

* * *

During the following days, Rushton sent more of his spies deep into the slums of Cairo. Every rumor and sighting of al-Banna was noted and followed up on. After a dozen reports of seeing the man from Heliopolis to Zamalek and south to the pyramids, Rushton was beginning to believe that his own network had been seriously compromised. In reality it had. The British had no friends among the Egyptians that made up the Muslim Brotherhood, but they did have many paid informants. Twice, Rushton's informants had been discovered talking with the targets they were supposed to be watching, a case of the classic double-cross. The British, not liking to be fooled, suggested to certain people that the informant might be double-crossing the Brotherhood. The men disappeared. Sixty-three years of colonial rule, no matter how benign and veiled, as the British called it, would not change the fact that white Europeans held political and financial control over Egyptian Arabs. The two world wars changed the relationship some, but for the common Egyptian, the day-to-day grind of survival changed very little. Any worsening of their condition was laid at the feet of the British and their Egyptian sycophants.

Six decades of British spy craft paid off the afternoon of the second day. Rushton received a note that a senior banker with the Egyptian national bank, and a known high-ranking member of the Brotherhood, had been invited to a meeting at the el Azhar Mosque the following morning. The message, from the banker's appointment secretary, said that the banker was ordered to tell no one about the meeting. The secretary added a comment that the message was composed in a manner that usually meant he was to meet with the senior leadership of the Brotherhood.

"Do you think that al-Khaldi will be there?" Rushton asked Sophie late that evening.

"There is only one way to find out," she answered. "Can you have your people quietly and inconspicuously surround the mosque and watch who enters and leaves? I do not want them to apprehend al-Khaldi. I still want to know what he has in mind and what his connection is to Dietz. We may also be able to follow al-Khaldi to Max."

"You think he's there against his will?"

"You don't know Max as I do. He will never be anywhere against his own will. If anything, he is finding a way to become more deeply involved in the whole operation. Hell, in time, he may even try to control it. Our goal now is to understand the magnitude of the operation. If it is an attack, it will take more than Max to stop it. We need to be prepared to confront multiple targets. Colonel, this may be the start of a revolution. If it is, there may be hundreds of coordinated attacks across the breadth of Egypt against us, maybe even as far as Palestine and the Levant."

The el Azhar Mosque, Cairo
October 1945

Abdul al-Khaldi stood in the main court of the el Azhar Mosque; its highly polished white marble floor appeared as though water had been thinly spread across its surface. Dozens of beautifully designed Arabic archways enclosed the court. The soft gray and white tile and marble façade above the arches gave support to the three dominant minarets and dome that extended up into the blue sky. He was trying his best to remain calm; the elders he was to meet with had left him impatiently waiting for more than a half hour.

Finally, a young boy crossed the court and bowed to the Algerian. "They wish to see you now, Master. I will lead you to them; they are in the library." Without waiting for an acknowledgment, the boy immediately turned and walked toward the far corner of the court.

They walked through the interior of the mosque. Hundreds of intricately decorated columns populated the space, and the floor was overlaid in rich red wool carpeting. Seated in an alcove of the library, six men waited. Two were dressed in black *jellabiyas* with white turbans; the others wore European business suits and dark red tarbooshes. They watched suspiciously as the Algerian followed the boy into the room.

"*As-salamu alaykum*," al-Khaldi offered in greeting to the men as they rose from the cushions.

"*Wa'alaykum salam*," they said in unison, as they touched their hearts, lips, and foreheads in greeting.

"It is good to see you again, Sheikh Hassan al-Banna," the Algerian said, acknowledging one of the men in a black suit. "Your family, they are well?"

"Yes, and thank you," the founder and leader of the Muslim Brotherhood answered. "And how is our dear friend Mufti Amin al-Husseini? Is he well and still in France?"

"Yes, I saw him just a few weeks ago. He gives thanks to Allah, and greetings to all of you."

Al-Banna motioned to the boy who then left; the others lowered themselves to the cushions. Without exception, they watched the Algerian closely.

"Will we see the Mufti soon? He is missed," one of the men asked.

"Yes, he has been gone too long with that German," another said. "I am not convinced that the Mufti has had the interests of his brothers here in Egypt and Palestine in his heart. We have heard things, scandalous things."

"I assure you, my brothers, that the Mufti has all of you in his heart and cannot wait to return to Egypt and his home in Jerusalem. The Nazis supported him during a time when many would not."

"Or could not," another interrupted. "The British have been very forceful since the Palestinian revolt almost ten years ago. They have kept their boot on our necks."

The boy brought in a tray of tea and small cakes. He set it down on a small table in the center of the group, then left.

"Please," al-Banna said, pointing to the table.

"The Mufti frightens the Americans and the British," the

Algerian continued. "And, as you can see, he has found a temporary home in France, at least for now."

"What could scare the Americans?" another offered. "At the moment, they control the world."

"True, but they could have easily demanded the Mufti and his advisors, demand that he be turned over to them. Nonetheless, he is in France, untouched, and not even under house arrest. Our meetings went well—he is healthy and strong. His dream for Egypt and Palestine and all the Arabic countries is for us to be free of the British and the French. The end of the war in Europe has created a vacuum here; neither of those countries wants to continue the war. A case in point, the British just a few weeks ago, in their quaint democratic way, have voted out Churchill—he is no longer prime minister. The Mufti also told me that he believes that these countries are financially destitute. That they would be glad to rid themselves of the Middle East and all the troubles we cause."

"And to save money," another, in a suit, said.

"Correct, but it will also allow them to turn their back on the bigger issue, the Zionists. They will try to save face. However, they would like nothing more than the Jews to just go away."

"I fear that will never happen," a voice offered.

"One thing at a time, my brother. We must first make the British and the French so uncomfortable that they see only one way out—to leave Egypt, the Levant, and even the Arabian Peninsula. To make them see there is no future for them here."

"That will be very difficult," al-Banna said. "They have deep vested interests here far beyond the political and military. In the long term, they are here for a single financial reason, our oil. That is the reason they fought to keep the Germans from invading our world, and it is the only reason they remain. Soon we will be nothing more than the world's petrol station."

"The Mufti understands this," al-Khaldi offered. "That is

why we Arabs must take control of this invaluable resource. We must be the ones to dictate its price. We must control our religious and financial destinies."

"And how does he propose to go about this?" al-Banna asked. "We have tens of thousands in the Brotherhood, all willing to fight for the future of Egypt, and with our independence, the rest of the Middle East will follow. However, we have no weapons; we have nothing to fight with beyond a few rifles and pistols. The British, even in their current condition, will not just pack up and leave."

"One only has to look around and see how the British have become complacent. The terrace at Shepheard's Hotel is a very good example. They grow fat and lazy. The Mufti believes that we need to take advantage of this complacency while the government in England is in chaos. To strike now will reinforce Britain's war weariness."

"Again, I ask, how does the leader see this happening?" the banker asked. "Will the legions of past jihads come down from heaven and strike down our enemies? Will the Prophet come with his armies? We cannot fight the British with sticks of sugarcane and hide behind bales of cotton."

"The Mufti's time in Germany wasn't spent wastefully. He formed alliances and friendships with very important and influential men in the Nazi government. He—"

"They lost their war; they are all dead or in prison. What good are they to us?" the banker interrupted.

"They are not all dead or arrested. In fact, there are many here in Egypt—now, right this moment, in Cairo and Baghdad. They have escaped the Americans and are here serving the Mufti and others in need of professional military help." The Algerian looked slowly across the men, studying each face. He saw their interest, as well as their questions—he also saw fear. "Do you know how to form an army, Sheikh al-Banna? Do you know how to procure weapons, how to use them? Do any of you know war tactics? No, of course not. You are teachers, lawyers, imams, bankers, and shopkeepers, all noble professions in the Prophet's eyes, yet war is coming, and we will also need warriors."

"And guns," the imam said.

"Yes, and guns. Toward the end of the European war, many of these professional German soldiers escaped arrest and came here. I have met with a few who are very good at what they do, and they will help us."

"For a price, I'm sure."

"Of course. These are professionals—they will be paid for their efforts and for what they also bring: their expertise and their special skills."

"And what can these men who ran from Europe and the Americans, with their tails between their legs like a beaten dog, have that we can use?"

"The Mufti and his friends were able to secure thousands of German and Italian weapons and munitions. Much of this was stored in secure locations during the war in Greece and in Italy, and now has been shipped here to Egypt."

"Here? In Egypt, now?" al-Banna asked.

"Yes, I have seen these weapons," al-Khaldi said. "They are here. In fact, many are now in Cairo. With these weapons, we can take control of the country, throw out that pretender who is king, and return this land to Egyptians and to the Prophet."

"I again ask you, how will this be accomplished?" the banker said.

"My friends, the Mufti has told me he intends to secretly return to Egypt within a few weeks. When he arrives, he will meet with you and lead the revolution."

"Here? The Mufti is coming here?" the banker said. "And Palestine? Is not the Mufti Palestinian? Do not his interests lie there, in Jerusalem?"

"Yes, as he has said many times in his broadcasts. Jerusalem, like the holy places of the Hadj, is important and essential to Islam and our future. We Muslims must control these places to protect them from the infidels and unbelievers; and we have, at this moment in time, the ability to make this happen. The Americans want the Jews to succeed in Palestine; they will assist them in establishing a Jewish empire in this, our world, our Arab world. So, it is not just the British and French that must be overthrown, it is also the Jews. Now is the time, before they become too strong."

"Why will the Americans allow the Mufti to come here? Why will they let that happen?"

"They, like the British and French, are also tired of this war—the Mufti says that is why he is still free. Besides, the French are reasserting their independence and have shown the Americans that they will not be left in the shadow of an American future in Europe. Therefore, I can faithfully say that the leader has friends in very high places and will return to us in a few weeks. It is up to you to prepare the ground for the Mufti's return."

"How can we be sure that this isn't some suicidal attempt at revolution? It is all well to have guns and bullets, but the British have tanks and airplanes."

"On the day of the announcement to the world of the Mufti's return, he has ordered that the Brotherhood attack the British military sites in Egypt. It will be heralded to all of Egypt by the flyover of Cairo by one of the greatest gifts from the Führer, a fantastic airplane that flies faster than any airplane ever built. This jet, as it is called, will announce to the Brotherhood the start of the revolution."

The Algerian knew what they were thinking—he'd had the same thoughts and fears. Would they actually be able to seize control of their country again, throw off the centuries of Ottoman and British rule, and stop the obvious expansions of the Jews into the region? Was salvation coming in the form of a Jerusalem-born leader? Was Haj Amin al-Husseini the man who would lead them to the Islamic caliphate and fulfill the prophecies? It was one thing to sit and discuss revolution over tea; it was wholly another to take up a rifle and storm the oppressor's battlements.

* * *

The meeting broke up, and the men departed in small groups and pairs and met their aides in the mosque's hallways and parking areas. Within minutes, everyone who attended had left. Three nondescript cars were parked in the corners of the lot. Each held British agents taking pictures and making notes. Sophie and Rushton sat in a vehicle that commanded the best view of the main exit from the mosque.

When Sophie saw the last group, she said, "That's him, Michael—al-Khaldi. Can your men follow him?"

"Yes, they are ready."

"Good. Tell them to be careful. He's a slippery bastard."

37

Cairo,
October 1945

Petrov's personal apartment was in a nondescript area of north Cairo. It was unknown to her bosses and listed under a false name. It was critical to have a safe house, someplace she could escape to. Even her partners, like the now dead Semitov, never knew about her refuge. She stood in front of the long mirror in the bedroom and inspected every inch of her alabaster white skin looking for a mark or blemish. Pleased by what she saw, she dressed and put away the few things she was able to salvage from her apartment. Most probably by now, the British had ransacked hers and Semitov's apartments on the Corniche.

She was sure the American, this Dwight Loomis, was a spy, a government agent, sent to find her and neutralize her. He was here to poach Dietz and take the Nazi to America. She would never forgive him. Her new goal was simple—find the American, or whoever he was, and kill him. And that woman he was with—she would never forget her face. She would find her and make Loomis watch as she killed his woman, and then she would take the same dagger and put it in his heart.

The police report stated that a shooting had taken place in the courtyard of an apartment complex on the northern end of Zamalek. The influence of the people who lived in the building was demonstrated when the address was not included in the published report. She guessed that there were important people living in the building, citizens—Egyptian and others—who demanded and received privacy. At the scene, an unidentified man was found sprawled on the cobblestone, two bullets in his chest, one to the head. Another body, believed to be the doorman and father of six, was found nearby. There were no other witnesses, or at least, no others had come forward. The small article in the paper said that the police believed the unidentified man may have shot the doorman before he was shot by persons unknown. Petrov knew who the unknown killers were, and in time she would make sure that others in Russian intelligence would also know it was the Americans. Memories are extremely long in the spy game.

Petrov wondered why the American appeared at Dietz's apartment—it took a lot of Russian money to find that apartment. One person in the Muslim Brotherhood, a driver for one of the leaderships, who loved rubles more than Egypt, provided the information to her. He remembered the man's face when he delivered a message from the Brotherhood but did not know who he was. That was all she needed. Semitov watched the apartment and confirmed that Dietz lived there; he also confirmed that members of the Muslim Brotherhood also frequented the apartment. While the involvement of the Brotherhood complicated their effort, Petrov was sure they picked the right time to intercept the Nazi. Unfortunately, the American arrived. Maybe Semitov deserved what he got. After all, the boy said nothing and Semitov did go too far. However, men like Semitov were ubiquitous in postwar Russia—she would easily find another. Right now, she needed to understand why the American and the woman did what they did to save the Nazi.

Returning to her usual luncheon rounds, Petrov strolled into the lobby of the Semiramis Hotel, bought a package of Dunhill's, and went out to the small terrace that overlooked the Nile River to have a pre-luncheon cigarette and a Campari. The crowd was small, mostly British officers owing to the British barracks directly across the boulevard. A few older women of means, most probably Spanish or South American by their looks, sat in a far corner. A couple sat on the far side of the terrace having lunch; the woman's back was to her. The man, a British colonel, was hunched over and involved in a close and very private conversation. Petrov speculated about an assignation. After a few minutes, a sergeant appeared and whispered in the officer's ear; the man nodded. The soldier left. The officer returned his attentions to the woman as he drank his iced tea. The woman then withdrew a small booklet from her clutch and noted something in it. She closed the booklet and returned it to the small bag. The woman, dressed in a lightweight flowered summer dress, had strong shoulders—Petrov thought her athletic. Her jewelry was just a watch, no rings. Yes, a tryst with a British officer; he was handsome, after all. She had many lovers over the years; men were such pushovers. The couple intrigued her. Her drink arrived and she sipped the Italian liquor, indulging herself in her role as the voyeur.

The woman gathered her clutch and leaned into the officer. As she stood, he stood; and then she turned toward the lobby. Petrov was stunned; it was the American's girlfriend. *What gods had I pleased to win this break?* She watched the woman cross the terrace—*striking* and *handsome* came to mind. While she could never call another woman beautiful, this one came close. She walked confidently and with purpose. Petrov assumed she was heading to the ladies' room. *It is a chance that might never come again.*

Petrov stood and motioned to the waiter. "I'll be back in a

moment; please hold my table."

"Yes, Madame, of course."

Petrov walked through the terrace and followed the woman down the hallway toward the small, discreet sign for the ladies' room. The woman never looked back; she pushed the door in and disappeared. Smiling, Petrov held back a moment and waited. When she approached the door, a small Egyptian girl pushed her way out, a flustered look on her face. The girl excused herself in Arabic and fled down the hallway. Petrov ignored the insolent child. *Rude Egyptians.* She opened her purse, removed the small Beretta, and held it close to her side.

The aromas of perfume and sandalwood assaulted her nose as she entered; the humid air, thick and rich, unnerved her. Turning the corner, she was stunned by the barrel of a pistol placed on her forehead, and before she could raise her own pistol, another object jammed itself into her back.

"Move quietly into the room," a man's voice ordered. "I am going to take the pistol from your hand. Comply, or my friend will damage that pretty face."

Petrov did as ordered; two pistols significantly reduced her chances of responding to the challenge. She looked at the woman and realized why the American, Loomis, was interested; up close, she was stunning—black hair, green eyes, just the right amount of makeup. However, the pistol, a black Walther PPK, was more sinister than any accessory. Petrov's Beretta departed from her hand.

"Move into the room," the male voice said. "Hands on your head. Back to the wall."

She moved, her eyes never leaving the woman.

Petrov heard the door's lock click. The man walked into her view; it was the colonel from the terrace.

"Are you sure it's her? She's not as cute as I remember," the woman said.

"Positive. I have a hundred photos of Natalia Katrina

Petrov in a file. This is definitely her—aren't you, my little Russian cabbage flower?"

"I hate cabbage," Petrov said. "It's the food of peasants. I lean toward caviar and champagne."

"Who doesn't?" the women answered. "Where is Max Adler?"

Petrov crinkled her nose and forehead. "I suggest introductions before we begin."

"No harm," the woman said. "I am Sophie Lacrosse, French Security Directorate."

"Colonel Rushton, His Majesty's British 8th Army."

"Yes, I'm sure that is *exactly* who the two of you are," Petrov answered. "At least I have names to the faces, no matter how incorrect."

"Who is this Max Adler? I do not know a Max Adler," Petrov said.

"Do you know a Dwight Loomis?" Sophie asked. She noticed Petrov's eyebrows rise at the mention of the name.

"I might, why?"

"I will ask the questions, you will answer," Sophie said.

"Maybe yes, and maybe no."

"Right now, yes is the better answer."

"Then ask the right questions," Petrov said.

"Do you work for Soviet intelligence?"

"You know as well as I do that there is no such thing as Soviet intelligence. Everyone running that country is an idiot. That's why I'm here. I will live a lot longer here in Egypt than almost anywhere in Russia. So, this Dwight Loomis has another name—interesting. I used to know a Max—cute boy, killed at Stalingrad. I like the name Jakob; it's a strong name. Your boyfriend is cute, very cute. Do not lose him; he would be a good catch."

"Here is how it's going to go, Miss Petrov," Sophie said. "Whether you tell me what you know or not, Colonel Rushton will have you wrapped up like a fish and put in the women's section of the local British prison until you can be sent back to England. There you will be dealt with as all spies should be."

"Ah, that's what I thought, MI6. I see it in your eyes; they light up when you talk about Britain. Yes, definitely MI6. Phooey on the French, *oui*?"

"You are compromised."

"Miss Lacrosse, I was compromised a long time ago."

Petrov was moved to the MI6 Egyptian headquarters. After five hours of interrogation, it was agreed by Sophie, and the bureau chief of Security Intelligence Middle East, that she probably did not know where Max was. Since Miss Petrov might be a valuable asset and the Russians most likely did not know that she had been arrested, it was suggested that she be sent to London. There she might provide additional intelligence or possibly be convinced to assist them.

"One never knows in intelligence how the game will be played," Sophie said.

The next afternoon, Sophie and Rushton watched as Petrov was loaded onto a British air transport. Surprisingly, Petrov waved to Sophie as she climbed the steps.

Shubar District
October 1945

Max awoke to the scratchy sound of a key turning in the lock of the steel door to his cramped room. He'd guessed his narrow cell, at one time, was used for towel storage. The door opened, and Gottlieb stood in the glare of the overhead hallway lights.

"I'm not sure what I have to do to prove myself to you and Herr Dietz," Max said as he stood in the space between the cot and the wall. "But right now, a bathroom would be helpful."

"Down the hall and on the right. As to proving yourself—I don't fucking care. You easily could be one more body lost in the desert," Gottlieb said. "Who'd miss you anyway?"

"My girlfriend for one. Ask Herr Dietz; he will tell you about her. She gets lonely. She might mention my absence to the police."

"The newspaper reports that it was a robbery that went wrong. The guard—who, by the way, was a decent fellow with a family—was shot by the dead man, who was then fatally shot by an unknown person. There were no witnesses."

"And Herr Dietz, did they question him?"

"No, he's one of more than a hundred tenants in the building. He returned home early this morning, answered their questions, and was allowed to return to his apartment—all neat and tidy. The major said you knew who the man was?"

Max studied Gottlieb, not sure what story to concoct. The sling on his left arm intrigued him. Postwar Germany was in chaos, and control of all information was through either the Americans or British. He was certain it was impossible that any German, still connected to the old regime, could confirm or deny anything he said.

"While in the RSHA, I saw the man's photo. He was a Russian agent, Georgian. He had been seen in Istanbul and Athens at the end of the war."

Gottlieb looked at Max. "A Russian spy, how convenient. Now he's dead. That makes everything so much simpler."

"It is what it is. I spotted him watching the hotel and guests that frequented Shepheard's terrace; in fact, he was on the terrace the day of the attack on Herr Dietz in front of the hotel. I've noticed him on and off over the last few weeks. I saw him in Shepheard's after I came back from the warehouse move. We followed him; he went to Herr Dietz's apartment. When I saw he was targeting the major, I intervened. I could not stand by and watch the major be kidnapped. Curious thing—where were you during all this? Herr Dietz would not say. It should have been you protecting him, not me. Was that when your shoulder was injured?"

"Where I was is not your concern. Come with me," Gottlieb said.

"I have nowhere else to go."

"Don't be insolent."

"I can be even more insolent if you like. How about a truce, Hans? We have more than enough to do without getting on each other's nerves. And someday, I predict, we are going to be best friends."

"An excellent idea, Max," Dietz said from the door. He looked around at the closet's accommodations. "Comfortable?"

"I do not need a suite," Max said. "However, if you're asking—these arrangements are just fine, Major. I've slept in barns in the dead of winter. The Ritz couldn't be nicer."

"Swine," Gottlieb said and started to move toward Max.

"Stop it, you two; you're acting like schoolgirls. Hans, I need you to finish the inspections of the arms. There are two men from the Brotherhood here to work with you. They are associates of al-Khaldi. He has informed the Brotherhood of the Mufti's intentions and schedule. There is much to do. Herr Adler will help me."

Gottlieb took one more glance at Max, then left.

"He's a good soldier, Herr Adler, and we have worked together a long time. After Africa, he joined me during the final months of the war, especially in Yugoslavia. It is too bad we were not able to use our advanced weapons then; they would have turned the enemy."

Max, remembering his narrow escapes during the past winter, thought of an odorless and invisible gas drifting through the forest and settling into foxholes and shivered. "Yes, Major, I'm sure it would have done exactly that."

They walked through the room where the gas canisters were being filled. Two attendants stood to one side watching the valves. Both wore rubber suits and gas masks.

"Are we okay? Their outfits aren't very comforting."

"Yes, we are safe. Only one type of gas is exchanged at a time. As you can see, the other tank is not even in the room. When these six canisters are filled, they will be placed in storage, then the others will be filled."

"Fascinating," Max said. "It does not look that difficult."

"These men were selected for their dedication and experience. The chemicals are similar to modern pesticides. They understand both the need for care and the risk."

"And if the room is contaminated?"

"We are very careful not to let that happen."

"But if it did, what then?"

"Without proper protective gear, they would die. Then the material would drift through the building and eventually out into the neighborhood. Until it naturally breaks down or is incinerated in an extremely hot fire, it will be fatally toxic to every living thing that encounters it for a period of hours, maybe days."

Max looked at the tanks and the men; for once, he did not have a comical remark or quip.

He needed to get the information to Sophie; she would know who to pass it on to. During the tour, Max noticed the lack of telephones or radios. In fact, he'd not seen a telephone anywhere in the warehouse or the garage area of the facility. He knew that Dietz had to talk to the other base, wherever that was, as well as his contacts with the Brotherhood. So, he assumed that somewhere in the building was a telephone or maybe even a two-way radio. He had two options: find a phone and hope that he could make a call outside the building without being caught, or to get out of the building and find a phone or some way to get a message to Sophie or the major. Neither looked promising.

After two days moving crates of rifles and ammunition, as well as fastening canisters full of the most toxic stuff he could ever imagine to the bed of one of the trucks, he was certain that a phone did not exist.

"The weapons, are they secured and counted?" Gottlieb asked that evening as what was called dinner was served—a dish of rice, boiled mutton, and thin fried bread. They ate in a room off the machine shop that was informally called the office.

"Yes, secured. The counts are on the clipboard. I could use

a beer," Max answered.

"So could I," Gottlieb said with a smile.

Shocked by Gottlieb's flash of humor, Max pushed on. "Why are you here? You could be in South America, South Africa, any number of places. Argentina needs men with our skills."

"True, but my loyalty to Herr von Dietz goes back many years. So, for now, where he goes, I go. Besides, he needs my help—he is the scientist, and I'm the soldier. After finishing school, I joined the army. After a few years, I was asked to join the Schutzstaffel. That is an honor I am proud of; I was assigned to the IG Farben chemical factory in Wuppertal-Elberfeld. That was in 1942. When the major returned from Africa, I was assigned to work with him."

"The major mentioned Africa and the Eastern Front."

"Yes, we were testing a new form of chemical weaponry—aerial dispersion. I flew the plane; he managed the control devices."

Max, alerted to the phrase *aerial dispersion*, asked, "Were they successful?"

"In a limited way. The major has adjusted the formulas. We will see. Where did you see action?"

"I was twenty-four when the war started," Max said. "Believe it or not, I was in New York City then. I took a boat to South America, then to Africa, and eventually Germany. So, like you, I am a survivor. I don't know anyone in my graduation class at Bad Tölz that is still alive. I spent most of my early career in France and Italy. I'm fluent in both languages. I was in Rome, where I was stationed at the embassy. Then mobilized when the Americans landed in Salerno, but later was assigned to SS-Captain Erich Priebke's police force in Rome in early 1944. Later that summer, I was reassigned to Berlin and Schellenberg's RSHA. In time, I was transferred to Skorzeny's command, due to my American and English language skills."

"And you're here because?"

"I want to live. I sure as hell do not want to be in Germany or anywhere in Europe right now. We SS are on a 'mandatory-arrest-if-caught' list. Hell, if the wrong people catch you, like the Zionists, they will just put a gun to your head, no questions asked. We were soldiers doing what we were ordered to do—there must be some protection for that, doesn't there? Every SS member who's been caught is in prison waiting trial; I preferred the open desert to a cold prison. Otto Skorzeny told me to find von Dietz. When I first met the major, I told him that. So, after a crash landing and other adventures, here I am."

Max knew that Gottlieb was probing, looking for inconsistencies, but then again, the story was crazy enough that even he believed it, or at least most of it.

"I noticed in the warehouse crates with British weapons, especially uniforms and grenades," Max said. "A bit of larceny by the Brotherhood?"

"Yes, the Arabs are thieves, at least some of them. We've traded food and other valuables for any weapons they find or can liberate. The uniforms might come in handy at some point, to help confuse the enemy."

"Yes, I worked with Skorzeny as an American cultural resource when he was putting his fake American soldier force together during the Ardennes action. It's nice to have a supply of British uniforms. I suggest that you wash them and roughen them up. You don't want your army to look too much like a bright coin, do you?"

Hans nodded his assent.

"And be very careful of those grenades—they are British 77s," Max added. "I'm sure the fool that stole them didn't realize they were phosphorus grenades. We ran into them in Italy. The British used them when we set up positions in steep ravines and caves. When they explode, the shrapnel burns like the fires of hell. I've seen men dig the burning bits of metal out of their arms with bayonets and daggers."

Gottlieb walked across the room to a cabinet bolted to the wall and pulled out a drawer, then reached inside and unlatched the cabinet from the wall. It swung open about a foot.

"I discovered this compartment a few weeks back," Gottlieb said. "Our Arab friends in the Brotherhood are quite religious and frown on liquor—that's why you don't see any on the shelves. But, Max, I do have these." He carefully pushed the cabinet with his right shoulder, avoiding pressure on his injured left. He retrieved two bottles and set them on the desk. One was cognac and the other schnapps. "I suggest a toast to our fallen brothers, and a toast to us, and the future."

Gottlieb retrieved two glasses from a drawer in the desk and poured two cognacs. When Gottlieb presented the liquor, Max stood and took a quick look into the space behind the cabinet. On the top shelf sat a phone; its wire hung down from the base and disappeared out a hole drilled in the wall.

"To our comrades," Gottlieb offered.

"To fallen comrades and friends," Max saluted back.

Cairo,
October 1945

Dietz said to Max, "Come with me. I have an appointment, and I want you there and armed."

"Trouble?" Max said. "My pistol is in my room."

"Get it; we will leave in an hour." Dietz turned away and left the laboratory where Max had been finishing the final inventory of the remaining canisters. A half-dozen smaller containers had also been manufactured; these were aligned on the table. Tags on them read that three had been filled. Three were still empty, their tags unmarked. By his calculations, the two large tanks in the chemical laboratory were half full; the rest of the larger canisters were now secured in the trucks. Dietz still had not told him where the trucks were going. He checked his watch; he had a half hour left to himself to meet Dietz—just enough time to finish with the small containers.

Max stood next to the Mercedes waiting for Dietz, his Browning pistol secured in a holster under his jacket. A thousand paranoid thoughts raced through his head. The biggest was—what would he do if he were recognized? He was close to finding out what Dietz and the Mufti had in mind for Cairo but still did not know. Dietz walked out into the garage with Gottlieb. They talked for a few moments, then Dietz came to the automobile. Gottlieb handed him a briefcase, said something, then left.

"The Abdeen Palace. We are expected at ten sharp. Any later and we will not be allowed in. I assume you know where it is?"

"Yes, sir," Max said and closed the door after Dietz settled into the rear seat.

They drove through to Bab el Hadid and then south past Shepheard's Hotel, Ezbekieh Gardens, and the Grand Continental Hotel.

"Go to the north entry of the palace, not the main gate. We are expected. After we enter, turn left, and I'll direct you to one of the buildings on the east side of the complex. I want you to stay with the automobile. I will only be in the building for a short time."

"I won't let you go in there alone," Max protested.

"That's quite all right—nothing will happen. I am meeting with one of the king's generals. I have something to show our appreciation for his diligence and assistance during the past few months."

The guard at the gate looked at the letter that Max handed him—it was a pass from the general that Dietz was going to meet. Max then drove through the massive complex to a parking area that fronted a four-story stucco and limestone building. The sign read "Army Headquarters, Cairo." Max parked.

"I will only be a moment; I want you to be ready to leave as soon as you see me walk down the steps of the building. It is imperative that we leave the area as fast as possible."

Max opened the door for Dietz, who retrieved the leather case from the floor of the car. He stood next to the Mercedes as Dietz walked up the steps to the building. The car sat idling.

Arabic voices caught his attention, and he turned toward

the sound. A group of six men, all in suits and tarbooshes, were crossing the street and headed toward him. Max instantly recognized the tallest member of the group; it was Abdul al-Khaldi. The Algerian saw him, and then looked at the Mercedes.

"Herr Dietz, he is inside?" al-Khaldi asked. The others in his group stopped.

"Yes, sir," Max answered. This was a complete shock.

"Excellent."

Al-Khaldi turned back to the group and waved his hand toward the entry. After three steps, one of the men in the group took al-Khaldi by the arm, leaned in, and said something. After a moment, the two men separated themselves from the other four and walked to the side of the landing; the man was extremely demonstrative. Twice he looked at Max, then continued talking with al-Khaldi. Max was stunned—he knew the man, but it took a few seconds for the face to register. It was Habin Hassan, the Syrian that he and Faber interviewed a few months earlier outside Berlin. What the hell was he doing here? Max adjusted his coat and felt the comforting tug of the shoulder strap of his holster.

The Algerian turned toward Max and started to walk toward him. Beyond the man, Max saw Dietz exit the building and walk quickly toward the group, a grim look on his face.

Max went on the offense and began to walk toward the Algerian and the Syrian. "What the hell is that man doing here?" he yelled at al-Khaldi in French as he pointed at Hassan. "Why is this man with you? Why are you talking to this fucking traitor?"

Al-Khaldi turned and looked at Hassan, then back at Max. Dietz had reached the group; he wondered what Max was yelling about.

"Herr Adler, what the hell is going on?" Dietz asked. "We need to leave."

"You will have to ask Herr al-Khaldi why he is dealing with a traitor to the Brotherhood, the Mufti, and to the cause. That man works for the Americans. He was arrested in Berlin. I was informed that he told them everything about the Mufti's associations here in Egypt."

"He is a liar," Hassan screamed as he reached inside his suit coat and began to draw out a pistol. "It is him that is—"

Max's pistol fired once, hitting the Syrian mid-chest, knocking him to the pavement. "Traitor," Max yelled and fired again.

The others scattered away from al-Khaldi and Dietz.

"We need to leave, Herr Dietz, now!" Max yelled.

Johann von Dietz took one look at the man on the pavement, then quickly walked past the Algerian, saying nothing. He climbed into the back seat of the Mercedes as an alarm began to blare from speakers mounted at the highest corners of the building. The sound was penetrating.

Looking out the rearview mirror at the five men left standing on the landing, Max floored the accelerator and managed to leave the palace grounds before the entry gates could be locked.

"What the hell went on back there?" Dietz asked.

"I can ask the same thing, Herr Dietz. What was in the briefcase?"

"Who was the man you shot?"

"A traitor, an American collaborator. He is a Syrian named Habin Hassan, or was. He was an aide to al-Husseini; I met him in Berlin. He is also a liaison with the Mufti's organization. Or at least he was, until we found out he was passing information to the Americans. The end of the war overwhelmed us, and he disappeared before we could take care of the traitor. I never saw him again until he walked up with al-Khaldi. I assume that he recognized me and was going to make sure I didn't tell anyone what I knew."

"Lucky for you and us," Dietz said.

"And the general?"

"I assume dead. That was the reason for the alarms."

Max looked at Dietz in the mirror.

Dietz saw his eyes. "A test. The general has been asking for more and more money. I trust no one who wants more money; they will easily turn to another cause that will meet their ever-growing financial demands. The general expected a briefcase full of English pound notes. What he found when he opened it—after I left the room, of course—was a device that activated a canister of SARIN gas. I assume that the alarms went off when they discovered his body. I did not stay around to see the extent of the collateral damage. As a scientist, though, I would be very interested."

Max looked up the boulevard and the traffic congestion; they needed to disappear into the labyrinth of the Shubar.

"Did you know that al-Khaldi was going to be in the building?"

"No. When I left the building, I was as surprised as you. Two of the men with him were government officials, senior administrators for army and police affairs. I did not know the other two. If the man you shot was associated with al-Husseini, then it can only mean that the Mufti is coming here. I expect that he is orchestrating some type of internal coup or revolution."

Max's mind raced—everything about what Dietz was doing, the Algerian's presence, the possibility that al-Husseini was coming. In fact, seeing Hassan, he was sure the Palestinian was coming. That could be the only reason for the man being here in Egypt. His people in the OSS must have let Hassan go. Shit—what was going on?

"Al-Khaldi acted as though he knew you were here, Major. Would anyone else know about your meeting?"

Dietz thought for a moment. "No, and the only source would have been someone in the facility. It concerns me."

"Shall we go back to the facility, Herr Dietz?" Max asked. The squealing of a streetcar required him to speak loudly.

Dietz, deep in thought, stared out the open window. "What did you say?"

"Shubar. Shall we go back to the facility?"

Dietz paused, then looked at his watch. "No, take the boulevard to the Ismailia Road. We are going to the Sinai."

"Sinai? Why are we going to the Sinai?" Max asked.

"To see wonders and marvels, Herr Adler. Things that would have changed the war."

The drive, in the brutal heat across the Sinai to the airfield, took more than three hours. As they ferried across the Suez Canal at Ismailia, Max now understood why the Germans wanted to sweep through Egypt and take this thin ribbon of water that connected southern Europe to the rest of the world. Max felt the same way when he flew over Gibraltar on his way back to England and saw the gateway between the Mediterranean Sea and the Atlantic Ocean. Two strategic points into the Mediterranean—the ancient western door at Gibraltar and the modern eastern passage of the Suez Canal. The control of both would ensure the control of the whole Mediterranean Sea and all the countries that surrounded it. That was why the British fought to take and hold these entryways. That was why they were in Egypt. It wasn't the cotton or the sugar. It was to manage and control the whole world.

Max followed Dietz's directions. The roads were open; an occasional truck or small group of Bedouin on camels were all they saw. As they approached a range of mountains that extended along the southern horizon, Dietz had him turn off the main road onto a gravel track that headed up into the sunburnt foothills. After another hour they crested a ridge and were confronted by a gatehouse and fence that extended up and over the ridge on either side. The guard snapped to attention and saluted the major with the Nazi heil. Dietz left the car and talked with the man. They saluted, and Dietz returned to the automobile.

"They switch off every three hours in this heat. Bruno is a good man. He was with Gottlieb at IG Farben, another one of our escapees. Turn here and follow the road down into the valley."

After passing through a narrow cut in the hills, Max was surprised to see a runway and cluster of buildings under camouflage netting spread out in the valley below. Dietz directed him to a shady spot within a grove of palm trees. A tall man stood in the shade, waiting.

"Max Adler, this is Captain Klaus Bitner—he is our pilot."

Bitner extended his hand—Max shook it. "Welcome to the ass end of hell, Herr Adler."

Colonel Rushton said to Sophie, "Your partner has been busy this morning. He was seen when two inexplicable events took place on the grounds of the Abdeen Palace before lunch. A man was shot dead on the steps of army headquarters, and a general and three officers were poisoned to death in their third-floor offices."

"Max, you've seen Max?" Sophie asked.

"Yes, he was there with Dietz," Rushton said. "I've included a photo of Max in the set of suspects passed out to the police. The dead man on the steps was abandoned by his comrades who quickly escaped after he was shot. The general and his aides died after a man matching Johann von Dietz's description left a briefcase for the general. They don't know what the poison was, but it was very fast acting, brutally effective, and left no obvious residue. Our chemical warfare experts are working with the Egyptians to try and sort out the agent. It was reported to act like mustard gas but faster and deadlier."

"The man on the steps?"

"The passport on his body was Syrian, but he had custom stamps for Germany during the Reich, France during the last few months, and an Egyptian entry stamp earlier this week in Alexandria. His name was Habib Hassan—does that ring any bells?"

Sophie paused for a moment, and then said, "Yes. We interrogated him in Berlin. The Americans had him, and after they were done, I took a shot. Couldn't find anything to arrest him for—he was held for a month or so and then released. Then, like most, he disappeared. He was one of al-Husseini's aides in Germany, who I assume is still in France. This is not good. Max was identified?"

"The shooter of Hassan is described as a tall blond German. He was standing near a car that is like the red Mercedes that you described the night Semitov was killed, the car that Johann von Dietz was driving that night. And Dietz got into that car after leaving the building; the tall man was the driver. Hassan was shot with a large-caliber bullet, possibly a .45. The same caliber bullet found in the body of Semitov, along with yours, of course. In time, someone will try and match the slugs. I am assuming, for the moment, that Max *is* the tall German. We are having the guards look at the photos."

"Are you suggesting that Max has gone over to the enemy?"

"No, but he is leaving dead people in his wake; not a way to keep a low profile, even here in Cairo. Additionally, this poison gas attack on the army has the government, and us, worried. There is an unconfirmed report that a Bedouin settlement deep in the Sinai was gassed a week ago by an airplane that screamed like a banshee. More than fifty people died, as well as all their horses, camels, and sheep. A shepherd with one of their flocks was halfway up the mountain and watched it happen. When he reached the camp, they were all dead."

"And he lived?" Sophie asked.

"Yes. It seems the gas doesn't last long," Rushton said. "Just enough time to contaminate and then kill those it contacted or breathed, just like in the palace. Two gas attacks in less than a week—I do not believe in coincidences."

Sophie had been anxious about Max before these incidents; she was now afraid. What had Max gotten himself into? She was certain that he'd not joined Dietz, that was a given—no matter what Rushton might hint at. The Syrian must have recognized Max and he had to do something to protect his cover. Rushton's report also described the other five men with Hassan; one of them might have been the Algerian. Why they were at army headquarters was a mystery but not a surprise. She knew that factions and opposition groups were spread throughout the government. Now with al-Husseini in the mix—obvious through this dead Syrian—it was going to get even more bloody and deadly.

* * *

Max lit a cigarette and walked through the grove of trees to a spot that overlooked the runway, his view reaching out and above the heat shimmer that vibrated the air above the macadam.

"The major says that you have saved his life a few times," Captain Bitner said.

"Yes, right place and the right time," Max answered. "Lonely stuck out here, I imagine."

"I've been in worse places during the last eight years. Spain was terrible, and so was an airfield south of Benghazi in 1942. Here, at least, no one tries to bomb you to hell and back. Herr Dietz says that you shot someone this morning."

"A traitor, someone who was infiltrating our operation. It needed to be done. I hope the damage is minimal."

"I've bombed cities and troop emplacements, strafed trains, shot other pilots out of the air, even high-altitude attacks on American and British bombers. But I've never actually killed someone face-to-face—strange, don't you think?"

"War is like that," Max said. "It's not something I live for, even if it's our duty. High altitude? I thought our planes had difficulties over thirty thousand feet."

"We can go much higher. My Me 262 can almost reach forty thousand feet. There were other conventional fighters, like the 109, that could go as high, but they took forever to get there. At five hundred miles an hour, I can get there quickly."

Max began to understand what was happening. He remembered the Me 262 that strafed him and Faber in the Ardennes. What would have happened to the Allies if there had been hundreds?

"The jet performs well in these conditions, the heat and dust?" Max asked, probing.

"Exceptionally well. Fuel and parts are the issues. After this operation over Cairo, maybe I will fly the plane somewhere else. I certainly can't build another one. My hope is that the engines can hold together for a few more sorties. Where were you based?"

Max gave Bitner the same story he'd given Gottlieb and Dietz, praying that the details would be the same. When you lie as he'd been lying, he hoped no one would take notes and compare his stories.

As he walked back to the main building, his mind began to understand the pieces of the puzzle: jet airplane, poison gas, Cairo, remote airport, al-Husseini, Hassan, the Algerian, weapons and uniforms, and senior members of the Muslim Brotherhood. It all added up to an attack on the British and Egyptian armies and a takeover of the Egyptian government. Now, he really needed a phone.

Dietz waved to him from the one building that looked marginally more hospitable than the others. "Dinner, Max."

It was a great meal, almost rivaling Shepheard's. The chef, a German soldier from Munich, prepared a feast of sauerbraten, fried potatoes, and real German beer. Dessert was a real chocolate cake with thick sugary frosting. There were six men at the table; the three soldiers sitting at the end generally talked amongst themselves and Max could see they were in awe of the major. For Max's part, he kept his mouth shut and only responded when asked questions. He wasn't sure when a question was a probe or an innocent remark. Soldiers were soldiers, and they told their war stories. However, these were Nazi soldiers. The three men had survived six years in the army, Poland, the Ukraine, and later Italy and eastern France. Their stories were about killing the Allies. When they began to talk about the Jews, Max politely excused himself.

The evening had cooled, and again there was the same acrid taste of the desert on his tongue. It cut through the rich fattiness that his mouth carried from dinner.

"Are you okay, Max?" Dietz asked as he joined him under the palms.

"Fine, sir. Just a very strange day." He offered the major a cigarette from his pack of Lucky Strikes.

"American cigarettes? I miss our Ecksteins, but whenever I could get American cigarettes, that was a day to celebrate. Where did you find these?"

"Shepheard's has them. I hope they don't toss me out. All my things are still in the room."

"Do you want me to send someone to get them—to keep them safe?"

Max thought for a moment. There was nothing that could compromise him in the room; that, he was sure of. If, however, someone was to go into the room—he was sure it was being watched—maybe Rushton could pull information from the man.

"Thank you, yes. I'm not sure when I'll get back there. I prepaid for a month; I do not seem to be getting my money's worth."

"You mentioned that you were involved with bringing

al-Husseini to Germany from Italy. What was the man like?" Dietz asked.

Max, realizing where this was going, answered, "I never met the man. I was handling the logistics and the baggage. Others were involved in the man's travel arrangements; I'm not even sure how he got to Berlin. I know that his bags and cases went by train."

"And that's where you met the man you shot?"

"No, that was in Berlin a few years later when the SS Handschar units in Bosnia were being formed," Max said. "Hassan—that was his name—was involved. We at the RSHA knew he was communicating with the Americans—that's why I was surprised to see him here. I am not sorry I shot him. I was upset knowing the man was a spy. He was responsible for the deaths of many of our men. He also recognized me, I'm sure of it, and was preparing to draw his weapon."

"A fortunate coincidence for us. Do you know what this is?" Dietz waved his arms in a broad arc.

"Obviously an airport. One of the Egyptian government's?"

"No, it is mine—at least for now. It was secretly built during the war by our people with the help of the Brotherhood. We were hoping to use it after Rommel took the canal—that, unfortunately, never happened. For now, the British don't know about it. This is where we will start the revolution."

"I had assumed as much, considering the weapons and the uniforms. And with what you have in the Shubra facility, a formidable beginning."

"More than formidable. My goal has been to drive the British and the Egyptians to their knees, to make it impossible to speedily react to our offense. It is a new form of blitzkrieg. I will make it impossible for them to react, and at the same time fill them with a monumental fear. A fear that if they do retaliate, they will die."

"But why are we here, in the middle of the Sinai Desert?" Max asked. "The enemy is west of here, and northeast as well, in Palestine. You are doing amazing things, what can be done from here?" Max's questions were probes that appealed to Dietz's ego. The Nazi was proud of what he'd planned. Max had a very good idea now what he had in mind, but the specifics were critical—especially the when.

Dietz blew the smoke from his American cigarette into the dark night. Other than the billion stars that filled the clear desert night, its tip was the only visible light.

"I do not trust you, Max Adler," Dietz began. "Captain Gottlieb does not trust you. That is our nature. However, I have a debt to you. The type of debt that a man does not turn from, no matter the issues of trust or conviction. We are all that is left of our nation's failed attempt to change the world. We few grim, worn-out soldiers fighting here in the Sinai Desert. We have now become mercenaries, soldiers willing to die for money."

"And that leaves me here in the desert with you," Max said. "And a crazy pilot and trucks full of poison gas and eventually a bullet in the head. Yes, Herr Dietz, history is full of perversions as well as validations. I assume that we are going to attack the British and be the catalyst that starts the revolution?"

"Yes, all revolutions start somewhere. The Mufti is returning to Egypt in five days; when he does, we will begin. Captain Bitner will fly over Cairo and strategically place the SARIN over the British barracks at Kasr el Nil and the Citadel. Within an hour, the British will find it impossible to organize any meaningful reaction to the Muslim Brotherhood's attack on critical government buildings, military bases, power stations, communication centers, and the Suez Canal. As the revolution grows, it will include the universities, airports, and ports. We cannot attack like we did in Poland and the Low Countries—we do not have the manpower—but we do have a population that wants the British gone. They will provide the support to the Brotherhood."

"Why is Abdul al-Khaldi here?" Max asked.

"He is al-Husseini's man. I believe he is mad. But I had no choice in the selection—al-Khaldi hates the French and will take a portion of the SARIN to Damascus where he will remind the French of all the pain they have caused Algeria."

"The fool will be caught before he gets there," Max said.

"Not my concern," Dietz answered. "May I have another of the American cigarettes?"

Dietz held the cigarette as Max lit it from the gold lighter he'd carried; it was a trophy from an SS officer.

"Handsome lighter."

"Thank you, a gift. Sadly, the man is dead; he died in Paris. We have left many on the battlefield; unhappily, we have little to remind us of them. Soldiers talk about their families. Yours?"

"Dead. The war has taken everything. My wife was killed in a bombing raid in the north of Germany while I worked at the Farben chemical factory. We had no children—our greatest regret. Now, maybe it is for the better. Germany is a disaster and will be for a long time. The French and British punished us for what they called the Great War. Now they will, like Rome did to Carthage, salt the earth of Germany. We will cease to exist. Those that were the instigators of our misfortune, the Jews, will get their own country as a reward. Thus it is for the losers and the victors."

"The dinner was excellent," Max said, changing the subject.

Also sensing the same need, Dietz answered, "The sergeant was a chef in a small restaurant in Bavaria. He even cooked for the Führer once—a distinct honor considering the safeguards required by the Führer's bodyguards. He showed up in Alexandria one day with two other men; they had managed to flee south through Austria and the Balkans. Eventually, they made it to Egypt; Gottlieb found them working in an Italian restaurant. And here, like you, they are."

"War does that. What are your orders, Major?" Max asked.

"Tomorrow we return to Cairo," Dietz said. "I have a meeting with al-Khaldi and the leaders of the Brotherhood to finalize the operation. I left enough confusion after the incident in the palace to leave people puzzled and, I hope, frightened. While the general supported us, he was becoming a liability; others who know of our relationship will wonder why it happened. All we need is five days; al-Khaldi will let me know the final schedule tomorrow. I also suggest that, until he understands why you shot al-Husseini's aide, you keep out of his sight. He'd just as soon kill you as call you a Jew."

The Sinai Desert
October 1945

The next morning, before sunrise, Dietz and one of the soldiers left the airport compound in the Horch to return to Cairo. Max followed in one of the converted British lorries. They reached the Suez Canal and waited for an hour for the ferry just as the sun rose over the desert; it promised another hot day. The loading onto the cramped boat was uneventful, except for the dozen camels that balked at climbing aboard. The camel herder had to beat them with a stick to make them board. Max found the wailing and braying humorous. The camels filled the stern along with a small drove of goats destined for Cairo. While they crossed, Dietz and the young soldier went forward to escape the stench of the livestock. Max, staying with the truck, saw this as his chance.

The previous night, after Dietz left him, Bitner had asked if he would like to see the Me 262.

"She's my baby, for how long I don't know, so if you'd like . . . ?" Bitner said.

"Absolutely," Max answered. An hour later, he was more than amazed and sure that if the Germans, two years earlier,

had produced this plane in quantity, the war would have possibly lasted another five years or even come to a different conclusion. On a workbench in the hangar, he saw a steel spring
clip and had an idea. He slipped the small clip into his pocket. Now, as the ferry neared the west shore of the canal, he
opened the hood of the truck, found the fuel line, and pinched
the rubber hose with the clamp. He estimated he had about a
mile of fuel in the line before it stalled.

They drove slowly through the village of Ismailia; the
British presence was obvious, but they were not stopped. A
mile and a half later, the lorry began to cough and choke. Max
pulled to the side of the road, then slowed to a stop. Dietz saw
Max stop, turned around, and pulled up next to the truck.

"What's the problem?" Dietz asked through the window.
Bruno, the soldier who was driving the Horch, sat behind the
wheel looking at Max.

"Acted like a fuel line problem. I have plenty of gasoline,
so it will take a few minutes to clear. Why don't you go on.
Either I'll catch up or reach the facility soon after you. There is
no reason for you to wait here."

"Do you want Bruno to wait with you?"

"No, he doesn't speak English. The reason you brought me
on board was my English. If a British patrol stops, I may need
to bullshit my way through this. Bruno might mess it up—sorry."

Bruno nodded and understood.

"Should take no more than fifteen minutes; the engine has
to cool down," Max said. "There's a repair shop across the
road. If I need something else, I can talk to them. You go on,
Herr Dietz. I will see you this afternoon, at the latest."

Dietz said something to Bruno. The man nodded again
and slowly accelerated into the morning traffic. Max watched
them until they disappeared out of sight. He lit a cigarette and
walked to the back of the truck. Ten minutes later, the cam-

els and goats from the ferry ambled by, braying and bleating. When his second cigarette was finished, he crushed it in the gravel, went back to the engine, removed the clip, and climbed back into the cab. After three tries, the engine caught and idled like nothing had happened. He turned back onto the highway and went in the same direction that Bruno had headed. The day before, when he and Dietz had driven through Ismailia, he noticed a sign for a British outpost located at the gateway to a marina built along this northern flank of Timsan Lake. Reaching the outpost, he slowed the lorry and pulled into a parking spot behind the building. The truck was hidden from the main road.

As he stepped down from the cab, a British soldier approached, his rifle up and ready. "Can I help you, sir?" the corporal asked.

"Yes you can, Corporal. I need to speak with your lieutenant," Max said.

"About what, sir?"

"His ears, Corporal. His ears only."

* * *

Thirty minutes later, Max was back on the road. The call to Rushton went well, better than Max had hoped. It took ten minutes to explain to the corporal's lieutenant why he, an American, needed to talk with Cairo and a Colonel Michael Rushton, 8th Army. It took another ten minutes of phone transfers to eventually find Rushton. And ten minutes more to unnerve Rushton. While he was talking with Rushton, he looked out the window of the guardhouse and saw Dietz and the Horch pass by, heading back toward the canal. He quickly finished his conversation.

"Michael, I need to go," Max said. "Meet me at the railway station tonight at nine o'clock. I will try and explain everything." He thanked the lieutenant, climbed back into the truck, and got back on the highway.

Five miles down the road, he looked in the rearview mirror and saw Dietz's face in the windshield of the Horch. Bruno, his arm out the window, was waving him over to the side of the road.

Max climbed down and walked to the vehicle; Dietz remained inside.

"Are you okay?" Max asked, trying to take the advantage.

"It was you we were worried about," Dietz said. "When we drove back, we didn't see you. Where were you?"

"Responding to nature, sir. After I cleared the line, I pulled into a gas station, took a piss—you passed me as I walked to the truck. You didn't need to come back; everything is okay."

"I was concerned," Dietz said.

Like hell, Max thought. "We need to get into Cairo before it gets too hot. Bruno, lead on. I will stay on your bumper the whole way." And he did.

After they returned to Cairo and the vehicles were secured, Max and Dietz walked through the laboratory.

"According to al-Khaldi, the Mufti will arrive in four days," Dietz said. "I think they are fools; they need months of preparation. When we went into Poland, the blitzkrieg planning took almost a year. They believe they can overpower a country with the strength of their will and Allah. Personally, I think that will is overrated; a hundred thousand well-armed soldiers are far better."

"Are you sure that the gas will accomplish what you are hoping it will?" Max asked as he looked at the two half-full tanks. "There are many variables and unknowns."

"The gas will perform as designed. It's the rest of the operation that concerns me."

"The rest? Yes, the Arabs, they are problematic. There are too many factions, too many opposing goals and desires. The religious leaders want one thing, the secularists another. What,

Herr Dietz, do you mean by 'the rest'?"

Before Dietz could answer, Gottlieb walked into the room; two Brotherhood soldiers accompanied him.

"Major, we need to talk," Gottlieb said. He looked at Max. "Alone, sir."

"Yes, Hans. I will see you in the office," Dietz responded.

"Sir, this is critical."

Dietz sighed. "Never a dull moment, right, Max? What is it, Hans—the Muslim Brotherhood, the Mufti?"

"Sir," Gottlieb said impatiently. "These men will remain here with Adler." He turned to Max. "We will be back in a few minutes." He headed out the door; Dietz shrugged and followed his second in command.

The two Egyptians, automatic weapons across their chests, just stared at Max. One pointed to a chair. "Sit," he said in German.

"Rather stand," Max answered.

One of the men looked at the other, then glared at Max. "Sit, now."

It was obvious to Max that the men were not accustomed to the weapons they held. The MP-40s were new; he thought he still saw grease along the edge of the barrel.

"Do you know how to shoot that weapon, soldier?" Max demanded. "Have you been trained in their use?"

They exchanged looks again.

"Adler, they know what they need to know," Bruno said as he walked into the room. He held a Luger. "I told them to just aim the barrel and pull the trigger."

In that split second, Max saw his opening. He pulled his Browning and fired one round into the chest of the first Egyptian, the second into the other man, and then swung the weapon toward Bruno. The German had ducked out of the doorway, but for only a second. He fired three shots wildly back into the room.

Max dove behind one of the tanks. "Not good, Bruno—one poorly aimed bullet will kill us all. I'd rather take a bullet than suffocate in a cloud of gas."

The shooting stopped. "Good thinking," Max yelled, as he worked his way to the door at the back of the room. Reaching the door, he fired three times into the wall to the right of the doorway, pulled the door open, and ran down the hall. Bruno, hit by one of Max's lucky .45 slugs, held his broken right arm and impossibly tried to return Max's fire.

Max slid to a stop outside the gymnasium where the weapons he hauled in from the delta were stored. He looked into the dimly lit space. Half the crates had been removed, but the three crates filled with British phosphorous grenades still sat where Max had last seen them. Next to them were two crates with the conventional German potato-masher style grenades; he slipped two into his belt. He slid a hand truck under the British crates and rolled the boxes back down the hallway to the room full of chemicals. Bruno was gone. Max hoped he had a minute to do what he could to neutralize the gas in the tanks; a minute before Gottlieb and Dietz would return to finish what the two Egyptians were ordered to do.

He rolled the crates full of the British grenades between the tanks of poison gas. If he were right, when they exploded, they would burn at a temperature over five thousand degrees, more than enough to destroy the tanks and the gas. He slowly backed away.

"I'm extremely disappointed in you, Adler," Dietz yelled from the opposite corridor. "While we were in the Sinai, Hans found out that you are not who you say you are. He says that you are an American agent; I told him that could not be true. I said you were a German, strong, a believer."

Max worked his way back to the hallway and stood just outside the door. Dietz was distracting him, which meant Gottlieb was working his way around the gymnasium to outflank him. He needed to move fast.

"It's even more bizarre than that, Herr Dietz," Max yelled, as he withdrew the first of the grenades from his belt. "I *am* German. I was born in Berlin. I fought for my new country, America, and I am your worst enemy—I am a Jew." He pulled the cord of the first grenade and tossed the stick into the room and immediately repeated the action with the other grenade. He slammed the door shut and began to run down the hallway, counting as he ran. *One, two, three* . . . Before he reached four, the wall thirty feet behind him exploded, then another blast immediately followed. By the time he reached the door that led to the garage, the three crates of phosphorous grenades exploded. The heat would melt steel.

The garage still contained the truck he'd driven from the airport, the roll-up door was open, and the Horch was missing. The fire behind him burned like a raging and roaring animal. More explosions followed. In minutes the building would be entirely engulfed. When it reached the ammunition, the weapons, and the other explosives, its intensity would increase exponentially, threatening the whole quarter.

He drove the truck out of the garage and into the narrow streets of Shubar. Already the sounds of fire trucks and emergency vehicles echoed through the passageways. He turned south and headed toward the train station. Assuming they survived the fire, he had no clue as to which way Dietz and Gottlieb would go. Dietz's apartment? He doubted it. Back into the desert? Again, the only way was over the Suez Canal. Within minutes, after he talked to Rushton, the ferries would be watched. Where could they hide?

42

Misr Train Station, Cairo
October 1945

Max walked into the cavernous Misr train station and scanned the benches that lined the gilded walls. He first saw Rushton, then, standing next to him, Sophie. She spotted him.

"Never do that again," she said, intercepting him.

"What? Run off with the bad guys?" Max answered.

"I'd rather see you run off with another woman than that Nazi."

"Do you know where Dietz is?" Rushton asked. "I have all of Cairo looking for him."

"Right now, Colonel, there's a huge fire burning in the Shubar. Hopefully, all the poison gas is destroyed."

"Poison gas?" Sophie said.

Max explained everything that had happened during the last few days.

"They intend to make an aerial attack with poison gas on the British barracks at the river and the Citadel, hoping to knock out any British reaction to the Muslim Brotherhood's attack on the primary targets in Cairo and Alexandria. This is all set in motion by the return of Amin al-Husseini, the Grand Mufti, to Egypt. When he arrives, he will give the signal that starts the attacks. That is why al-Khaldi is here, to coordinate."

"You have not heard," Rushton said. "The Mufti is still in Paris; it seems he's gotten to like the bourgeois Parisian life. After your call this morning and the mention of the Mufti, I contacted London. The French have restricted his movement, at least for now. There is no way he can be in Cairo in three days. And after what you are saying, they will be watching him even more closely. So, if the Brotherhood is going on the offensive, it won't be with their greatest inspiration."

"And al-Khaldi?" Max asked.

"He is also missing. We were watching the house where he was staying; a banker with the Brotherhood was providing him a bed. Since you shot Hassan, he has been missing. We do not know where he is."

"Then where are Dietz and Gottlieb?" Sophie asked. "If they escaped the chemical facility, they could be anywhere."

"Even more critical to the whole operation is Dietz's private airport—that's where the attacks will start. Get me a map and I'll show you where it is. It's hard to find from the highway, but one of your Spitfires could spot it in minutes. It's about one hundred and twenty miles east of here in a valley."

"Maps are at headquarters," Rushton said. "They cover the whole region from Tripoli to Palestine."

Max grabbed Sophie's arm. "Palestine, that's it. Damn it, I should have known. Michael, Dietz said something this morning that caught me by surprise. He said, 'the rest of the operation concerns me.' I didn't understand what he meant and he never had a chance to explain. I know it's Palestine, Jerusalem in particular. Dietz was using al-Husseini to fund him, get him the necessary equipment he needed to mount the attack on Egypt—but it's not Egypt. He's left that to the Egyptians. He is after the British, but the British in Palestine. Al-Khaldi will get what he needs to go to Syria and Damascus, probably park a truck in front of the French legation, or army headquarters, turn on the gas, and walk away. The damage would be psychological, as well as physical. Dietz will do the same thing. A target like the Dome of the Rock or the Western Wall, kill as many Muslims and British as possible, and the blame will fall on the Jews and Zionists. Or, in less than a half hour, he could fly the jet to Jerusalem, douse the whole region, and be instantly gone before your people could even get to your airplanes. Jerusalem is rich in targets—the King David Hotel, the neighborhoods that surround the Dome of the Rock. Hundreds, maybe even thousands, would die. He'd get his vengeance on the British and the Jews."

Stunned by the assumption, Rushton and Sophie looked at Max, yet there was nothing they could say that could counter what Max said. It made too much sense; the war Dietz had fought was against the British and the Allies, and under the maniacal paranoid leadership of one man, Adolf Hitler. Dietz and Gottlieb were true believers; all this preparation was one more battle, in their never-ending war, against the Jews.

"We need to see your maps and find Dietz," Max said.

The Suez Canal

Gottlieb looked his watch—it was almost midnight. The boat they'd hired to take them across the Suez Canal, like almost everything in Egypt, was late. The Horch sat in the parking lot of the marina, hidden between two boats on blocks. It might be a day or two until it was discovered. He hated to leave Bruno in the back seat, he'd been a good soldier, but the wound to his arm and shoulder proved to be more than he could survive. He bled out before they could stop it. He'd fought with Gottlieb for three years, including the Ardennes. It was such a waste to die by the hand of a traitor.

"They are late," Dietz said.

"Yes, sir. They will be here," Gottlieb said.

"Bruno Altman was a good soldier; we will not fail him."

"Yes, sir. We will not."

The day before, after the incidents at Abdeen Palace, Gottlieb met with a furious al-Khaldi. So furious, Gottlieb was glad that he'd carried a pistol when he met the Arab. He wasn't sure if al-Khaldi would take the death of Habib Hassan out on him.

"Where is this Adler?" al-Khaldi demanded. "Where is that son of a bitch?"

"He left with Herr Dietz—they will be gone a few days; why?" Gottlieb was lying; he didn't know where Dietz was.

"Adler is a Jew. As Hassan lay dying on the steps, he told me everything about Adler. He said that the man interrogated him in Berlin; the man was an American officer, an American Jew. Adler, or whatever his name is, works for the American OSS. He is here to stop us. And it is your fault, you and Dietz, that that man is here."

When Gottlieb returned to the facility, he tried unsuccessfully to reach Dietz at the airport by radio. He had no idea where the major went, but he was certain that Adler was with him. Dietz owed too much to Adler to question him—a blood debt was a strong bond. Gottlieb returned to the chemical facility early that morning, hoping that Dietz had returned. It was when he walked through the gymnasium and heard the voices of Herr Dietz and Adler that he confirmed that they'd returned. That was when Gottlieb told Dietz he had something important to tell him. Ten minutes later, as the building burned around them, they escaped. They put the wounded Bruno in the rear seat of the Horch, and with the two of them in the front seat, they fled toward Suez, hoping to cross the canal before the British would be alerted.

Halfway to the canal, in the town of Heliopolis, they stopped at a mosque known to have Brotherhood connections.

It took three phone calls to find al-Khaldi.

"Adler burned down the laboratory," Dietz said.

"You fool," al-Khaldi answered. "I do not trust any of them, the Americans, the British, and now you. You put your Reich first, in front of Allah and the Quran. You are all infidels; you should be discarded like apostates and Jews. Where is Adler?"

"I don't know, probably with the British," Dietz said. "There is a woman with him, a French agent."

"Black hair with green eyes?"

"Yes."

"She is a whore and a British agent; she works for MI6. How could you be so stupid?"

Dietz said nothing as he let it all soak in. Yes, how could he have been so stupid? But then again, their schedule—the real schedule—was only known to Gottlieb and himself. At least he'd not told Adler the real reason for all this.

"Are we ready to start?" Dietz asked. "Can we move up the schedule?"

"Everything has changed," al-Khaldi said. "The Mufti will not be coming in four days; the French will not let him leave France. They have taken his passport. He is well—thanks be to Allah—however, I have told the Muslim Brotherhood that we must wait. There are too many preparations that need to be completed. The Mufti ordered us to stand down, but to continue to prepare."

"We cannot wait. The gas in the Shubar laboratory is destroyed. All that we have left is in the desert at the airport, and it is too volatile to wait. If it is not used in the next few days, it will be worthless."

"We will make more," the Algerian said.

Stupid and ignorant man, Dietz thought. "Impossible. We must go now."

"Allah will provide." The phone went dead.

"Fucking idiots," Gottlieb said. "They are worthless."

"We need to get back to the airport—from there, we can replan our attack on Jerusalem."

An hour later, a light flashed from just above the water in the canal, and a small boat drifted to the dock. A young boy, illuminated by Gottlieb's flashlight, jumped to the dock and tied a rope around a pole. He waited, looking into the blackness that surrounded the flashlight.

"Are you coming, effendi?" a voice said from the boat. "In a few minutes, the British will be all over the shore. We must go now."

The boy helped Gottlieb and Dietz into the dhow, and in minutes the boat drifted out into the slack water. Dots of light from structures on the far bank reflected off the mirror surface. The captain started the small one-piston diesel motor, its thumping barely heard beyond the confines of the low-slung wooden boat. Fifteen minutes later, they approached another dock on the east side. Gottlieb signaled the shore, and the response—a quick flash of a flashlight—was immediate. Dietz handed the captain a handful of British notes and then, without even stopping at the rail, jumped to the dock. Gottlieb followed.

In the parking area above the dock, Bitner stood waiting.

"Pleasant night for a sail," the German pilot said.

"Considering how fucked up the day has been, yes, it was almost pleasant," Gottlieb said.

Five minutes later, they were deep into the desert following a series of posts and milestones laid along the indiscernible edge of the gravel and asphalt road.

"Where's Bruno?" Bitner asked as they drove.

"Adler shot him," Dietz answered.

"Adler? Why?"

They told him. Bitner slammed his palm against the steering wheel. "Son of a bitch—I'll get him. I sure as hell will cut his throat from ear to ear; I will leave his carcass for the vultures."

The compound was quiet, no lights. In the desert night, if there were one light bulb burning, the camp would be seen from thirty miles. Two men stood guard in the dark, machine pistols held ready. They joined Dietz, and the five Nazis walked to the main house. After drawing tight the blackout shades, Dietz poured the men glasses of schnapps.

"To the Führer," Dietz said and saluted the dead leader. "*Sieg Heil*," was the response.

"I have some cold chicken if you are interested, Herr Dietz," the cook offered, as Dietz and Gottlieb wearily settled into chairs at the dining table.

"Yes, thank you, Wilhelm. Is there bread left?" Gottlieb asked. The chef nodded. "*Danke.*"

Dietz poured another round of schnapps and said, "It is now only us, my comrades. Right now, the Americans and British are trying to find us. It will only be a matter of time; we may not even have until the morning. We will have no help from the fucking Arabs. Everything we have planned and worked for must begin tonight—there is no time left." He again raised his glass. "To our fallen comrades, *prost!*"

British Headquarters, Cairo
October 1945

The map was spread across the massive table in Rushton's office; Max traced his finger across the roads that connected the Arab villages in the Sinai Desert.

"It has to be here, in this area," Max said, emphasizing the spot by tapping his finger on the map. "This is the road from Ismailia. I remember a sign that read two hundred and twenty kilometers to Be'er Sheva in Palestine. From Be'er Shiva it can't be eighty kilometers to Jerusalem. Even with bad roads, it would take less than six hours to cross the desert and reach Jerusalem." He looked at the clock on the wall; it read 10:16. "It will take us at least four hours to reach the base. We need to hit the airfield at sunrise. We must stop them from escaping to Palestine."

Sophie and Rushton looked over Max's shoulder. Off to the side stood another man, RAF Wing Commander Lt. Colonel Stanley Tillinghurst.

"I can have two Spitfires over that spot at oh-five-thirty," Tillinghurst said. "The Me 262 is formidable—we have to trap it on the ground. Once in the air, it would outrun anything I have. We will make the runway impossible to use. But it must be daylight. I'm not sending my boys near that airfield without knowing what defensive weapons they have. And besides, the surrounding mountains are three thousand feet high. My men need to see everything."

"I saw nothing more than small arms and automatic weapons—nothing heavy or antiaircraft," Max said. "There is a small two-seat Storch parked near the hangar on the eastern side of the airport, and under camouflage netting is a Junker 352. It was used to fly in the parts and support gear for the jet. There are three other outbuildings. I only saw Germans on the grounds; in addition to Dietz, Gottlieb, and the pilot, there were other personnel. There may be Arabs working at the base; how many, I don't know."

"Not an effective defense force," Rushton said.

"I don't think it was Dietz's idea to set up a defensible base; this is a staging area."

"You believe that Jerusalem is the target?"

"Yes, and I agree," Sophie said. "It's been confirmed from London that the Mufti is staying in France, for now. This revolution was to start with al-Husseini's arrival. Now, it is has probably put everything on hold."

"I agree," Max added. "Except . . ."

". . . Dietz has his own schedule," Sophie continued. "London says that if the gas is SARIN or something like it, it has a short life span before it degrades to ineffectual. He has no more of the raw product—Max saw to that. They also know that Max Adler is not who he said he was. Dietz will proceed as quickly as possible—it must be Jerusalem. An attack on Egypt would be a waste, nothing more than a gesture. Dietz wants to make a significant statement that the Reich is still alive, still relevant. The target can only be the Jews and the British."

With a call, Rushton martialed an offensive ground force in front of the barracks—they had six hours until the Spitfires hit the airbase.

The night consumed the headlights of the three British 8th Army lorries that drove east across the Sinai Desert. Dust blew from the Mediterranean Sea fifty miles to the north, throwing up ghostlike forms in the headlights' glare. Max and Sophie sat in the front seat of the lead truck; Colonel Rushton was in the second. Their truck and the others were filled with British commandos. The operational plan was simple—six men would move in and secure the perimeter of the building compound by oh-five-hundred. The remaining trucks would then crash the gates. Additional commandos would trail behind the vehicles and watch for any defensive operations. Once the base was secured, the Spitfires would strafe and make the runway unusable, trapping the aircraft. As always, planning is planning, operations are operations, and reality is reality.

At oh-four-hundred, after locating the approach road, the first group of six commandos dismounted and began the hike through the desert to the location that Max had located on Rushton's map. The distance was about one-half mile. The three trucks then moved forward, up the road that Max had driven only a few days earlier. Ten minutes after dropping the first group of commandos, the empty lead truck disappeared over a rise in the road. Max and Sophie had taken the second position in the convoy in the front seat with the driver. The explosion of the lead truck rocked their vehicle; their front windshield was shattered by the blast. The experienced driver slammed on the brakes.

"Mine, sirs. Goddamn mines. Bloody hell," their driver yelled.

Ahead, the vehicle furiously burned, the two following vehicles emptied their commandos who immediately disappeared into the early gray of the sunrise.

"Now what?" Sophie asked Max as they slid into a shallow swale along the side of the road.

"The commandos know what to do; we need to get to the jet." Max checked his watch. "The Spits will be here in twenty minutes; we need to find Dietz."

The two jogged along the side of the road. They did not have the time to check for mines, and they prayed that they were only in the road and not along the shoulders. The flames from the burning truck lit the road ahead. The driver waved to them from the opposite side of the road—he'd jumped immediately after the explosion ripped away the rear of the vehicle. Max expected to hear the chatter of small arms as the first wave of commandos reached the camp. Only silence greeted them; there were no other sounds aside from the crackling and popping of the burning lorry.

"Something's not right," Max whispered. "There should be some kind of action by now."

"The explosion might have driven them into hiding," Sophie said as she followed Max on his right flank.

"Possibly, but where?"

The space between the hangar and small warehouse—where the two lorries had been parked when Max and Dietz left—was empty. The only vehicles remaining were the Mercedes and the Horch.

"Shit, the trucks are gone," Max said. "We missed them. They got out."

Beyond the corrugated metal buildings, a high-pitched whine began to build, a sound that they had never heard. It kept increasing.

"The jet," Max yelled. "The jet is taking off." He started to run toward the sound, Sophie close behind.

* * *

The Sinai Desert

Bitner checked the gauges and dials—everything looked correct. He'd run from the hangar to the jet as soon as the mine exploded; he didn't care why the others hadn't detonated. He knew he needed to be in the air as fast as possible. The original plan was that he would follow Dietz and Gottlieb later in the morning, giving them enough time to reach Jerusalem. Then, at noon, he would strafe the grounds around the Dome of the Rock and the other holy places that surrounded it, then release the gas over the courtyards and surrounding neighborhoods. Then, if he were still alive, make a pass over the British Palestinian operations base at the King David Hotel. He had enough fuel to then fly to a small airstrip in a friendly part of the southern Sinai. After that, he could just walk away. That scenario had now changed. He had to attack before Major Dietz arrived. He knew that Dietz and Gottlieb would understand.

He slowly maneuvered the jet out onto the apron of the runway and held there waiting for the engines to warm. The wind, from the north, was acceptable; the silk yellow and orange windsock was perfectly pointed. He again checked the gauges. They were good. The sun, to the east, fired up an intense glow from a spot just below the horizon. He pushed the stick and the aircraft taxied to the end of the runway.

He ducked as the Spitfire roared overhead, not twenty feet above his cockpit. He watched it bank and carve an arc to the south. He needed to be in the air. He pushed the throttle, released the brake, and the jet jumped and quickly accelerated down the runway. Ten seconds—all he needed was ten seconds. The runway ahead of him exploded in a furious fusillade of bullets from another Spitfire that was bearing straight at him, no higher than thirty feet above the centerline on the pavement. Due to their respective angles, he could not fire his own 30 mm canons; he had no defense other than speed. Bitner pushed the throttle forward as far as it would go; the acceleration pushed him hard into the seat. The sound of steel on steel racked the jet. Abruptly, the plane jerked and veered right; he pushed the brakes and tried to realign the plane—

nothing worked. The second attacking Spitfire roared over his head, not fifteen feet above the cockpit. The jet slumped hard onto its right wingtip. He saw and felt the right engine explode, breaking away from the underside of the wing and tumbling along the pavement. The jet went into a slide and began to rotate on its one remaining landing gear and tire. The canisters of SARIN gas mounted to the underside of the airframe were forced up and through the thin metal skin of the underside of the jet; the lines connecting the canisters were ripped away.

After a dozen gyrations down the runway, the plane skidded to a stop. Bitner threw open the overhead canopy, jumped from the cockpit, and began to run from the aircraft, positive that it would explode. He stopped after he'd crossed the runway and turned to watch as hundred bullets, fired by the returning first Spitfire, hammered the jet. The wind was in his face; the smoke from the burning jet stung his eyes.

Bitner looked back up the runway toward the compound; in the sun's light, a group of men stood there watching. The pilot inhaled, trying to catch his breath; he coughed and tried again to fill his lungs. His eyes burned; he rubbed them. He again coughed, trying to clear his lungs. He turned back to look again at his jet—it was now furiously burning. He gagged and tried again to inhale; his lungs refused to work. He gasped again; blood and spittle covered his hands, and his bowels exploded. He dropped to his knees. His hands and arms shook spasmodically, and with all his remaining strength, he removed the Luger from its holster on his right hip, and with the little muscular control he had left, Bitner pushed the pistol's muzzle under his bloody chin and jerked the trigger.

Sophie said, "Holy Mother of God," as she watched the plane burn and the effect that the poison gas had on Bitner. "They were going to spray that stuff over a city?"

"Dietz said the British barracks in Cairo," Max said. "That was a ruse, or at least not the only location. Maybe, after the Cairo attack, the jet would then turn to Jerusalem. It would make the distance in less than forty minutes. But that fell apart when the Mufti stayed in France."

"Or, when they discovered that you were not a Nazi," Sophie said.

"Yeah, there's that too."

Colonel Rushton joined the small group at the end of the runway. "No one else was found; the pilot was the only man here. The Spitfires are returning to their base—there was no reason to keep them here."

"Don't let your men near that plane or the body of the pilot," Max said. "Give it at least twenty-four hours. The poison gas exploded out from the jet and engulfed Bitner, the pilot. Killed him. Fucking way to die."

"Not many worse," Sophie said.

"Dietz and Gottlieb escaped during the night, while Bitner waited. We spoiled his timing," Max said. "We didn't pass them heading to Cairo, so they could only be going east toward Palestine. How the hell are we going to find them?"

"Only two ways to go," Rushton said. "North or east. The road along the coast will have heavy traffic and is longer—too long to coordinate an attack in Jerusalem. They could go east and head for the gate at Nitzana—that's a hundred miles, and the road is wide open. There's a border police garrison there. After that, they would head north through Be'er Shiva. But, bloody hell, they could be anywhere."

"They have a three- to five-hour head start," Sophie said. "Maybe they haven't reached the border."

The group walked back toward the compound. The smoke from the destroyed jet, the savior of the Nazi dream, drifted west away from them, the remaining poison gas consumed by the burning jet fuel.

The commandos joined the group. Other than the driver of the first lorry, who walked with a slight limp, no one was lost or injured.

"We were lucky," Rushton said. "We just missed the bastards. I'll radio Cairo, and they can pass the word to the Middle East Command. They can try and intercept the trucks."

Max lit a cigarette and walked in the early morning light toward the massive Junker hidden under the netting. He saw the Storch and stopped.

"Sophie, dear," he said, turning to the MI6 agent. "Do you think you can fly that thing?"

"If it has a motor, a full fuel tank, and wings, I can fly it." She had already started to jog to the airplane. Ten minutes later, she climbed out and gave a thumbs-up to Max and Rushton. "At least they painted it—it doesn't scream, 'I'm a Nazi,' all over it."

Max smiled and rolled up the maps he'd found in Dietz's office and slipped them under his arm.

"You people are crazy," Rushton said. "Command says that there's a front moving in. Out here that means the possibility of a haboob."

"A what?" Max asked as he walked toward the plane.

"A massive dust storm can mess with radios and communications," Rushton said. "And you do not want to be in that airplane when they hit. Be bloody careful."

"We will be all right, Michael, don't worry," Sophie said. "We can cover more of the desert in that airplane than anyone on the ground, radios included. I've heard a lot about their maneuverability. Should be exciting."

Rushton advised them, "If the storm hits, you have two options—land and stay put or try and fly over it. Personally, I'd try and outrun it."

"I don't need exciting right now, Sophie," Max answered.

"Get canteens of water and something to eat," Sophie said. "It has a radio on board. Major, alert the border we are headed their way; it might also be a good idea to put your RAF in Palestine on alert. We may need them, and make sure they know about us. I don't want to crash due to friendly fire. So, lover boy, you ready for a plane ride?"

* * *

The trucks had been repainted to match the British Mandate vehicle colors, and the doors had been stenciled with the appropriate regiment identifications for the Middle East Command. The men were dressed in British uniforms. Dietz and Gottlieb were going to bluff their way into the heart of Palestine and Jerusalem. Bitner said he'd try to rejoin them in Baghdad if everything worked as planned. They said their goodbyes. The pilot would place mines in the road that led to the gate after they left. Dietz and Wilhelm were in the first truck, while Gottlieb and Otto followed in the second. For the first two hours, they drove in the dark—the road east was empty. After about seventy miles, headlights appeared and a small convoy of four similar British trucks approached. They passed on their right. Wilhelm waved to the lone driver in each truck until their taillights disappeared. They continued driving toward the yellow haze of the rising sun. Camels and sheep appeared along the shoulder; a young shepherd waved.

A disheveled village of stone and concrete block buildings appeared as they approached a crossroads. A road sign pointed north to Al Arish and Rafah. Below, it read, "Palestine Mandate Border—Prepare to Stop."

Dietz held the bundle of papers, which consisted of supply manifests listing the contents stacked in the back. The crates were British military supplies, which sat over a false bottom covering an elaborate system of valves and canisters—an arrangement like the system on the jet. It was a simple process of parking the vehicles near the British barracks or the newly located United Nations Palestinian headquarters and activating the timers that controlled the valves. Dietz had to believe that Captain Bitner would carry out his operation as planned. After Bitner attacked Cairo with the gas, he would strafe the targets in Jerusalem. Dietz would activate the timers mounted behind the seats. With the chaos of the aerial assault, Dietz hoped that the British would overlook their trucks. The gas, when discharged, would drift through the adjacent neighborhoods, effectively creating a suffocating hell on earth.

They pulled to the side of the road, a mile short of the border. Both Dietz and Gottlieb lit cigarettes; Wilhelm and Otto joined them. They then checked their weapons in case they had to force their way through. If that happened, the whole operation would fail. Dietz, the only one who could speak decent enough English, would do the talking. It was the only time Dietz wished that Alder hadn't been who he turned out to be.

Along the northern horizon, a cloud of dust appeared, and lights from within the cloud flickered on and off. It advanced slowly toward them. They were the headlights of an approaching convoy; it was coming from the north. Their paths would intersect at the crossroads.

"Captain, I think we are in luck," Dietz said as the convoy neared them. "Mount up—let's see if they will allow us to join them."

They waited until the ten British Army trucks had passed and then they slipped into the space left at the end. A single jeep held back, covering the rear of the convoy. The driver waved them in, and they joined the line of trucks. The convoy slowed as it reached the gate at the border but did not stop. Within minutes, they were through and following the road to Be'er Sheva.

Eastern Sinai Desert
October 1945

Two thousand feet above the convoy, a single airplane coasted along the same road. It held back and stalked the two trucks that joined the convoy.

"Smart move," Max said as he watched the convoy maneuver through the border crossing. "Five minutes later, we would have lost them."

"Are you sure it's them?" Sophie asked as she banked away from the road, but never letting the convoy out of their sight.

"Has to be. We saw no trucks other than the small group heading toward Cairo, and the British will intercept them. These two must be Dietz."

The twelve trucks and two jeeps were on a northerly heading that would take them to the ancient biblical city of Be'er Sheva. In every direction were ragged mountains and endless desert. Somewhere, in this part of North Africa, the Sinai changed to the Negev Desert. To Max, it all looked the same, burnt ochre rock and buff colored and sand. The only visible marker was the column of dust rising from the convoy a few miles ahead. Sophie made a slow arc away from the convoy;

her speed was three times that of the convoy's. She did not want to get ahead of the trucks. Their hope was that Dietz would not see them through the dust. She pointed over her shoulder to the north.

"We are running out of time; that's the haboob."

"Shit," Max said, looking at the dark wall of sand and wind. "How long?"

"Maybe an hour—we have to stop these trucks, now."

* * *

The Germans tied handkerchiefs over their faces and slipped on goggles. The dust kicked up by the ten trucks ahead of them permeated everything. Dietz stayed ten feet behind Gottlieb. Three miles past the border, the road changed from rough oiled gravel and sand to macadam; the dust settled, and the air became breathable.

Wilhelm touched Dietz's arm and pointed. "Company," he said and pointed to the passenger's-side mirror.

"What is it?" Dietz asked.

"A Storch, similar to ours at the compound."

"Similar? Or is it the same one?"

"Can't tell, but there can't be another around here. Is it Captain Bitner? Did something go wrong with the jet?"

Dietz let the idea muddle around in his head. He doubted that Bitner would have left the airfield in the Storch; he would do whatever he could to fulfill his mission. Besides, following them would have served no purpose; it might even alert the British. Someone else had to be flying—and he was certain that person had to be Max Adler.

"Where is he now?" Dietz asked.

"They are staying back and away. Maybe they are afraid the British might shoot at them?"

"Signal the captain. Make him aware of the plane."

Wilhelm pointed his arm out the window at the aircraft;

Otto flashed his headlights acknowledging the plane. Through the dust he saw the driver and passenger of the jeep look up as well. The column did not slow.

* * *

Max said, "We can't let them get to Be'er Sheva, let alone Jerusalem. They must have a similar dispersal system built into the trucks as the jet. They need to be stopped here."

"Does the road straighten out ahead of us?" Sophie said, looking ahead. "Someplace where we might be able to land?" She looked again to the north at the storm wall.

Max ran his finger along the road map. "Maybe five miles, over that ridgeline. Looks straight on here."

Sophie accelerated and banked away from the road. "See if you can reach Rushton—we are going to need a lot of help."

"Roger that."

As Sophie flew over the ridgeline, she spotted the mile of straight and flat road. Max tried to reach Rushton. All he received was static and incidental confused chatter he could not break into. "The storm is throwing out a massive amount of interference. We are on our own, my little desert flower. Like old times, just you and me and the nasty Nazis."

"There's a bunch of the good guys there, too—the British," she said, looking down on the convoy a few miles back.

"Those Limeys are going to be in for a surprise—the war's not over."

The convoy came through a pass in the ridge and began the run down the straightaway that gently sloped into a broad valley. Sophie brought the aircraft around and aligned it with the centerline of the road; telephone and power lines draped from pole to pole along one side. She dropped the Storch until she was ten feet above the pavement and coasted along. Her goal was to stop the plane a few hundred feet from the lead truck, obstructing the convoy. She slowed the airspeed until the wheels just kissed the road; she then let the plane settle onto the road. The convoy braked, then stopped. Sophie taxied the plane to within fifty feet of the lead jeep.

"You stay here and keep the motor running," Max said. "I'm not sure where this will lead. If that son of a bitch activates the gas, I want you out of here."

"I'm not going to leave you here," Sophie protested.

"Thanks. Love you, too, but get the hell out of here anyway."

Max climbed out of the airplane and checked the wind's direction—it was quartering across the convoy. The wall of the sandstorm was maybe twenty minutes out. Any poison gas would be blown away from them, or at least that's what he hoped. Through the door, Sophie handed him an MP-40. He slipped it over his shoulder and then adjusted his Browning. From the lead jeep, an officer, a lieutenant, dismounted.

"Good God, man, what the hell are you doing?" the officer said. "Get that fucking contraption off the road. We need to get to Be'er Sheva. I do not want my men caught by that storm." Two more soldiers, from the lead truck, joined the officer. Both carried carbines.

"Have you been contacted by Middle East Command?" Max asked.

"No. How could we? No radios. And even if we did, that storm would make it impossible. We came down from al-Arish with supplies. That thing has chased us most of the way. Now, who the hell are you?"

"Middle East Command. Two trucks joined your convoy just before the border. We need to—"

Before Max could finish, the snapping of pistol shots rang out from the rear of the convoy.

"What the hell is that?" the lieutenant yelled. "Get back there, Corporal, and find out what the hell is happening."

Just as the corporal left, a sergeant stumbled up to the

group; his breathing was hard, and a bloody stain spread on his upper arm.

"Lieutenant, they took the jeep," the sergeant yelled. "They shot Private Timmons—bad leg wound." He then saw the Storch. "Good God, what the hell is that doing here?"

"Who shot you?" the lieutenant shouted, as two more of the men in the truck joined them and grabbed the sergeant.

"Those trucks that joined you at the border, Sergeant— they still here?" Max said, walking up to the group.

"And you are?" the sergeant asked.

"No time for that. Are those two trucks still there?" Max asked.

"Yes, they're still there, but the four men in them took the jeep. They turned around and headed back up the road."

One of the soldiers stripped off the sergeant's shirt and wrapped a gauze bandage around the wound on his arm.

"What the hell happened?" Max demanded; out of the corner of his eye, he saw Sophie approaching.

"It's just a scratch—got worse at El-Alamein. When we stopped, I pulled up to the two trucks that joined us. I got out and walked to the second truck. When I reached the door, a Luger was pointed down at me by the driver. A man yelled, in bloody English, to stop. We did as ordered. Four men then climbed down from the two trucks, all of them armed, two with machine pistols—fucking German machine pistols—like the one you are carrying. They were in British uniforms. 'Get out,' they ordered. Timmons tried to stop 'em, and that's when they shot him. Then they took some equipment from both trucks and put it in the jeep. They looked like flamethrowers— double canisters and all. They put them in the back of the jeep. Then one of them climbed back into each of the trucks, spent a few seconds, then climbed out. Ten seconds later, they were headed back up the road the way we came."

"Shit." Max turned and jogged back to the airplane, then

stopped and walked back to the soldiers standing at the jeep. "Again, tell me what they took out of the trucks."

"Who the hell wants to know?" the lieutenant demanded.

"I'm Max Adler, captain, American Army, OSS. The pilot of that airplane is Sophie Norcross, British intelligence, MI6. The men in those two trucks are Nazi fugitives. They are carrying enough poison gas in those trucks to kill everyone in Be'er Sheva. Get it?"

"Bloody hell. As I said, two shoulder packs, each with two canisters, like flamethrowers. They set them in the back of the jeep, the men climbed in, and they left."

"What did they do in the trucks?"

"Don't know. You said they are carrying poison gas?"

Max and Sophie were already running down the shoulder of the road to the end of the convoy. Max pulled himself into the cab of the first truck and looked around—nothing out of the ordinary. He pulled the back of the seat forward. Wedged in between the seat and the back wall of the cab was a simple timer, six inches by six inches. It was mechanical and ticking— ten seconds remained until the end of the sweep of the small hand closed the connection. Max spun the mechanical timer back, found the two leads that disappeared through the truck wall, and disconnected them. He ran to the other truck, found another timer. This timer still had two minutes left. He disconnected the wires.

"Nick of time?" Sophie asked as he climbed down.

"Proverbial."

The sergeant and lieutenant pulled the jeep to the side of the truck.

"They had set the timer to activate the poison gas," Max said. "We stopped it. However, the stuff is still incredibly dangerous—will kill you in five minutes. Set up guards to keep the locals away until the bomb squad can get here and take charge. You need to send someone on ahead to let Command know.

We are going after the jeep."

Five minutes later, they were at one thousand feet and following the road back toward the border. The black wall of the storm filled the horizon.

"We've got maybe ten minutes before we turn back," Sophie said. "Any longer and that thing will swallow us alive. The grit will eat this motor."

"Got it," Max yelled over the roar of the engine. "There, a mile ahead—I see them."

"Then what are we going to do? Those canisters must be more of the SARIN. It may be the last of it, but Dietz will try and use it somewhere."

"I still believe he's headed to Jerusalem. Get lower—maybe I can hit them with the Schmeisser."

Sophie swept in from the left side of the road until she was a hundred feet off the desert floor; the jeep was five hundred yards ahead of them.

"It's going to be close; the sand is beginning to hit the windscreen," Sophie said. "They are speeding up—they've seen us."

"Lower; watch the power lines," Max yelled as he slid open the small window on his left.

"Any lower and the power lines won't make a fucking difference."

As they paralleled the jeep, two holes appeared in the side window behind Max.

"They're shooting at us," Sophie yelled.

"Really? Lower!"

She dropped another twenty feet; the jeep was less than a hundred feet away. The sound of the engine and the storm made conversation impossible. Max pushed the barrel of the machine gun out the window and aimed it at the jeep. As he started to pull the trigger, the Storch jerked up and away. When he looked down, the jeep had disappeared into the storm. Sophie quickly accelerated and banked the massive wings of the aircraft away from the advancing storm, its tail already engulfed by the raging, grit-filled gale of the haboob.

**The Negev Desert
October 1945**

Gottlieb drove the jeep with its four occupants into the wall of the storm. Without any protection, they were engulfed in blinding sand and dust. Breathing became impossible. After twenty minutes, Dietz tapped him on the arm and motioned to the side of the road; Gottlieb slowed and pulled the jeep into a shallow ravine. The four men took shelter on the leeward side of the jeep, and each did the best they could to keep the fine dust out of their nose and mouth. It was late in the afternoon when the wind finally died, and they were able to stand and shake off the desert.

"Will the jeep start?" Dietz asked.

"The men will get it started," Gottlieb answered. "They are trying to clear the intakes and filters. With luck, we will be on the road in an hour. Where are we going?"

Dietz retrieved his leather map case and unfolded a map of Palestine and the Negev Desert. There were few villages with names, and only three of the largest cities were shown—Be'er Shiva, Hebron, and Jerusalem.

"There are dozens of small tribal settlements, and even

some Israeli kibbutzim throughout the region," Dietz said, pointing to the spot where they had waited out the storm. "We have about one hundred and twenty kilometers to go before we reach Jerusalem. How many checkpoints and roadblocks are along the route, I don't know. They are looking for us. They have had hours to start the search while we were stuck here in the storm. We can go along the eastern side of Palestine through Hebron. None of us know what the roads are like, but if we try even farther east, past Be'er Shiva, it is longer but less populated. With luck, we can make it in six hours—it will be night then."

"We can't do it in this jeep—everyone will be looking for it," Gottlieb said. "We need to find another vehicle."

"Agreed, but we need to move from here," Dietz said and pointed again to the map. "The crossroad here goes north and south. I suggest south, then wrap around until we can go north. Maybe we'll find something in one of the villages."

"And the target in Jerusalem?" Gottlieb asked, shaking the dust from his shirt.

"Here." Dietz circled an area on the west side of the city. "It's the headquarters for the British and foreign services." Dietz then slipped the map and case into a shelf under the dashboard.

The jeep started; Wilhelm called it a miracle. There were three jerricans of gasoline secured to the sides of the jeep; they poured one of them into the gas tank. They also cleared as much of the sand from the vehicle's interior as they could. Gottlieb then drove south. An hour later, they approached an Arab village that was nothing more than a collection of collapsed concrete block and stone buildings, a small grove of half-dead palm trees, and a deserted petrol station. For all intents, it looked abandoned.

"We can stay here for the night or continue north," Dietz said to Gottlieb.

"I prefer driving north at night—less chance of being spotted by aircraft. The British will be looking everywhere for us; we need the cover of night."

"I agree. See if there's anything here to eat—we leave in ten minutes."

The men searched through the buildings and found nothing. Even the well pump was broken. They had exactly five liters of water left for the four of them.

"It's enough," Otto said.

The sun sat low on the horizon; it would be dark in an hour. They would leave then.

"Company," Wilhelm said to Gottlieb. "On the horizon beyond the crest of the road, I saw a truck. It is headed this way."

"Pull the jeep around the corner of the building," Dietz said. "Let's see who it is."

Gottlieb and Wilhelm took positions behind a large collapsed sign; through the rust, it read "British Petroleum." Dietz and Otto crossed the road and stood against the side of one of the buildings. As the truck cleared the last set of low hills, it headed directly toward the abandoned village. At a hundred yards, Gottlieb and Wilhelm walked into the center of the road and signaled the truck to slow down. It appeared to slow, then suddenly the engine roared as the driver accelerated. It bore down directly on the two men. Gottlieb stood his ground until the last second then jumped out of the way. The driver, an Arab, fired wildly at them with a machine gun. His passenger fired a pistol at Wilhelm, narrowly missing him. From the side of the road, Dietz and Otto fired their machine pistols, hitting both the driver and the passenger. The out-of-control truck swung back and forth across the road, until it slowed and rolled to a stop against the side of a building.

The truck sat there sounding like a wounded beast; dust swirled around the vehicle. An unseen hand appeared on the frame of the back of the truck and then pushed away the canvas rear panels. In the cover of the truck's dark side, a boy jumped to the dirt and ran to the shelter of the building and hid in the shadows.

The four men cautiously advanced to the truck. The driver was slumped over the steering wheel, the passenger collapsed against the side door. Both were dead.

"Check in the rear," Dietz said.

Wilhelm pulled open the canvas and climbed into the truck. The bed was filled with dozens of boxes, stacked five and six high, though some had toppled over during the aftermath of the shooting. He opened three of the boxes. Inside were cigarettes, bottles of liquor, and women's underwear.

"Major Dietz," Wilhelm called out. "They were smugglers. The truck is full of contraband."

Dietz looked into the back. "This will work for us," he said. "Get the bodies out of the cab, and strip them of their robes and *kaffiyehs*. We'll transfer the gas canisters to the truck. Check the fuel; if we need gasoline, transfer it from the cans in the jeep."

The truck was a prewar Citroen. The paint had been sandblasted away over the years, and the rust had eaten through the door panels. Under the crates of smuggled goods, the road could be seen through the wooden floorboards.

"I want to be out of here as soon as we can," Dietz said and walked back to the jeep. He lifted each of the canister systems and placed them on the ground. He checked for leaks, then laughed to himself—if there were leaks, they all would be dead.

He carried each apparatus to the truck and placed them behind the cartons; with straps, he secured them to the truck's interior side panels.

"The fuel tank is half full," Gottlieb said to Dietz. "With the rest of the petrol in the last jerricans, we should have more

than enough fuel to reach Jerusalem. We have nothing to si-
phon the gas from the jeep. This will have to do."

"I'm sure it's enough. Get the men on board. We are leaving."

They hid the jeep behind the building and covered it with
rotten tarps found inside the gas station. They put the smugglers' bodies in the jeep.

Ten minutes later, they turned back onto the gravel road
and continued north. A kilometer outside the nameless village,
a rusted sign read, "Hebron—60 kilometers."

The boy watched everything. Why did the British soldiers
kill his father and uncle? Why would they steal the truck? Why
would they hide the jeep?

✳ ✳ ✳

The Storch—kicked in the tail by the storm—soon outran the
dust and wind. Max leaned in from his rear seat and yelled in
Sophie's ear, "That was close."

"You don't like my flying?"

"I love your flying—it's the best flying I've ever enjoyed.
What I really want is a good landing. Any ideas?"

"We have about a hundred miles of fuel left. If we head
north, we can stay ahead of the storm and get there before
it's too dark to land. North of Jerusalem, there's an airfield at
Atarot—it's the main British airport near Jerusalem. Try calling
them."

As Max picked up the microphone, a flash of brown and
sand camouflage roared past them at three times their speed.
The Spitfire rocked its wings as it passed.

"Jesus, that thing scared the devil out of me," Max yelled.

"Right there with you," Sophie said as she slowly inhaled
and adjusted the yoke.

The Spitfire came around and then slowed to pace them;
their radio crackled.

"Good afternoon, Lieutenant Dingle here. I sure as hell

hope that you are Norcross and Adler. If not, I'm authorized to shoot you down. Over."

"We are Norcross and Adler—save your ammunition. We need to get to Jerusalem; it's critical. Over."

"Understood. Take a bearing of twenty degrees east. The airport is about thirty-five nautical miles. I'll stay with you."

"Roger that and thank you, Lieutenant Dingle. Over."

Sophie adjusted their bearing and headed north. The Spitfire stayed near but had to circle. At the Storch's slow one hundred miles an hour, the Spitfire's engine would have overheated.

Forty minutes later, they were taxiing to the rollout area of Atarot Airport. They were directed to a spot between two Avro York transport aircraft. Sophie, looking at the massive British airplanes, believed they could easily park beneath one of the wings.

Standing in the lobby of the small reception building stood Michael Rushton.

"How did you get here so fast?" Max asked as they walked to another jeep parked outside the building.

"When the word got to Cairo about the poison gas, Middle East Command sent a crew in a de Havilland Dragon to the Nazis' airfield. After the demolition and chemical crews had been dropped, I hitched a ride here. I figured there were only a few places you could go after the storm passed through. I also sent the Spitfire to look for you. What about Dietz?"

"Lost them," Sophie said. "They disappeared into the storm, we turned, and after the Spitfire found us, landed here. I assume that you've not heard anything?"

"Nothing. Are you still thinking they are headed here?"

"Fairly certain," Max said. "Especially now that they have, or what I guess to be, portable dispersion systems for the gas."

"Bloody hell."

Max explained about the convoy, the Nazis' escape, and

the timers and the on-board poison gas systems on the trucks. He also voiced his speculations about the portable canisters.

"I now know what the small tanks I saw in the Cairo facility were for. The larger ones were for the jet and the trucks, the smaller ones were for 'just in case.'"

"For just in case, what?" Sophie asked.

"In case the others failed."

An RAF soldier walked smartly to Rushton and saluted. He handed him a paper. He read it.

"They found the jeep," Rushton said. "It had been abandoned in a deserted village about twenty miles from where you stopped the convoy. It was confirmed with the license plates. There were two dead Arabs inside. No gas canisters. They also found a boy who, after being convinced that they were real British soldiers, told them that after they had killed his father and uncle, they took his father's truck."

"He didn't say what kind of truck?" Max asked.

"Yes, the kid said it was a Citroen. It was his job to keep it running. He also wanted to know, if we find it, could he have it back with all the cigarettes and booze that was in it. His mother would not be happy if he loses it."

"Nice kid," Sophie quipped.

"Out here, everyone has to make some kind of living," Max said.

"And they also found a map case under the dash," Rushton said. "A route was shown from the airfield in Egypt into Palestine, confirming it was Dietz. On another map, one of Jerusalem, a location was circled."

"What was it?" Sophie asked.

"The King David Hotel."

The Negev Desert

Dietz sat next to Gottlieb, who drove the Citroen at its top speed of just over twenty-five miles an hour. If the engine didn't seize, the transmission didn't lock up, or the tires fall off, it would take them all night to reach the southern settlements of Jerusalem. The left headlight—the right had shattered during the crash—barely lit the road ahead of them. Wilhelm and Otto had found uncomfortable spots to sit in the rear on old hemp bags. Dust kicked up from the road boiled through the cracks in the decking, choking them.

"Dammit, I left the maps in the jeep," Dietz said, slamming his hand on the dashboard. "I forgot them. If they find the jeep, they will know where we are going."

"So what? We will still make this happen," Gottlieb answered. "Our challenge right now is getting to Jerusalem—no matter how."

"I marked the King David Hotel. If they find the maps, they will know."

"Assuming they find them! They don't know where we are or what we are driving. That's to our advantage. We push on— there are a thousand targets in Jerusalem."

"But only one that will avenge my family and my country," Dietz said. "If I could, I would swim the Atlantic and place our weapon on the steps of the White House. But I can't. We are soldiers, and we can only fight with what we have. Hans, we will still attack the hotel; we will find a way."

"Excellent."

In the black of the desert, a cluster of lights materialized and seemed to float above the road. The roadblock appeared out of nowhere when they crested the ridge. As Gottlieb slowly approached, the dim light of the single headlamp threw a baleful light on the two jeeps that blocked the road. A manned machine gun was mounted on the right jeep, and four well-armed men stood in front of the jeeps. One man waved a flashlight at the oncoming truck. Gottlieb slowed to a crawl.

Dietz called out to his men in the back. "A roadblock. Wait for my command; there's a machine gun on the right. When we stop, take positions on the sides. If we have to fire, make sure you take out the machine gun first."

* * *

Jerusalem, October 1945

Max and Sophie managed to get a bite to eat and a few hours of fitful sleep. Before sunrise, they entered the Jerusalem headquarters of MI6, with Rushton.

"Have you been here before?" Max asked Sophie.

"No, this is my first time to Jerusalem. When you were in the Ardennes, I was in Moscow. Here, in the Middle East, everything is crazy."

"And getting worse," a lieutenant colonel offered, as he walked into the room.

"Colonel Drake, this is American OSS Captain Max Adler, and one of ours, Sophie Norcross," Rushton said, making introductions. "Colonel Drake is the MI6 commander here in Palestine."

"Sorry to hear about your OSS shutting down; good group of lads. But in today's world, best to leave it to the professionals."

Max wouldn't take the bait. What was it with these British assholes? "Well, at least we still have a few tricks up our sleeves, as the Japs are finding out."

Drake, clearly realizing that the conversation was not going to go his way, began, "Since the Irgun's terrorist activities and the Stern Gang's assassination of our minister, Lord Moyne, eight months ago, Jerusalem has been in virtual lockdown. Nothing in, and almost nothing out. We know the Jews use the sewers and tunnels, bring in weapons at night, and take every chance at disrupting our military activities. It will get worse before it gets better, if there can ever be a better. So, I believe we can keep this Nazi of yours outside the city."

"Mine, Colonel Drake?" Max said angrily. "SS Major Johannes von Dietz is not *my* Nazi. Right now, he wants to unload about thirty-five pounds of poison gas in the King David Hotel. Today, for all intents, he is *your* fucking Nazi."

"The King David Hotel is the most secure facility in Jerusalem, maybe in all of Palestine. He won't get there. No one can get there." Drake said.

"Colonel, he doesn't have to 'get there'—all he has to do is get near it. The winds will carry the gas. Their original plan was to fly over the hotel and spray the gas over buildings and grounds. He was also going to attack it from the ground in two trucks that your soldiers are now guarding somewhere south of Be'er Shiva. That plan literally exploded yesterday morning. So, right now, Dietz is trying to accomplish the same thing but on a smaller scale. Thousand can still die. I've seen what this gas can do."

"I was in the trenches thirty years ago in Verdun, young man. You don't have to tell me what poison gas can do."

"Dammit, this is not the same," Max shouted. "Three out

of four died from mustard gas, less with phosgene. This gas is called SARIN; it is almost one hundred percent fatal. It is colorless and odorless; you won't know you're affected until you are dying. Do you understand?"

The colonel stared at Max, then harrumphed. "He won't get near Jerusalem." Drake turned and marched out the door.

While still in earshot, Max yelled, "Colonel, it's my guess he's already here."

The three intelligence agents looked at each other.

"See what I have to put up with?" Rushton said. "Between you and me, Britain should get the hell out of here. Leave this land to the Jews and the Arabs. They will sort it out."

"All-out guerrilla war?" Max said. "That doesn't seem like a good option."

"There are few good options in this country," Rushton said. "Every Jew in Europe wants to immigrate here. Every Palestinian and Arab wants them to stay in Europe. And with the terrorist Amin al-Husseini radicalizing his people here, and smuggling in weapons and ammunition, it will only get worse."

"And we've confiscated any weapons the Zionists have, leaving them defenseless," Sophie added.

"They will be used on us before they can use them on the Arabs. What option do we have? Dietz and his poison gas? Hell, for all I know he will just give it to the Palestinians."

A soldier knocked on the door and handed Rushton a message; he read it.

"They rushed a roadblock east of Hebron. Killed three British soldiers and severely wounded two others. They left one of theirs—he's dead."

"Did they get away?" Max asked. "Was the dead man Dietz?"

"No way to know," Rushton said. "I'll send his description and try to get a confirmation. The report says they may have wounded one of the men in the cab. It's not confirmed. Sunrise is in one hour, and these three men are less than ten miles from here—and the roads are filling with morning traffic."

"Can we lock down the city?" Sophie asked.

"As Drake said, it is locked down," Rushton said. "Nonetheless, goods and food still have to come in. Besides, Command barely has enough men to protect the government offices and barracks. There are a thousand ways in—they only have to find one of them."

* * *

Dietz wrapped the length of cloth he'd cut from his robe around Gottlieb's right arm; the bleeding had stopped; the wound was shallow. The door of the truck managed to deflect the bullet's effect.

"I'm fine, sir. I can still use my right hand. It's my left shoulder that's really hurting," Gottlieb said. "The last sign said Jerusalem was five kilometers—we are almost there."

"Pull over, I'll drive," Dietz said. "I will see that Wilhelm's family understands his sacrifice."

"To die in a fucking desert at the hands of the British after everything that he and I had been through the last four years. It will be avenged."

"Yes—he will be."

They were running out of time. The truck was known. British soldiers would be converging to this part of Jerusalem—every vehicle would be stopped. The hills to the east glowed pink with the start of a new day; along the sides of the road, Arab and Palestinian vendors and traders walked toward Jerusalem. A few pushed handcarts, while others carried goods on their heads. The wealthier vendors used donkeys to carry bags and even small pieces of furniture. Dietz slowly drove the truck into the busier section of the Arab quarter. Off to one side of the road, a shop served tea and coffee. A cluster of half a dozen itinerant vendors stood talking and smoking outside the shop; four donkeys were tied to a rail next to them.

Dietz said, "I have an idea."

Dietz slipped the truck into a gap between two buildings; the early morning shadows hid the truck. He then walked over to the men smoking and drinking their tea. They eyed the German cautiously.

"Does anyone speak English?" he asked.

A thin young man, with a stringy beard, spit on the ground. "Who wants to know?"

"I do. I am looking for two men who want to make their fortune today. Two men with donkeys, who will discover that Allah is smiling on them. Which of you men will it be?"

"You are nothing more than a British spy. Why should we help you?"

"I assure you, I am not a spy. In fact, in all confidence, the English are looking for us right now. However, I have a greater opportunity than what those British pigs will offer you. Again, I ask, which of you want to make your fortune?"

Two teenagers joined the thin speaker. "Yes, we are interested; we are brothers."

"You are fools—they will only trick you," the others in the group said. They stood, spit on the ground, and then led their donkeys away.

The three men walked to the back of the truck. When Dietz pulled the canvas panels back, Otto stood there with his machine pistol. The men tried to turn and flee.

"Stop, he won't hurt you," Dietz said. "Here is the opportunity. I want to trade you the contents of this truck for your two donkeys. In fact, I'm going to leave this truck here with the keys. The three of you can decide how you want to share this bounty."

Otto opened one of the boxes and showed them the cartons of cigarettes. Dietz could see them counting the boxes and doing the math in their heads. One touched the side of the truck as if caressing it, then looked at his donkey.

"That animal is stubborn and obnoxious," he said. "You a fool to make us such an offer?"

"Yes, I may be a fool, but I need an answer, now," Dietz said.

Gottlieb walked around the corner of the truck, his arm bloody. Dietz watched one of the men blanch at the sight.

"Your answer, now. Otto, show them what's in the other boxes."

Jerusalem, Palestine

The three Germans, still wearing the smugglers' filthy robes, pulled the donkeys along the side of the steep road. Above them stood the city of Jerusalem and the massive structure of the King David Hotel. Two trucks full of British soldiers passed and ignored them as they slowly climbed the steep road. The Germans were lost among the hundreds of Palestinians, Arabs, and Jews walking the same route. Even during a time of civil war, commerce had to move forward. The Palestinian Arab population stood off to one side of the conflict between the Jews and British, watching and waiting. The British, like the Turks before them, would soon be gone. And after the British left, they would remove the Jews.

The men found a spot of shade and turned their backs to the narrow street that climbed to the hotel. If spotted by the British, their eyes and complexions would give them away. Under their robes, each carried a machine pistol and a Luger. The two donkeys, now carrying the canisters wrapped in heavy cloth, stood to one side, shaking their heads trying to ward off the relentless flies.

"The wind is perfect," Dietz said. "The gas will slowly drift through the compound. We will position the animals along the road in front of the hotel and secure them to a railing or a tree. If there are other peddlers, even better. I will set the timers for noon, giving us enough time to escape. I will take one donkey to the west side. Otto, you and Hans go around to the east."

"This is not turning out the way we planned," Gottlieb said, grimacing in pain. "We were to strike a blow that the British and the Jews would never forget. Captain Bitner must be dead, or if for some strange twist of fortune he is not, we will be dead by our own gas when he attacks this mountain. We will accomplish little. There has to be another way to use these weapons, one that will strike at their heart."

Above them stood the hotel, its broad stone façade sharp and hard above the ancient houses and structures that tumbled down the hill below it. Dietz scanned the city that had wrapped itself around the face of the sacred hill called Mount Zion. Beyond, he caught a flash of the morning sun off the massive lead-covered Dome of the Rock.

After a moment, Dietz said, "What if we were able to set the sons of Abraham on each other? Turn one against the other?"

"I don't understand," Gottlieb said.

"Imagine an avalanche, one small insignificant stone that begins to tumble down a mountain. It hits another and another until the whole mountain begins to collapse. If we wanted to cause such an avalanche of cultures, what would you strike? What small pebble would take down the mountain?" Dietz pointed at the dome of one of Islam's holiest places. "There, and below the shrine, the singular object of every Jew's reason to come to Jerusalem—the ancient biblical foundation of the Temple Mount, the Western Wall."

Gottlieb smiled. "Yes, Major, I understand. We will start our avalanche there."

* * *

Ali Mohammed, Sami Farsoun, and Khalili Farsoun could not believe their good fortune. Allah had finally smiled on them. They watched the foolish Europeans dressed as Arabs walk up the road, the donkeys grudgingly pulling along behind them. It was good to be free of the stinking animals. After ten minutes of rummaging through the back of the truck and opening the cartons of cigarettes, liquor, and women's silk underwear, they calculated that by the end of the day they would be so rich that they might even be able to afford wives.

"We need to move this truck," Sami said. "Who knows who might try and steal it? Ali, we can take it to our mother. She has room to park it near the chickens. We can then figure out how to sell the cigarettes and liquor; she may have an idea."

Ali had known the Farsoun brothers his whole life. Their mother was a good woman, and she would help. He looked at the keys in his hand, but why should he split the treasure with the brothers? After all, he was the first man they had approached, the first they had talked to. He jingled the keys the man had given him and watched the brothers climb down from the back of the truck. Sami held a bottle of brown liquid, and since he could not read, the label meant nothing, but Ali knew it was liquor, a forbidden drink—but worth a fortune to the right sinners. Sami took a swig and nearly coughed up his breakfast; his brother laughed. Sami held up the bottle to Ali, who shook his head. The brothers disappeared around the back of the truck. Ali went to the driver's side, quietly opened the door, and slid into the front seat. He looked at the keys, the dashboard, the various pedals, and mechanisms. He had spent some time in his uncle's taxi and had diligently watched—it did not look that difficult. He slipped the key into the most obvious spot, turned the key, and the motor fired up with a grinding cough.

"What the hell are you doing?" Sami yelled from the far side of the truck. He opened the door. "You can't leave without us." He slid into the middle of the bench seat; his brother followed. "You can drive this truck, can't you?"

"Sure, it's just like my uncle's taxi. You ready?"

Ali grabbed the gear stick and pushed the gas pedal. The motor roared, but the vehicle did not move.

"You are supposed to push that pedal then wiggle the stick. I've seen it a thousand times," Khalili said and pointed.

"Right; forgot."

Ali pushed the clutch pedal and jerked the gear stick; the truck lurched and, remarkably, did not stall. He slowly pushed on the gas pedal; the truck began to move. A big smile came to his face. Using the steering wheel, he guided the truck out into the busy road. A taxi sped past, its horn blaring.

"Down the hill—you're doing a good job."

Ali pushed the gas a little more, the truck picked up speed, and the whining from the engine increased.

"I think you need to shift it again—that's what I've seen," Sami said. Both of his hands were on the dashboard, an uncomfortable look on his face. Ali took a quick look, all he saw was panic.

Ali pushed in the clutch pedal and the whining lessened. He pushed the stick to the right and let out the clutch. It surprisingly engaged, and the truck picked up speed. It was approaching its top speed of twenty-five miles an hour, but with the steep downhill grade of the cobblestone road, the truck would be well beyond that. Ali pushed down hard on the last pedal, the brake. The truck slowed but not enough. Ali tried to control the direction of the vehicle; he overcorrected. It swerved from one side of the narrow street to the other. People ran to get out of the way. More vehicles honked and drivers waved hands out their windows in rude gestures. Ali prayed to Allah, thought of his short life, and then drove the truck into the side of a stone house more than five hundred years old.

* * *

Just outside the MI6 offices, Max and Sophie stood on the terrace overlooking the ancient biblical city of old Jerusalem. Distinct villages clung to the sides of the hills, as they climbed Mount Zion. These incongruent communities merged and became the citadel that enclosed the cradle of the great Western religions, and for most believers, the holiest of places.

"What a view," Sophie said.

"And five thousand years of history, religion, war, and . . . hope," Max answered.

"Always the cynic. This is your home; these are your people."

"Yes, maybe so. However, we Jews are a pragmatic people, almost a race, certainly an ancient tribe. To think that there, under that black Islamic dome, all the fears and hopes of my disparate tribe are focused. For a kid from the North Side of Chicago, it is quite a wonder. Even my parents have not been here—I probably should find a postcard."

"Cheapskate."

Rushton joined them. Following him, in a British sergeant's uniform, a young man stood at attention, olive complexion, black hair, and very dark eyes. Sophie found him exceedingly handsome.

"We found the truck," Rushton said.

"Where?" Max asked.

"Imbedded in the side of a building at the base of that hill there, Mount Zion."

"They got that close?"

"No."

Rushton told them about a patrol sent to investigate a truck that crashed into a building. The three banged-up Palestinian boys spilled their story of trading their donkeys for the truck and the contraband in the back. "They are lucky to be alive.

The guards almost shot the truck up; it fit the description of Dietz's truck—in fact, it is the same truck. Now our Nazis are on foot. One of the boys said that they were headed toward the King David Hotel. The boy was confused. One man from the truck spoke English, but all were dressed as Arabs. They were climbing the road up the hill—that was last they saw of them."

"Dammit, on foot now," Sophie said, then looked at the young man.

"Captain Adler and Miss Norcross, this is Sergeant Avi Baum. He is with British intelligence. You are going to need a translator and guide. He was born in Jerusalem."

Sergeant Baum smiled. "A pleasure to meet you."

"And you, Sergeant," Max said and then looked across the valley toward the Temple of the Rock. "Sergeant, how many men do you have around the hotel?"

"There's maybe a hundred thousand British soldiers here in Palestine. Right now, at least ten percent are guarding the hotel and its approaches."

"How many are guarding the Western Wall and the Dome of the Rock?"

"That's hard to tell. We try to keep a low profile there—causes fewer problems with the locals: Jews and Arabs and even Christians. Maybe a few hundred. Why?"

"We know that Dietz is not a fool; he knows that we know he's here. He's counting on his luck and smarts to put himself someplace where he can cause the most damage and death. Before he's caught, he will set the timers on the devices—ones that are probably like the ones on the trucks. They need time to escape; they are not suicidal. Dietz realizes that there are too many chances to be caught before he gets to the hotel; right now, he needs a target. It's my guess that he's changed his tactics and is now headed to the Temple Mount. An attack there will have everyone blaming each other; it could be the fuse that ignites everything. Even the truth will not change the excuse for violence and the deaths. Sergeant, Miss Norcross and I need a jeep."

* * *

Dietz, Gottlieb, and Otto tried everything to cajole the two donkeys into following them; twice they stopped and would not move.

"Maybe if I shoot one, the other one will get the idea," Otto said.

"They are either too stupid or too smart, not sure which," Gottlieb said. "I'm leaning toward smart; their future does not look good."

"We need to change. We can't carry the canisters, it's too obvious." Dietz looked up the road to a small restaurant that had a few tables sitting in the shade. A jeep was parked outside. Two British officers sat at one of the tables.

Two minutes later, Otto, still dressed in his Arab robes and *kaffiyeh*, walked up to the back of the jeep and yanked out one of the officers' leather satchels and bolted toward a gap in the buildings.

"Bloody hell, you little bugger, stop," yelled the officer. Both men raced after the man and disappeared into the same alley. Seconds later, they were both unconscious and tied up. The Germans stripped off their Arab robes, Gottlieb replaced his bloody British blouse with one of the officers', and pulled the keys from the lieutenant's pocket. The three strolled back to the jeep, the two donkeys in tow. The quizzical look on the restaurant owner's face demanded an explanation.

"They are chasing the thief," Dietz said. "We are to take the jeep and meet them at the top of the road—he gave me a few shillings to pay the bill. We will come back for the animals later. Until then, they are yours."

"I don't want those stinking animals," the owner protested, but the payment calmed him, and after tying up the donkeys, he walked back into the restaurant. Gottlieb and Otto, seeing the cakes and coffee left by the officers, stuffed them into their faces. They untied the canvas bags from the donkeys and gingerly placed them in the back of the jeep and climbed in. Dietz looked up at the face of Mount Zion, took a deep breath, and began the drive up the winding road to the Temple Mount— only a few hours more, he thought.

"Where are we going to place the weapons?" Gottlieb asked as he climbed into the driver's seat.

"I'll know when we get there," Dietz answered.

* * *

Sergeant Baum was at the wheel of the jeep as he drove Max and Sophie through the labyrinth of old streets and alleys that led to the Damascus Gate on the north side of old Jerusalem. Rushton stayed at MI6 headquarters to manage the operation. Numerous checkpoints had been set up along the roads surrounding the city, manned by British soldiers and uniformed policemen. All along the street's shops and stores, queues of women stood waiting for the few goods they could purchase.

"The Zionist Irgun terrorists have been active during the last few days," Baum said. "There have been a few explosions around the city. They check everyone now. This tightening has affected food and other supplies."

They parked near the British guard post that oversaw the Damascus Gate. The surrounding walls, made of massive limestone blocks, extended upward to a crenelated battlement over the arched entry. A mismatched collection of old buildings extended outward from the stone walkway that led from the street. Merchants hawked their goods under tents and awnings.

"Sergeant, can we drive in there? This is a military priority," Sophie asked, pointing at the gate.

"Ma'am, not a chance. Once you get in, there's not a street wide enough to allow you to go a hundred feet in any kind of vehicle except a motorcycle. Inside you walk or have a donkey—that's it."

"How about the other gates?"

"Same thing. Park outside, walk inside."

"Now what?" Sophie said, turning to Max.

"They are faced with the same problem, but they have donkeys—at least that's what the Palestinian boys said. There has to be ten thousand people in there."

"More like thirty thousand," Baum said. "And it is up and down steps and stairs as well—you would be lost in ten minutes. The important places are on the eastern side, about fifteen minutes from here. Signage points out every imaginable religious shrine, monastery, church, and synagogue squeezed into this half square mile of adulation and adoration. If you get lost, follow the signs to the Damascus Gate; it will get you back here."

Baum parked near the guard post constructed of stacked sandbags. He talked with the two soldiers, then retrieved his Sten gun from behind his seat and set it against the jeep. He pulled the antenna out on the walkie-talkie. "Com check, over . . . Roger. Going through the Damascus Gate . . . Roger." He turned to Sophie and Max. "Are you ready to travel back in time a thousand years?"

Old Jerusalem, Palestine

They found a tourist map in the jeep. As he studied it, Dietz began to form a plan. He told Vort to follow the road they were on; ahead there should be a sign for the Dung Gate. The pain on Gottlieb's face was obvious. Every bounce of the jeep made him jerk. Tears ran down the soldier's cheeks.

"Slow down; it should be on the left," Dietz said.

Vort and Gottlieb looked closely at the massive stone wall that paralleled the road. Signs pointed to a gate, but there was no road.

"If the gate is here, there is no place to enter with the jeep," Vort said as he slowed to a stop across from where the gate was supposed to be. People were walking toward a spot along the wall. "Are we going to carry the canisters inside?"

"Yes. The map shows a location for the Western Wall, one of the most revered locations for the Jews. It would only be appropriate to discharge the canisters here. Above it is the Dome of the Rock and the Aqsa Mosque."

Dietz helped Vort with the straps to one of the devices, then Vort did the same for Dietz.

"I can carry one of them," Gottlieb said.

"We're good," Vort answered. "But stay close."

Dietz watched the street traffic, then crossed the road toward the southern entry into the old city; his men followed. A policeman stood to one side when he saw Dietz in his officer's uniform; he saluted and waved the three men in.

"No wonder the British have problems here," Gottlieb whispered. "We could be anyone. He didn't even blink about the backpacks."

"Sometimes we all believe what we want, Hans."

Falling into a line of Arab women carrying baskets filled with bread, the three men, with their grisly sacks of death, disappeared into the small gate at the base of the ancient stone wall.

* * *

Max, Sophie, and Baum walked quickly south and wove their way through the narrow cobblestone alleys. In places, they would climb a set of stairs; then, at the top, climb down another set.

"Major Rushton told me about Dietz and his second in command, Gottlieb," Baum said. "He also said there were two others?"

"There's only one now," Max said. "The other is dead, killed at a checkpoint south of here. Gottlieb and the remaining soldier are experienced survivors of the war. Do not take them lightly."

"Anyone who would set off poison gas in this place has to be taken seriously. He told me you are the only ones who can identify these men. Is that true?"

"Yes, unfortunately. And if they are dressed as Arabs, they will easily blend in."

Baum's radio squawked. "We are almost at the intersection between the Jewish quarter and the Armenians." He listened a long minute. "I'll tell them. Out."

"There has been no sign of Dietz, but a new development. Three men matching their description stole a jeep from two British officers at a restaurant and left two donkeys. The officers were assaulted and tied up."

"When was that?" Sophie asked.

"About a half hour ago. It was on the far side of the city, at the base of Mount Zion. We are looking for the jeep. Like us, they can't drive into the old city. They will have to park and walk in."

"Great," Max said. "Half a square mile of some of the densest development in the world and we have to search every alley? Where would you go, Sergeant? Where would you take out your retribution?"

They began to jog again, Baum in the lead. The radio squawked.

"Baum." Again, he listened. "Roger, out."

"I have a good idea now; they found the stolen jeep near the Dung Gate on the far south side. It's near the Western Wall and the shortest connection to the entry to the Dome of the Rock and the al-Aqsa Mosque."

"How far?" Sophie asked.

"A thousand feet."

"Then go, go," Max yelled. "Go!"

They ran east toward the minaret that stood high above the expansive terrace atop the massive foundation of the Temple Mount.

"Below that minaret is the Western Wall," Baum yelled, as they pushed their way through the crowds that flowed like a human river toward the holy shrines.

"We turn here," Baum said and made a hard right. His pace did not waver. "One hundred feet."

As Baum had promised, at one hundred feet, the claustro-phobic alleys and corridors abruptly ended, and a narrow plaza opened before them. Hidden in the shadow of the late morning stood the dark face of the Western Wall, the two-thousand-year-old wall that once supported the Second Temple built by Herod in the decades before the birth of Christ. This exposed portion extended for over two hundred feet and faced a narrow, stepped plaza. However, for the Jews, this was also where Solomon built his temple a thousand years before Herod. Max knew instinctively that this was where Dietz would try to resume the murder of Jews that had been stopped in Europe.

Max turned toward Baum; the man was talking on the walkie-talkie. All he heard was, "Dammit."

"What's happening?" Sophie said.

"A policeman watched three men enter the gate; two were carrying bags. He didn't pay them much mind; they were all in British uniforms."

"How long ago?" Max asked.

"Maybe ten minutes."

The three scanned the narrow plaza; clusters of people slowly moved throughout the holy place. More than two dozen men in dark clothes and long coats stood at the wall nodding and praying. An equal number of women, in fringed shawls and covered heads, also stood facing the ancient wall. To complicate the situation even more, British soldiers walked among the worshipers. None were Dietz or Gottlieb.

"We need to split up," Max said. "That housing, Sergeant. What's that?" He pointed to the buildings that fronted the wall.

"That's the Moroccan Quarter."

"You go there. Look for three very nervous British soldiers; they will be wearing backpacks—maybe. Sophie, you go to the end of the wall. I'll cross to the far end and . . ." He squinted at a group of men walking the arcade in the shadows of the Moroccan Quarter. "There—that's them. Sergeant, call for support and to get these people out of here. If they set off those canisters, thousands will die."

Max and Sophie ran toward the same arcade that fronted

the wall the Germans had entered at the far end. Max prayed that they had not seen them.

* * *

Soon after Dietz and his men had passed through the Dung Gate, they found themselves on a twisting alley that headed uphill. If it weren't for the Jews pushing their way forward, they wouldn't have been sure if this was the right way in or not. The last sign read in Hebrew and English, "Western Wall," with an arrow. After walking through a confusing series of corridors, Dietz cautiously looked around a building's corner. Beyond stood the massive façade of the Western Wall and the base of Solomon's Temple.

"We're here. Now what?" Gottlieb asked.

"This is all wrong; it's too confined," Dietz said. He pointed to a short passage behind them that ran perpendicular to the wall. "Set the bags down, there." He pointed.

Gottlieb and Vort gently set the bags in a shallow and low alcove off the passage.

"I didn't realize how enclosed everything is. The gas will not drift far before it loses its effectiveness." He pointed to the top of the wall. "We have to go up there. From there, it will drift over all the quarters—Muslim, Jew, and Christian alike."

"This will kill Christians?" Vort asked. "I'll not be a part of that."

"You are a soldier," Dietz said. "I'm ordering you to pick up that bag. We are going to climb to that terrace. The wind is coming from the east. The gas will spread over all the quarters that surround the temple."

"I'm not a soldier anymore—I chose to be here because of the Jews," Vort said.

"You are staying, Otto. I'm ordering it," Gottlieb said. Sweat poured down his face. "We have fought together for four years, survived every unimaginable horror, and we stand here to make one more effort for the glory of the Reich. Pick up that bag."

Gottlieb pulled his pistol, the muzzle rising and now pointing at Vort's heart. Vort looked at Dietz, who had also drawn his pistol.

"There is no glory in this," Vort said and reached down to grab one of the bags. "No glory at—"

"Do not pick that up," a voice yelled from up the passageway. "Step away, or I will shoot."

The Western Wall, Jerusalem

Max and Sophie defiantly stood at the end of the passageway, the noon sun behind them. Their shadows, and the distinct silhouettes of pistols in their outstretched arms, stretched down the stone paving burnished by a million long-dead feet.

"I said leave the bags where they are," Max again demanded, this time in German, "and drop your weapons."

Dietz answered by firing into the blinding sunlight. Gottlieb and Otto quickly raised their weapons, and the staccato shooting echoed throughout the labyrinth of alleys and passages. Max and Sophie, seeing Dietz's initial move, dove around the corner of the building.

"Give it up, Dietz. In five minutes, there will be a hundred soldiers surrounding you. This is pointless."

"Is that Max Adler and, I assume," Dietz said, now tight against the wall, squinting into the sunlight, "his Italian whore as well?" He did not lower his weapon.

"This madness must end here," Max said. "There's nothing to be gained by killing thousands of innocent people. Just leave the bags and come with us."

"Tell me one thing, Herr Adler—who are you? Herr Gottlieb wanted you dead from the first day. I was sentimental; I should have allowed him to kill you. I welcomed you like family?"

"You, and Germans like you, have never been my family." Max watched as Baum pointed behind him and signaled that he was going to go around the Germans. Max nodded. "My family left Germany when Germans like you no longer appreciated us. My country is America now, the country we chose; it has welcomed us. Germany became sick with a cancer that only cleansing fire could destroy. The Allies provided the fire. Put your weapons down."

Max saw Gottlieb turn to a sound behind him. Standing on the steps above was Avi Baum, his Sten gun pointed directly at Gottlieb.

"You heard the man—drop your pistols," Baum ordered.

Dietz turned to Max. "You. You said you were a Jew? "

"Yes, I'm a Jew."

"Then you must die."

The other German suddenly grabbed the top of one of the bags and with one swing of his arm flung the bag at Max and Sophie. The sound of steel crashing against stone was only slightly muffled by the coarse cloth of the bag. Everyone froze and stared; time was stopped. From the seams and torn side of the canvas, a red fog began to emerge. The man who threw the bag screamed and fled up an adjacent passageway, hoping to escape the expanding crimson cloud that held close to the ancient stones. Gottlieb yelled something in German and raised his machine pistol toward Baum. Three bullets from Baum's Sten shattered his chest before he collapsed into the red mist.

"Herr Dietz, is this how it will end?" Max demanded, the mist now around his ankles.

"Run, Sergeant," Sophie yelled at Baum. "The poison has already killed us; run. Don't let anyone else down here."

Seeing the red fog, Dietz yelled, "No, no. This can't be. The SARIN was in the canisters—the dye was never in the canisters. It can't be." He glared at Max. "You!"

"Yes, Herr Dietz, I refilled the small canisters in Cairo. I could not change all the others before we escaped the fire. Put the pistol down, Dietz. You are all alone—there is nothing more. This is over."

"There is always a way out." He swung his Luger up at Max and fired. Max spun to his right from the impact of the bullet but was still able to fire twice, hitting Dietz in the chest. Sophie followed with two pistol shots of her own. The German dropped to his knees, and then he, too, disappeared into the crimson cloud. Max, staggered by the bullet, put his hand against the limestone wall and turned to look at Sophie. She slipped her shoulder under his arm and pulled him out into the sunshine. The red fog tumbled down the steps behind them and began to slowly dissipate.

* * *

Standing over Max in the hospital, Sophie demanded, "Why didn't you tell me that you had changed the canisters?"

"I didn't know they would end up here," Max answered. "Back in the laboratory, I only had enough time to change two of the small canisters. There were six on the table when I left. I was going to change the other four but didn't have time. We were lucky."

"Luck? You don't believe in luck. You had no idea that if that Nazi had flung the other bag, we would all be dead."

"What?"

"The other bag had a contraption like the first. Only those canisters held *real* SARIN gas. If that device had ruptured, we and a hundred, maybe a thousand other people would be dead."

Max looked at Sophie and a smile grew. "We Jews are a rational people. We never believe in luck or the stars. However, there's the notion of *mazal*, or luck. My mother always said to trust and believe in God and work hard to make your own luck."

"You are an idiot. As I said, we were lucky," Sophie said.

"Damn straight," Max said.

"Someday I want to meet your mother and thank her for creating the most cynical and annoying man I've ever met or fallen in love with."

"She will tell you that I'm also spoiled, headstrong, willful, with a touch of self-importance."

"Yes, there's that, but after the last few years I think I know you fairly well. I have my own list."

"And what is on that list?"

"None of your business."

Colonel Rushton tapped on the doorframe.

"Max Adler or whoever you are, you look good for a man that missed dying by about three inches. You were lucky." Max looked at Sophie and grinned.

Ignoring their looks, Rushton added, "Sergeant Baum sends his best. When he heard you were a Jew, it confused him. He thought you were just a fool American. I shouldn't tell you this, but when I gave him what history I know, he said that there is always a place here in Israel for men like you."

"Michael," Sophie said to her friend. "There are a lot of places that can use a man like Max Adler."

"Good God, can you two hear yourselves? What about al-Khaldi, any word?" Max asked.

"After the laboratory fire and Jerusalem, he seems to have vanished," Sophie answered. "Our Brotherhood sources give conflicting stories. One said he left to return to France and al-Husseini, another said he went back to Algiers to throw out the French, and one hinted that he went to Damascus. We are watching everywhere."

"And did he take one of the canisters?" Rushton asked.

"I don't think so," Max said.

"So, he's in the wind."

"Yes, he's in the wind."

* * *

Chicago, December 1945

Max left the embrace of his mother and said, "Mother, Sophie and I are going down to Skeets. Is there something that you need? I can pick it up before we come home."

"There's a list on the kitchen counter. Your father will be home at six," Mrs. Adler answered, touching the cheek of her son.

"We'll be back by then." Max picked up the list from the counter and walked out into the entry hall. Through the glass of the front door, snowflakes drifted in the still air. He put on his black cashmere overcoat and fedora. From behind, Ruth Adler wrapped a red wool scarf around his neck, turned him around, and tucked the ends inside the coat. He bent down and received a kiss on the cheek. Sophie, all bundled up in a thick fur coat, smiled at the motherly attention.

"And you look lovely. Make sure he stays wrapped up; someone has to take care of him."

"Yes, Mrs. Adler. He is such a pain."

"You do not know the half of it. Do you have your gloves?"

"Yes, Mother."

"And the list?"

"Yes, Mother."

"Good. On it are a few things I forgot for Chanukah. Tomorrow morning the ladies are coming over, and they want to hear all about Jerusalem. Only Mrs. Spitzer has been there, and she wants to hear about everything that's new."

"There is nothing new in Jerusalem," Max said. "But, much of everything that was old is new again. We will be here."

Later that morning, Max set the bag of groceries on the

wooden floor of the North Side saloon, pulled out one of the old stools for Sophie, and then sat next to her. They were the only customers at the ancient mahogany bar. Mr. Skitsenbaum, the wiry bartender from Poland with a wooden leg to replace the real leg he lost at Chateau-Thierry, set a glass of Tennessee bourbon with ice in front of Max.

"And for the lady?"

"Whatever he's having," Sophie answered.

"Excellent choice. One for yourself, Skeets—it's been too long. There's been a lot of—"

"If you say water under the bridge, I will punch your arm, hard," Sophie said.

Max smiled and kissed her cheek. "Thanks, Skeets, I've dreamed of this for more than a year." He raised his glass to Sophie and the bartender. "This is to us, and every damn survivor of the last six years. Why we are still alive, I haven't a clue—I guess we were just lucky. *L'Chaim.*"

The End

REVIEWS PLEASE

Today authors rely heavily on the reviews posted by our readers. As an independent self-publisher this is even more important than traditionally published books. If you have enjoyed this novel, please take a few minutes and post a review on Goodreads and Amazon.

About the Author
Gregory C. Randall

Mr. Randall is Michigan born, Chicago raised and Californian by choice. He makes his home in Northern California. Mr. Randall is the author of fiction and non-fiction works available through the usual outlets and Amazon.com.

For more on Max Alder and the other characters in the writing universe of Mr. Randall, please visit his website.
http://www.gregorycrandall.info

Made in the USA
Middletown, DE
02 September 2021